Logan was a cabdriver ~~that had happened out a~~ have to be a real fool n~~o~~ was connected. Still, t~~he~~ couraging signs back at the trailer. Everything had looked normal. Except for in the bathroom. Certain things had been missing. No toothbrush; no razor; no shaving cream; none of the things were there that a guy would grab and throw in a bag if he had to leave in a big hurry. But then Logan had to be scared. Maybe he was just afraid to spend the night in the trailer. Maybe he'd gone to a friend's place for the night to think things out, to try to decide what to do with the money.

Maybe.

Maybe not.

One thing was for sure. The cabdriver was on a winning streak. He'd already missed being blown away twice in the same night.

NIGHT OF THE RUNNING MAN

This book is for Deborah Ann, who with only a smile used to make sunrises.

ACKNOWLEDGMENT
With special thanks to Richard Matheson for much appreciated help and encouragement.

NIGHT OF THE RUNNING MAN

LEE WELLS

A GOLD EAGLE BOOK

London · Toronto · New York · Sydney

*First published by St Martin's Press, Incorporated
First published in Great Britain 1988
by Gold Eagle*

© *Lee Wells 1981*

*Australian copyright 1987
Philippine copyright 1987
This edition 1988*

ISBN 0 373 62112 4

20/8807

Made and printed in Great Britain

PART ONE

1

THE MINUTE THE GUY was in his cab, Jerry Logan wished he hadn't picked him up.

He looked back over his shoulder at the guy. "Where to?" he asked him.

"Airport," he said. "TWA, and step on it for me, okay?"

Jerry reached over and slapped down the yellow metal flag, starting the meter. He turned out of the circular hotel drive into the night traffic of Las Vegas Boulevard. Step on it, my ass, he thought.

The thing was, the guy was a nervous type and that always had the bad effect of rubbing off on Jerry and making him nervous, too. And of course, the guy was in a big hurry. That type was *always* in a big hurry. Now a lot of the drivers didn't mind shoving the old foot through the floor every once in a while, risking the ticket for the tip, but Jerry had never liked doing it. He didn't like doing anything in a rush. When he had gotten out of the army back at the end of the Korean War, he'd made himself a promise that he'd never double-time to a damned thing if he could help it and he'd done a pretty good job of sticking to that promise over the years. But it wasn't only the guy being nervous and in a hurry that bothered him. It was hard to explain, but there was something about him that smelled like trouble. When you pushed a hack in a wide open town like Vegas, you got to where you kind of developed a sixth sense about the people you picked up. You could just feel trouble when it got close to you. The way hookers could feel Vice when they were around. But a hooker can always pass on the action. Once a guy was in your cab, you were pretty much stuck with him unless he was drunk and making trouble or something like that. He looked at the guy in his mirror. He guessed him to be in his middle to late thirties, about average height. He was a little on the skinny side and had a very smooth complexion, almost like a little boy's, and this very fine, very yellow blond hair. He seemed familiar somehow, but Jerry was pretty certain he'd never seen him before. He noted all these things about the man's appearance because there had been a lot of holdups lately and information like that could come in handy later.

Richard Widmark!

Yeah, he thought. That's who it was. The guy reminded him of Richard Widmark, the actor, when he was younger. That would be a good thing to remember, too.

"Hey," the guy said. "Can't you kick it in the ass a little, huh? I don't want to miss my plane."

"What time's your flight?"

"Nine-thirty."

Jerry pulled back the sleeve of his jacket and looked at his watch. It was just a little past eight-thirty now. "No sweat," he said to the guy. "You'll make it easy."

The guy didn't answer. They came to the end of the Strip and turned off on the airport road. It was nearly deserted. Hardly anybody ever left Vegas on a Saturday night. He thought he could feel the guy watching him, feel his eyes on the back of his neck. He sincerely hoped he wasn't planning on trying anything. He was thinking that if he had to draw a holdup man, he would prefer it to be a *calm* holdup man, when the guy suddenly leaned forward over the back of the seat. Jerry felt his shoulders stiffen. The guy's face was close to his own and he could smell his after-shave lotion. "Hey, listen . . ." Richard Widmark said, "you really step on it for me, get me out to the airport in a hurry and *this* is yours."

Jerry glanced to his right. Between the guy's thumb and index finger was a folded-in-half one-hundred-dollar bill. He felt relief go all through his body, and he relaxed. He thought about telling the guy again that they had plenty of time, that it didn't take an hour to get out to the airport. But a bill tip! Richard Widmark was a big spender. "You got it," he said to him.

"Good enough," the guy said. He sat back in the seat again.

Jerry pressed down on the gas. So what the hell, he thought. You get a ticket, you get a ticket, that's all. It had to happen someday anyway and it might as well be for a hundred bucks. That kind of tip didn't come along every day. Not even in Vegas.

About ten minutes later, the trouble started.

Jerry noticed the car because it was coming up on him so fast and because the driver had his brights on. He waved his hand back and forth, but the creep wouldn't dim them down. Here he was doing almost sixty, and this guy was tailgating him. "So go *around* me, you goddamned moron!" he yelled. He was about to make a comment to Richard Widmark about all the clowns on the road these days, but when he looked in the mirror at him, he couldn't say anything because of the sinking feeling in his stomach. The guy was down on his knees in the seat, peering out the back window at the car behind him. And he was holding a gun.

"Hey, mister..." Jerry began.

"That car is after *me*!" the guy said, and his voice sounded like he was choking on something or he had a bad cold.

"Now look, man," Jerry said to him. "I don't want to get in any trouble." The other car was right on his bumper now, its bright lights flooding the inside of the cab.

"You listen, stupid!" the guy screamed at him. "They catch us and it's your ass too. I'm not bullshitting you. Now you better *drive*!"

Jerry swallowed hard, braced himself in the seat, and tightened his grip around the wheel. *Oh, God!* he thought. He stomped on the gas and the cab snapped forward. Up to seventy, seventy-five and still the lights behind him only dropped back a little. Eighty, and the wheel was already vibrating badly in his hands.

"They're going to catch us!" the guy was yelling at him. "They're going to *catch* us!" The speedometer needle quivered up near the ninety mark. Lights blurred by at the side of the road. A *cop*! He thought wildly. *Please, God, let there be a cop!* The wheel was shaking so badly now that he could feel it clear up through his arms and then he suddenly saw where they were and he started pumping the brake. "What're you *doing*?" the guy was yelling at him again, but there was no time to answer be-

cause the airport turnoff was there then and he jerked
the wheel, whipping the cab into it, feeling the rear end
start to drift away almost instantly and then a cyclone
fence on the other side of the road was coming right at
him. He fought to hold the wheel, trying to steer with
the skid and they were away from the fence, back across
the center line, into the wrong lane, tires shrieking, just
missing a big white car, its driver swerving off onto the
shoulder, honking his horn furiously, and then, somehow, he had the cab again.

Jerry let his breath out in a loud rush and he was aware
for the first time that his teeth had been clamped down
hard on his lower lip and now he felt the pain and the
warm little stream of blood running down his chin. In
his mirror, he saw that the other car had made the turn,
too, but the hell with it! That was all, baby! No more!
He hit the brakes and pulled over to the side of the road.
Even before he'd stopped the cab, he heard the back
door open and then the guy was running past his window toward the terminal building, and he sat there and
watched him go, legs pumping, the tails of his sports
jacket flying, the fine blond hair blowing wildly on his
head as he looked over his shoulder at the car that now
shot past the cab, barely missing the opened back door,
and Jerry stared as he saw what was going to happen—
what *was* happening. The thin blond man was running,
the headlights getting brighter and brighter on his back
and then he stopped, whirled around, the gun was in his
hand ready to shoot only there was no sound of a shot.
There was only a little thudding sound and a short, high-
pitched scream as the grill of the car smacked into him
at the waist, tossing him into the air, his arms and legs

sticking out in different directions as though he were trying to make some kind of comical leap. Then he was lying in the street and the car was in front of him. The driver made a sudden screeching U-turn and headed back toward the cab where Jerry was sitting and watching it coming and he couldn't seem to move and he thought, *they're going to kill me now*, and then the car was right across from him in the other lane and he had a blurred glimpse of white faces through the side windows as it shot by him and back out of the airport grounds to the highway and he was still sitting there at the wheel and all he could think of was that he was not dead.

He stared out the windshield at the man lying in the street. People were getting out of their cars now, walking cautiously over to the body, jabbering excitedly, pointing. Get away from here, he thought. *Get away from here!* He reached over the seat and pulled the back door shut. He turned the cab onto the road and drove slowly around the gawkers, past the body in the street and out to the highway. He concentrated on his driving, trying not to think about anything else, and he was halfway back to the city when it all hit him hard in the stomach and suddenly he had chills and was shaking badly. He pulled the cab into the driveway of an old abandoned motel and got out. His legs wouldn't hold him and he went down on his knees in the cool gravel beside the cab and was sick. He stayed down for several minutes and then, still trembling, managed to pull himself up and light a cigarette. He leaned on the hard, cool roof of the cab, sucking in deep gulps of air. Off in the distance, the bright, many-colored lights of the Strip danced against the black desert night. *"Oh, Jesus,"* he said softly. *"Oh, Jesus!"*

2

LATER, AFTER HE'D DRIVEN INTO a gas station and washed his face, he went over to Ernie's for a drink. He felt incredibly empty and tired, but he didn't want to be alone. He wanted people around him.

And he wanted to hear the news.

Ernie's was a quiet little bar at the edge of the city limits. The customers were older cabbies, truckers and the guys that worked on the big hotel-construction jobs that always seemed to be going on along the booming Strip. The place was nothing fancy. It was a man's bar, dark, cool and smelling of beer and the fresh sawdust that covered the scarred wooden floor. Ernie, a great big fat man who used to drive for Greyhound, looked up and waved to him as he came in the door. Ernie and a few guys at the bar were watching an old Bogie movie on television. Jerry didn't recognize any of the guys at the bar, and he was glad of that. He sure didn't feel like shooting the bull with anybody. He sat down at one of the little green tableclothed wooden tables at the back of the room and ordered a double bourbon on the rocks with a water back. The waitress brought it and he tossed off half the bourbon in one swallow without touching the water. He took his cigarettes out of his pocket, lit one and laid the pack down on the table next to his drink.

The big question in his mind was whether anybody had seen the guy jump out of his cab. If anybody *had* seen him, then he was involved and it wouldn't be too long before the cops would be coming around. He didn't like the idea of having to talk to the cops. The whole thing smacked of the Mob. Things must be changing, he thought. In the old days, nobody ever got hit in Vegas, no matter what they did. It was bad for business. People came here for fun and laughs. Having somebody get murdered in a city of fun and laughs was a downer. That guy, whoever he was, must have done something pretty heavy for them to run him over like that. He was sure the guy was dead. The way that car had been moving when it hit him, he couldn't be anything but dead. He took another sip of his bourbon and looked at the cigarette jerking nervously between his fingers.

He had finished his drink, ordered another one and felt a little steadier when the news bulletin came on the TV over the bar. He clenched his fists under the table and listened as the newscaster told how a guy had been the victim of a hit-and-run tonight out at the airport. The dead man had been identified as one Eric Nichols, an employee of the Silver Tiara hotel on the Strip. The news guy went on to say that several people in the airport lot had witnessed the car hitting Nichols, and then speeding away. At present, no motive was known for the killing.

That was it. The Bogie movie came back on.

Jerry sat back in his chair and took a big slug out of his drink. Thank God! There had been no mention of a cab or of a cab *driver*. And thinking about it now, it made sense. He had been sitting off on the side of the road when it had all gone down. The people saw only the guy running and then getting hit. Nobody had noticed where he'd come from. Well, that settled it. He wasn't involved and he sure as hell was going to stay not involved. God, he felt so tired! What a night. What a sonofabitch of a night! And all for a bill tip that he never got anyway. He wondered if maybe the guy might have dropped it in the seat. Probably not, but he'd take a look anyway. Now it was time to get his ass home and get some sack. He downed the last of his drink, left some money on the table and waved to Ernie as he went out. He took his time driving home, and it wasn't until he'd parked the cab in front of his trailer and gotten out that he remembered the tip. He opened the door, and the yellow dome light went on. There was no sign of the bill on the seat. He looked down on the floor and it wasn't there, but something else was and for a minute, he thought he was going to be sick again.

Richard Widmark had forgotten his briefcase.

Inside, he locked the door of the trailer, threw the case on the couch and went straight over to the cabinet above the sink, took down a bottle of bourbon and a glass, poured himself a good belt and tossed it down. He stood there holding the empty glass and looking over at the black briefcase. He wondered what was in it. You're probably a hell of a lot better off if you don't know what's in it, he thought. But then what difference did it really make? He *had* the damned thing now. If he knew what was in it, maybe he'd know what to do with it. He splashed some more of the bourbon into his glass and carried the bottle over to the couch. He put it and the glass down on the coffee table and picked up the case. It was locked. He went over to a drawer, dug out a screwdriver, and in a few minutes, he had the latches broken. He lifted the lid and knew right away that he was in a whole lot of trouble. He had never been so close to so much money in his life.

He dumped the case upside down on the couch. There was nothing in it but money. Neat stacks of hundreds, fifties and twenties all with those little white paper bands around them like banks used. For a few minutes, he just sat there looking at it all. Then, because he couldn't think of anything else to do, he began counting it. It took awhile, and when he'd finished, he got up and went over to the door and made sure that he'd locked it. He parted two of the plastic blinds over the window with his fingers and peered outside. The neighboring trailers were dark, the trailer park silent, asleep. He went back over to the coffee table, picked up his glass, emptied it and splashed in some more of the whiskey. He couldn't take his eyes off the pile of green paper on the couch. Sweat trickled slowly out of his hair and down the side of his temple.

Five hundred thousand dollars.

That guy—Nichols, the newscaster had called him—he must have been trying to skip with all this money. That was why they'd been after him. And now *you've* got it, he thought, frustration rising up in him. And you can bet your Aunt Minnie's ass that they'll be after you, too. Damn that guy! Why didn't he take his fucking case with him? So here you are, he thought, with five hundred thousand dollars of the Mob's money. Wasn't that just terrific? And what're you going to do with it?

Give it back?

Back to *who*?

He could just take it to the cops. Oh, sure. That's brilliant. Go ahead, he thought bitterly, take it to the cops, tell them everything. Then you'll be a witness against the Mob. That's beautiful! Why don't you just run an ad in the paper—WILL THE DRIVER OF THE HIT-AND-RUN CAR AT THE AIRPORT PLEASE CALL JERRY LOGAN. I SAW THE WHOLE THING AND I'VE GOT YOUR MONEY…

He sipped at the bourbon, trying to calm down. Okay, he thought. *Okay*… You've got it now. Just think a minute. They were probably already checking on him, he reasoned. It wouldn't be difficult for them, not here in Vegas. They'd just send somebody to the cab company, talk to the drivers and narrow it down to him being the one who was at the airport. And that would be all, baby.

Or would it?

Maybe they don't want you, he thought. Maybe they just want their money. After all, you weren't the one who took it. Okay, sure, you were there and you saw the car hit the guy, but the whole thing had all happened so damned fast that he'd never gotten a good look at the men inside the car. He wouldn't know them if he saw them on the street in the morning.

Right.

But *they* didn't know that.

Well, he sure as hell wasn't going to wait around to find out what they had in mind for him. He'd just have to get the hell out of here, that's all. He'd leave the money in the case for them to find. They'd probably figure he'd left town and they'd know he was scared, and because he was a cab driver in Vegas, he'd most likely guessed the score and had enough sense to keep his mouth shut. Maybe they'd just let it go. He'd leave tonight, too, not wait around. They might not expect him to get out so fast. He'd just throw some stuff in a suitcase. He was glad that he only rented the trailer. He started putting stacks of money back into the dead guy's briefcase. He'd put over half of it back when he stopped.

Five hundred thousand dollars.

More money than you'd probably see if you lived three lifetimes, he thought. He picked up a packet of hundreds, riffled them like a deck of cards. His throat was dry, and he could feel his heart pumping. He swallowed hard. Maybe, he thought. Maybe one time in a man's whole life, a really big chance comes along. He has nothing to do with it. It just happens, and he can either grab it or let it go. He looked around the trailer.

Home.

Forty-six years old and this was home. This crummy little trailer and it didn't even belong to him.

What *did* belong to him?

Nothing. Zip.

Only the clothes on your back, he thought, and the money you got from driving that fucking cab outside. Hustling your ass off every day of the week, carrying around people who had plenty of money, hauling them from one good time to another and hoping for some fat tips to offset half-the-meter at the end of the shift that the cab company paid you. Half the meter. So you could eat, pay the rent, get a haircut, buy beer, throw a few nickles in the slots and bargain with a hooker for a piece of ass now and then when you felt you had to do that.

Always hustling.

And where did it get you? Noplace. You just went around and around in a circle like a dog chasing his own ass. And then one day you'd probably get it the way that other driver, Ryan, had a few months ago. Ryan had stopped at this coffee-and-doughnut place to grab a cup to go. He'd just sat down in the cab with the coffee and bang! A heart attack. He didn't even have time to close the door of the cab and he fell out and laid there in the gravel of the coffee-and-doughnut place. He was already dead by the time the paramedic guys got to him. A coffee-and-doughnut place. Wasn't that just terrific!

He drank the rest of the bourbon and tossed the glass down on the couch next to the money.

And now, right here in front of him, was opportunity. A one-shot chance to gamble big like the high rollers in the casinos who got treated like kings. A chance to bet on yourself, he thought. You lose and it's your ass for sure, but then what the hell've you got here that makes losing such a big deal? What's so great about all of this? And then he remembered something a guy had told him one night in the cab. The guy was a high roller in town on a junket from New York. They'd started talking about gambling, and the guy had said never to think about losing. Never. If you started thinking about losing, you'd ruin it for yourself.

It didn't take him twenty minutes to get ready to leave.

He put a few clothes and toilet articles in his old beat-up suitcase, dug his old army ditty bag out of the closet and stuffed the money down into it. Then he closed the dead guy's briefcase and put it with the other two bags. He didn't want them to find it when they came to the trailer, and he was certain they would be coming. Then he walked up the hill out of the trailer park and waited in the darkness near the bus stop until the bus came along. He had plenty of change for the bus. He'd kept the whole day's take from the hack. No half-the-meter this time. He wished he'd had time to *sell* the damned cab. He would've felt good about doing that.

He looked around the bus. It was pretty empty. The only other passenger besides himself was an old guy in a night-watchman's uniform, and he was asleep in the seat with his lunch box between his legs. He felt scared, but he felt excited, too. He wasn't so tired anymore. In fact, it seemed to him that he hadn't felt so awake in a long time.

3

A FEW MILES AWAY, in a large private office in the Silver Tiara Hotel on the Strip, a short, fat man paced furiously. The fat man, whose name was Al Chambers, was almost completely bald, and now his smooth, pudgy face was flushed tomato red with anger. He wore several very expensive rings on both hands and he fiddled with them as he walked, twisting them around and around on his fingers. A tall, good-looking man in his middle thirties sat on a white leather couch watching him.

"Right at the airport!" Chambers said. He smacked one plump fist into his palm and shook his head in disbelief. "They chase the no-good sonofabitch all the way to the airport and then they run him down in the parking lot! In the fucking parking lot! In front of people! And still they don't get the money back for me!" He ceased pacing and glared at the tall man on the couch as though he expected him to comment on this, but the other said nothing. "I told them—stop the bastard before he ever gets to the airport, but they let him get away." He shook his index finger at the man on the couch. "Nichols had that money with him when he got in that cab and he didn't have it when the dumb asses ran him down. You get that money back and you fix that cab driver!" He took a small slip of paper from his pocket and handed it to the other man. "I don't want any loose ends, right?"

The tall man waited for a minute, making sure that was all the other had to say to him. Then he got up from the couch. "I'll be in touch," he said quietly. He gave Chambers a little smile, turned and walked out of the suite, closing the door softly behind him. Chambers stared at the door, frowning, his lips pressed tightly together. He didn't like the tall man. He might be cool and quiet and all that bullshit, he thought, but he was still a wise ass. It was the smile that irritated him. It meant that the tall man sensed he was in trouble because of what had happened at the airport tonight.

And he was right.

The tall man stood in the stillness of the heavily carpeted hall and waited for the elevator. He was glad to be away from Chambers. Chambers was a slob. His office had been a mess, papers everywhere, ashtrays full of his disgusting, chewed-on cigar stubs. A real slob. The elevator bell dinged sharply in the empty hall. The tall man stepped in, rode down to the casino floor and went out through the hotel lobby to the parking lot. In a few minutes, he was driving toward downtown Las Vegas.

The tall man's name was David Eckhart. He was thirty-five years old and quite wealthy as a result of wisely investing the money he'd earned over the years from killing people for a living. He had been working at this particular occupation since he was twenty-one, and though he had been arrested several times, he had never spent more than four hours in a jail in his life and he had never been convicted of anything.

He was a man who carefully cultivated discipline and common sense. His living habits were designed in the manner of the professional who knew that he must rely totally upon himself and his own personal skills if he hoped to continue functioning successfully in his chosen line of work. He kept his body in good physical shape and easily passed for a man in his middle twenties. He did not smoke or gamble and drank only to be able to handle it. At sixteen, he had run away to Miami from his parents' home in Detroit to escape their constant drinking and the things he saw them do under the influence. He never saw either one of them again and hadn't thought about them in years, but to this day, he held a deep contempt for drunks. It was, in fact, that very contempt that had indirectly led him into his present occupation.

After he had run away from home, money became a problem for the first time in his life. It had been the one thing that his upper-middle-class parents had never denied him, and he hadn't liked being without it. He'd gotten a job bussing tables in the restaurant of one of the big hotels along Miami's Hotel Row.

The young Eckhart was bright and observant, and he came to notice certain people in the restaurant who always seemed to have plenty of money yet did not appear to have any kind of steady job, since he often saw them there at all hours. One night he mentioned his observations to one of the boys he worked with and was tersely warned that these were very important customers of the hotel. He was to be nice to them at all times and not to talk about them at all. Eckhart took this advice to heart and added his own touch to it. He began being *very* nice to these people. He remembered little things they liked and didn't like at the table, and before too long, he found himself working as a waiter instead of a busboy. He also began doing certain little favors for them outside of his waiter duties. He ran errands for them, picked up their clothes from the cleaners, went to expensive department stores in town and brought back things they had ordered, and in time, he was asked to observe certain people in the hotel at their jobs and then report back on what he had seen.

Eckhart went out of his way to do a good job, and the people he worked for liked him. He wasn't a hotshot, back-talking punk like so many of the others. They liked the way he did exactly as he was told without asking any questions and the way he was always well mannered and showed the proper respect. Because of his polite and withdrawn nature, it is doubtful that any of these people at that time ever gave the slightest thought to the boy becoming a contract killer. Then one night a few years later, an incident occurred that made them look at him in a whole new light.

It had been a few days before Eckhart's twenty-first birthday. He had left his job at the restaurant and was working as a kind of personal assistant to an elderly man known to the police as a fairly high-ranking figure in the organized-crime structure of the city. On this particular night, Eckhart, the old man and one of the old man's bodyguards had just left a nightclub after having dinner and were waiting on the front steps for another body-guard to bring the car around. Suddenly a man, ob-viously quite drunk, came lurching out through the door behind them, yelling at them to get out of his way, but before they could oblige him, he shoved his way through them, causing the old man to stumble and fall to the sidewalk.

Even before the bodyguard could act, Eckhart was all over the man, grabbing him by the hair on top of his head, spinning him around and smashing him hard in the face. The man let out a cry of pain and went down. Still holding onto his hair, Eckhart stepped forward and drove his knee viciously once, twice into the man's face. The bodyguard moved to intervene, but a word from the old man stopped him. The second bodyguard came roaring up in the car and was also stopped. The three then watched as the drunken man, who was much big-ger than Eckhart, grabbed him around his ankles and the two went down on the walk. They saw Eckhart take several hard blows that brought blood to his face but did not seem to faze his rage. Finally he managed to get on top of the man. He held his arms down with his knees and began beating him until both were covered in dark blood under the streetlights. The old man gave the sign to the two bodyguards, and it was all they could do to pull Eckhart off the man.

The old man had watched the fight with keen interest, taking careful note of the dark fury in the boy's face, which he took to be an expression of Eckhart's concern for him, but which was, in fact, the explosive triggering of his deep hatred for all the drunken man had symbolized to him. It was not too long after this incident occurred that the old man made Eckhart one of his bodyguards, and shortly after that, he was offered his first money to kill.

The old man's chief bodyguard took him aside and carefully explained the situation. He was told who the victim was to be and why they had deemed the action necessary. It was emphasized to him that he did not have to take on the job, but if he did choose to do it, he would be paid fifteen thousand dollars in cash. He was to think about it and give his decision the following day. All that night Eckhart laid awake considering the proposition, going over the pluses and minuses, immediate and long range. By ten the next morning, he had made up his mind and went downstairs to see the old man, who was having his coffee and waiting for him in the library of the huge house.

The old man said good morning, told him to come in and to close the door so that they could talk in private. He poured Eckhart coffee from a gleaming silver pot, then sat back in his chair and looked across the desk at the young man, waiting to hear what he had to say. Eckhart sipped his coffee, set the cup back down in the saucer as his other hand brought the gun smoothly out of his belt under his shirt and, leaning forward, bracing his elbow on the desk, he looked straight into the shocked, disbelieving face and shot the old man twice through the head.

His life changed with those two shots.

TODAY, AMONG PEOPLE whose business it is to know such things, Eckhart is regarded as one of the best in the country. A heavyweight. One who can be counted on. He has never married, having decided that a wife along with close friends were luxuries that someone in his line of work could not safely afford as long as he was actively engaged in that line of work. He plans to retire in two years. There is absolutely no one who is aware of that fact. When the time comes, he will simply and suddenly disappear.

He was downtown now. He looked out the windshield at the heavy traffic, like a used-car lot on the move. The sidewalks were jammed, too. Though it was after midnight, everything was bright as day in the brilliant explosion of neon. This was the bargain part of Vegas. Everything was a little cheaper down here than in the posh hotels along the Strip. Glitter Gulch, the locals called it. All kinds of people were to be found here. Tourists, cowboys, punks, construction workers, kids, old women, old men, hustlers of both sexes—name it, it was here. Eckhart frowned at the scene. It was all too loud, too tacky for his taste. Like a cheap carnival. He seldom came down here.

He stopped for a light and thought about the job he had undertaken.

He didn't like Al Chambers, but not because of anything the man had ever done to him. The two men knew each other only slightly. It was that Eckhart didn't like the Chambers type—loud, pushy, a big shot in love with his own importance. Chambers was president of the Silver Tiara, a solid hotel and casino operation owned for the most part by August Gurino, an old ex-mobster from back East. Chambers was a man of some juice in Vegas. He had told him as much as he'd thought was necessary tonight: that Nichols, one of his trusted men in the hotel, had tried to rip off quite a lot of money from the Tiara. Five hundred grand, to be exact. Nothing really all that unusual. Things like that went down from time to time. Chambers's goons were supposed to have stopped the guy, but they screwed it up good, and now he had called in Eckhart to clean up their mess. Eckhart had taken the job because the money was good.

But something was missing.

Part of Eckhart's talent—a part that he kept to himself—was his exceptional ability to tune himself into the emotions behind the words that people said to him. And he had picked something up from Al Chambers tonight in spite of the man's power and position.

Chambers had been afraid.

Eckhart was sure of it. He had felt it in the man. So there was something more behind this whole thing than just Nichol's greed. He wondered what that something was.

The light went green and Eckhart tapped the wheel with his fingers, thinking, easing the car along in the traffic.

And now there was this cab driver.

Eckhart looked over at a chunky-faced man standing on the corner, wearing a bright lemon-yellow T-shirt and

polyester slacks. On the front of the T-shirt was an inky
drawing of a naked man with his arms wrapped around
his stomach, and underneath the drawing, the words, I
LOST MY ASS IN LAS VEGAS. Eckhart sighed, shook
his head and drove on. Drawing Nichols for a fare had
been a bad break for this cabbie, whoever he was. He had
seen what had happened out at the airport with Nichols
and now he had the money. Chambers was too jittery to
take any chances. The cabbie had to go. Bad luck for
him.

He parked the car in a lot and walked the couple of
blocks up the street to the small, gray metal Quonset hut
that served as the dispatch headquarters for the cab
company. The long, rounded room was empty except for
the dispatcher and one of the drivers, who was sprawled
in a chair in the back reading the sex ads in one of the
hustle papers. The room was badly air conditioned and
stank heavily from sweat and cigarette smoke.

Eckhart walked up behind the dispatcher and stood
looking down at the man's enormous back. The dispatcher was talking into a mike, breathing heavily
through his mouth, his enormous belly rising and falling under his faded, food-spotted green shirt. A large bag
of M & M's lay ripped open next to the mike, and now
and then he would shove his plump, sausagelike fingers
inside the bag, grab a few of the candies and pop them
into his mouth as he barked instructions to the drivers
out on the street. When he had given all the fares he had
on the lined yellow tablet in front of him, he turned
around in his swivel chair and looked up at Eckhart. A
sparkle flashed into his small brown eyes and he gave the
tall man a big grin, exposing a row of crooked front teeth

that were the faded yellow of rotten bananas. "Need a cab, mister?" he said.

Eckhart handed him the piece of paper that Chambers had given him back at the hotel and smiled. "What else?" he said.

4

THERE WERE NO CUSTOMERS in the coffee shop in the Las Vegas train depot. The waitress, a thin dark little woman in her fifties, was slouched behind the counter reading the *Reader's Digest*. When Jerry Logan came in, she looked up at him and frowned, put down her magazine and came over. "What're you gonna have?" she asked him.

Jerry looked at her. "Uh . . . a beer," he said. "Just a beer."

The waitress shook her head. "No beer," she said. "No liquor of any kind."

"Oh . . . yeah. Right. Just coffee, then, and maybe a piece of pie."

All he really wanted was to be on his train and moving, but he had a forty-five minute wait before it was due, and he hadn't liked the out-in-the-open feeling he got in the station waiting room so he had come into the coffee shop. At least here, he could see all around him and cover anybody who came in the station door.

"What kind of pie do you want?" the waitress asked him. She pointed to several pieces on dark-blue saucers inside a glass case. "We got blueberry, cherry there, apple . . ."

"Apple," Jerry said quickly. "Apple's good."

She took the pie out of the case, put it in front of him and poured the coffee from the steaming round glass pot. Jerry looked down at the pie and knew he would never be able to eat it. You have *got* to settle down, he thought. This is only the first of it.

He looked out through the door of the coffee shop at the almost-empty waiting room. He wished there were more people in the station. It was funny, he thought, all the times he'd dropped people off here in the cab, but he'd never had a reason to actually come inside the place. Nobody thought about taking a train anywhere these days. At least, he hoped nobody would think about it.

The waitress had decided that she didn't want to read anymore. She poured herself a cup of coffee and leaned against the counter. "Where you headed?" she asked him.

"Chicago," he said, not thinking at all.

Oh, that's good, stupid! Go ahead. Tell everybody where you're going!

"Lost all your dough already, huh?" she said, smiling at him.

Jerry shrugged, grinned at her. "You know how it is," he said.

She sipped at her coffee, set it down on the counter, nodding. "Oh, I know how it *is*, all right. Boy, do I know! Let me tell you something—I wouldn't bet a nickel in this damned town, you'll excuse my language. The things people do here!" She made a face and rolled her eyes. "They're *crazy!* Like they blow it all, you know? They go bust. So what do you think they do? They go and they cash in the return part of their tickets home so they can go out and gamble some more! There's places here—'' she pointed out the window, ''you can see them from the highway—that have those advertising signs telling you how they'll cash in your bus or train ticket for you. Like they were doing you some kind of *favor*, for Christ's sake!'' She looked closely at him. ''You lose much?''

''Not too much,'' he said.

Not yet, anyway.

The old man who operated the ticket cage came in then and sat down at the other end of the counter, and the waitress went over to him.

The first places they'll look, he thought, are the airport, the bus depot, and then here. They'll bet on the airport because it's the fastest way out of town. He wondered how well they would be able to check out what he had done. Would they think they had just missed him at the airport or would they have a way of finding out whether or not he had ever been there? That same thing was true for the train. He had heard that they could find out anything they wanted to find out. He wondered if that was really true.

Bang!

His whole body jerked, and he whirled around, spilling the coffee on the counter and on the front of his shirt.

Bang! Bang! Bang!

Down the counter, the old white-haired guy from the ticket cage was pounding the glass sugar container on the countertop. Jerry smiled, started breathing again. Terrific! He thought. Settle *down!*

"Something the matter with the pie?"

He looked up. The waitress was standing in front of him again, looking down at the untouched piece of apple pie.

"No," he said to her. "I thought I wanted it at first, but it's too late for me." He frowned and tapped his chest with his finger. "I eat too late, I get heartburn."

She made a sympathetic face. "Yeah, I know what you mean," she said. "I get it, too." She picked up the pie. "Listen," she said, lowering her voice, "you didn't even touch it, so I ain't gonna charge you nothing. What the hell." She put the pie back up in the glass case and slid the door shut.

"Thanks," Jerry said. He took a dollar out of his wallet and laid it on the counter. "For you," he said. He stood up. "I've got to get going."

She gave him a big smile and picked up the dollar bill, and he looked right at her and noticed for the first time how pale and tired her face looked. "I appreciate it," she said, still holding the bill. "A place like this—no good tips, you know?"

He picked up his bags. "You take it easy on yourself now," he said to her.

"Yeah," she said. "You do the same. And listen, the next time you come in, remember what I said about this town. It's crazy!"

He grinned at her. "It sure is," he said. "And I'll remember." He walked the length of the counter past the back of the old guy from the ticket cage. Suddenly he couldn't stand being inside anymore. The building seemed so old and depressing, and he felt like it was closing in on him. The waitress with her tired face and those heavy purple bags under her eyes that looked like bruises, but were really from having to work such long, late hours at her age. He wished to hell he could've left her a thousand-buck tip! He would have, too, by God, but later, there were sure to be people checking on him, and the less he was remembered, the better.

Outside, a cool breeze was blowing and the fresh air felt good on his face. There was nobody around anywhere. He walked away from the lighted door of the depot and over into the shadows at the side of the building. He set his bags down and lit a cigarette. The breeze was getting stronger, turning into a chilly wind, the way it often did in the desert, and he reached back under the collar of his jacket and turned it up around his neck. He huddled in closer to the side of the building, shivering a little. It could get pretty cold in Vegas in October. A lot of the tourists were surprised by that. He looked off through the blowing, clear night at the twinkling lights of the city and thought about all the people having a good time, forgetting their worries and hassles even if it was only for a weekend. They could knock Las Vegas all they wanted, but the city had a place. He was going to miss it. He wondered how long it would be before he could come back here again. Maybe never, he thought.

He threw his cigarette down and was stubbing it out with the heel of his shoe when the train whistle screamed and sent his heart right up into his mouth. He grabbed his bags and watched it coming big, black and noisy down the track toward him. Come on, baby! Come *on!* He wanted to be on it and moving away. This train made a lot of stops at a lot of little and big towns between here and Chicago. For all they would know, he could've jumped off at any one of them. He would get on the train, order a double of the best bourbon they had and then try to come up with some kind of a plan. He had to know just what he was going to do by the time he got off the train.

He left his suitcase and the dead man's briefcase in his sleeping compartment and kept the bag with the money in it with him. Then he went back out to his seat in the main car and sat down by the window. The only other person who got on the train with him was a young, sleepy-eyed army private. Jerry looked at the kid and remembered when he'd been doing that whole thing, sleeping in chairs in bus and train depots and dragging that damned heavy duffel bag around. He'd really hated it then, but thinking about it now, it seemed like an incredibly simple life. It also seemed like a hundred years ago. The train lurched slightly, and then they were moving, a feeling of deep loneliness swept over him and he felt unprotected and vulnerable. The train picked up speed and moved out in the desert darkness. Well, he thought, you're in it for sure now. It was time for that bourbon.

He drank the first one in the club car and carried the second one back to his compartment. Once inside, he closed the door and bolted it tight. Then he tossed the bag with the money down on the little bed and kicked off his shoes. He grinned to himself, feeling pleasantly high from the drink, and wriggled his toes inside his socks and sat down on the bed next to the bag. "I'm going, going, *gone*, fellas!" he said to the little room. "You missed me this time!" He put his drink between his knees and pulled the bag over to him, unzipped it and turned it upside down, dumping the stacks of money out on the dark blue bedspread.

Five hundred thousand dollars.

He sat there staring at it, awed at the possibility that he had a chance—a slim one, probably, but still a chance—of keeping it all. He lifted his glass in a toast to himself. *"Hey, lady…how about a break this time, huh?"* he said softly.

He drank.

His eyes closed, opened, closed again. The whole incredible night whirled through his mind. He was so tired. He had to get some sack. He stuffed all the money back into the bag, zipped it shut again and put it down by the bed. He stretched out, his head sinking down into the wonderfully soft, clean-smelling pillow. The compartment was warm and snug. He should get undressed, he thought. His left arm was hanging out over the side of the bed, the drink still in his hand. Slowly it slipped down out of his fingers. He never heard it hit the floor.

5

ECKHART RIPPED THE LITTLE TRAILER to pieces.

Nothing.

He stood looking down at the cheap coffee table in front of the couch, breathing heavily from the effort, his usually neat black hair hanging down over his forehead and touching his eyebrows. He had come straight to the trailer park after talking to Rodney, the dispatcher at the cab company. He'd had no problem getting Jerry Logan's name and address from Rodney once he'd shown him the license number that Chambers had given him at the hotel. Taking down that number had been the only thing that Chambers's goon had done right.

Rodney had been happy to see Eckhart. Seeing the tall man always meant money. Rodney had a weakness for the hookers but couldn't afford them on his salary. Because of his dispatcher's job, he was in a good position to hear things that went on in town, and from time to time, Eckhart saw to it that Rodney had the money to entertain his sexual appetite, so the man was always eager to help. He had even peeled Jerry Logan's photo off his work-file card and given it to Eckhart. The picture was a real bonus, and he had given Rodney an extra hundred for being so on the ball. Eckhart reached down over the coffee table and picked up the empty glass from the couch. He sniffed it, made a face and dropped it on the floor. He looked around the trailer thoughtfully for a minute. Then he left.

Driving back to the Strip, he carefully went over the situation in his mind. Logan had the money. He was sure of that. He could feel it. He found it hard to believe that the guy would try to split with it. Logan was a cab driver in Vegas. After everything that had happened out at the airport, the guy would have to be a real fool not to guess that the money was connected. Still, there had been some discouraging signs back in the trailer. Everything had looked normal. Except for in the bathroom. Certain things had been missing. No toothbrush; no razor; no shaving cream; none of the things were there that a guy would grab and throw in a bag if he had to leave in a big hurry. But then Logan had to be scared. Maybe he was just afraid to spend the night in the trailer. Maybe he'd gone to a friend's place for the night to think things out, to try to decide what to do with the money.

Maybe.

Maybe not.

One thing was for sure. The cab driver was on a winning streak. He'd already missed being blown away twice in the same night.

6

JERRY LOGAN GOT OFF the train in Springfield, Illinois. It was a big enough town for him to be able to do the things he had to do, and it was just a short flight away from Chicago. The train trip from Vegas had been quiet and uneventful. He'd had plenty of time to think, and he had a plan. It was a little crazy, but at least it was something. He only had his suitcase and the bag with the money now. The second night on the train, he had gone out onto the little observation porch of his car and hurled the dead man's black case into the darkness of whatever state they had been passing through at that moment. He hadn't wanted to take it with him at all, but he'd felt that it might help him a little if they didn't find it right away back in Vegas.

The cab from the train depot dropped him off in the middle of the Springfield business district, and he walked until he found the kind of hotel he was looking for. There were hotels in the downtown sections of every

city in the country: a decaying red brick dump that ca-
tered to transients and elderly people on fixed incomes
who couldn't afford to move. It was a hotel where people were nameless, where they went in and out the door
like flies and nobody noticed anything about them, or if
anybody did notice, didn't give a damn.

He checked in and paid the desk clerk, a surly-faced
old hag in a blue print dress who was a dead ringer for
Broderick Crawford. He signed the register as Mr.
Leonard Rodman. It was the name of the cabbie who'd
brought him from the train depot. He'd read it off the
guy's hack license pinned to the visor. Not that it mattered at this dump. He could've registered as Clark
Gable, but he wanted to get into the habit of using the
name for later.

The bellhop, an old man in his sixties, bald and
sweating, put his bags down in the room and looked at
him, his dried, cracking face impassive until he saw what
kind of tip he was going to get. Jerry handed him a dollar, thinking of the waitress back in the train-depot coffee shop in Vegas. The dried, colorless lips split into a
smile. The bald head bobbed once. Then he turned and
left, closing the door. Jerry walked over to the window
and raised it. The cold air hit him in the face. Okay, he
thought. Okay. You've got a plan. You've got a place to
stay, but you've also got one hell of a lot of things to do
and they all have to be done by tonight. He didn't think
he could afford to spend more than a day and a night
here. He had to be on a plane to Chicago in the morning. Speed was on his side. He wanted to keep it there.

7

"FLORIDA?" ECKHART SAID. He looked at the well-dressed young man sitting across from him in the booth of the hotel coffee shop.

"Yeah," the young man said. "Waitress at the train depot remembered him."

"Where in Florida?"

The young man shrugged. "She couldn't remember," he said. "She's an old broad. She wasn't sure he even said the name of the city he was going to. She said he was a nice guy." The young man grinned at Eckhart. "Nice and stupid, right?"

Eckhart didn't reply. He reached inside the breast pocket of his jacket and took out a sheaf of clean new bills bound together by a thin, gold, monogrammed money clip. He peeled away a fifty-dollar bill and laid it in the saucer of the man's coffee cup. "I've got it from here," he said. The other looked at him, nodded, picked up the money and went out.

Eckhart stared out the window at the heat waves rising off the Strip and thought about this cab driver, Logan. The whole business had started to look different to him. The young man who had just left was wrong. Logan wasn't stupid. That had been no dumb run he'd made. The guy had been thinking all the time. Leaving by train and leaving right away, that had been smart. Finding him in Vegas would have been a piece of cake. Now he was out of the city. Well, at least he knew the general direction the guy was heading. There was one more thing that he wanted to check out.

He left the booth, paid the check and went out into the dazzling desert sun. Walking to his car, he started thinking how he would handle it if he were the one running with the money. The situation would present a lot of interesting problems, but he was pretty sure that if he were the one doing it, he could pull it off. He was just as sure that the cab driver would not be able to pull it off. Logan had been lucky. Damned lucky. But as anybody who lived in this town for any length of time could tell you, nobody stayed lucky for long. Winning streaks sooner or later went bust.

IT WAS WELL PAST MIDNIGHT when the waitress from the train depot entered her apartment. She was tired and the calves of her legs were aching badly, which meant that she couldn't go right to bed. She'd have to soak them in Epsom salts or she'd never be able to get to sleep. She thought again about the man who had come into her coffee shop asking about one of her customers. It had been on her mind off and on all night. The guy had said that he was a cop and he'd flashed an ID, but if that stiff was a cop, she was Kate Hepburn. She'd been in this town way too long not to recognize his type. She wondered what kind of trouble the nice guy was in who hadn't been able to eat his pie and who had left her the buck tip. She made a hobby of studying her customers, and she had noticed that the guy was pretty damned nervous, but she'd figured it was probably because he had to go home and explain to his old lady how he'd lost all his money at the tables. She flipped on the light switch by the door and something hard hit her across the back of her neck.

Eckhart caught her before she hit the floor.

When she came to, it was very dark and she didn't know where she was. As her head cleared, she was aware that she was outside, but she couldn't see anything. The wind was blowing hard, and she was very cold. Her arms were stretched straight up over her head and her face was brushing against a gritty wall of some kind. She was not standing on anything and couldn't feel anything under her feet. She thought that she was tied and hanging by her arms but then she lifted her head and looked up into the man's face and her breath caught in her chest and her eyes widened as she saw that she was not tied at all, that he was holding her by her arms and the fear froze her as she looked past him at the wide, curving concrete wall and suddenly knew where she was, knew that this man bending over her in the darkness was holding her out over *the edge of the Hoover Dam* and the sudden understanding of the deep emptiness beneath her feet dried up the scream in her throat and she could only make little gasping, whimpering sounds and stare wildly up into his face.

The man's head bent closer to her, his face shadowy in the half-clouded moonlight. When he spoke, his voice was very soft, almost soothing. "I need you to tell me something," he said. "You tell me the truth and I'll pull you up out of here and you'll be fine. You lie to me . . ."

The tight grip left her arms and she was falling, screaming.

Only to be caught again, this time by her wrists.

"You *lie* to me," the soft voice went on, "and I'll *know* if you're lying, and I'll let you fall. When they find your body, they'll think you either committed suicide or fell off the dam. It happens all the time.'' The voice paused, waiting for this to sink in. "Now, do you understand what I'm saying to you?"

She tried to answer, but at first her voice wouldn't come and then she got out, "Yes, yes," and nodded her head twice.

"Good," the voice said to her. "Now, a couple of days ago, you talked to a man in your coffee shop at the train station. A man in his forties, about average height. He was leaving town. Somebody came around later asking you about this man, about where he went, and you said he went to Florida. You also said that you thought he was a nice guy so I guess you must have liked him." Eckhart looked straight down into the frightened eyes, hardened his voice. "What I want to know is, did you like him enough to lie about where he was going?" He jerked his head suddenly at the woman, indicating that she had better think before she answered. "The *truth*, remember..." he said.

The sockets of her arms ached with a burning fire from her own weight pulling at them. She looked up into the man's face and heard her voice start to talk, her words sounding tiny in the heavy wind that whipped around the enormous dam.

Eckhart listened to her, watching her face, and when she had finished, he knew that she had told him the truth and he let go of her then and felt her wrists and fingers brush quickly through his hands and then she was gone down into the darkness, the wind sucking away her scream.

He walked back down the road to his car and took his time driving through the still night into the city. It was too bad about the woman. He had never liked having to do things like that, having to close out people who just happened to get in the way of things that were going on, but now and then, you had to do it. You had to do it because you always had to be careful that you didn't leave anything behind that could pop up later at some bad time for you and put you away. The waitress was pretty smart in her own way. She probably wouldn't have talked to anybody about what had happened tonight. She probably would have been too scared to even mention it to her friends.

Probably...

Which really meant that there was always a chance that given another time and different circumstances, she would talk about it. And she had seen his face and heard his voice.

He looked out through the windshield at the pale white highway under the desert moon.

You always have to be careful, he thought.

Back in his apartment, he made two quick phone calls and then began packing a bag to leave for Chicago.

8

JERRY LOGAN SAT BY THE WINDOW in his cheap hotel room in Springfield, Illinois, and tried to fight off the fear and desperation that were crawling all over him. He had not turned on the lights and it was dark in the room now. It had taken him all day to get together the things he needed for his plan. He looked over at the dark lumps of packages that he had dumped on the bed. Now that he was actually going to carry out the plan and it was no longer just something in his mind, he was having serious doubts about it. The whole thing seemed insane to him. Who did he think he was, anyway? What the hell made him think he could get away with all that money?

The Mob's money.

He remembered stories he had heard. Things they had done to . . .

"Shut up!" he said out loud. "Just shut up!" It was way too late now for this kind of crap. Okay, he told himself. Okay, so the plan was crazy. Crazy things worked sometimes just because they *were* crazy and people weren't expecting them. And besides, he had to try it. It was the only plan he had and there sure as hell wasn't time to come up with another one. He had to stay ahead of them. He had to keep his edge.

He reached down to the floor beside the chair and picked up the bottle of bourbon he'd bought during the day, and holding the glass up in front of the street-lighted window so he could see, he poured another shot. He sipped at the whiskey and looked out through the window past the rusting, rotting, half-torn-away screen down to the street below. The wind was blowing hard and the thin glass rattled inside the old wooden window frame. It was raining, and the traffic hissed slowly along from corner to corner. He looked at the wipers on the cars, snapping back and forth across the windshields in front of the small, unrecognizable faces, and thought about all the people eager to get home from work out of the wet, have dinner, watch TV and relax. Enough of this shit, he thought. He wished that he could go out and have himself a real night on the town, but he knew it was not a good idea. Pull this off, he promised himself, and you'll have plenty of good nights on the town.

He wondered what London would be like.

On the train, he had decided that was where he would go from Chicago. He had chosen it because it was a place he'd always wanted to go to and because there would be no problem with the language. He was pretty certain that he couldn't stay in the States. They'd be bound to track him down sooner or later. His chances would be better in Europe. He stood up, feeling a little calmer from the bourbon, some of his tension and anxiety gone. He had to get things ready for the morning, but first he'd better eat something. He went over and switched on the lights, put on his jacket and went downstairs and across the street in the rain and brought back two big Sloppy Burgers and a cup of coffee. It was a hell of a dinner for a guy with five hundred thousand dollars to spend, but it would have to do for now.

By midnight, he had gotten everything ready. He wound his travel clock and set the alarm for five. Then he went into the bathroom and took a long hot shower, taking his time, soaping himself up slowly, letting the water pound away on the back of his neck, and when he came out, he felt pretty relaxed and thought he would be able to go to sleep. He turned out the little lamp by the bed and got under the blankets and lay there listening to the rain and the muffled noises down on the street and after a while, sleep came to him. He slept, but his sleep was not deep, always right at the edge of being awake, and several times through the early hours of the morning, he opened his eyes and looked over at the green, needle-thin hands of the travel clock and thought, it's okay. I can sleep some more, and once when he did this, he dreamed.

He was inside a building in the dream. He did not know what the building was or where it was, only that it was very old and he was running up a flight of curving, rickety steps inside it. The stairwell was very dark and he knew that someone-something was coming up the steps after him and he was afraid and he was running very fast, gulping in his breath, his feet slamming down again and again on the old wooden steps and each time his weight would hit a step, he would hear a sharp, cracking sound and think that it was breaking away under him and he was going to fall through. He wanted to stop running so fast because he couldn't see too well in the darkness, but he was much more afraid of what was coming up behind him and so he tried to run even faster, only now the incline of the steps seemed to be getting steeper and it was harder to run and his chest was burning and his side was starting to ache the way it had years ago in high school when he was running the mile.

And then he saw the door—at the very top of the steps.

He drove himself, pumping his legs still harder, and he could feel the muscles twitching in his calves as he went up-up-*up* and hit the next-to-last, then the last step and he reached out, grabbed the doorknob, jerked it open, leaped inside and slammed it shut, looking, feeling frantically for a lock and finding an old slide bolt, but it was rusted tightly in place and panic crawled up his back as he tore at it with his fingers because he knew that whatever was after him was almost at the top of the stairs by now and then the bolt gave way and he rammed it into place. Forehead pressed against the door, gasping, he tried to listen over the pounding of his heart for any sound outside and at first there was nothing and then after a few minutes, he heard it, a shuffling, rustling sound.

From behind him in the room.

He spun around, pressing his back against the door, cold fear chilling up into the hair at the back of his neck because he knew then that whatever had been chasing him up the steps was not outside at all now but was somehow in the room with him. The room was almost completely dark. The only light came from under the bottom of an ugly, scorched-looking paper shade pulled down over the single window at the far back of the room. His eyes were adjusted to the darkness now and he stared into it, but he could not see anything and he let his breath out and swallowed and thought that maybe he had been wrong about hearing something, that it was probably his imagination because he was so afraid, and then off in a far corner, a huge shadowy figure moved out away from the wall and started toward him.

He wanted to run and it was in his mind to do that, but his body seemed to be made of cement, unmovable, and he could only stare as the figure came closer, got bigger, and he could hear the old wood of the floor creaking under its footsteps and then the figure was only a few feet away from him and he looked up into the face only it wasn't a face at all but a misshapen skull, stripped clean of flesh and bleached white, with eyes that were punched-in holes, a mouth of teeth that were twisted into a hateful grin, and his own terror broke his body loose then and he whirled around to rip the lock away from the door and run.

Only the door was *gone!*

He found himself facing the wall, digging his nails into it, and he felt the figure looming up closer and closer behind him and he screamed then, a long, loud, terrible scream that jerked him suddenly awake, sitting up in the hotel bed, sweat covering his face and his chest, his eyes darting wildly around the room looking for the thing, but it wasn't there and the only sound was the nervous ticking of the travel clock in the still night.

He did not sleep anymore after the dream and he was awake to push in the alarm half an hour before it went off. He got up and turned on the lights against the dark and the predawn chill in the room. He folded his arms across his chest and rubbed his hands briskly up and down the backs of them, kneading his shoulders with his fingers. Then he went into the bathroom and pushed the little soft white rubber stopper down into the drain and filled the yellowing basin with hot water. He took one of the white hand towels from the rack, soaked it in the water, wrung it out and wrapped it around his face, holding it there for a couple of minutes, letting it soften his beard. When he took away the towel, his face in the mirror was flushed red as though he had a sunburn. He picked up the can of shaving cream, foamed a mound of it into the palm of his hand and spread it over his face, rubbing it in. He felt very tired. His eyes burned, and now and then as he was shaving, tiny clear spots would flow slowly across his line of vision. He stopped for a minute, thinking about the coming day.

The razor trembled in his fingers.

BECAUSE IT WAS SO EARLY in the morning, the commuter flight to Chicago was only a little more than half-full. A tall, blond stewardess with beautiful green eyes came cheerfully down the aisle with coffee and pastry. He took the coffee and wondered how close they were to him by now. They probably knew that he had taken the train out of Vegas, and that would give them something to wonder about. Would he go straight to Chicago or would he jump off in one of the hundred little towns along the way and try to hide for a while? They wouldn't know the answer to that one. They'd have to check, and that would take time. You've done okay, he thought. The whole damned thing had started on Saturday night. He'd gotten out of Vegas early Sunday morning, into Springfield Tuesday morning and now it was Wednesday morning and he was on the last lap. He sipped at the hot black coffee in the white Styrofoam cup and looked out through the little oval window of the plane at the flat, gray Illinois sky. The really tough part was coming up in Chicago.

He ran through his plan again in his mind. He had everything. He was all set. The passport had been the hardest thing to get, but money had talked as loudly in Springfield, Illinois, as it had in Las Vegas and a passport in the name of Mr. Leonard Rodman was safe inside his breast pocket. He looked down at the expensive tan leather briefcase in his lap. All the money was inside it. He had dumped his old army ditty bag and his suitcase in a Goodwill bin down the street from the hotel in Springfield. The new briefcase went well with his new suit. He didn't like the suit, didn't feel comfortable in it, but then he'd never felt comfortable in any suit. Still, it served a purpose. He looked like any of the other middle-aged business types on the plane. He fingered the latches of the case and resisted an urge to open it a crack and take a quick peek at his money.

His money?

Not yet, he thought. Not yet!

And in his mind, he saw it all happen again—the thin blond man who'd looked like Richard Widmark, running in the Vegas airport street with the car lights getting brighter and brighter on his back, and when the plane began its descent into Chicago, he said a fast prayer. It was the first time he could remember praying since he was a kid.

9

ECKHART WAS BORED.

He got into Chicago Wednesday morning, and passed out copies of Logan's work photo to certain people who were being paid to help him locate the cab driver. Eckhart gazed out over the vast terminal building full of people. His lips tightened into a frown. What a bitch of a place to have to look for somebody, he thought. O'Hare was the biggest international airport in the world. Well, if he didn't find him by tonight, he'd either missed him or he'd gotten off the train somewhere along the way. He was pretty sure the cab driver hadn't done that. He felt reasonably certain that Logan planned to get the hell out of the country with the money and that was why he'd come here. There were flights to everywhere in the world from this airport.

He was sure now that his assessment of Logan back in Vegas had been correct. The man was no fool. Nine guys out of ten would've hotfooted it straight to L.A. from Vegas and tried to get the first plane out of the country from there. If Logan had done that, he'd be dead now. Los Angeles International had been the first place Chambers had had covered after he found out his goons had blown it for him with Nichols. Eckhart's eyes went over faces in the churning crowd. The whole thing was a mess now. A damned rabbit hunt in the bush. Even if he did luck out and find the cab driver here, he still had a touchy problem.

He was going to have to take him out in this crowd without causing a riot.

10

JERRY LOGAN WALKED CAREFULLY toward the Pan Am ticket counter.

He was sweating heavily, and the tie he was wearing was like a rope chafing his neck. His eyes jumped and bounced off every face that came toward him in the crowd. He knew it was risky as hell coming in here like this, but it was the only way. He still had the airport security check to get through, and if it turned out that there was any problem with the money, he didn't want it to happen while he was in the middle of working his plan. Things could easily get too difficult for him to handle.

He gave the agent his ticket and waited while the man checked it against the reservation list. He realized that he was clenching his teeth. *Take it easy.* He just felt so out in the open in this crowd. Finally the guy was finished and handed him back his ticket, smiled and told him the gate number of his flight and wished him a pleasant trip. Jerry nodded, made an attempt at returning the smile and then quickly walked away from the counter. He took a deep breath and looked at his watch. He had a little over two hours before his flight.

Now the security check.

There was nothing to be done about it. He had to go through it. The briefcase now not only contained the money but also the things he needed for his plan. But even so, there was no way he would've ever checked a case with five hundred thousand dollars in it. He didn't trust any airline that much.

He stepped into the end of the line and looked over at the young security guard on the other side. The guy didn't look any too damned friendly. He didn't know what the hell he was going to say if they stopped him, made him open the case and asked him what the hell he was doing with so much cash. He'd just have to cross that bridge when he came to it.

The line moved pretty fast.

His turn now.

He walked through the short aisle past the metal detector and then stood watching as the case came up X-rayed on the little TV screen in front of the guard. They both watched it. Jerry glanced at the guard. Even with the other stuff on top, you could still see that it was all money. But the line behind him was filling up and the guy only looked at him for a second as the case came through and he picked it up off the conveyor belt.

Made it!

Jerry grinned to himself as he moved away. *You made it! You crazy bastard!* Maybe they didn't care what the hell you had in your bag as long as you couldn't hijack a plane with it. One thing was for sure. Morning or not, he badly needed a drink.

He found a little cocktail lounge near the departure gate for his flight. In spite of the early hour, the place was packed, but he lucked out and saw a guy getting up to leave as he came in and he got a little table in the back alongside a floor-to-ceiling window that looked out on the field. He ordered a double Jack Daniels on the rocks with a water back and lit up a cigarette. The cocktail waitress came over with the drink and put a little square napkin down on the table in front of him. The napkin had a pen-and-ink reproduction of the airport on it.

The waitress put the short glass of Jack Daniels down on the napkin and then set the taller glass of water down next to it. "You want me to run you a tab," she asked him, "or are you in a hurry?"

Jerry pulled back the cuff of his shirt and looked at his watch. What the hell, he thought. He had some time. "Keep me a tab," he said to her. "I'll probably have another one at least." He yawned suddenly as he said it, and the waitress laughed.

"Rough day already?" she asked him.

"Yeah," he said. "Rough day already."

The waitress smiled at him. "I know what you mean," she said. Then she moved away to another table across from him.

Yeah, he thought, watching her. You *know* what I mean! He picked up the Daniels and swallowed half of it in one gulp. If only you did, baby, he thought. *If only you did!* He took a drag on his cigarette and looked through the smoke at the other people in the lounge. They were mostly business types who, from the way they were drinking and talking, were on those expense-account vacations they passed off as business trips. The whiskey began to relax the tension in the back of his neck and along his shoulders. He glanced down at the expensive leather briefcase between his feet. Ain't this a bitch! he thought. Five hundred thousand dollars! He smiled. You're crazy! You are for sure *crazy!* He sipped at his drink and realized how nice it was to be able to afford good whiskey. How much better it tasted than the three-thirty-five-a-fifth stuff he'd been drinking for so many years. He thought about a lot of the other things in his life that he'd never been able to afford. He had a lot of catching up to do. He finished his drink and checked his watch. He had time for one more and then he'd put his plan into action.

11

THE YOUNG AIRPORT SECURITY GUARD was on his break. He looked around the coffee shop, saw two other uniformed guards sitting at a table and went over to them. They both grinned at him as he pulled out a chair and sat down.

The two other guards were older men, and both were retired cops. "So, what's goin' on, ace," one of them, a tall, thin man with a homely face, said.

The younger guard, whose name was Bates, waved for the waitress. Then he looked at the two men across the table from him. "Man!" he said. "You guys are not going to *believe* what I saw this morning!" The waitress, a pretty brunette, came over to the table and Bates looked at her, his eyes lighting up. "Hey, Rita!" he said. "Uh, just dump some mud in a cup for me and bring me a piece of that cheesecake."

"That's all?" the girl said, smiling at him.

"Yeah," Bates said to her. "I'm not too hungry."

"See, honey, he's on a diet," the other guard, a heavyset, red-faced man, said. "He's got to watch his figure, you know."

"I don't think it's *his* figure that he's watching," the homely guard said. The other guard laughed. Bates blushed and shook his head. The waitress laughed and went to get Bates's cheesecake and coffee.

"You like that cheesecake, huh?" the red-faced guard said, still teasing Bates.

"Boy!" Bates said. "You fuckin' guys have had your minds in the sewer so long, it's a wonder you don't stink!"

"Well, come on, damnit," the homely guard said. "What was it that you saw this morning that we ain't gonna believe?"

"Yeah," the jolly, red-faced guard said, winking at his friend. "Let's hear it. What'd she look like. Go *on!*"

"It wasn't no *girl*," Bates said.

"Ohhh, oh," the homely guard said. "I think we got trouble with this boy!"

"Just shut up and listen," Bates said, ignoring him. "I'm on the line this morning, you know? Well this guy comes over, middle-aged guy, nice suit, briefcase—like that? Well, Kathy runs him through and I'm lookin' at the screen and I'll tell you, I could not fucking *believe* it!" He paused dramatically and looked at each of the two older men. "There was nothing in that briefcase but money! *Cash*, baby! Oh, he had some other stuff on top of it, but it was mostly just money."

The homely guard shot a glance at his companion, then back at Bates. "You sure?" he asked him.

"Hey," Bates said. "I ain't bullshitting you! A whole damned briefcase full of money. Enough to set all our asses down in Hawaii for a while."

"You ask him about it?" This from the jolly, red-faced guard.

"Hell, no, I didn't ask him about it. It was just money. But let me ask you guys something—now you tell me— what kind of man carries around that kind of loot? You think maybe he was a gangster or something like that?" Bates had come to Chicago from West Virginia and was forever convinced that the city was still the main stronghold of dark, swarthy-faced hoodlums in shiny silk suits.

The jolly, red-faced guard shook his head. "Nah," he said. "He was probably just one of them rich old bastards that don't trust their money to banks. There's a lot of them around. You'd be surprised."

The homely guard nodded in agreement. "Yeah," he said, "they think that if they ain't got cash, they ain't got money, but damn, that's taking a big chance! There's guys hanging around this airport—if they knew somebody was carrying that kind of money on them!'' He whistled softly.

"Yeah, but you can't tell them,'' the jolly-faced guard said. "Then the first time the dumb bastards get hit over the head, they come crying to us.''

The waitress came back with Bates's coffee and cheesecake. The two older guards had to leave. Their break was over. Bates was glad they were going. He'd been working himself up for three months to ask the waitress out, but he sure as hell couldn't do it with those two hanging around gawking and grinning at him.

12

JERRY LOGAN WAS ON his fourth Jack Daniels on the rocks. He felt a lot better now, more relaxed. He knew he was a little drunk, but he didn't care. It felt great to feel this good. He hadn't felt this good in one hell of a long time. There was something to be said for good booze, he thought. He grinned suddenly, and a mountainous woman sitting at a table with three other mountainous women grinned back at him. He laughed, picked up his glass and swirled the whiskey around in it.

Yeah, there was something to be said for good booze, he thought, still smiling. And there was something to be said for having five hundred thousand dollars in cash in a briefcase under your table while you were drinking it, too! He took a sip of his bourbon. *Thanks, lady,* he thought, *for staying with me this far. Just don't leave, please.* Though he had not let himself think about it very much, though he had worked to keep it out of his mind, he had never actually thought he would make it this far. And now here he was in Chicago with a plane ticket to London in his shirt pocket, drinking Jack Daniels.

He picked up his glass and drained the last of the whiskey.

Maybe you worry too much, he thought.

Yeah. Maybe he gave them way too much credit. They might not even have the slightest idea where he was now. Hell, they could be hunting and sniffing around every little burg between here and Vegas, looking for him. Well, you just keep right on looking, boys, he thought. Look until your goddamned eyes pop out! He leaned back in his chair and put his arms over his head, stretching and pulling at the muscles. His head felt pleasantly light. He looked around the little cocktail lounge. It didn't seem to be as noisy with voices as when he'd first come in, though the place was still full. He looked at his watch. He had just a little over an hour before his plane.

Then he thought of something that made him laugh.

What if, he thought...what if he didn't need his plan at all? He hit the top of the table with his fist. Huh? Wouldn't that be a kick in the head? After all the worrying about it on the train and back in that roach hole in Springfield, and then not even to have to use it! He picked the package of cigarettes off the table, pulled one out, dropped it, picked it up again and lit it. Okay, he thought...let's just think a minute here about this. Suppose you were wrong. Suppose they *did* know you were here. Yeah . . . suppose they knew you were sitting right here in this very airport in this very bar.

What're they going to do?

Bar's full of people. Airport's full of people. There's guards around. Guards with guns. Somebody comes up to you, he thought, gives you any shit, you make a big stink, you yell your goddamned head off. He lifted his glass and drank the little bit of water in the bottom from the melting ice. He knew then exactly what he was going to do.

Nothing.

He'd just stay right here at this little table and have another drink and wait until it was time to get up and go right outside there to the gate and get on that big bird to London.

London, England!

Sonofabitch!

He was drunk. He had five hundred thousand dollars and he was going to London, England.

"Waitress!" he yelled.

13

ECKHART'S EYES BORED INTO the swirling crowd of people dragging suitcases, clutching tickets and children.

Ridiculous!

He shook his head and rapped his knuckles impatiently against the wall where he was standing. The whole thing was ridiculous and stupid. The place was too big. There were too many people. And even if he hadn't missed Logan, it would take a goddamned hawk to spot him in this zoo, and even then the hawk would have to have luck with him. The hell with it! he thought. You gave it a good shot. You've earned your money. Nobody's going to fault you for losing Logan. The whole thing was Chambers's fault and he knew it. He'd just have to take the fall for the money and he knew that, too. Tough shit. It couldn't have happened to a nicer guy, Eckhart thought, smiling. He'd go now and call him. He'd just tell him that they missed the guy, that was all. The fat slob would yell and scream, but screw him.

He remembered that he didn't have enough change to make the call to Vegas. He found a change machine against the wall and broke some singles into quarters, nickels and dimes. There was a security guard standing near the machine and he asked him where he could find a pay phone. "Whole row of them right down there around the corner," the guard told him. Eckhart thanked him and walked away.

As he headed for the phone to call Chambers, he wondered what the slob would do now that Logan had gotten away to wherever with the money. He'd probably still try to track him down, but that wouldn't be so easy now that he was out of the country. He remembered Chambers's nervousness, his fear. How would Logan's getting away affect what was bothering him. Maybe, Eckhart thought, it had something to do with Gurino, the owner of the hotel. Gurino had a reputation as a decent, solid citizen in Vegas, but he had heard stories about the old man, about his early days in Detroit. Maybe that was what Chambers was afraid of. Losing five hundred grand of Gurino's money. If the whole thing really was Chambers's fault, that might be it. Eckhart smiled thinly. Well, different people have luck at different times, he thought.

One thing was for sure. If Chambers had gotten on the wrong side of August Gurino, he had good reason to be nervous and afraid.

14

JERRY LOGAN SAT AND WATCHED a huge 747 come roaring down on the tarmac outside the window of the airport cocktail lounge and thought about the incredible way things could happen in a man's life sometimes. You got yourself into a job and you worked it day after day until you finally knew it, and maybe after a while, you knew that you really didn't like the damned job, that you'd like to be doing something else, but you didn't know what, exactly, so you just went on doing what you were doing and you knew you were in a rut, but you were so busy just living, trying to keep your head above water, that you learned to live in the rut and then, bang, one day something happens. You didn't have anything to do with it happening, but it wakes you up fast and all of a sudden you got a good, close look at your life and the way things were with you. He thought about how different things were now from the way they'd been not even a week ago. Pulling the cab up in front of the trailer sometimes as late as three or four in the morning depending on what shift you were working and your back'd be aching and you'd be tired as hell, but you knew you wouldn't be able to go to sleep right away because you were still wound up so you'd go make a bologna sandwich, pop open a can of beer and watch some old movie on TV until you were tired enough to go to bed or you just dropped off to sleep on the damned couch. And sometimes on nights like that, he would think about what a lousy, boring life he was leading and how he really didn't have anything or anybody. Oh, sure, he had a few friends around town, but not really *anybody*.

Now he picked up his glass and shook the little ice crystals around in it, drained the last of the Daniels.

Go on, he thought. *Say it.* You're drunk now, you can say it.

He didn't have anybody to *love*.

Yeah ... and ... come on, you drunken bastard!

And he didn't have anybody to love *him*.

There! Out! Said! You going to cry next, he thought. You've always just loved crying drunks.

Why was it, though, he wondered, still indulging himself, that he'd never married, had kids, a house and all of that stuff? He'd always thought that he'd end up doing it sooner or later, but somehow it had never happened. It just seemed that it hadn't taken as long for him to get older as he'd thought it would. Or something like that. Who knows? Who the hell knows the reasons for anything?

"Excuse me ..."

He looked away from the window. A young guy holding a newspaper stood looking down at him. "I've got a little while before my flight," the guy said, "and I was wondering if you'd mind if I sat down here and had a quick drink?'' He gestured at the packed bar. "Place is so full,'' he said.

Jerry shrugged. "Yeah, go ahead.''

"Hey, thanks a lot,'' the guy said. He borrowed a chair from a larger table across from them and sat down. "I really appreciate it. I'm not too good at flying without a drink first.''

Jerry nodded. "Yeah, I know what you mean,'' he said. He turned around then and went back to looking out the window. It was a rude thing to do, but the hell with it. He didn't feel like getting into any stupid conversations with anybody. And besides, the guy looked like a salesman or a lawyer or something like that. Some glad-handing hotshot. He'd driven hundreds just like him back in Vegas and he'd had to be nice to them then. Well, he sure as hell didn't have to be nice to them now. He lit up a cigarette and stretched his legs out from under the table until the toes of his shoes touched the glass at the bottom of the big window.

He heard the waitress come over and the guy ordered his drink, a Harvey Wallbanger, which figured, and he thought again how all those types looked so much alike. It was really something. Like their hairstyles all seemed to be the same and it looked like their hair wouldn't mess up on their heads if they were standing in a typhoon. And it was the same thing with their clothes. Like they all went to the same tailor. Nice, expensive suits, vests, colored shirts and snappy ties. And they were all very big on smiling. Smiling and shaking hands. They were absolutely terrific at smiling and shaking hands.

He looked out at the field and watched a little truck towing a long string of flatbed cars piled high with luggage out toward a waiting plane. He smiled at himself, at his prejudices. Okay, he thought, sure, there's probably a lot of those kinds of guys that are okay. It was just that so many of the ones he'd talked to back in his cab in Vegas had been nothing more than well-educated, smooth-talking bullshit artists on the make for number one.

Well educated, huh?

And you quit in the middle of high school, right? he thought. Yeah, but there had been no money in the house then and his mom had been working behind the counter at that stupid, cheap-paying department store in St. Louis. She'd come home tired as hell every night and she was always worrying and talking about the damned bills. Oh, they were making it okay, but that was about all, and he hadn't been able to stand it after a while, so he'd quit school and gotten a job pumping gas to try to bring a little more money into the house. He remembered how sad his mom had looked when he'd told her he was quitting, but he remembered, too, that she seemed to be proud of him the first time he cashed his check and brought her home the money, and even now, thinking about it, he didn't regret what he had done.

And so yeah, he thought, maybe he *was* a little jealous of some of those guys.

He took a long drag on his cigarette and blew the smoke at the window, watching it hit and spread out over the glass.

He wondered if maybe his old man was alive someplace.

His old man had been a prick.

He never knew him and only faintly remembered what he looked like, but from what he'd been told about him by an aunt (his mom would never say a word), the old man came home from work one day and took all the money and anything else of value that was in the house, and nobody ever saw him again. Maybe he wouldn't think all that badly of the bastard if he'd just taken off. He could maybe understand a man doing that sometimes, but he should have left her something. He shouldn't have taken everything. He looked down at the expensive leather briefcase between his feet and wished that his mother were still alive, that she was a nice blue-haired old lady and he could set her up in Miami or somewhere like that, do something nice for her.

He dropped his cigarette on the floor and rubbed it out with his shoe.

You're terrific, you know that? he thought. Really terrific. A few drinks and bang, it's nostalgia time. He thought about having still another drink and turned back around to the table and picked up his glass, but then decided against it. He didn't want them to have to carry him onto the damned plane.

He put two fingers into the glass and picked out a little piece of melting ice and popped it into his mouth, and the young guy sitting across from him said, "Hey, did you see *this*?" He had his newspaper spread out on the table in front of him. (*The Wall Street Journal*, which also figured.) He was pointing to something he'd been reading.

"What's that?" Jerry said, not giving a damn what it was.

"I can't believe this!" the guy said, shaking his head. (Like radio announcers, Jerry thought. That was another thing. They all sounded like goddamned radio announcers!) The guy turned the paper around on the table and pushed it across to him, pointing to a column in the center of the page. Jerry looked down at it and the guy moved his finger away and said, "You just keep right on looking, Mr. Logan," only now the voice was softer and very, very serious. "You just act like you're reading that paper and you listen and keep your fucking mouth *shut*!"

Jerry stared at the suddenly meaningless jumble of black type and felt all the strength drain right out of his body.

"You do *anything*," the voice hissed, "except what I tell you, you fucking thief, and I'll waste you right here at this table, and don't think I won't do it, either. Nobody in this room'll have the time or the balls to stop me. Now, you've got some money in that briefcase that doesn't belong to you. I'm here to get that money back and that's *all* I'm here for. We're going to get up and go out of here and you're going to show me that money. If it's all there, you can split and consider yourself one lucky man, because if it was my money, your ass'd be dead tonight. Now, you hear what I'm saying to you, shithead?"

Jerry Logan did not look up from the paper. "Yeah," he said quietly.

Eckhart looked closely at the man, reading him. It would be okay now, he thought. He had made him believe. He thought he had a chance of saving his ass and that was all that mattered to him now. That was always

the best way to handle it. You caught them flat, laid a real
Edward G. Robinson number on them. Then you let
them think they still had a chance. It worked every time.
"Okay," Eckhart said, dropping money on the table for
the drinks. "Let's go!"

15

IT HAD BEEN NOTHING MORE than dumb luck that had
led Eckhart to Jerry Logan. He had been standing in the
phone booth looking up Chambers's number in his address book, when he'd heard his name called out over
the PA system. He was to come to the Air France ticket
counter for a message. As he approached the place, he
saw one of the people paid to keep an eye out for the cab
driver. He had been privately informed that this particular individual was something of a small-time strung-out
bettor, into a shylock over the ponies and out of fear, had
enough sense to keep quiet. He had felt a rush of adren-
aline as he walked up to the woman and looked at her.
"Well?" he said.

She flashed him a smile and raised her eyebrows.
"You'd just be surprised at the things a girl can hear
working in a little coffee shop at the airport," she said.

And he had listened to the story that had been told to
her by some security guard who was obviously hot to get
into her pants, and when she had finished, he had not
been too optimistic. It didn't sound like his cab driver—
the expensive-looking suit, the briefcase and all that
business—but still, the man carrying so much cash had

made it something that he had best check out. It was also possible that Logan thought he was home free by now and was spending some of his new money on a new image. He had then gone to each of the people he had searching for the cab driver and passed on these new additions to the man's description, and in less than half an hour, one of them had spotted Logan in the little cocktail lounge. Eckhart had stopped on the way there to buy a newspaper as a prop and had stood inside the crowded bar, pretending to look for a place to sit down while he studied the man sitting alone by the window. True, the clothes were wrong and so was the expensive leather briefcase under the table, but the face belonged to a Las Vegas cab driver whose lucky streak had just run out on him.

16

JERRY LOGAN REACHED DOWN and gripped the sides of his chair and scooted it back from the table. He got up, and they were walking then past the tables of laughing and talking faces and he wanted to scream at them to look, to see what was happening here, but he only kept moving with this tall man so close behind him that he could feel his elbow brushing against the man's jacket. His whole body felt very heavy, but he did not feel drunk anymore, only light-headed, and he wondered if he was going to faint and then they were through the bar and they moved out the door and into the wide expanse of the terminal building and Jerry saw people, lots of people everywhere, moving every which way.

Then he ran!

Running, hot-faced, with terrible fear-chills shooting all through his body, mouth open, heart thundering in his ears, he ran past people, into people, between them, shoving them aside, hearing their angry and puzzled voices behind him, cutting quickly around a corner, but he was too close to the wall and the briefcase smacked into it, the shock of the impact jarring through his hand into his arm and then his shoes were sliding and he was falling forward, his arms shooting out in front of him as he went down hard on the floor.

People all around him, hands pulling him up, curious faces looking down, voices . . .

"What is it?"

"Is he okay?"

"Well, he shouldn't have been running like that!"

And back up on his feet then, standing inside the small circle of curious, staring, faces and he wanted so badly to keep them around him like a wall, make them move with him and protect him, but he knew that he had to get away and he heard his own voice saying words at them. Yes, he was okay—fine, now. Late, he was late, that was all—why he'd been running—and yes, yes, he *had* better be careful, thank you, yes . . .

And he broke away out of the circle.

Walking fast, but not running now, looking around for the tall man, but he didn't see him. Then he saw the little white sign that read MEN, and he cut over to it, went inside, going straight into one of the stalls and he had only enough time to bang the metal door shut behind

him, flip the bolt and bend forward, hitting the chrome
rod that flushed the toilet with a watery roar, drowning
out the sounds of his being sick.

17

ECKHART HAD NOT EXPECTED the man to run. He had
seen the tiny droplets of sweat form along his upper lip
and the deep, shocked fear in his eyes and usually they
didn't have it in them to run by then. They just sat there
with you and waited and sometimes they looked at you
and sometimes they looked straight ahead out the window like the guy had that time on the beach of that small
lake in Jersey. They had both been sitting in the backseat and he had placed the gun so close to the guy's head
that the tip of the barrel had touched the curling black
hairs of his sideburns and the man was still looking out
through the windshield when he'd pulled the trigger, the
gun bucking hard once in his hand.

But this one had run.

And he had not been able to run after him without
drawing too much attention to himself, and now he
would have to search him out again, try to follow the little human trail a man leaves when he runs in panic
through a crowd—clusters of people talking and looking off in one direction, the things they said, remarks
that told you your prey had passed this way.

Only this time it didn't work.

The hunting ground was way too big and there were

too many people moving around, covering up the trail, and abruptly it ended.

Eckhart's eyes scanned the crowd, the frustration building up in him. *Goddamn* this place! he thought. There must be at least fifty exits to the terminal building, and Logan was probably already on his way out one of them. Well, enough was enough. He wasn't going to go through the whole number of trying to find him again. He turned around and started to walk out of the building when he thought of something that made him stop.

The unexpected.

That was what had been behind the cab driver's luck from the beginning. He had not done any of the things that one would logically expect a man in his situation to do. Like running with the money in the first place when he had to know it was connected to some big people after what he'd seen happen to Nichols. And then leaving Vegas that same night, and on a train yet. And now, just when you're sure you've got his ass, he cuts and runs on you. Logan had to be really scared now that he knew somebody was right on him. Most guys would run straight into the city, try to lose themselves for a while. And they'd be caught, too. Because you had to know *how* to hide in a city like Chicago, and the average man just wasn't skilled enough to pull it off. The word would be out on the street with enough money behind it, and the guy would be found inside of a week or two. Eckhart rubbed his hand over his mouth.

Would Logan know that? he wondered.

Yeah, he thought. He would know that. Or he'd figure it out. He was a careful man. And scared or not, he would still be thinking and he would see that his chances of hiding were probably not worth a damn, that there would be too many eyes looking for him. So he'd do just what nobody would expect him to do.

He'd stay right here in this airport and try to get on whatever flight he'd been waiting for when he was spotted. He'd do that, Eckhart told himself, because, risky or not, it was still his best bet in the long run. He began walking back in the direction of the little cocktail lounge where he'd grabbed the cab driver. People who are waiting for a flight will usually try to find a bar that's as close to the gate of that flight as possible. So, he thought, it would be a matter now of trying to get inside Logan's head, trying to guess where it might be that he was planning on going. There would be no point in checking the various airlines. He was sure Logan would be ticketed under another name. As he approached the cocktail lounge, Eckhart knew the whole thing was at best a crapshoot, but then maybe the cab driver's luck *was* starting to burn out and maybe he was due for a run of his own.

18

JERRY LOGAN SAT IN THE little stall of the rest room. He sat very still, his eyes closed, his head between his knees, his arms hanging limply down beside his legs, the tips of his fingers just touching the cool, moist tile floor. He was concentrating very hard on trying to control, to slow down his ragged breathing and make his body stop trembling. *Easy...*he told himself. *Just breathe. In...and out...nice and...easy.* In...out...

Minutes passed.

And slowly the blind terror that had gripped him so tightly began to give way, and he sat up and opened his eyes. He unbent his fingers from their cramped grip around the ends of the briefcase in his lap and massaged them. His shirt was unbuttoned at the neck, the knot in the dark blue tie jerked loose and in the white glare of the circular light in the ceiling, sweat glistened on his face and his throat. He stared straight ahead at the gray metal door of the stall, listened to the sounds coming from the other side of it.

Footsteps and voices.

Luggage clumped down on the floor.

Jets of water being turned on, turned off in the sinks.

Urinals flushing.

And he wondered if the tall man who wanted to kill him—and he was certain that was his intention—might be waiting for him to open the stall door and come out. Had he seen him run into the rest room? No, he thought. There had been too many people in the way. But you didn't look *behind* you when you came in here, he thought. You don't know. He could have seen you.

He reached inside his shirt pocket for his cigarettes and took them out, a new pack, unopened, and he couldn't seem to pick away the damned thin red strip of cellophane around the top of the pack to open it and frustrated, he tore the whole top away and dug one out, bending it. The book of paper matches was soft and damp from being so close to his skin and he was afraid they wouldn't light, but they were okay and he lit up, drew the smoke deep and let it out. Then he looked at his watch.

And nearly cried out. His plane left for London in twenty minutes.

You can't stay here! his mind screamed at him. If that flight leaves without you, what are you going to do, huh? What are you going to *do!* He looked down at the brief-case in his lap. He *had* to try the plan, he thought wildly. It was all he had. No choices now. He took another drag on the cigarette and dropped it down between his knees into the toilet. Then he stood up and put the briefcase on the back of the bowl and opened it.

19

ECKHART SAT IN THE telephone booth. He left the glass door to the booth half-open. On the little metal shelf beneath the phone, he had spread out an assortment of quarters, nickels and dimes, but he had no intention of making any call. He had chosen this particular booth because it faced out on the departure gate of what he hoped would turn out to be Jerry Logan's flight. Four gates circled the little cocktail lounge where he had found the cab driver, and all four of them were for flights out of the country: two to Europe, two to the Orient. He knew that he could easily have picked the wrong one. And to make matters worse, the departure times for all four flights were nearly the same. He couldn't go run-ning from gate to gate, because he knew Logan would be watching from somewhere and spot him. And if he did luck out and have the right gate, the cab driver probably wouldn't show up until the very last minute so he'd be able to go right on board and not have to wait around out in the open. There was no doubt in Eckhart's mind that if he did see Logan again, it was going to be touch and go. The departure gate of the flight was nearly full now, and as his eyes searched from face to face, his hand went inside his coat pocket and lightly he moved his fingertips over the hard, smoothly polished handle of the knife.

Eckhart smiled.

Nobody ever suspects the ordinary, he thought. So all you had to do was to make the ordinary dangerous. Make it your weapon. When he had emptied his pockets at the airport security check, they had seen the knife, but nothing had been said about it. That didn't surprise him. There was nothing about the look of the knife to arouse any kind of suspicion. It was, after all, just an ordinary pocketknife. It even had a bottle opener on one end of it. Lots of men carried them.

Except this one was different.

If they had taken the time to open the knife and examine it more closely, they might well have had second thoughts, for one of the blades, the middle one, was much thinner than the others and of the very finest stainless steel. This blade had been honed sharp as a scalpel, and the slightest touch of it against the skin would draw blood. Eckhart had had the blade custom fitted to the pocketknife several years ago in Germany, and since that time, it had served him well on several occasions. He had known that he wouldn't be able to get a gun into the airport without having to involve too many people in his plans and that was something he never liked doing. He didn't even like having to pay the people to help him look for the cab driver, but that had been necessary and it was an involvement of an indirect nature. And besides, even with a silencer, there were too many things that could go wrong using a gun in a place as crowded as this airport.

But the knife, that was another thing entirely.

It would enable him to use the thick, moving crowd of people to his advantage. He needed only to get in close enough to Logan to have body contact with the man and then he would use it quickly, grab him as he fell and call for help as if the cab driver had fainted or had had a heart attack. Then, in the confusion that would be sure to follow, he would grab the briefcase and slip away.

Only one problem made him uncomfortable.

Eckhart tapped the little metal shelf with his knuckles, making the coins on it jar tinnily. His lips tightened and irritation flashed in his eyes.

The victim knew his face.

That was something he had never had to deal with before. Surprise had always been his ace, and now it had been taken away from him. Now he would have to come up on his man from behind, get to him and use the blade before he turned around and saw him or all hell would break loose for sure.

20

JERRY LOGAN WALKED CAREFULLY through the crowd toward the departure gate of his flight to London. Voices swirled around him, but he heard them only as gibberish. Behind the dark sunglasses, his eyes darted from face to face looking for the tall man, but he did not see him. He looked ahead of him at the gate area full of people now waiting to get on the plane. His eyes picked over the faces of the passengers, but the tall man was not there, either. They would be letting everybody board the plane any minute, he told himself. Just take it easy. Concentrate. Pay attention.

Back in the rest room, after he had gotten ready and was about to open the stall door, a sudden wave of anxiety and trembling had come over him and it had been all he could do to make himself reach out and open the metal latch of the stall door, and then he'd done it only when he'd heard a lot of voices outside. But when he had stepped out, there had only been the usual assortment of men one would expect to find in the rest room of a large airport. Two portly men in their fifties, dressed in sports clothes, obviously traveling together and both obviously drunk. A lone sailor, a couple of straight business types and a man with a dark-haired little boy in a bright green Snoopy T-shirt. They had all turned to look at him when he'd jerked open the stall door, and it occurred to him that he must have looked frightened. The man with the little boy had even asked him if he was all right, and he'd said that yes, he was fine and moved away out the door of the rest room and as he had stepped out into the crowded terminal building, a strange thing had happened.

He had thought about dying.

And it struck him as odd that he'd never really given any thought to that, and yet strangely, the idea itself had not frightened him very much. He'd felt only that he wanted to get on with this whole thing, to try to make it work all the way to the finish, no matter what the hell the finish turned out to be. It had crossed his mind that there really hadn't been too many things in his life that he had ever finished.

"Is this your first trip to London?"

Jerry turned his head slightly and looked into the smooth, cheerful young face of the airline attendant who was walking beside him to the gate and who, out of some sense of professional duty, had decided that they must have a conversation. "Yeah," Jerry answered. "I've always wanted to go."

"Ahh!" the kid said, nodding vigorously. "You're in for a treat. It's one of the greatest cities in the world!"

"Yeah, I know," Jerry said, wishing to God the kid would shut up. He had enough things to think about without having to keep up small talk, but they were up to the roped-off gate then and they walked into it and he felt a sudden feeling of relief, but it only lasted for a second because something happened that he had never thought about happening at all.

The kid told him he might as well sit down.

Jerry looked at him. "The aircraft is not quite ready for boarding yet," the kid explained. He made a helpless gesture with his hands. "Afraid we're running a little late this morning."

"How long do you think it'll be?" Jerry asked him. His voice sounded funny to him.

"Ah, it shouldn't be more than another ten minutes or so," the kid said.

I have to go on *now!* his mind screamed into the smiling face, but he let himself sit down in the chair and the kid turned away and walked out through the double glass doors that led out to his plane and he was alone then. He sat bolt upright on the edge of the chair, his fists clenched tightly together on top of the briefcase in his lap. He had been so careful, he thought bitterly. He had worked out the time so closely. He would get to the gate and then go right on the plane, one, two, just like that, and now he was sitting here. They were supposed to be ready! Why in the hell weren't they ready?

He looked around at the other passengers inside the gate and then behind him past the ropes at the bustling terminal. Okay, he thought. He took a slow, deep breath. Okay. You're here, at least. Just try to relax and keep your eyes open. Ten minutes, the kid had said. That was all. Just ten minutes; not very long. And maybe what you hoped for happened, he thought. Maybe the tall man had already left the building. Maybe when you ran, he thought you were going for the cops and he took off. He forced himself to unclench his fists, rubbed his open palms over the smooth top of the briefcase, staring down at the sweat smears on the leather.

Ten minutes.

21

ECKHART HELD THE QUARTER in his fingers and rubbed one edge of it down hard on the little metal shelf of the phone booth, scratching through the gray paint. His eyes narrowed and his jaw muscles tightened as he looked out at the gate that was now full of people preparing to get on the flight.

No cab driver.

If he had picked the right one, Logan should show his ass any minute now. Inside the gate, a ticket agent in a bright blue blazer was talking on a white telephone behind the counter. He hung up the phone and pulled over a microphone and began to announce that the flight was now ready for boarding and would all the passengers please make certain that they had not forgotten any of their carry-on belongings before they left the gate area.

Eckhart stood up. His right arm hung straight down at his side, the fingers of his hand curled slightly upward, the handle of the knife resting inside them, the blade out of sight up the sleeve of his coat. A simple flick of the wrist and it would be ready to use.

He glared at the people inside the gate as they began getting up and gathering their debris. Frustration started to rise from the pit of his stomach up into his chest because he knew that he had chosen the wrong flight. Only then he saw one of the passengers inside the gate do something, a little something and if he had not been watching so closely and if the man had been standing instead of sitting down, he would have missed it, but he hadn't missed it and it was enough. Incredible! he thought. All this time!

His shoulder banged into the door of the phone booth as he moved quickly out of it and into the crowd toward the gate, his eyes locked on the blind man in the dark glasses and loud sport shirt who was sitting up at the very front of the gate. The blind man with the full head of black hair that he'd be willing to bet would come off in your hand if you pulled on it.

The blind man who had just looked at his watch!

22

JERRY LOGAN DROPPED THE CUFF of his shirt like it was red hot. *What are you doing!* he screamed at himself. *What the hell are you doing!*

He had forgotten all about the damned watch. He was supposed to have taken it off and put it in the case before he left the men's room. It had just been habit that had made him forget it. He never took the thing off, not even when he went to bed. You better stay awake, he told himself. You just better the hell stay *awake!*

He looked over at the ticket agent behind the little counter, who was now reading off the names of the people who were on the standby list for the flight. He would read a name off the list and then wait a minute to see if the person was there and if the person was, he'd then ask if he or she preferred smoking or nonsmoking seats and then give the person a ticket and go on to the next name. How many names were on that list, Jerry wondered. Five? Ten? Come on! Come *on!* He couldn't sit in that damned chair any longer. Slowly he stood up, turned and looked at the crowd and then over at the entrance to the gate.

And it was like something heavy had just struck him in the chest.

Already through the gate entrance, heading toward him, smiling, was the tall man.

People were moving out of the way to let him through; a friend hurrying to say good-bye to another friend before he left on his trip.

Only this friend had something shiny in his hand.

He wanted to run, but it just wasn't in him to do that now. He opened his mouth to yell for help to some of the people around him but there was no saliva in his mouth, and he tried to swallow but couldn't do that either, and now the tall man was much closer and he could see the features of his face, the tight smiling lips, and all of a sudden he just didn't care anymore. He closed his eyes behind the dark glasses, felt the tall man come up on him, felt his hand grab his shoulder and then, "Okay, we're all ready for you, Mr. Rodman!"

Eyes open again. The face of the young flight attendant smiling at him. He looked past the kid.

At the tall man not five feet away. His eyes watching them, his face alert, undecided.

"We're really sorry for the delay," the kid was saying, "but we're all set to go now. We'll get you on board and then the rest of the passengers. Here, let me take that for you." He took the briefcase out of Jerry's hand and began guiding him firmly by the arm toward the double glass doors that led out to the plane. He felt his breath coming in fast, short bursts through his mouth and a crazy, wild kind of exhilaration. He let his weight lean into the arm of the young attendant, looked back over his shoulder at the tall man.

And a little smile started to form on his lips.

The smile got bigger, turned into a wide grin and then a short, sudden bark of a laugh exploded up out of him. He shoved his arm straight out at the tall man, the middle finger of his hand raised in the well-known gesture of contempt.

The other passengers stared at him.

The tall man was not smiling.

The double glass doors banged shut behind him.

23

ECKHART STOOD AND WATCHED his man get away. Some of the people inside the gate were looking curiously at him. He put an embarrassed look on his face, shook his head, then turned and began walking back toward the exit. Once he was outside the ropes and back into the moving crowd, he palmed the knife and dropped it into his coat pocket.

He felt tired and he had a slight headache, but strangely enough, he suddenly wasn't all that upset that Logan had gotten away. He was really something, he thought as he stepped into the phone booth and slid the glass door shut. The guy was really something. Eckhart took out all the change he'd gotten earlier and again spread it out on the little metal shelf. He took a small, tan address book from his pocket. As he lifted the receiver, it occurred to him that maybe he wouldn't wait another two years to retire. What was two years, anyway? Could be a lot, he thought, depending on how you looked at it.

The dime clunked down into the phone box. He put his finger into the O slot, spun the dial.

"Operator," a pleasant female voice said. "May I help you?"

Eckhart looked down at the opened page of the address book. "Yes," he said quietly. "I'd like to place a call overseas. To London, England."

24

AND ON THE PLANE, tears of relief rolled slowly out of the corners of the blind man's eyes and down his cheeks below the frames of the dark glasses. They might still come after him, he thought. There was a good chance they would, but there were things he could do. There were plenty of things he could do now. He looked down at the briefcase in his lap. The plump, middle-aged woman in the dark blue suit sitting next to him kept glancing at him nervously as though she wanted to say something but couldn't decide what. He snapped open the latches on the case with his thumbs and turned his head slightly toward the woman. She looked away.

He raised the lid of the case only enough to slip his hand inside, felt the stacks of dry paper under his fingers. He swallowed and took a deep breath, let it out slowly. Incredible! he thought. Really incredible! He snapped the case shut again and leaned back into the wonderful softness of the high-backed seat, and the stewardess came over with the champagne he had ordered.

He turned toward the woman in the dark blue suit and, smiling, asked her if she would like to join him in a glass. She smiled, surprised, and said that she would be delighted. The stewardess poured. The woman looked at him, holding hers, only half-smiling now, suddenly a little uncomfortable at drinking a toast with someone who could not see. Jerry smiled at her. "To a good trip!" he said.

The woman smiled, more relieved. "To a good trip!" she said quickly. They drank their champagne and settled back, the awkwardness eased, the ceremony over.

Jerry put the briefcase down on the floor in front of him and put his feet on top of it. The booze was free in first class, but he would only have the champagne now and then he would sleep for a while. He was so tired, his body and mind numb, drained, empty.

But he felt like he had to have the champagne.

And silently he lifted his glass, drank another toast, this one to himself. It felt good to drink a toast to himself. And it struck him that for maybe the first time in his life, he honest-to-God had something that was worth celebrating.

PART TWO

25

THE MAN IN THE BED was sleeping soundly.

He was lying on his side with both knees drawn up to his belly and he had the blankets piled up high around the side of his face so that only the top half of one ear and some of his hair were visible. The hair was tousled and very blond. Near his head on the bedside table, the numbers glowed softly red in the dark face of the digital clock-radio. The man's soft snoring was the only sound in the room save for the muted, quick little flap as the numbered minute tabs flipped over the clock. The man stirred in his sleep, shifted his positions a little, his huge bulk moving under the blankets.

The telephone rang, shattering the silence of the bedroom. He opened his eyes for a second, then closed them again, uttered a muffled curse into the sheet against his lips and pulled the pillow tighter around his head. He was never a deep sleeper, and once awakened in the night, he often had a difficult time getting back to sleep.

Ring. Ring. Ring.

Earplugs, he remembered angrily. He'd kept meaning to buy the damned things, give them a try, to see if they would be of any help against the disturbances that often ruined his sleep—wrong numbers in the middle of the night, cars backfiring on the street—but he could never think of the damned things during the day when he was out. Well, the hell with it. He wasn't getting out of bed to answer the thing. He'd let it ring. Whoever it was would get tired of holding the receiver up to his ear after a while.

Ring. Ring. Ring. RIINNGGGG . . . !

He endured it for maybe another two minutes.

Then with a loud, angry curse, he flung the blankets away from his face, jumped out of bed, noting the time as he got up and stumbled across the dark bedroom in fury, ready to bring the full wrath of hell down on whoever was on the other end of the line only he never did that because as soon as he had snatched up the receiver and barked a "Yes!" into it, he heard the faraway, tinny-sounding voice of the operator saying that she had a person-to-person call from a Mr. David Eckhart for a Mr. Derik Mills and all he said was, "This is Mills speaking," and then he waited, suddenly very awake, listening.

The conversation was brief.

Mills actually said very little except to ask a question now and then, and there was not the slightest trace of anger in his voice now. After he had hung up, he went back to the bed and sat down, his mind going over the conversation, thinking about what he would have to do. He sat there in the dark for several minutes and then got up, turned on the lamp on the bed table and walked into the bathroom to take a hot and then a cold shower, and half an hour later, he was driving through the chilly, deserted London night. He rolled his window down and took a deep breath of the air that smelled faintly of rain.

Now that he was awake, he found he didn't mind being up and about with the city to himself.

He thought about the call that had come in from the States. It sounded like Eckhart had botched this one. Mills chuckled softly. He knew how much it must have galled Eckhart to have to call to enlist his help. The two had worked together three or four times in the past, with Mills assisting mostly, helping Eckhart with details, but he had never been allowed at the completion of any of those jobs. Eckhart wouldn't permit it.

The two men did not like each other. Not that there had ever been any conflict between them. Perhaps it was only that the two of them were in some ways very much alike. They were close to the same age, Mills a little younger, and both were strong, ego-oriented personalities. But Mills worked for someone else and Eckhart chose whom he worked for. Eckhart expected more deference from Mills than the other would give him. But then you didn't have to like someone to do business with him and take his money. And Eckhart did always pay well.

Mills went over again the things he would have to acquire before he could go to work on Eckhart's job. Not all that much to it, really. He'd just have to wake up a few people, that was all. They'd complain a bit, but the money would take care of that.

Only one thing bothered him. He wished Eckhart had given him more freedom with the man he was after.

In the soft yellow glow of the lights on the dashboard, Mills smiled. Still, the part that he did have to do had some interesting possibilities.

The smile widened in the shadowy face.

Oh, yes, he thought. Some interesting possibilities. Exciting ones, too!

26

THE LADY PLACED THE CREAMY WHITE receiver of the telephone down in its cradle and leaned back into the lush comfort of the leather recliner that perfectly matched the phone.

The Lady loved white.

White was so . . . so clean, bright!

She stretched, and her white satin robe fell open around her long golden thighs. She looked down at her Piaget watch, its diamond-clustered face sparkling against the deep tan of her thin wrist. It was only a little after nine. She was seldom up this early in the morning.

But then the white phone had rung.

There were two phones in The Lady's lavish six-room apartment. If the red phone had rung, she wouldn't have bothered to answer it, would probably not have even heard it, in fact, because the phone-answering machine would have grabbed it on the first ring. The red phone was her public phone. It was even listed in the book.

Not under her real name, of course. Nobody in Las Vegas knew her real name. The Lady had a thing about keeping that a secret. Her real name was a special part of her that she wanted to keep all to herself. There were some mornings—not many, but some—when she would wake up and feel like being the woman that name belonged to. Those mornings usually meant that she would spend the day alone, thinking, reading, talking to no one. They weren't sad days and they weren't happy ones. They were just "real name" days. But today wasn't one of them.

And the white phone was special.

Only five people had the number of the white phone. Five *men*.

All very important men. All very wealthy. The president of a large advertising agency in Los Angeles. A very quiet, well-mannered Japanese man, also from Los Angeles, who was the chief stockholder in a company that manufactured luxury yachts. The owner of one of the largest hotels and casinos in Las Vegas with similar interests in New York and the Bahamas. And an older gentleman who had made his million in the stock market before he'd been thirty and who had retired to Las Vegas.

And a man about whom she knew almost nothing except that he was independently wealthy as a result of various shrewd investments. She knew him only as Dave and felt pretty certain that that was not his name. Of the five, he was the most attractive physically, and The Lady found him the most interesting. Probably, she realized, because she knew so little about him personally.

It had been Dave who had just called on the white phone.

The five men who had the number of the white phone did not share that number with anyone. The Lady was not one to need or want referrals. She had acquired all five of these men through her own careful efforts and had told each of them that if he ever gave her number to anyone, she would never see him again. So far, nobody had ever called on the white phone who was not expected. And that fact made The Lady feel very good. It told her that in spite of the power and importance of these five men, she was one stand-up piece of ass that they did not want to risk losing, and knowing that gave her the feeling of having a little corner of power over them.

Not that The Lady needed their assurance.

She had been pure, raw dynamite in the looks department ever since she'd been about fourteen, and there hadn't been one boy with any red blood flowing in his veins back in her high school in Cincinnati who wouldn't have given up a year of his life and done it with a smile on his face, too, just to spend a few minutes in the sack with her. Not that great looks were all she had going for her. No way. Not a phi beta kappa, maybe, but still a magna cum laude from Ohio State and that wasn't chopped liver, as her dad used to say. She had not especially liked college, mainly because she was anxious to get going somewhere with her life, but she had stuck it out, studied her ass off because she'd decided that if she was ever going to mix with the kind of people she damned well intended to mix with, she'd have a better chance if she was equipped with a good education. She didn't have the slightest idea at that time just what it was that she planned to do with her life, but whatever it turned out to be, she wanted to be ready for it. She had taken her degree in fine arts.

The Lady smiled. That was a private joke that never failed to amuse her. There were fine arts . . .

. . . and there were *fine* arts.

After graduation, she had gone to New York to give professional modeling a shot. She was pretty sure she actually was beautiful, so, it seemed a natural thing to do. If she'd been a man, thin and six foot five, she'd have headed somewhere to try to play basketball.

In a remarkably short time, she had found herself getting jobs as a print model, and in time, those jobs had led her to television commercials. And not once, not one time, had she ever fucked one of those advertising stiffs for a job. Oh, she had let some of them think that it might turn out that way, sure, never by saying anything directly, of course, but just by communicating enough hints to fire up their fantasies. Later, a few of them had been mad as hell when she hadn't come across, but by then, she had already done the job, and once she'd started being seen in print and TV, the snowball had started its downhill roll and one job had led to another. Her agent got excited about her. The photographers got excited about her and talked her up to the ad agencies and the agencies caught the fever and talked her up to their big clients. There was no doubt that she had one great future in the business and so they had all been shocked stupid when she'd up and told them she was quitting cold turkey, that she didn't want to do it anymore. It was no big thing, she'd told them. She was just tired of it, that was all, which was only partly the truth. She was no dummy, no beautiful, empty-headed kid with misty dreams of stardom or any of that shit. She had taken a good, close-up look at the business and at the other top girls who had been in it for a while and she had seen the one thing she hated the most in life.

Boredom.

She saw that it would not be too long before she'd be bored silly with dolling herself up and trooping all over the fucking city to stand for several hours with some photographer while she smiled and held up a can of deodorant or hair spray. And on top of all of that, she could see that the business itself was so fickle. One year you were a hotshot top model and everybody was coming in their pants over you and kissing your ass every time you turned around, and then the next year some new face zoomed into the city and all of a sudden none of them wanted to talk to you anymore. You were yesterday's news. "Sorry, baby, but you know how it is. Things change, right?"

No way. If she'd wanted to live with bullshit, she'd have been a farmer. She didn't know what she was going to do, but she wasn't all that worried about it. She had plenty of time and she had some money. Something would turn up.

Something did, and almost right away.

The man's name was Harlan O'Connor.

She had met him on her last big assignment before she'd decided to hang it up. O'Connor was president of one of the biggest cosmetic corporations in New York, and she had been chosen as the girl to hype Touchable, the company's newest perfume. Harlan O'Connor was a darkly handsome man in his late fifties, who kept himself trim and fashionable partly out of ego and partly because he had discovered since his wife died that he still had quite a healthy appetite for beautiful women.

Harlan was not looking for a serious relationship or another marriage. He was, directly and happily, looking for a good lay.

Or rather, as many good lays as he could find, and he was in a position to find plenty. He had thought about it and decided that at his age and in his position, he could afford to be very direct. When he met a girl that really knocked him out, he would invite her to spend an evening with him. Then, if it turned out that he still liked her, he would tell her just where he was coming from. He was not looking for anything heavy, and if she was, well, then, it had been a nice evening and thank you. But if the girl wanted to play, they could have a great time. He could promise her that. They would do everything, go places—Paris, Rome, London, wherever. He would never come to see her without bringing her a gift. And he was never pushy or crass. He liked women; admired them, in fact. After all, he'd built his life's business around them. To him, his direct approach, telling a woman just what he wanted and what she could expect from him, was a sign of his respect for her. He wasn't trying to be like a lot of men, slinging a line of shit, telling the girl that he was in love with her and promising her the moon just to get her in the sack and then crapping on her head later. Still, he was aware that a lot of women would consider him a sexist prick for his attitude, but that was okay, too. He just wouldn't go out with any of those women. Live and let live.

The Lady sent earthquake vibrations through Harlan O'Connor.

The ad agency had brought him pictures of several girls they thought might be on target to push Touchable. The Lady's photograph had been on the top of the stack. He had looked down at it and never even looked at the rest. She was perfect, he told the agency, and ordered them to hire her at once and set up a conference so that he could meet her. The first time he saw her in person he truly understood for the first time how a photograph could not do certain people justice.

The raw beauty of her had stunned him.

He had tried to recover himself, to make himself look at the other people around the conference table once in a while, and he had managed to get through the meeting, talking about the Touchable image he wanted to present, how he had high hopes that it would become the top of the line for the company, but it was just a rehearsed script to him. His mind was far from perfume and advertising. He could barely keep his eyes off her, and now and then it seemed to him that he saw something in her eyes, a little smile when she looked at him, that made him feel she was reading his mind and knew exactly what he felt, what he was thinking. The thought of being in bed with her somewhere, anywhere, almost made him dizzy.

When the meeting was over, they had all shaken hands. Her skin had felt so soft, and he had looked right into those large, pale gray eyes and wondered what the hell he was going to do with himself if she wouldn't go out with him.

He didn't want to come at her like King Kong, so he waited three weeks before he called her. During that time, the president of the ad agency had told him over lunch that Touchable was to be the girl's last job, that she was quitting the business. A real shame, the ad man had said. Wasn't it a bitch! All the great-looking broads that bust their asses to get the kind of break this girl had and what does she do? She hangs it up. They were all crazy. All of them.

The first night out with her, Harlan O'Connor knew he was in trouble.

They had started with drinks at the Oak Room of the Plaza, and he couldn't ever remember feeling so guarded and protective of a woman. He noticed faces and it seemed to him that there wasn't a guy in the place who didn't look at her and hurt because he wanted her, and who didn't look at him and hate him just because he was with her. He had never wanted a woman so much in his life and though he kept pushing it out of his mind, he was actually afraid that he might not be able to stick to his usual arrangement with her. He felt that if he wasn't careful, very careful, he might fall in love with her, for God's sake. But he managed to keep his head and finally, after they'd had dinner and were finishing a bottle of wine, he'd come right out and told her just what he had in mind. She was very attractive to him, he said. He liked being with her, enjoyed her company and that there were to be no strings involved and never would be. They could have some wonderful times, he told her. And if she said no, she didn't have to worry that she would lose the Touchable job. That was business. This was personal.

When he had finished, The Lady had looked at him for a minute, keeping her face impassive, and that had to be the longest minute of Harlan O'Connor's life. Then she looked right into his eyes and made his whole year when she said that it all sounded like fun to her.

And it was, too.

For the next four months, she spent almost all her waking hours and most of her sleeping ones with Harlan O'Connor. Life with him was dazzling and more exciting than she'd even dreamed about it being. They went everywhere—the theater, the most elegant restaurants in New York, Paris, Venice. It seemed he knew everyone. They met film stars and politicians. They did cornball things right out of the old forties movies, like going to Coney Island and buying one great big ice cream cone and sharing it, and some nights they just stayed at Harlan's incredible estate on Long Island, the servants sent away, the two of them messing around putting together a big dinner, sipping wine while they did it, later ending up making love on the big white fur rug next to the stone fireplace. They made all the society columns, the wags noting that Harlan O'Connor's newest flame seemed to be "burning longer than any of the others." And during it all, they both stayed away from ever talking about a relationship or where they might be headed or what might happen with them. Harlan made a point of sticking to his old pattern, going out with a few different women now and then, some famous models, a film star or two, and The Lady never batted an eye, going out too with some of the eligibles that were hot on her trail and they both knew it was all bullshit and that sooner or later, they were going to have to face up to things and come clean with each other.

And finally, late one night on the company's private jet en route to Madrid, it happened.

They had the plane all to themselves. It was a business trip, but Harlan had opted to go himself and take her so they could be alone. They were cuddled in a seat with a blanket over them, looking out the little oval window at the night, not talking for a long time until he said, "There's something I want to talk to you about. Something I want you to know."

The Lady looked at him. "If there's something you want me to know, then I want to know it. What?"

"I'm almost old enough to be your father," Harlan started. Then he laughed. "Hell, not even almost. I *am* old enough to be your father. But the thing is, I'm in love with you anyway. I've thought about it a lot and nobody means as much to me as you do and there's no sense in bullshitting myself that that isn't the way it is. So now that I've told you that, I don't know what else to say except that I'd like you to marry me."

"You want me to *marry* you?" The Lady was truly startled.

Harlan nodded. "That's right," he said, laughing at the look on her face. "I *know*. I know what I told you. I never wanted to get married again. I'd had that. I wasn't even looking for a serious relationship. I just love women and I like a great sex life. And when I told you that, it was the truth."

"But you want to marry me?" The Lady was smiling now.

"Yeah. I didn't plan it that way," Harlan said. "I really didn't think I could get into all of that, that falling-in-love business." He shrugged, shook his head, amused at himself. "It's ridiculous. No, it *is!* Listen to me! I'm fifty-eight years old, and if you say yes and you marry me, the chances are we're not going to have all that many years together anyway. I'll probably kick the bucket and you'll end up a rich young socialite widow and everybody'll just say that you married me for my money anyway." Harlan laughed again. "But the thing about it is, I don't give a damn about any of that if you don't. I want you to be with me all the time. When you're not, you're just on my mind anyway.''

"You're sure you don't want me to just live with you?"

Harlan sighed. "To tell you the truth, I thought about that," he said. "But that's not what I want. I want you to be my wife. You know, I told you, my first wife and I never had any kids."

"You want to have kids?"

"Just *listen*, okay? We never had any kids and now she's dead. Okay, so it's too late for me to do that now. I'm a rich man. I've worked hard and I'd like to leave my money to somebody I really care about, somebody I love, instead of just letting Uncle Sam come in and clean me out." He looked right at her then. "Well?" he said. "Come on. Let me have it. Are you in love with me or not? I don't know what the hell I'll do if you're not. Get really drunk, probably."

"Of course, I'm in love with you," she said. "And yes, I'll marry you. I just don't like the idea of everybody thinking it's because of your money."

"That's what they'll think, though," Harlan said. "But as long as you know differently and I know differently, what the hell do we care what anybody thinks."

"Can I ask you something?"

"Go."

"How do you know that I *wouldn't* be marrying you for your money?"

"I've tried to know people in my life," he said to her. "To read them. I've had a lot of gold diggers come at me. I don't think you're like that, but if you are, then you've fooled me pretty good."

The Lady smiled at him. "You don't have anything to worry about," she said. "You're a terrific guy. You've made me feel wonderful so many times. I don't care if you're *eighty*-eight. And that's the truth." She laughed then and looked away from him.

"What's funny?"

"You really want to know?" she asked, grinning at him.

"Let me have it."

"It's just that at first, I went out with you for the same reasons you went out with me."

"What do you mean?"

"*What do you mean?*" She laughed, mimicking him. "I wanted to have a good time, too," she said. "But I wasn't hot to get into some big, heavy relationship. What you were looking for was what *I* was looking for, that's all."

Harlan stared at her. "I'll be damned," he said. "Are you serious?"

"I'm not kidding," she said. "That's the way it was."

"And now," he said, studying her face, "you're in a 'big relationship' anyway. . ."

The Lady chuckled softly. "Yeah," she said. "How about that?" She reached out, took his hand. "Just when would you like to get married, Mr. O'Connor?" she said.

"I have to go to Paris the middle of next month," he said. "Why don't we do it there? It seems like a great city to get married in to me. I'd just as soon not go through that whole thing of getting married in New York, with the press and all of that."

"Paris sounds great to me," she said.

He put his arm around her then, pulled her over to him and kissed her lightly on the forehead. "I'll be really good to you," he said softly, as if to assure her of a lot more than that.

"I know," she said.

And she knew he would be. She felt how much he cared for her, felt it past the words themselves. She understood, too, that some of the sadness she heard in his voice was there because he was wishing things were different, that he were younger so they would have more time, but she knew she couldn't let herself get sad about that, couldn't let it bother her or it would cut in on the time they did have. She loved him. She was as certain of that as she could be at her age, and you had to start trusting your feelings sometime. She really didn't care that he was so much older or what anybody might say about that. You fell in love with the person, not with how old or young he was. The thing about marrying him for his money did bother her, but he was right. As long as they knew differently, what did they care. It surprised her that she was so ready to marry him, though. She wasn't very impressed with what she'd seen of marriages so far in her young life, the way they started all big and wonderful and full of fireworks and then came apart like a cheap skirt. But still, she thought, they might have a little better shot at making it work than most because along with loving each other, Harlan was older, had his feet solidly on the ground, and maybe he could help her balance some of the craziness in herself that she knew was there.

And all things considered, she might have been right, too, but she never got the chance to find out because they'd only been back in New York a little over three weeks when another man happened into their lives, a tall, skinny, buck-toothed, desperately strung out junkie named Curtis Pinkney, whose connection had just laid the bad news on him that the price of feeling good had gone up ("In*flation*, my man!), and Curtis had found himself seventy bucks short of happiness and fading fast, and so when he'd shoved this older dude off the sidewalk in between the two buildings that night, he had had no idea at all that such a straight, establishment-looking dude would turn hardass on him and try to fight back, and having that happen along with the way he felt and all the other shit in his life, well, it was just too much, man, and like he told the cops later, he didn't think at all, he just freaked out, went flat, whacko nuts for a few minutes and started cutting the motherfucker, yelling and screaming and cutting him even after he fell down and he only stopped when he saw people looking at him, scooping him from the sidewalk, and then he split the scene, but by that time, Harlan O'Connor had lost way too much blood and he was already dead by the time the paramedics slammed the back door of the ambulance on him.

THE LADY LEFT TOWN as soon as she knew for sure that he was dead.

No talking to anybody. The phone off the hook while she packed her things, working at not thinking about anything at all except putting stuff in her suitcases, leaving her apartment, and in the taxi on the way to Kennedy, picking Las Vegas as the place she was going because she saw a billboard along the road advertising one of the hotels on the Strip, and it was not until she had gone through the whole thing of flying there, finding a place, renting it, moving in and unpacking and putting things away that she finally ran out of things to do and had to face it all and she'd ended up very late one night, maybe three or four in the morning, alone in the Jacuzzi of the apartment building with champagne, drinking it straight out of the bottle with both hands and crying her eyes out over Harlan O'Connor in the hot, windy desert night.

SO MUCH FOR LOVE and all that.

At least for a while.

It would probably happen to her again when she was ready for it to happen. She'd meet somebody who would be special enough to do it. But not now. Now she was busy. As the highest paid, most selective and discreet prostitute in Las Vegas or possibly the whole country, The Lady had plans. She thought of Harlan now and then, thought of him warmly, fondly, but she no longer hurt or brooded over him. She had done that for a while, gotten it out of her system, and then she had looked around trying to decide what she was going to do with herself. Ironically enough, the idea for her present enterprise had come from Harlan himself.

She had decided that what she needed was a good, solid bank account, enough money so that she would have the time free to really think and plan what she wanted to do with her life without having to worry about how she was going to live while she was thinking and planning. If you had assets, you used them. She knew that she didn't want to be another Vegas hooker. She had taken a good look at that scene, the same way she had taken a good look at the modeling scene in New York, and she knew it wasn't for her. The whole thing was too crass. Hanging out in some hotel bar until some jerk hit on you and then going back to his room with him, not knowing the guy or what he was like, what he might do, and on top of it all, you had to pay the bell captain of the hotel so you could work there without Vice coming down on you. No. That was all way too risky, and there was not that great a profit involved. There had to be a better way of doing it.

And then she had remembered Harlan.

She remembered how direct he had been with her that night at the Plaza. The way he'd presented her with his very own special proposition. Here it is. Take it or leave it. That was good. That was classy and up front. She had spent a couple of weeks planning just how she would do it.

What she would offer.

Then she had gone into action.

It had all taken some time because she was being careful and selective, but eventually, through a series of prearranged contacts under the guise that she "just would like to meet the man," she'd had dinner with certain important people whom she felt would be perfect for what she had in mind.

And the whole thing had turned out to be incredibly easy.

She would have dinner with the man a few times, get an idea of what he was like and make sure that she liked him. If she did, she would sleep with him.

Once.

Then the next time they got together, she would quietly and directly make him her business proposal. Whenever the gentleman wished to see her, he could do so. He had only to call a certain number. He would always come to her place; she would never come to his. He would come for the evening and spend the night. It would all be very much like being with a girl friend or mistress. His favorite cocktail would be there when he walked in the door. There would be comfortable lounging clothes that he could change into. They would be bought just for him, and no one else would wear them. She would prepare him a scrumptious gourmet dinner of his favorite dish, and the wine would be one that he had picked out. The charge for the entire service would be two thousand dollars to be paid in cash. She knew, she would tell the man, that this was a lot of money, but then her service wasn't intended for everyone, was it? It was designed for the special men who could afford it, and there were only a few. He must never give her phone number to anyone else under any circumstances, or she would never see him again.

The Lady had approached six men with her offer.

None had refused.

One of the six, the vice-president of a large import-export firm based in San Francisco, had been with her for a while but then had been transferred to Tokyo. Before he had gone, he'd told her that she would be the only thing he was going to miss about the States.

The Lady decided to leave her list at five. She saw each of these men at least once a month and often more when they could arrange it.

The Lady did well.

She was careful not to delude herself. She was a prostitute. But out of fairness to herself, she also knew that she was special. She was a refiner of her craft. Frank Sinatra was a nightclub singer, but that label hardly served to cover the man or the full extent of his talent. She had given the subject of prostitution a great deal of careful thought before she had actually started her own particular enterprise, tried to decide at gut level just how she felt about it because Harlan had taught her that what you yourself thought was always what was the most important. And she had come to the conclusion that for her at least, what she was doing was simply not a moral issue. She had a solid, basic product that was marketable and she had worked at making that product of a higher caliber than her competitors'. It was essentially a matter of honing her particular talents until she was a master at using them. She would've done the very same thing she had attempted to be, say, a championship ice skater or a top hairdresser. She had read a great many of the important studies on prostitution and felt that most of the conclusions reached by those studies simply did not apply to her. They did not fit the way she felt about what she was doing. She most certainly did not hate men. She loved men. Always had. And she did not harbor any deep desire to be humiliated or any of that nonsense, or if she did and it was that deep, that secret, then it didn't bother her anyway. And she did *not* have contempt for her clients. The reverse was true. They were all well-bred, well-educated gentlemen who treated her like the lady she felt she was. She was not in love with any of them, but she didn't have to be. She was fond of them all. She also was very much aware that she would not be plying her particular trade for very long. The same was true with boxers or championship football players. That was okay, too. She had never intended her enterprise to be a life's career. It allowed her to live well and to amass a great deal of money so that she would have the time she needed to decide just what she really wanted to spend the rest of her life doing.

She was twenty-four now.

The way she had it figured, another year or two would do it. Then The Lady would cease to exist. By then she would have her plans down cold, and she could do whatever she damned well pleased.

27

NOW THE LADY LOOKED at the white phone and thought about the man who had just called her. She had known it was him because of the hour. He was the only one who ever called her in the morning, and because he was special to her in a way, she allowed it. She saw him less than she saw any of the others, and that fact made him more interesting to her, his not needing to see her any more than he did, maybe once or twice every six months. Another thing that made him more attractive to her was that she didn't really know anything about him. The others tended to talk about themselves, but not this one. He was an attractive man, this one, always a little reserved and nervous with her at first, but after they had been together for a little while, a half-hour or so, he got over it, and where it counted, he was more exciting than any of the others, and she always enjoyed her time with him.

She got up from the white recliner and walked barefoot into the kitchen, the white satin nightgown swishing softly around her ankles. *Kitchen* hardly seemed a sufficient term to describe the room, airy and beautiful, tiled in rainbow mosaic, with lots of dark wooden cabinets and a large window that faced the sun. The Lady loved the sun in the kitchen in the morning. She loved the sun period. It did special things for her, made her feel healthy and beautiful, and she could never be out in it without coming in feeling sensuous and sexy, and to hell with how it was supposed to age you. You aged anyway, and she'd just as soon be tan and old as pale and old.

She walked over to the counter and poured a cup of steaming, rich-smelling black coffee from the tall silver service. She loved the aroma of this coffee. It was a very special mixture from Colombia, and the little red-nosed man who owned the coffee store downtown always kept several pounds of it for her. Holding the thin, fragile white cup in the saucer, she walked into the bedroom. She looked at herself in the dresser mirror. Pretty good, she thought. Just up, no makeup and her hair was kind of tangled, but still pretty damned good. It didn't bother her that she was hung up on her looks. The hang-up was one of her secrets. Outside of her apartment, she never did anything around other people—men or women—to give the impression that she was pleased with her appearance. The Lady smiled. But then she didn't have to do anything. The looks on the faces of the women and comments by the men did it for her.

She glanced again at her watch. Dave would be here around six for dinner. She had a lot to do.

AT FIFTEEN MINUTES TO SIX that evening, she was sitting on the white sofa in the living room sipping champagne when the red phone rang. She reached over and picked it up, listened for a minute, then said, "Yes, thank you. Please do," and replaced the receiver.

He was downstairs, and now that the desk had gotten her okay, he would be on his way up to her.

She took another drink of the champagne, her eyes going slowly over the large living room.

Everything was perfect.

She had turned the indirect lighting in the ceiling way down, and with the fire burning in the fireplace, the room was all soft, inviting shadows. The scent of her Joy perfume hung faintly in the air, mixing with the scent of the two sandalwood candles that burned at each end of the long, dark wooden bar, their flames reflecting in the row of gleaming liquor bottles.

Perfect.

And she was perfect, too. The dress was deep blue, almost purple, like the color of the sky sometimes after an evening storm, low cut but tastefully so and slit up the front so that it fell open at the middle of her thighs when she crossed her legs. She tilted her glass again and drank, feeling the bubbling fizz on her lips. God, but she loved champagne! It always made her feel so good, so warm! And the secret was, you never drank too much of it. Only enough to give you that good feeling and then you stopped. Champagne was special.

The doorbell chimed softly.

The Lady got up from the sofa and walked across the deep white rug, pausing to set her glass down on the end of the bar as she passed it. She opened the door. The man looked at her, a little smile on his face. In one hand he held a small gift package wrapped in bright red.

"Hi!" she said softly, and she reached out and took his hand, led him into the apartment, closed the door and turned the bolt. Then she put both arms around his neck and, rising slightly up on her toes, kissed his lips, a soft kiss, short, but just long enough and with just enough pressure. Then she stepped back and, still holding his hand, looked at him, smiling, her eyes sparkling. "It's good to see you," she said, meaning it.

The man smiled back at her, offered the package. "You, too," he said.

She took the gift and then stood there looking down at it in her hand and then back up into his face. She saw his body relax as though he had just put down some heavy load that he had been carrying for a long time or as if some worrisome problem on his mind had just been solved. His eyes drank her in, going slowly over her, this shockingly beautiful woman. The heavy, midnight black hair that fell to just past her bare, golden shoulders, the ends of it curling down over the thin straps of the blue dress, touching her breasts. The slash of tan leg that was now visible through the slit in the front of it. He was not a man to show a lot of emotion in his face, but The Lady still caught the little light of pleasure that came into his eyes as he looked at her, and she loved him for it. "Come on," she said. "I'll fix us a drink before dinner."

The man went over to the sofa and sat down. He un-buttoned the jacket of his sport coat and sat back watching her as she poured the Martel into a large crystal snifter and then refilled her champagne glass. She put the two glasses on a drink tray along with the little package and carried them over to the sofa. The man took the cognac, and she put the tray down on the heavy dark-glass coffee table. The Lady lifted her champagne and looked straight into his eyes. "To seeing you," she said softly, and they drank.

She opened the gift then, fussing with the paper, being careful of it the way she always was, and then when she had the small, dark purple box in her hand, she held it up near her ear and shook it a couple of times, laughing girlishly at the suspense she was creating, and then she opened it.

The thin, white-gold bracelet gleamed. She made a little gasp, took it out. "Beautiful! God! So pretty!" And she put it on and leaned over and kissed him again. The man had watched her through all of this ceremony, enjoying it as much as she did or as much as she pretended she did, because he was never really sure about her in such situations. They touched glasses again, and The Lady looked closely at his face. "You look tired," she said. "Rough day—or," and a gleam of mischief flashed into her eyes, "have you just been out playing around too much?"

He laughed. "Just a lot to do lately," he said. "A lot going on."

"Am I ever going to learn just what it is that you do for a living?" she asked him.

The man laughed again. His eyes went away from her face, came back. They had played this game before. "Am I ever going to learn just what your real name is?"

he said to her, imitating exactly the tone of her own question, and then it was The Lady who had to laugh because people did have their own secrets, and even if they were only important to the person who had them, they were valuable and needed somehow. "Thelma Ginch," she said, putting on a straight face. "How many times do I have to tell you that? It's a simple name, a cinch to remember. Ginch. A cinch."

The man chuckled softly, took a longer pull at the Martel and then leaned forward and put it down on the coffee table. He took the champagne glass out of her hand and set it down next to his. "Thelma Ginch," he said softly. "Got it." And he reached for her then and she came into his arms all warm and alive and soft and delicious-smelling and he kissed her, running his fingers up through the silky black hair, holding the sides of her head gently but firmly, kissing her and kissing her, and her arms went around him, pulling him against her, her nails caressing, then digging, then caressing the back of his neck and she let him have her tongue then, just the tip at first, teasing, and then more and more of it and the blood started to pound in his temples as she took one hand away from his neck and ran it slowly down over his chest into his lap, rubbing, massaging softly, and he moaned half-aloud and his own hands went away from her hair and then down to her bare shoulders and he began pushing her backward on the sofa, but suddenly she pulled away from him, her hand gone from his lap, pushing against his chest, and he looked at her, her face flushed red as she said, "I think we'd better have another drink or my dinner is going to burn."

"Hell with the dinner," he said, almost whispering, and he reached out for her again, but she laughed and twisted away, jumping up from the sofa, looking down at him, her eyes bright. "Huh, *uh!*" she said. "I worked too hard, and we are *going* to have dinner!" The long red nails flashed up through the black hair as she pushed it away from her face. She grinned at him. "You really ought to get your mind on something else besides sex once in a while, you know."

"You bitch!" he said to her, but he was laughing too now, settling down a little, getting control again.

She scooped up their two glasses from the drink tray and headed back to the bar, shaking her head. "I go to all this trouble," she said, mock injury in her voice. "I fix him this terrific dinner and what does he do? He calls me *names!*"

And as he watched her refilling their glasses, he was struck once again by what a one hundred percent totally knowing female this woman was, because now he was actually *glad* that she had stopped him, that she had made him be content with only a taste of her, and now, all through dinner, he would be thinking about what was coming in the long night that lay ahead of them and it was exciting to have those thoughts. And knowing that somehow she understood all that made him want her even more, and hours later, after dinner, after having wine on the floor, when he had her the first time on the thick fur rug in front of the fireplace, both naked, warm, entering her slowly with delicious difficulty at first and then easier, deeper and deeper, feeling her moving under his thrusts, trying to get all of him, kissing him, talking warm-breathed, softly in his ear, urging him, and then near the end, her long legs locked tightly around his back, he gave himself up to her, felt himself go completely, crying out, filling her, and something else broke loose inside him too with the doing of that and he buried his head down in her shoulders, biting her hard, losing himself, what he was, who he was, all lost in her screams as she went with him.

And afterward, holding her against him, she sleeping then, her beautiful face relaxed, her breathing even, he felt a kind of peace for a little while, but then he felt it starting to come at him from not so far away and this was the part, the time that over the past few months he had not understood but had learned to dread, and he felt it coming closer now, settling over him like a thick fog and it was a feeling of hollow, desolate loneliness, but that was not all of it. He was not a man often afraid, but fear was a part of it, too, and lying in the silent, warm, fire-flickering darkness, Eckhart stared into the hearth at the jumping yellow and blue flames and was afraid. The fear had no name and that made it worse for him and he was suddenly cold, shivering, his shoulders shaking, and he moved in closer to the soft warmth of her body and that seemed to help some, made him feel warmed, yes, and safer, yes, that, too, and he stayed there close against her for a very long time into the night before he closed his eyes and slept.

He woke a little after dawn, and with the pale daylight washing in through the long white curtains that covered the three-walled picture window of The Lady's apartment, he found that he felt better, more like himself. The cold, nameless terror of the night was still remembered, but without the power it had in the darkness, like a bad dream fading. They had slept all night on the fur rug in front of the fireplace, moving over to one side of it sometime in the night and then pulling it over them like a blanket. Now, awake, one arm resting over her bare hip, Eckhart was aroused and wanted her again. He began lightly caressing her breasts, her stomach, her skin wonderfully soft and smooth under his touch. The Lady moaned softly in her sleep and moved in closer to him. He let one hand move down her leg and rested it between her thighs, pressing softly, kissing the back of her neck, and she turned over suddenly into his arms and they made love, urgently this time, and he held her for a while and then picked her up and carried her into the bedroom, warm and naked against him, and still holding her, he bent down and flipped back the spread and the blankets on the bed and put her down on it, covering her and sitting down beside her as she snuggled deeper in under the blankets and smiled up at him sleepily, the heavy black hair tangled and looking even blacker against the bright whiteness of the big pillow.

And he was not at all aware of the exact moment that it began happening to him, was not aware that he was suddenly frowning at her or of the questioning look on her face because she did not understand the frown. All he felt was a fast, rushing feeling of shock and cold fear of her as he saw for the first time how very dangerous she was to him. How, when he was with her, he did something that he never, never let himself do. He let go of himself. He stopped being careful. He left himself open, completely open, let go of all the very things that had always kept him alive!

He let himself be vulnerable!

*And it seemed like someone was shouting the word .
deep, booming voice inside his mind. VULNERABLE!
VULNERABLE! And, my God! he couldn't have that!
That couldn't be allowed to happen! No, no, no! He couldn't
let that be! Why hadn't he seen it before? He should have seen
it! She was the only one. The only one with whom he let
himself be unprotected.*

His whole body feeling cold, he reached down for her.

*He did not see the questioning look fade from her face, turn
into a little smile as she reached up for him, her slim, tan arms
going around his neck, pulling him down to her, feeling his
hands again caressing her face and then suddenly her entire
body went rigid, as she felt the strong fingers pressing, and
then she wasn't thinking anymore at all, the panic grabbing
her, and she was reaching wildly to claw at his face when
she felt the hands raise her head up from the pillow, felt her
neck twist sharply to one side and a dazzling white explosion went off in front of her eyes.*

Silence in the room. For several minutes.

Eckhart sat staring down at her, his eyes locked un-
seeing on her face. His hands still tight around her neck.
All right now, he whispered, his chest heaving. All right
now. Close, but all right now. Yes . . .

More minutes went by.

His hands came away from her throat. The glaze faded
from his eyes. He reached down and lightly stroked her
face, pulling a wisp of the black hair from one of her eyes,
pulled the blankets up a little higher around her.

Eckhart smiled.

God, what a beautiful woman!

He sat up straight, stretched his back. He'd let her
sleep, he thought. She wasn't used to being up this early

in the morning. He couldn't stay for brunch with her the way he always did anyway. Not today. He had the meeting with Al Chambers and then he had to be at his own place near the phone. Quietly he got up from the bed. He wiped the back of his hand over his forehead, frowned at the sweat that came off on it. It didn't seem that hot in the room to him. He hoped he wasn't coming down with the damned flu or something. He'd read in the papers that there was a lot of it around now. He walked naked into the bathroom and washed up, and when he came back out she hadn't moved, was still sleeping. He went on out into the living room and dressed. On his way to the door, he stopped at the bar, looked at the bottle of champagne and at the opened little purple box containing the white-gold bracelet. He smiled remembering the way she had looked when she'd opened it. She was really something, he thought. He reached inside the pocket of his sport coat, took out the cream-colored envelope with the four new five-hundred-dollar bills in it and propped it up against the bottle of champagne. Then he let himself out, turning the bolt and hearing it click solidly behind him as he closed the door.

On the way down in the elevator, Eckhart thought about the day ahead of him. He'd go back to his apartment now, shower, shave, change clothes and then go over to the Silver Tiara to see Al Chambers. He'd bring the slob up to date, tell him that he hadn't lost his ass yet, that he still had a chance of getting his money back and taking care of the cab driver, too. Eckhart grinned.

Then would come the good part.

He would break the news to the slob that this possible second chance in London, if it worked out, was going to cost him another ten thousand dollars in addition to the thirty grand that they had initially agreed on for the job. Eckhart could already see the look of outrage that would come over the pig face at that bit of news. But Chambers would pick up the tab. He was sure of that. If he thought there was a chance—hell, half a chance—of his getting back his five hundred thousand, he would pay and gladly. That had been the main reason he had flown back to Vegas from Chicago—to tell Chambers about the extra ten grand and to have the fat man agree in person to the increase in the fee.

That had been the *main* reason.

That and to see The Lady.

He thought of the night just past and knew that he would be thinking about it, tasting it for days to come, and though it would fade, it would hold him until he saw her again. And he wondered, as he always did after each time with her, whether if their situations had been different, something could have come of them.

The elevator stopped. The double doors slid soundlessly back. Eckhart stepped out and walked across the thick red carpet of the lobby toward the front entrance. The young clerk on duty looked up from the desk, recognized him and smiled. "Good morning, sir," he said pleasantly. Eckhart nodded to him and returned the greeting. He went out of the building into the sunny, blue-skied desert morning and started down the street toward his car, smiling, amused at his private fantasies, his right-out-of-the-fucking-movies thoughts about ever having something with The Lady. He reached into his pocket and took out his keys. Incredible! he thought. The Lady was a . . .

No, she wasn't!

There was no way, just no way at all that he could ever think of that woman and the word *whore* in the same sentence. And he didn't give a damn that that wasn't logical, that she accepted money for sex. Whoever and whatever she really was, neither that word nor any of the others fit her in the slightest. She was somehow above all that. He came to his car, got in and headed toward the Strip, pushing her out of his mind.

He turned his thoughts to Derik Mills, the man in London whom he'd been forced to involve in his job.

He didn't like Mills.

Not that the man had ever done anything to him. It was just that he never felt comfortable around deviants of any kind. You had to be so careful with them, because they were difficult to read. You never knew what they were going to do next, the looks on their faces seldom reflecting what was going on in their heads. But Mills had a lot of street contacts and he could be trusted to do what he was being paid to do and not step out of line. Mills wouldn't let greed get the best of him and try anything with the money if he was able to find Logan. And that was a big *if*. Eckhart had his doubts. London was a damned big city.

It would probably occur to Mills to try something, Eckhart thought. The temptation would sure be there. Five hundred grand was a lot of money. But Mills wouldn't try anything because he worked for some very powerful people in London, people Eckhart had done business with in the past, who valued him as a Stateside contact. These people would not take kindly to one of their employees doing anything that would cause Eckhart trouble, and Mills was aware of that fact.

Another reason Mills wouldn't get greedy was Eckhart himself. Mills was a dangerous man and had done much violence in his life, but he knew that Eckhart was equally dangerous, and more important, he knew that Eckhart had no fear of him and would most certainly come after him and try to kill him if he ever did attempt anything underhanded.

Of course, none of this mattered if Mills failed to find Logan.

Well, he would know about that before too long. After he had met with Chambers, he would go back to his apartment and wait for the call from London. He didn't envy Logan if Mills was able to get to him.

Back in his apartment, Eckhart had just come out of the shower when the phone rang. He knotted the large, white bath towel around his waist, walked into the living room and picked it up.

"Hello."

"Yeah," Chambers said. "I been calling. What the hell took you so long to get back, anyway?"

"I got hung up," Eckhart said evenly, the tone of his voice making it clear that that was the beginning and the end of his explanation. He wasn't about to tell the slob that he had gone straight to The Lady's place from the airport instead of going to the Tiara the way they had agreed when he'd called from Chicago.

"I been goin' nuts here for chrissake!" Chambers said.

"I just got out of the shower," Eckhart told him. "I'll get dressed and I'll be at your office in about half an hour."

There was a brief pause on the other end of the line and then Chambers said, "Listen," and his voice was suddenly lower, and Eckhart caught something else in it, too. "I ain't at the Tiara now. I'm out. I'm at a pay phone. Why don't we just, uh . . . why don't we meet at that little gin mill across from Circus Circus? It's a good place to talk. We ain't likely to get interrupted by anybody we know. Okay?"

"Sure," Eckhart said. "Wherever you want."

"Okay, about half an hour then."

Chambers hung up.

Eckhart put the receiver down and stood staring thoughtfully out through his living-room window at the high mountains that cut sharply around the far horizon. There had apparently been some developments while he was gone. That had not been the old Chambers on the phone just now. The old Chambers would have been mad as hell and yelling because he hadn't called him the minute he was back in town. And the old Al Chambers wouldn't have been caught dead in the kind of place he'd just suggested that they meet. He was the kind of man who always preferred doing business on his home turf, so that could only mean that he no longer felt comfortable talking in his own office at the Tiara. Eckhart wondered how serious things had become for the fat man. Serious enough, he thought. The thing he had caught in Chambers's voice had again been fear. In spite of the man's attempt to hide it, it had come through to Eckhart. Fear was something he could always sense. He went into the bedroom to get dressed.

THE LITTLE BAR across the street from the Circus Circus hotel bore the highly uninspired name of The Lucky Number. It was typical of the little joints that made their money in the shadows of the big hotels around them on the Strip, catching the tourists who would wander in, lured by the signs outside the place that screamed in big red letters LIBERAL SLOTS! A JACKPOT EVERY TEN MINUTES! DRINKS FROM THE WELL 80 cents! FREE SALAD BAR! and so on.

Chambers had been right. The place was pretty empty at this hour of the morning. There were a couple of guys at the bar and a group consisting of one older man and two older women at a table in the center of the room who had Midwest stamped all over them, and that was it for the customers.

Eckhart saw Chambers sitting in a booth back near the bright red-and-blue flashing jukebox and walked over to him, the front of his shoes drifting over with a light layer of the fresh sawdust that covered the hardwood floor. Eckhart wondered why in the hell the guys who owned places like this always seemed to feel they had to dump that shit on the floor. It fucked up your shoeshine and made the whole bar smell like a goddamned lumberyard. These places shouldn't even be on the Strip anyway, he thought. They should be downtown where the Okies got off on that kind of shit.

He sat down opposite Chambers in the booth and looked at him. Chambers seemed thinner somehow, or maybe it was just his face. He was wearing a bright red sport shirt with black stitching around the collar, white pants and white shoes. The shirt changed, Eckhart thought, but never the white pants and shoes.

"So . . ." Chambers said, looking at him.

Eckhart couldn't resist. "Classy joint you picked here," he said.

"It'll do," Chambers said. And then, still playing his game, he said, "We talk in the hotel, there's always somebody interrupting me. You been there, you know how it is."

A cocktail waitress, a blonde with too much eyeshadow, wearing a short red outfit, came over then. Pinned on her blouse was a big, bright yellow button in the shape of a sunflower, and on the face of it, written in bold black letters, were the words, HI! I'M PAM! WHO ARE YOU? Chambers already had a martini in front of him. It was only half-empty, and Eckhart wondered if it was his first.

He looked up at Pam and told her to bring him a Perrier with a twist. "Perrier, twist!" she repeated. "Right!" She glanced at Eckhart's sport coat and blue silk shirt, and with an ability as native to Vegas as desert sand, she made a good guess in her head at how much each of them cost, and since she didn't get too many guys in this dump who could afford threads like that, she really turned on the smile for him and made a teasing comment about the Perrier and was Eckhart on the wagon. Eckhart smiled at her and said that it was just a little too early for him to drink yet. Pam turned and walked back to the bar then, hoping the guy was looking at her ass and that he at least liked what he saw enough to lay a good toke on her when he left because the old fart with him had stingy written all over his face.

When the waitress was out of earshot, Chambers leaned forward slightly, his elbows on the scarred black Formica tabletop, the clean, pink fingers of both hands locked together. "So tell me, huh?" he said to Eckhart. "What's doing with all this business?"

"I called a guy," Eckhart said simply. "In London. I told him what to look for. He finds it, I'll go get it; that's all."

Chambers expelled a hissing breath of air through his nose into his bunched fingers, his eyes studying the tall man's face. Eckhart noticed the fingers tightening, relaxing, tightening. Chambers was *very* nervous. "Who's the guy?" he asked.

"A contact," Eckhart said.

"You *know* him?" Chambers said. "You work with him before? He straight?"

Eckhart only looked at him, the faintest trace of a frown coming over his lips. It had been a stupid question, and the other man knew it.

Chambers unfolded his hands, made a fist and smacked it once, twice into his palm. "What a mess," he said. "What a fucking mess!" His voice was a little louder now, agitation clearly audible in it, anger sparking in his eyes. He glared at Eckhart. "How in the hell did you ever let him get away from you to London?" he snapped. "Huh? You tell me that? London! Sonofa-*bitch!*"

Before Eckhart could answer him, Pam returned with his Perrier. She took it off the tray and put it down in front of him, bending forward enough so that he got a good close shot of her boobs. She looked at his jacket, touched it for a second with one of her fingers, said, "Nice!" and then, turning away again, went over to one of her other tables.

Chambers seemed to get a little control over his anger during the brief interruption. Okay, Eckhart thought. He's picking up the tab. He hired you. He's got a right to know. So he told him everything that had happened back at the airport in Chicago. Well, not quite everything. He did not mention how he had planned to take care of Logan. That was none of Chambers's business, and if he was curious, he kept his curiosity to himself this time and didn't ask.

When Eckhart had finished, the fat man sighed and shook his head. "He's still hot," he said. "That fucking guy is really hot."

That was true, Eckhart thought. Logan *was* lucky, but that was only part of it. The man had something on the ball to go along with his luck, but all he said now to Chambers was, "It can't last forever."

"What kind of odds you give your guy in London?" Chambers asked him.

Eckhart shrugged. "Fifty-fifty," he said. "Maybe a little better than that. He's got a description of the guy. He knows his flight number. But then it's a big airport. There'll be a lot of people, just like in Chicago."

"He grabs him," Chambers said, trying to sound casual, "you just going to London to get the money?"

"I'll go and do my job," Eckhart said.

Chambers nodded, sipped at his martini. The thin glass trembled in his hand.

"There's something else," Eckhart said to him. "If he manages to get him and I have to go over there, it's going to cost you."

Nothing from Chambers for a minute. Then, "How much more?" he asked, trying to keep the anger out of his voice and not quite succeeding.

"For all of it," Eckhart said, "another ten thousand."

"I gotta lay out another ten grand because *you* fucked up and lost the guy in Chicago!"

"You're damned lucky I even *found* him in Chicago!" Eckhart snapped. "And he would never have *been* in Chicago in the first place if you'd handled things the right way, and you know it."

Eckhart had him on that one. He knew it and Chambers knew it, too.

"Okay, okay," he said. "You got the money." He glanced around the darkened bar then and finished his martini. He looked across the table at the tall man and seemed to come to a decision about something. "I'm going to lay it out for you," he said. "Where I am about this whole thing," and some of the toughness faded out of his voice then. "My ass is in a sling."

Eckhart didn't reply. He waited. He knew Chambers was hating having to tell him whatever he was about to tell him.

"That money is important," he said. "I'm getting a lot of pressure."

"Heavy pressure?" Eckhart said, and normally he would never have asked something like that, would never have pursued anyone else's personal problems, but he felt that strange, scary feeling rising in him again about all of it, and since he was involved physically, he felt he needed to know as much as he could find out.

Chambers picked up his glass, caught Pam's eye and waved it at her. She nodded and ordered another one from the bar. "*Very* heavy pressure," he said quietly.

Chambers had just told him that he was in danger of being killed if the money Logan had stolen was not recovered.

And while that fact in itself did not mean anything to Eckhart, it did serve to make him all the more confident that whatever this restless, bad feeling of his had to do with, it was a warning to him that he had better stay alert. Losing five hundred thousand dollars of certain people's money in this town could easily be considered serious, but for someone of Chambers's position, getting killed for the loss represented extreme and unusual punishment. That he might be chastised in some way would not be out of line, but to have him killed—August Gurino again came to Eckhart's mind.

"So when are you gonna know?" Chambers asked him. "About your man in London?"

"Later this afternoon," Eckhart said, and Pam was back then with the martini, bending over as she served it. She smiled at Eckhart and went away. You better put it to him flat out, Eckhart thought. He *needs* you now. "When you first called me in on this thing," he said to the fat man, "you told me the money wasn't yours. Whose is it, anyway?"

Chambers stared at him, his mouth falling open, truly astonished. "You really think I'd tell you *that!*" And the words came out too loudly and he caught himself, lowered his voice, leaned closer to Eckhart again, looked dead into his eyes. "What the fuck's with you, asking me something like that, huh? You believe me, you don't have to know anything like that, you understand? That's none of your business, a thing like that!" He stopped then, shutting himself off with an effort that was clearly visible on his face. "You just do what you're being paid to do, okay?" he said. Chambers sat back then, picked up his martini glass again and drank half of it down.

Eckhart decided to back off. For now. He would wait until he knew how things had gone down in London. Then he would ask that question again.

And he would get an answer.

28

JERRY LOGAN STARED OUT through the window in the back of the taxi at the unfamiliar England night. Every once in a while, a light from something, a passing car or a building at the side of the road, would flash into the cab and reflect right off the window beside him and he would catch his reflection in the glass.

He looked so *unhappy*.

And he was.

Why? he thought.

And that was one damned valid question, considering all he'd gone through and his present circumstances. He'd almost lost his ass, had gotten lucky and saved it and now he was on his way into London, one of the world's truly great cities, and aside from still being tired all over and having a dull ache in his shoulder from falling in the airport back in Chicago, he had nothing to complain about. He had been scared shitless when they'd taken him off the plane back at Heathrow, because he figured there was at least an even chance that the tall guy had maybe wired or phoned ahead and had somebody waiting for him.

His flight had landed a little earlier than it was supposed to, so he still had time going for him. He'd kept his eyes open behind the dark glasses to see if anybody was watching him, but that hadn't worked too well because he'd noticed a lot of people watching him to one degree or another and then he'd realized that was just because he was a blind man being escorted off an airplane and people always tended to look at somebody like that. Still, nobody had seemed any too interested, and the Pan Am attendant had been very polite and concerned about him and had escorted him outside the building up to the line of taxis, put him in the first one, had his luggage put in the back and then instructed the driver to take him to the Hilton in the city, and he was on his way.

He had picked the Hilton because he was ready to stay at a nice hotel after that roach hole back in Springfield. He knew that staying there could be risky. If the tall guy did have somebody looking for him, the most logical thing would be to have all the big hotels watched and then if they found him, wait and try to grab him one night in his room. But even knowing that, he'd thought, the hell with it. He was going to stay someplace that was pleasant. This was really the beginning of everything new for him, and he wanted to start it off right. And besides, there was always the chance that he was giving the tall guy too much credit. Maybe he didn't even have the kind of connections in London to suddenly get somebody on his ass right away like that. So really, all things considered, things weren't too bad.

And on top of it all, he had the money.

He, Jerry Logan, had, by God, five hundred thousand dollars in cold cash in this briefcase he was holding in his lap!

He looked down at it, ran his palm over the smooth leather top. He took a last drag of his cigarette and stubbed it out in the little ashtray in the armrest of the door.

So how come he felt so damned depressed?

The only answer he could come up with didn't make any sense.

There'd been nobody to meet him at the airport.

Stupid.

Because first of all, he didn't even know anybody in London who could've met him at the airport, and the real truth was, he'd been afraid there *might* be somebody there to meet him. Like maybe some three-hundred-pound, box-headed goon with no neck who was a buddy of that tall creep's. But still, he felt that he had gone through so much to get here that it just seemed like there should've been somebody there, damnit, to shake his hand and say something like, "You made it! You crazy sonofabitch! You made it!" And when there hadn't been anybody, he'd suddenly realized how totally alone he was now.

Stupid. But there it was anyway.

Well, he consoled himself, things were going to get better. He planned on doing a lot of new things. Things he'd always wanted to do. And he'd be meeting new people as he went along and that should help get rid of the loneliness. Maybe he'd even meet a girl. Sure, why not? Somebody nice, special. It could happen. He wasn't old yet, and while he wasn't any Redford or Newman, he wasn't a bad-looking guy, either. Thinking about all that helped some and he lit up another cigarette and leaned his head back against the top of the seat.

The cab smelled pleasantly of smoke and old leather, and the smell seemed distantly familiar to him somehow, but he couldn't place it. Then he remembered that his grandfather's room in their old house used to smell like that. He'd just been a kid, and the old man had been living with them and he'd hardly ever opened the window in his room because of the drafts, he'd said, and he would sit in there at night sometimes before he went to bed and smoke his pipe, and all the furniture in the room was his and all of it was old and some of it was covered in leather and sometimes he would go into the room and play Chinese checkers with the old man and the room would smell of his pipe smoke and that old leather-covered furniture. He was surprised that after all these years he could still remember something like that, but not nearly as surprised as he was now to see that the cab driver was turning into the driveway of this house and then he was gunning the cab straight into the little garage next to the house, and he didn't need anything else to happen to know that he was already in bad trouble, and so he went for the door beside him, slamming down the handle, and he got it open okay, but that was all he did because the cab driver was no dummy and he had pulled in so close to the wall of the garage that you could only open the door about a foot before it banged into it, and unless you were a small child or a midget, there was no way that you were going to get out, and he had to forget about the door on the other side now because the driver already had it open and he was down in kind of a squat with his arms outstretched like you always see the cops doing in the movies and there was nothing else to do then so he just froze, didn't move at all, only stared at the man and the muzzle of the gun that was pointing through the door dead at his face.

Then out of the cab.

Out of the garage.

Into the house.

The cab driver close behind him all the way, like the tall man had stayed close behind him back at the airport in Chicago, and this guy was just as tall as that sonofabitch only bigger, a lot bigger, and it was funny because even when he'd ordered him out of the car, his voice had been really friendly sounding and polite and Jerry wondered if he was really a cab driver and his first guess at that one had to be no, but here in England where everybody tended to sound well mannered, who could tell for sure?

And wasn't this something, he thought.

He wasn't all that afraid. Here he was in London thinking one minute that he had made it and now he was in this house with this great big sonofabitch with a gun behind him, and cab driver or not, it was a sure bet that this guy was connected to the tall man and the good Lord only knew what was going to happen now, and he just wasn't feeling all that afraid. Oh, scared, sure. Stomach tight and heart was overdoing it pretty good, but not afraid like he had been, say, back in that little airport bar in Chicago. It crossed his mind that maybe when you'd been through some really bad, scare-the-holy-shit-right-out-of-you-and-turn-your-hair-white fear—that if you got through it, then maybe you weren't so afraid the next time things got bad for you.

The cab driver walked him into the living room of the house and motioned with the gun for him to sit on the couch. The room was large and carpeted in green shag, and the furniture was mostly all wood and expensive-looking. And that answered one question for him, because no hack he'd ever known could have afforded a spread like this.

The guy put the briefcase down on the floor next to a big brown leather chair, and Jerry looked at him. Big, blond, handsome face—looked like he kept himself in good shape. He looked like the kind of guy sporting-goods stores liked to hire as salesmen. The guy walked over to him now, still holding the gun, but now he had it down at his side to show that he really wasn't worried about anything. He gave Jerry a really friendly sales-man smile and said, "We have quite a while to wait. Would you care for a drink?"

Jerry looked up into very pale blue eyes, nodded.

"Let me tell you something first," the blond guy said, "just so that you'll be aware of the way things are. If you just relax, stay where you are and don't try to cause any kind of flap, we'll get on fine. But if you do attempt to give me any trouble, you may be very sure that I will shoot you. I won't kill you, but I will shoot you and then you'll still have quite awhile to wait only you'll be wait-ing in a great deal of pain." Again the smile, only this time Jerry thought he saw something funny in it. Something was different in the voice, too, but he didn't know what it was exactly. "Now," the guy said, "do we have an understanding?"

"Yes," Jerry said. For now, anyway, he thought.

"Excellent!" the guy said. "Now, what would you like to drink?"

"Bourbon," Jerry said. "On the rocks."

The guy walked over to a small portable bar against the wall and poured from two bottles. One bourbon, one Scotch. He put both glasses on a small drink tray and brought them over, tray in one hand, gun in the other. Jerry took the whiskey. "My name's Derik Mills," he said in that pleasant, friendly voice. "Your first name is Jerry, am I correct?"

Jerry nodded.

Derik Mills walked over and sat in the big brown leather armchair. He put the gun down next to his thigh, took his drink off the tray and put the tray on a little table next to the chair. He sipped once at the drink, looked at Jerry and shook his head. "You've gotten yourself into quite a nasty mess, Jerry," he said. He glanced down at the briefcase on the floor. "Tell me, have you ever done anything like this before? Stolen money, I mean?" This was said quietly, the handsome face interested.

Jerry lifted his glass and drank, the whiskey making a slow, soothing, burning feeling down his throat into his stomach. "No," he said.

Mills nodded. "I didn't think so," he said. "You see, or perhaps you've already guessed, I'm not a taxi driver," and when Jerry didn't say anything, "I work at a gaming casino here in London. My principal function is to collect debts owed my employer from certain people who enjoy gambling on credit, but who don't enjoy paying up when they lose. That, you see, is a form of stealing. Well, one deals with that type often enough and after a while you come to recognize them when you see them. They have a certain look about them. You, however, do not have that look."

Nothing from Jerry.

Mills smiled, drank.

And Jerry looked at the distance from the couch where he was sitting to the chair where Mills was sitting and at the gun next to his leg. There was nothing he could try now, he told himself. Maybe later, though he didn't know what the hell it would be since there wasn't a chance that he'd get anywhere with this guy in a fight. He saw the pale blue eyes looking right into his then and he felt like Mills had read his mind, but all he said was, "You'd have done much better for yourself, Jerry, if you'd just gone out and robbed a bank. The police, well, they would have only put you in jail, but the ones you're mixed up with now . . ." Mills put a doubtful frown on his face, took another sip of his drink. "A different story altogether, you know?"

"How did you manage to fix it so they'd put me in your cab?" Jerry asked him suddenly, because talking was sure all he could do at the moment and it helped take his mind off the possibilities of who or what they were waiting for.

Mills chuckled softly. "Not a terribly difficult thing to arrange," he said. "I knew they would be bringing you out to the taxi that was parked at the center of the walkway in line with the terminal door, so I merely gave the driver whose cab was already in that spot a few pounds and he gladly gave it over to me. And getting the taxi was no real trouble either. You can acquire just about anything you want if you have the money."

Jerry looked at him then, didn't want to ask, didn't want to know, but asked anyway. "Who told you to wait for me? The guy that was after me back in Chicago?"

"That's right," Mills said cheerfully. "David Eckhart, an old associate of mine, in a way. You were lucky to get away from that one, let me tell you." The friendly smile was back. "But then I guess he really hasn't lost you, has he?"

Silence from Jerry.

He drank the last of the whiskey and put the glass down on the coffee table in front of the couch.

"Another?" Mills asked him.

"Yeah, thanks," Jerry said. Mills picked up the gun, fixed him a new drink and freshened his own, brought it over to him. Jerry took the glass from the offered tray and said, "Is that who we're waiting for—that guy from back in Chicago?"

Mills put the drink tray down on the coffee table, sipped at his glass, nodded, and Jerry looked at him. He was close now. He had a glass in his hand. The gun, too, but maybe a straight punch right in the nuts right over the table and . . .

No good, he thought.

Because it was clear across the room to the door, and even if the guy dropped the gun, which he might not, you might miss with the punch, and he looked like he could probably run, and then there was the briefcase. He wasn't going anywhere without it. Not now. So wait, he thought. Wait until you got a better chance, but then he thought that maybe it was too bad that he hadn't gone ahead and taken a shot at him because looking up at the guy now, he saw that funny look in his eyes that he'd noticed before, and it was back in his voice, too, when he said, "There's something I have to do," and Jerry thought he meant something he had to do in the apartment like maybe make a phone call or go to take a piss or something like that, and when somebody has just served you a drink, you're kind of not planning on anything happening until you've finished it, and so when Mills just bent down suddenly and smashed the muzzle of the gun against the side of his head just above his ear, he was caught completely by surprise and all he heard was a quick little splitting sound like when your shirt catches on a nail or something and rips.

MILLS LOOKED DOWN at the inert figure on the couch. He had hit him with the flat of the barrel. There was a little blood in the hair, but there wouldn't be any heavy bleeding. He had caught him completely by surprise. That look on his face! Pure shock! Mills smiled slightly, thinking about it. His pale blue eyes were bright, excited.

As soon as he came around, things would start to get interesting.

He took another swallow of his drink, tossed the gun down in the big leather chair and, carrying his glass, went over to the telephone. He picked up the receiver and dialed the operator, read the number in Las Vegas to her and waited while she put the call through. When Eckhart's voice came on the line, Mills said, "Success.

See you before long." Then he hung up. He finished his drink and put the glass down on the table next to the phone. Now he had things to do.

First he had to find some rope.

WHEN JERRY LOGAN opened his eyes, the room was blurry at first, so he closed them again, waited a few minutes, and then opened them again, and this time things were in focus. His head felt swollen on one side and he reached up to touch it with his fingers, to see how bad it felt, but he couldn't do it. He looked down then and saw that his hands were lashed tightly to the high-backed wooden chair he was sitting in. He tried to move his feet, but they were tied, too. The ropes were too tight around his wrists. His hands were a purplish color and tingling, the veins thickening under the skin. He had one real bitch of a headache, like a power drill going through the side of his head. He heard footsteps then and looked up to see Derik Mills walking over to him, a fresh drink in his hand.

"So! You're awake!"

Jerry said nothing, watching him.

"Let me explain, Jerry," Mills said pleasantly. "You see, my friend in the States tells me that you have a real talent for running away. He asked me if I could see to it that you couldn't do that so easily anymore."

Still silence from Jerry.

Derik Mills's smooth, handsome face frowned. "I'm afraid you've missed lunch," he said. "And we don't have time for any more cocktails just now, but," and again the pleasant smile, "never fear!"

The smile widened.

"You'll be in on the entertainment!"

Mills turned around then, and Jerry watched him go into another room, a kitchen, probably, because when he came out, he was carrying a very large cooking pot, and whatever was in it was pretty hot because steam was rising off the top of it. Jerry felt his stomach muscles tightening. Mills set the big pot down on the floor in front of the chair. Jerry looked.

Water.

Boiling water.

Jerry knew that he'd been all wrong before about not being so afraid. He was very afraid now.

Mills lifted his glass and drank it all down. He put the glass on the floor and moved it away from him with his foot. He looked down at the big pot of water and then back up at Jerry. "Have to hurry along with this," he said in his very pleasant voice. "Can't let it get cold on us."

He reached into his back pocket then and brought out a long red silk handkerchief. He held it by both ends and twirled once, twice, three times. Jerry tried to keep his lips shut tight, but Mills was strong and he jerked his head back against his chest, pulling the handkerchief hard against his mouth until he had to open it and then his mouth was full of the taste of it and he felt Mills knotting it tightly behind his head.

Then he felt himself being tipped slowly over backward until the back of the chair was flat on the floor and he was looking up at some jagged cracks in the high plaster ceiling. Mills went around in front of him then, and he heard the sound of the heavy cooking pot being scooted briefly across the floor, then Mills's voice saying, "There! I think that should about do it."

Jerry turned his head and saw Mills's ankles and feet walking back up behind him, and then he felt the back of the chair being lifted up again and he bent his head forward and down, his chin touching his chest, his eyes trying to see, and what he saw for the first time was his feet.

His *bare* feet.

No shoes. No socks. Nothing. And, he realized, no feeling in his feet either. They were numb, the circulation cut off by the ropes. He hadn't even felt that his shoes and socks were gone, but there was no time to think about that now because Mills was balancing the chair on its back legs, rocking it back and forth and Jerry tried to yell at him through the handkerchief, but there was no doing that, and then the chair was tipping way back over again and then going forward very fast and maybe a second before he felt it, he got a glimpse of his feet going straight into the pot of hot water.

His scream seemed to fill his brain, the room, everything, but it came out only a gagged, muffled cry past the handkerchief.

Then, tipping backward again and the cracks way up in the ceiling were there, his feet, ankles all hot pain.

He was already screaming when the chair went forward again.

Splash.

Banging the back of his head hard against the chair, again and again, his back arching, the ropes cutting into his wrists.

Tipping backward again and the jagged cracks in the high, white ceiling seemed to jump like black lightning above his eyes, and then he was going forward again.

Splash.

Tipping backward . . .

Forward again . . .

Splash.

And back . . .

Forward . . .

Only this time the scream didn't come because the room just tilted to one side and turned over.

The pain woke him.

Incredible, hot pulsing pain as though he were sitting with his bare feet and bare ankles in a roaring fireplace. He felt the nausea coming and he closed his eyes and took in deep breaths through his clenched teeth. After a few minutes, he opened his eyes. He wasn't in the chair anymore. He wasn't tied up, either, and the handkerchief was gone from his mouth. He was stretched out on the couch, and Mills was standing there looking down at him. His face was flushed red and the lemon-yellow hair hung down over his forehead, just touching his eyebrows. He was holding another drink in his hand. Jerry looked at the liquid in the glass, at the crushed ice.

Derik Mills came closer to him, smiled his friendly smile. "There now! That wasn't all so bad, now was it?"

Jerry only looked back at him, hate in his eyes, holding onto himself, but God, the fire in his feet and ankles! He wondered how serious the burns were. He didn't know anything about burns. People often went into shock after a bad burn, he'd heard that. How did you know when you were going into shock?

"Would you care for this drink?" Mills asked him, the voice that of the always-alert host. "Probably be just the thing," he said. "Set you right up."

Jerry started to nod, to say yes, he did want it, but then the nausea came at him again and he closed his eyes and rolled his head over to one side of the couch, and in the darkness in front of his eyes, he felt like he was falling. When he opened them again, Mills was putting the cool, cool glass down into his hands and he pulled himself up into a partial sitting position, keeping his eyes on the glass, not looking down at his feet. He brought the cold, wet glass quickly up to his mouth, cracking the rim of it lightly against his front teeth, drinking, feeling the ice against his upper lip. It was Scotch in the glass, and he swallowed some of it and then took it away from his mouth, holding it. The fire in his feet and ankles throbbed and pounded.

"It's an interesting thing, pain," Mills said. "How much of it a man can stand. What it does to him. Did you know that the only time a lot of people are really alive and alert to themselves is when they are in pain?"

Jerry brought the glass back up to his lips, drank a little more.

"Well, later," Mills said, "when you think back on this, you'll understand what I mean."

Jerry looked directly at him then and the words broke their way out of his mouth. "You dirty sonofabitch!"

Mills sighed. "Jerry, Jerry," he said. "Don't you see, it's, uh ... it's like they said in that movie *The Godfather*—it's nothing personal. How could it be, after all? We don't even know each other. It's strictly business. Well, I'm going to read for a while now. It's been a busy day.'' He cocked his head to one side and smiled. ''You won't run off, will you?''

Jerry looked down at the glass in his hands and wanted so badly to throw it at the smiling face, but wanted more to keep the cool of it. Mills laughed, and then he was gone from view, the sound of his footsteps going away across the room. Jerry drank from the glass again, reaching into it with his tongue and bringing a piece of ice back into his mouth. He rolled it around in his mouth until it melted and then went for another piece, only he never got it because this time the nausea came too fast, too strong, and he moaned softly, felt himself going out again, the glass slipping out of his hands, tipping over on his chest, the cold liquid spilling over him.

And later, when he came out of it again, the tears coming instantly into the corners of his eyes at the pain, he was aware of a sound. A kind of . . . ? What? A kind of scraping. Slowly he turned his head and looked in the direction of it.

No. Not scraping.

Snoring!

Across the room in the big, brown leather armchair, Derik Mills slept, one of his arms draped over the rounded thick arm of the chair, the other resting limply in his lap, the fingers of his hand curled loosely around an empty glass. The gun lay beside his leg. Jerry Logan glared at him, the anger rising in his throat, his lips drawn back over his teeth in pain.

You are going to get him! he told himself.

Fuck it all! All of it! Everything! But you are going to get him!

And slowly, so slowly, pressing his palms down into the cushions of the couch, he raised himself up, and when his feet lightly touched the rug, a white bomb of pain went off in his head and he clamped his teeth down hard on his lower lip to keep from screaming, jerking his feet off the floor, his fingers digging into the cushions. He sat like that for several minutes, a drum pounding heavily inside his head. He had never known such pain in his life. Slowly the loudness of the drum subsided. Carefully he stretched himself out again on the couch, and then, headfirst, his hands down on the rug, he began to inch himself to the floor into the crawling position, his feet in the air.

Then he began crawling slowly across the room on his knees.

Each time a knee came down on the rug, the impact sent pain shooting all through his body, and the cuffs of his pants were wet and he felt them rubbing against the burned flesh of his ankles. Never mind! he told himself, staring at the sleeping man across the room. Never *mind!* Burns heal. Worse than this. They heal.

Crawling closer . . .

And then he stopped because he suddenly realized something: One of the really bad things about anger mixing with pain was that it clouded your thinking, made you forget important things. Things like what in the hell was he going to do once he got up to Mills? He knew he had to get moving, think of something quickly. The pain from his feet was pumping up through him worse than ever, and he could feel a layer of sweat all over his face. His eyes moved away from Mills in the chair, looking around the room for a weapon. He saw things, but they were all too far away. He looked back at Mills and then, down on the floor a few feet away from one side of the chair, he saw something that might do just fine.

Jerry started crawling again.

He was close enough now that he could see Mills's huge chest rising and falling under his red turtleneck sweater, and then he shifted his direction and crawled toward the floor lamp at the side of the chair and when he was close enough, he reached his hand out and his fingers curled around the cool metal handle of the exercise weight and slowly he rolled it back to him. It felt very heavy on the floor and he wondered if he would be able to lift it, but there was no time to worry about that now, and shifting his knees back toward the front of the armchair, he began to crawl again, rolling the weight slowly across the rug in front of him with one hand.

Just a little closer . . .

And then he was only a couple of feet away from the knees of the sleeping man.

A little bit more.

He moved his left knee forward, then brought the right up next to it, and the sound of Mills's snoring mixed with the sound of his own heartbeat hammering in his ears. He rolled the weight back up against his knee.

And felt the dizziness start to sweep over him.

He closed his eyes, his fingers squeezing tightly around the handle of the weight. *Hang on! Hang on!* he yelled silently at himself. Better. A little better. He opened his eyes. Better. Okay . . .

He set himself as best he could and slowly began to lift the weight up off the rug.

Up to his shoulder then.

And it *was* heavy, but he pushed, raised it up even with the side of his head and it was getting hard to keep his balance on his knees.

Up above his head now, stretching his arm up until it was extended all the way, the weight shaking in his hand.

Then the man in the chair opened his eyes and looked at him.

But too late!

Jerry threw himself forward, driving the heavy weight down into Mills's shocked face, one end of it hitting him solidly in the forehead and his balance was all gone then, and while Mills only grunted in pain, Jerry screamed. He rolled away from Mills's body and down on his back, jerking his feet high in the air. He lay there gasping and whimpering out loud as the hot pain whipped through him, his eyes shut tight, his head jerking from side to side on the floor. For the first time in his life, he felt like he really wanted to die. Nothing—not the money or what he'd gone through so far or even the fact that he'd nailed this bastard—meant anything. All he wanted in the world then was for the pain to stop.

It didn't, though.

But it did ease up a little after a while, and he couldn't just stay there on the rug for the rest of his life. He had to try to get his ass out of this house, which was going to be no easy trick, since he for sure couldn't walk. He turned himself back over on his belly and then got up on his knees again and looked over at Mills. Blood covered his face, and there was a deep gash in his forehead. One end of the weight lay on his thigh, the other end on top of the broken drink glass between his legs. Jerry Logan

had never been a guy to go crazy about getting revenge
in his life, but at that moment, looking at Mills in the
chair, he could not help but feel a coldly pleasant satisfaction that he had hurt this man back for hurting him.

Now he had to find the john. He crawled into the
bedroom and found a small one leading off it. He ran his
hand up the side of the wall and flipped the light switch.
Then he reached up and grabbed hold of the edge of the
counter and, holding his breath, quickly pulled himself
up on top of it, his weight resting on his feet for only a
second, but it was a second too long. The pain shot
through every nerve in his body and forced his breath out
of him in a short yell. He sat on top of the counter next
to the sink for a minute and wondered if he would even
be able to make it out of the house. You'll make it, he
said. Even if you have to crawl out, you'll make it.

He opened the mirrored door of the medicine cabinet
and looked inside. Aspirin, Q-Tips, a tin box of Band-
Aids and, thank God, a little blue box of rolled cotton
and some adhesive tape. He put them down beside him.
Then he reached down and pulled up his right pant leg.

Jesus!

His foot and his ankle were the deep red of a very bad
sunburn, and already small, clear blisters had bubbled
up all along the skin. He reached down and turned on
the cold water in the sink. Then he took the cotton out
of the box, unrolled a long strip of it, soaked it in the cold
water and then wrung it out a little. Starting at his toes,
he gingerly wrapped it around his foot and up to the top
of his ankle, where the burn ended. The wetness of the
cotton made it cling to his skin and the coolness of it was
wonderful against the scalded flesh. Then he tore away

another strip of it, left this one dry, wrapped it over the wet one and secured it to his ankle with the tape. He was hoping that the two layers of cotton along with his shoes might give him enough padding that he could at least walk a little. All he needed was to get out of the house and find a bus or a cab. Then he could go to a hospital and have himself treated. In a few minutes, he had both feet wrapped, and just having the cotton around them made him feel a little better.

Get going, he told himself. Carefully he eased himself to the edge of the counter and, holding onto the edge of it with both hands, he put his right foot down on the tiled floor of the bathroom.

He groaned out loud. *Sonofabitch!*

Okay, okay, so it hurts, he told himself. You expected it not to? He put his other foot down and stood there, holding onto the edge of the counter, his face drawn with pain, testing his weight. A lot of pain, no question about it, but maybe it would do. Now, Jerry thought, see if you can move.

He took a step toward the door and then another, stopped. Bad. Really bad, but he could live with it for a while. Slowly he made his way out of the bedroom and into the living room. He saw that Mills was breathing as he passed him slumped in the big chair and he wondered if he was dying. He couldn't worry about that. He didn't like it that he was leaving his fingerprints in the house. They were on the drink glass he'd had and they were on the handle of the exercise weight and on things in the bathroom, but he couldn't take the time to go around and try to wipe them off everything. He wasn't sure how long he'd be able to stay on his feet, so he'd just have to take his chances.

He found his shoes and took the laces out of them to make them as loose-fitting as possible, but the sides of them rubbing against his feet brought tears to his eyes. He picked up the briefcase and Mills's car keys and went over to the front door and opened it. The street in front of the house was dark and silent at this late hour. He went outside and closed the door behind him. In the garage, he found the right key, opened the trunk of the taxi and took out his suitcase. He dropped the keys on the floor of the garage. He wished he could take the car, but with his feet like this, he'd never be able to work the gas and the brake.

He left the garage and walked down to the sidewalk in front of the house, turned left and started making his way down to what looked like an intersection. It was slow going. The weight of the suitcase and the briefcase put more weight on his feet, increased the pain, and already the cool feeling from the wet cotton had gone. He walked for several blocks, stopping every once in a while because he had to stop, looking around, acting like he was trying to spot an address for the benefit of anybody who might look out a window and see him. Finally he reached the intersection, and he had to sit down on the suitcase because his feet were all fire by then.

He sat there for almost half an hour before he finally was able to wave down a cab.

PART THREE

29

THE LARGE BEDROOM was completely dark.

No light came in from anywhere once the lamps by the bed had been switched off and the heavy wooden shutters over the two windows had been closed tight. It had been necessary for Chambers to have the shutters installed about five years ago, because it was then that Rosylyn had developed an acute sensitivity to the light and she'd had to be fitted with the specially tinted glasses that she now wore all the time. She had found that even the slightest amount of light coming into the bedroom at night would serve to keep her awake. At first she had tried closing her eyes against it, trying to ignore it, but that hadn't worked. Rosylyn was a woman who had always needed her sleep. She was simply no good the following day without her eight or nine hours, and she had only recently gone through a very difficult and anxiety-ridden change of life and seemed to need her rest even more to help her keep her balance.

So Al had had the shutters installed in the bedroom. He had done so with unspoken reluctance, because while he needed air conditioning during the day, he hated it at night while he was sleeping. It played hell with his sinuses and he would wake up the next morning feeling like somebody had stuffed a wet towel up inside his head.

And then, too, he had always liked to sleep with the windows open at night during the summers back in New York, and here in Las Vegas, where winter always felt like summer to him anyway, he had kept them open year round. There was often a breeze in the desert at night, and he liked to lie in bed and feel it blowing across the room over his face. It helped him relax and get things off his mind from the day so he could sleep.

But for Rosylyn, he would learn to live with his sinuses and the air conditioning and without the night air in his bedroom.

Al loved Rosylyn very much.

He was not a man who found it easy to love people. There were those he liked, sure. Some he worked with, a few friends, but the truth was if he had awakened one morning and all those people had suddenly left the earth, he simply would not have missed them all that much. Growing up in New York's lower East Side during the Depression, he had not been a boy to form close attachments. He had been a loner, always intensely interested in his own life. He had not been particularly sensitive to the struggle his mother and father were waging daily against the poverty and desolation of the time, but he had been sharply aware of the stark results of that struggle. He saw they didn't have spit, that they lived in a bleak land of other losers who would probably stay there all their lives, working themselves to death just like his old man was doing driving a truck for twelve, sometimes fourteen hours a day, hauling dresses all over town. He'd leave before daylight, come home always after dark, gray faced and tired, move slowly through the front door, into the can to wash up, then out of the can to the dinner table, eating, not talking, not even to his wife except to say pass this or pass that and then, finished with the eating, up and into the living room to fall asleep in his old, faded, thin-upholstered armchair with the newspaper open but unread on his knees.

Little outward affection was shown in the house. Survival claimed the parents' energies and attentions. For the old man, it was his job. For Al's mother, it was giving her attention to her man—her anchor, as she saw it, against the daily storms. As long as Al and his brother Eric were not sick or in any kind of trouble, they were pretty much left to themselves. Al had not been conscious of any resentment toward them for this neglect, but the lack of attention did prevent him from being close enough to them to develop any kind of real understanding of what they were like or what they were up against, and so he never really saw or appreciated that the neglect was merely a by-product of their desperate and all-consuming efforts to keep a roof over their heads and food on the table. The fact that both boys managed to stay out of any serious trouble in that neighborhood at a time when getting into trouble was more common than staying out of it was a kind of testimony to the success of the parents' efforts. The old man had been strict, the rules of the house basic. You showed respect and you kept your nose clean or you paid the price. The black leather razor strap that dangled on a nail behind the bathroom door was the instrument used in payment, and tired or not, the old man was quite capable of swinging it when the need arose.

Often in situations like this, two brothers will become close, making up somewhat for the attention they were lacking from their parents. Al and his brother had no interest in each other at all.

As soon as he had been old enough, Eric had quit high school and joined the navy, because he had always thought, he'd said, that he'd like to be on a boat somewhere. When their parents had died, the old man first, of a stroke one night sitting in his faded armchair and the mother a year later, from grief, fatigue and loss of purpose, Eric was stationed in Europe and hadn't come to the funeral. Most of the time, Al never thought of himself as even having a brother. They simply had never been very important to each other.

Al had stayed in high school. He was a below-average student not from any lack of intelligence as much as a total disinterest in the subjects he was forced to study for his grades. He stayed in school because it gave him time to think about how he might make money. He was determined not to be like his dead-assed brother or a lot of the other kids in the neighborhood who quit school and took some asshole job because they were hot to get a few bucks in their pockets.

Alert and shrewd, he had looked around and saw that taking a job like that was the first step into the trap. He saw plenty of guys around who had quit school to take a job just for the time being, and the time being had stretched into years. His old man had taken a job like that, driving a truck when he was eighteen, and he was still driving one the day he'd died. Al became one of those young men whose intense hatred and disgust for the poverty around him created a daily-growing fever for just one thing.

Money.

Money was it, young Al decided. Anybody who really looked could see that. And Al really looked. On Saturdays he would go to the one street, the one place that made him feel really good, that made him forget all his troubles.

Park Avenue!

He had a favorite bench along the sidewalk, and he would sit there and watch the people go by. How they dressed, the way they talked, the cars they drove. His eyes gleamed. At the end of the year, luck was with him in the form of two happenings:

He graduated from high school.

And the Japanese took their first shot at Pearl Harbor.

At first, Al had been mad as hell about the war coming along just at a time when he was finally ready to get the hell out of his crummy neighborhood and get his life moving. For a while, he searched frantically for some method of getting around the draft, but the way things were in the country then with guys going in left and right, he didn't have enough time to come up with anything that would work, so he was forced to resign himself to the inevitable. At least, he hadn't really had any hard, definite plans about what he was going to do with the rest of his life or how he was going to make all the money he was damned well determined he was going to have. If he'd had those plans already, going into the army would've truly been unbearable to him. Now if he could just keep from getting killed, maybe he could find his direction while he was in uniform.

And that's what happened.

Thanks to Nathan Shapiro.

Shapiro, a tall, lean man with curly, inky black hair and quick, sharp eyes, had been the manager of the Regency Manor Hotel in Manhattan and had been drafted at the late age of thirty-one because he had been unfortunate enough still to be a bachelor and to be in perfect physical health. Nate Shapiro, to talk to, was a quiet guy who read a lot and was embarrassed a little by being in the army with so many young kids just out of high school.

That was one side of him. The other side was that he was a totally dedicated lover of beautiful women. They had the effect of a good belt of pure oxygen on him, made him feel alive! No matter how down in the dumps Nathan Shapiro might be at any given time, the sudden presence of a beautiful face, a great pair of legs or a pair of well-formed breasts, and poof! Like magic, he was cured, the bad mood gone down the toilet.

Shapiro was a lover of the good life. The taste of fine wine and gourmet cuisine assured him that all was right in the world. He frequented certain fine restaurants as though they were his own and loved them in much the same way that certain men coveted possessions of antiques or stamps. The Regency Manor under Shapiro's direction was already starting to get a reputation as a first-class little hotel. Shapiro was the perfect hotel manager. Intelligent and possessing a native charm, he kept a sharp eye on costs and made certain the place was well kept up. His well-dressed appearance and engaging manner made him a favorite of the guests. Nathan Shapiro was a happy man. He loved his life.

Who would've ever thought about some people thousands of miles away across the ocean suddenly coming around and fucking it all up for him?

In the army!

No beautiful women.

No fine wine.

No gourmet food.

And if all that wasn't bad enough, there was even a chance that he might get killed!

Nate Shapiro lay on his bunk at night in the basic-training camp, gloom oozing from every pore.

But as it happened, his bunk was next to the one occupied by Al Chambers. Most of the other guys in the barracks thought of Shapiro as a nice-enough guy, but they tended to feel inhibited around him because of his age, or rather because of their age. Talking with him reminded them that they were still kids at a time when they more than ever needed to feel like they were men. So they all more or less politely avoided him.

All except Al Chambers.

Al's radar had right away picked up signals from some of the things he had heard Nate Shapiro talk about. Signals of success. Signals of money. Al and Nate began to talk frequently, and Al found the man fascinating. Nathan Shapiro had been around. Shapiro showed him pictures of his apartment back in New York, the likes of which Al had only seen in the movies. Nathan Shapiro showed him a picture of this hotel in Manhattan where he had been—not a bellhop or a desk clerk—but the fucking *manager*, no less! And Nathan Shapiro had been making twenty thousand dollars a year when the Japs and Uncle Sam had shoved it up his ass.

Twenty thousand dollars a year!

And after all this shit was over and if he didn't get his ass blown off, Nathan Shapiro would be back in that life.

And Al Chambers wanted to be back in it with him.

So he set out to become the best friend Nathan Shapiro could possibly have in the army. The best! The two started being together constantly. They went to movies at the camp theater. To the camp library. Shapiro showed him books. Al started reading, not loving it or anything like that, but he could live with it, and hearing Nate talk about some of the books, well, he had to admit they were kind of interesting. They shot pool and drank beer, though Shapiro hated the stuff. And most of all, they talked.

Or rather, Nate talked.

Al listened.

Nate held him fascinated with stories of his life BDN, as he liked to refer to it. Before Draft Notice. He told him about the Regency Manor and how it was well on its way to becoming one of the finest little first-class hotels in the city of New York. He told of buying nice clothes, mouth-watering meals at classy restaurants, parties, cars and pussy so good it kept you thinking about it for days after you'd had it. He spoke of people, important people, who sought you out because you were the manager of the hotel, the guy who could take care of them, who recognized them when they came in with their important clients or girl friends. Al drank it all in and then he would climb into his bunk to lie there and dream about it all, going over it, tasting it, picturing himself a part of it, and his ambition would burn so hot some nights he wouldn't be able to get to sleep until hours after taps had blown.

But Al remembered to be careful.

He never once even hinted to Nate about maybe making him a part of his action after they got out. He had to play his cards carefully. He would have to wait until the time was exactly right before he brought up that subject, and that time didn't present itself until later.

Both Al and Nate were high-school graduates. Shapiro even had two years of college, getting the credits at night at NYU while he'd first been working as a desk clerk at the Regency Manor. Al could type a little, the result of a short infatuation his junior year with the idea that he might want to become a newspaper reporter someday. The life had looked to him like one that could be interesting and exciting and give a guy a chance to get around, go places and meet people. People with money. But when he'd tried to get on the staff of the high-school paper, he'd found he had no talent at all for putting words together, and the effort of the attempt had bored the hell out of him so much that the idea quickly dissolved out of his system. The point was, both men were educated enough for the army to use them in some capacity in the administrative area.

So of course both were promptly stuck in an infantry division.

The news of which absolutely crushed Al even more than the news that he'd been drafted, because he was absolutely certain that all his efforts with Nathan Shapiro were on their way straight down the toilet because he was more than likely going to be killed by some crazy Jap sonofabitch he didn't even know. His dreams became covered with mud. He was convinced he would never see the inside of the Regency Manor.

But sometimes a guy gets really lucky. His gut level hunches, the ones that he just knows are right on target, turn out to be dead wrong.

Like the night on New Guinea, when Al Chambers and Nate Shapiro had been absolutely certain that they were going to die.

They were in a foxhole, the two of them, the army hot on the belief that you should keep two guys who were buddies together as much as you could because it was good for their morale. Scattered somewhere through the thick, wooded night was the rest of their platoon. The word had been passed along that there was to be a full-scale attack on their position sometime during the night and that they better expect it to be a bitch because they were heavily outnumbered. The night was chilly and wet, with a wind blowing, and peering out over the top of the hole, Al couldn't see anything but the clumped-together trees and bushes darkly outlined in the clouded light of the moon. The two men waited, each with his own private, scary picture of how it might be: the dark woods around them suddenly erupting with wild, piercing yells and the dark shapes of running, bayonet-carrying figures.

But the word had been wrong.

The attack did not come in a sudden, frenzied rush. It came silently, with barely a sound through the trees and bush-tangled woods, flat on the ground, creeping slowly, carefully, a little distance at a time toward them.

Al tried to stop himself from thinking, to shut the door tight on his mind so he wasn't so afraid he went crazy when anything did happen, and much to his surprise, he partially succeeded. Sometimes a thought would get through to him about being shot up and dying, but he would think about something else quickly before it had a chance to really grab hold of him. Neither of them had uttered a word for hours, fearing that the sounds of their whispered voices might hide the sounds of something they needed to hear. But finally it was Nate who broke the silence and with it some of the tension when he whispered, "You know what I really need right now?" And Al whispered back, "What?" "A really great piece of ass," Nate said, and the word *ass* was just out of his mouth when the two forms threw themselves up and out of the darkness on top of both of them. Chambers went crashing backward down into the hole, his rifle ripped out of his hands, staying just outside of the rim of the hole where he'd been resting it, and then he was being pinned down, hearing the thrashing, grunting sounds of Nate's own struggle, desperate and close in the darkness.

He knew the man on top of him had a knife, because before he was able to find his wrist and grab hold of it, he had grabbed the long blade of the knife itself, his fingers clamping around its sharp edge, and it had cut deeply into the palm of his hand. There was no room to move in the hole, and the man forcing the knife was very strong, had leverage on his side and already the knife was close to his face, had nicked into his cheek once and he knew that the man was trying for his throat with it, and since both his hands were busy, he used the only other part of him available. Closing his eyes tight, he snapped his head up with everything he had, smacking it flush into the man's face and both grunted from the pain, but still the hand holding the knife was pressing down, and desperate now, Al brought his head up again, and again it found its mark and this time he felt the man's wrist give a little. Once more and the contact was a hot burst of pain and made his senses reel, but he felt the man's weight fall slightly to one side of him, the knife hand going up and out, away from his face. He twisted his body hard then and suddenly he was the one on top, and all thinking gone, he pounded down where the face should be in the darkness, feeling his fists hitting, and then somehow he had the knife out of the man's fingers and he drove it down, falling on his hand that held it with all his weight, and that finished it. Almost crazy now, he could still hear Nate and his attacker struggling, could see their dark writhing shapes only a few feet away from him and he yelled *"Nate!"* and Shapiro's choking voice came back, "On top of me!" and Al threw himself on the top figure, his arm finding and going around the man's neck, pulling it back, the knife in his hand working once, twice.

They both laid there, not moving or talking at all for a while, just sprawled out against the damp, dirt walls of the hole, gasping in the night wind, the two still figures, dark lumps in front of them, and both wondered if more would be coming. But no more came, and at dawn, another platoon moved up into the area to join them, and they learned that they had lost six of their own during the night.

They had climbed out of the hole and were starting to walk away when Nate reached out and grabbed Al around the arm. Chambers turned and looked at him. Tears showed in the corners of Shapiro's brown eyes. He squinted in the early-morning light. "I won't forget," was all he said.

And he never did.

After the war, Nathan Shapiro brought Al Chambers into the Regency Manor, making him assistant manager, and under Nate's expert guidance, Al learned the business fast and a few years later, when the owner of the Regency built a new hotel out in Las Vegas, they sent Nathan Shapiro west to run it for them as president, and Al Chambers became the manager of the Regency. By that time, Al was cooking. He was having a great time getting into his new life. He had a lot of different women. Nate had been right. Fucking was one of the best things a guy could do in life. It was right up there with making a lot of money, and he was doing plenty of both. Love and all the complications that went with it did not interest him in the least.

Then he met Rosylyn Greene.

She had been hired to work behind the counter in the hotel gift shop, and the moment he saw her dark-eyed, olive-skinned innocence, he had wanted to devour her in the sack. But even though she was impressed with his combination of polish and rough charm, and even though he was her boss, Rosylyn Greene made it dead clear from the beginning that she had one hell of a lot of stubborn respect for herself and for her time. At the age of twenty-three, she had no intention of wasting any of that time being one of the hotel manager's now-and-again pieces of ass. She was, by God, looking for a relationship, spelled, in case he wanted to know, H-U-S-B-A-N-D.

And so another old story claimed another victim.

The more she put him off, the more Chambers wanted her, and he came to forget his promise to himself that he would never let his life get screwed up by having too much emotion where a broad was concerned. Rosylyn had gotten in his blood. Mornings at his desk, he would storm at himself about the way he was feeling and behaving about her. He blamed it all on the goddamned movies he'd been addicted to as a kid. You saw that romantic, falling-in-love, one-girl-for-me shit so many times on the fucking screen that after a while it got inside you and just laid there like a puddle of gasoline in your brain until the right broad who could see it came along and dropped a match! He'd fire her ass, that's what he'd do, he thought. No! Better yet, he'd keep her on and then ignore the shit out of her, make her see what she missed with her snooty, closed-legs attitude!

But then that was mornings at his desk.

At night, he drank the best Scotch, ate in the best restaurants in New York, smoked great Havanas, played poker, fucked his brains out and couldn't get Rosylyn Greene out of his head for one minute.

They were married inside of two months.

And Chambers had never regretted it. For the mix turned out to be one with gold edges. Once she had a commitment from him, Rosylyn felt free to let herself love the man as much as she was capable of loving him. And she was capable of a lot of love. She proved to be as strong and patient after her marriage as she had been stubborn and resistant before it. She was an intelligent girl, observant and attentive, and she came to understand Al Chambers a hell of a lot better than he ever understood himself. In time, Al learned to give out of himself to her and to experience the sense of release that came with doing that and from knowing that on bad days, he could come home and find comfort with Roz.

He stayed rough around the edges to all he met on the outside, but he was a different man with Rosylyn. She was his balance. The years went by, and when he was eventually offered a part-ownership in the Regency Manor, he discussed it with her, confiding to her for the first time that the people who owned the hotel were not what you would call law-abiding, upstanding citizens, and since he worked for them, that made him not so law abiding and upstanding either. Rosylyn listened to him, and though she was not at all comfortable with the things he told her, she told him that she thought he was strong enough and smart enough to know what he was doing, and whatever he decided, she would go along with him on it. Al accepted the offer, and for the twelve years he ran the Regency, the hotel became incredibly successful and prosperous, and he and Roz prospered along with it.

Then one night Nate Shapiro called.

In the time since he'd left New York, Shapiro had become a rich and powerful figure in Las Vegas as president of the Silver Tiara Hotel and Gambling Casino. Now he wanted to retire with his wife, Ellie—for a woman had finally gotten to him, too—and travel and see some of the world, he told Al, before he was too old to give a damn about seeing it.

The two men had stayed in touch over the years, seeing each other occasionally, mostly when Shapiro had a reason to visit New York, since Al hated traveling and all the crap that went with it, the airline reservations, rental cars, dragging suitcases—it was all a big pain in the ass to him. But he had visited Vegas and found that he liked it—the warm, dry desert climate, the color and special excitement of the city. And so when Nate made him the offer to come out and take over the presidency of the Silver Tiara, he and Rosylyn had talked about it several nights over dinner and finally decided that they could live without New York with its cold winters and stifling summers, and they sold their house on Long Island and moved to Las Vegas.

And as he had shown Chambers the ropes of the Regency Manor after the war, Nate Shapiro instructed him in the particular ways of the Silver Tiara. Both men had joked about history repeating itself, and Chambers, in a good mood, had told his old friend—for in spite of his self-serving intentions years ago in basic training, that's what Nate had become, his old friend—that he was getting tired of playing student to his teacher and that this was the last time he was ever going to do it.

And that turned out to be true when only a little over a week later, Nate Shapiro died of a cerebral hemorrhage within ten minutes alone at home in his wine cellar.

For the first time that he could remember, Al Chambers missed somebody being around who had been around, and often on his walks through the Tiara, he would think about Nate Shapiro and how much he owed him, how much the man had helped to shape his life. Nate had truly been a man of his word. He had never forgotten that night long ago on New Guinea.

NOW, AWAKE in the deep shuttered darkness of the bedroom with Roz close to him, asleep finally, snoring softly, Chambers thought about his meeting with Eckhart in the bar that afternoon, and about this cab driver way the hell over in London with his money, and Eckhart's question about that money, and the ungiven answer to that question. He pulled his arms out from under the warmth of the blankets for a moment and closed his eyes and found himself wishing crazily, stupidly, that somehow daylight would never come, that he could just somehow stay here in the warm bed in the quiet darkness with Roz next to him and not have to worry about doing anything ever again.

30

CHRIS ALTMAN WAS HAVING one of those days when it seemed like at least once every hour, something went wrong. To start, she found out that the electricity in her house had apparently gone off sometime during the night and then come back on again, so that when the alarm by her bed had gone off at five this morning to wake her for work, it hadn't been five at all but actually a few minutes past six-thirty, and she'd walked into the hospital late and Nurse Madden, the senior on the floor, looked at her hard, said, "Tardy, Altman," made her equally infamous clucking noise with her tongue between her lips, turned and stalked away down the hall.

Once again Chris had thought that Nurse Madden had indeed missed her true calling in life. The woman would have been the absolutely perfect housemother at some starchy, exclusive school for girls, where she could have made a career out of watching them with her bony chicken face, nosing into their business and making sure each night that none of their horny boyfriends was hiding under the bed after lights-out. The job would've delighted her. The woman would have been in paradise. But no, she becomes a nurse and inflicts herself on the sick.

But that was only the beginning of Chris's day.

After Nurse Madden had made her exit and Chris had gotten her cup of morning coffee, an ash with sparks in it from another girl's cigarette had fallen on the wrist of the hand that was holding the cup and, flinching at the pain, she had thrown hot coffee all over the front of her uniform and had to go and change. Then at lunch in the hospital cafeteria, she'd bitten down into one of the croutons in her salad, heard the dull cracking in the tooth and sure enough, out had come a piece of the filling, which meant another trip to the dentist and more money out of the checking account.

The day went by. The list grew.

Mr. Thompson in Ward Three, a scratchy old man who had fallen down his porch stairs and broken his hip, had insisted on recuperating at home but had been forced by his daughter to stay in the hospital, had thrown his small glass of Jell-O pudding through the window just as Chris had entered the room.

Then a run in her stocking.

A nice long paper cut across her index finger.

Dr. Graham with the quick-as-lightning fingers had pinched her on the ass as she'd walked by him in

Administrations and, startled, she'd cried out, causing everybody in the whole damned lobby to look at her while he escaped, innocent as hell, down the hall.

And now, at four-thirty, half an hour away from quitting time, she had to go to Emergency because a man, an American yet, had just come in with a pair of badly burned feet! Steady, Chris, she thought as she walked through the double doors into the Emergency section. Be pleasant. You are a *nurse*. You will always be pleasant, goddamnit! Tonight, thank God, was her last night on this late shift.

The physician on duty in Emergency was Dr. Colin Sloane, a self-loving little snot just out of medical school and mad as hell because he thought of himself as right up there with Schweitzer or Salk and resented the fact that he had been assigned to Emergency. Sloane looked at the American's feet, told Chris what treatment he wanted done, scribbled out a prescription for pain pills and promptly left, no doubt to go back to his little office and drool over the latest copy of *Penthouse* magazine.

The American, a tourist named Rodman, did not look well at all. The burns on his feet were bad. An accident, she'd heard him tell Sloane. He'd had some water boiling on a hot plate in his hotel room and somehow had knocked it over on himself. Just not his day, he'd said. Chris thinking of the hot coffee down the front of her uniform, sympathized with him.

Still, there was something strange about the whole business, but if Sloane had noticed, he'd given no sign, or more likely didn't give a damn.

First, if the man had gotten burned at his hotel like he said, then why had he brought his briefcase with him?

And if he hadn't gotten burned at the hotel, then where *had* it happened and why had he chosen to lie about it?

None of your business, she thought, irritated then at herself because those were just the kinds of things that she could easily picture Nurse Madden nosing over if she were here. Dressing and bandages in hand, she walked over to the man, smiling pleasantly. "You know, Mr. Rodman," she said, "you should really think about staying here in the hospital where we can keep a watch on those feet of yours. You won't be doing much walking on them for a while."

Sitting on the padded table, Jerry Logan looked down at her as she applied the thick gray salve to his feet and ankles. "Ah, I'll be okay," he said to her. "I'll be seeing the doctor again at the end of the week," which was what the doctor had said to him before he left, but he knew he wouldn't be able to come back here, because if he could move at all, he'd be moving his ass out of London.

The burn dressing she was putting on his feet must have had some kind of local anesthetic in it, because now the pain didn't seem to be quite so bad. He watched her expertly wrapping the bandages and thought that he wouldn't mind coming back here if he knew for sure that he'd be seeing her again.

She was pretty. Oh, not beautiful, maybe, like the nurses you always see in the movies, but pretty for sure. Early thirties, he'd guess, maybe a little younger. Strawberry-blond hair, green eyes, the hint of a nice figure under the wrapping. Pretty. And she had a nice voice, too. Soft. Like she looked. It was funny, he thought. A lot of girls, pretty girls, looked like they would have a voice like that and then when they opened their mouths, they sounded like Howard Cosell. "You, uh, been a nurse long, Chris?" he asked her, reading the black name tag with the white lettering pinned to her uniform. Dumb, he thought as soon as he'd said it, but he felt like he wanted to talk to her. He realized that he really hadn't just sat and talked to an attractive woman like this in a long time. She smiled in a nice way, and if she thought it was a stupid question, she didn't let it show.

"Actually, no," she said. "Why? Am I hurting you and you're just keeping a stiff upper lip and all of that?"

Jerry laughed. "Not me. You hurt me and I'll yell my head off."

"Please don't," she said to him. "I've only been on this job a little over seven months. They hear a patient screaming in pain and I'll be in trouble."

"You've only been a nurse for seven months?"

"My first job, this one," Chris said. "Right out of school. Aren't you the lucky one?"

"You seem good enough to me," Jerry said to her. "I mean," he searched for the words, "you haven't hurt me, and, uh," he looked down at the bandages on his feet, "you make good bandages." Great! Really great! How could a girl resist a suave, romantic approach like telling her she makes great bandages!

She smiled at that, though, and then she looked at him, her eyes concerned. "It says on your card, Mr. Rodman, that you're not married."

"No," he said. "Almost was, once."

"Well, do you have anyone traveling with you or someone who could look in on you at the hotel? You really should have, because the more you stay off your feet, the better it will be for you.''

"No," Jerry said, and then not because he thought it would matter a damn to her but because he wanted her to know that he *was* by himself, he said, "I'm traveling alone, but I'll be okay."

"I don't know..." her voice was doubtful. "It may be more difficult for you to get around than you realize. Even with crutches."

And he knew then that he was crazy, because if there was one thing he didn't have the time to do in his life right now, it was to try to start up something with a woman, no matter how pretty she was or how much he thought he liked her, but he felt, really felt so damned much that he wanted to try to do something that would let him see her again, and the opening had been laid out for him when she'd asked about his living alone. He didn't have anybody at the hotel to give him a hand while the burns healed. Hell, he didn't even have a hotel room yet, for that matter, and he knew that part of all this was probably just him feeling sorry for himself, but to hell with it. She was almost through bandaging him now, and if he planned on saying anything to her, he sure as hell better say it, but he couldn't think of anything to say, damnit, but he had to say something, and so what he finally blurted out to her was really incredible.

"Would you help me?" he said. "I'm in trouble."

She stopped bandaging his foot and looked up at him, her face puzzled. "Trouble?"

"Uh, yeah," Jerry said, and for half a second he was seized by a totally insane impulse just to tell her everything, which no doubt would've sent her running out of

the room and down the hall to get the police or at least a
few big guys with a straitjacket, so he passed on doing
that and said, "See, the trouble is, I'm a bachelor and
I'm on vacation by myself, and maybe you're right. I
probably *will* need somebody to help me out until these
heal and I can walk okay. I was wondering if you, uh, if
maybe you had the time and could take on the extra job?
I could pay you really well. A hundred dollars a day,"
he said and shrugged. "Whatever you want. I mean, if
you could do it . . ." He stopped then, looking at her,
embarrassed at the way he'd been rushing his words together, but he'd gotten it out at least, and now he hoped
she wouldn't offer to give him the name of a private nurse
or something like that.

"Well, Mr. Rodman . . ." she began.

Jerry, he almost said to her, but he caught himself.
"Leonard," he said. *Leonard! Terrific!* "Len." Better.

"Len . . ." she said. "I really don't do any outside
work. I have all I can handle here, but I'm sure I can get
you the name of a good private nurse who would be fine
for you."

Okay, he thought quickly. Since this really seems to
be a year for firsts in your life, why don't you just come
right out and tell the girl what you're really thinking?

"I want it to be you," he said.

That really surprised her. Color rose into her cheeks.
She laughed. "Why?" she asked him.

"Because . . ." he said. "Because you seem really nice
and you're pretty, and how do I know what the private
nurse is going to look like . . ." *Go on with it!* "And if it's
all right with you, I'd think I'd like to get a chance to
know you, and if I just walk out of here and don't at least

tell you that, I'll be mad at myself wishing I *had* told you. I'm nice, really. I'm not just some crazy American tourist. If there's anything you want to know about me, just ask. I'll tell you.''

Well, *almost* anything, he thought.

Chris didn't say anything for a minute. She went back to the bandage on his foot. The shiny scissors in her hand flashed through the bright white gauze, and she applied the tape, finishing the job. She stood up and looked at him. There was a faint smile on her lips. ''What hotel are you staying at?'' she asked him.

AND AFTER SHE got off work, something unusual happened to Chris Altman.

She felt good.

She didn't even mind the thought of going home to the empty house so much. On the tube during the ride, she thought about what she had done, and she was genuinely surprised at herself. Surprised that she had, on some crazy impulse, agreed to see a man, an American tourist, of all things, whom she didn't know in the slightest. She told herself that it was, after all, a job, a bit of outside work, and the pay was certainly good, and they'd talked about her only coming three times a week at that, and God knows, she could certainly use the money and—

And that was all rubbish.

Sure, she could use the extra money. Who couldn't these days? But she was doing all right. She'd agreed to see him, she thought, because she'd *liked* him.

And wasn't that something?

Chris smiled to herself. It was true. She'd liked him, and though she had always hated the word, there had been something really *sweet*, damnit, about the way he'd put his neck down on the chopping block like that just to try to see her again, and she'd felt flattered by it all, by the schoolboy-schoolgirl atmosphere of the whole thing, and it didn't bother her that it was silly! It had been fun to feel that way. She hadn't felt silly in a long time.

He'd been dead—how long?

Three years, almost.

A long time.

No time at all.

Not after ten years of working hard, both of them, him trying to be a doctor, her trying to make sure that they could eat and have a place to live while he was doing it. It was an old story—unless *you* were the one going through it. And there were the fights about the money that always seemed to occur on the days when she got paid, because she would know that it was all going to be gone for bills and to support them, and that would get to her sometimes, frustrate her and make her angry at him because she was working every day, making money but never having any for herself. Nothing for a good time now and then, or for new clothes, and thinking about all of that on the way home would feed her irritation, and by the time she got there, she was primed and ready for anything that would set off the fight, and when it happened, he would go off too because he had his own irritations, his own frustrations—the time it was taking him to be what he wanted to be, the shredding of his pride because he was taking from his wife instead of giving to her like he wanted to do. And so the explosions would come. Words would be shouted that would hurt them, erode what they had together. But they were of good stuff, and later, sometimes a day or two if it had been particularly bad, she would spend the money and fix one of their special candlelight-and-wine dinners, and later they would make love and then lie there in the darkness, the fight gone, the words forgotten, and close together, sipping from one glass of wine, they would talk softly of their plans, almost whispering, sharing bright secrets in the night.

And then had come a Saturday in September.

Near the end of the struggle for them. He was out of school and in his residency, still working hard, but not on that day, he'd decided. He'd take off, get away from it all, play eighteen holes in the morning and then they would go out. They'd make a night of it, he'd told her. Dinner, champagne, the works, and it all would be his treat for a change.

The sun had just started to go down when the policeman had come to the door, frowning slightly because he wasn't certain at first that he had the right house, and then when he was sure of that, "I'm sorry but I'm afraid there's been a motor accident . . ."

Endings.

And then, after it all, after the details, after the flat being full and then empty of friends, relatives and advice, she had settled down to deal with it all. The bed that suddenly seemed way too large. The not wanting or being able to sleep, and when she did, the deep, unstoppable hurt that would wake her crying so many dark mornings before dawn and make her not care at all about getting up, putting on the coffee, getting dressed, going to work. The hurt that with the months she learned to live with from Monday to Friday, but that would come down on her like a building after five on Fridays and eat her up through the weekend, and you could only take so much of that before it started to do things to you, before it set you on a course down the years that would leave you bitter or lonely, or you could see the possibility of that happening and the fear of it would be greater than the fear of the present, and you would try and make your-self give a damn enough to do something about your life.

And so she had decided to become a nurse.

And then it was working hard, studying, going to classes, hardly being home at all, and when she was there, it was to go to bed, and her body gave her no choice but to fall asleep. She was perceptive enough to see that she was trying to burn it all out, to get rid of some of her own pain in the myriad pains of other people, and that being a nurse, she felt closer to him, to what he had been involved with, and while that probably wasn't healthy, as some friends had pointed out to her, it had helped her nonetheless. And through it all, she had not been able to bring herself to care about being with a man, though with the passing of what was considered a proper amount of time, she had been approached by several men and had politely declined their invitations. And now today, for whatever reasons, she had felt something pleasant from a man with badly burned feet whom she had never seen before in her life, and she felt good about it without really understanding her actions at all.

THE TAXI DRIVER went around and helped him out, and a uniformed doorman came over and the two of them got him inside the Hilton. He had come straight to the hotel from the hospital, and while his feet felt better inside the protection of the bandages, they were too thick for him to get his shoes on over them, and that bothered him because he'd kind of been counting on the shoes and the cuffs of his pants to help hide them. Now the bright white bandages advertised him in the crowd.

He registered, and the bellhop took him upstairs to his suite in the wheelchair the hotel had for him. He had made arrangements to rent the chair, and Chris would be bringing him a pair of crutches when she came to change the bandages.

Once inside the suite, he began to feel uneasy about being there, about staying in London just because he'd happened to meet a good-looking nurse. He felt like he should be on a plane to somewhere else.

Bad move, he thought. Stupid. Like getting smashed back in Chicago instead of right away putting your plan into action like you should've done.

But he was here now, and, thinking about it, maybe it was not such a bad move after all. Traveling with his feet bandaged the way they were, he would certainly leave a trail of people behind him who might remember him. Here he could stay inside the hotel, stay off his feet and give them a chance to get well. And here he would have Chris coming to take care of him three times a week. It was nice to think about having her around to look at and to talk to.

He rolled the chair over to his suitcase, opened it and took out a fifth of Jack Daniels. There was a little tray of glasses on the table by the window of the living room, and he wheeled himself over to it, poured himself a straight shot and looked down at the lights of the city. Yeah, he thought, sipping the whiskey, maybe it *is* better that you're here. It's risky, but not as risky as being out in the open and not able to walk, much less run, if anything happened. There were a lot of hotels in a big city like London. It would take time to check them, and he wasn't registered under his own name.

He took another sip, frowned, remembering something.

He had thought they would have to check all the little towns between Vegas and Springfield too, and look how quickly they'd found him in Chicago. He wondered how they had done that. Then he remembered that he had screwed up and told that old waitress in the train depot where he was going. Maybe they'd talked to her and that was how they'd known to go straight to Chicago. Not her fault, he thought. She didn't know anything, and he was sure those guys could be pretty persuasive when they were trying to get information.

He wondered about the tall man, too.

Boy, had he been wrong about him. Mob guys weren't supposed to look like IBM salesmen. He wondered who the tall man was working for. Whose money was it that he now had in his briefcase on the bed? And that skinny, nervous blond guy who had looked like Richard Widmark—where the hell did he fit into all of it?

Questions you'll never know the answers to, he thought.

It was really something. He had never believed in fate or any of that kind of stuff, but it made you stop and

think. If that guy, what the hell was his name? Nichols?
Yeah. That's what the guy had said on the TV that night
at Ernie's. If Nichols had just walked out of the Tiara a
few minutes earlier or later, he'd have gotten into another cab and he wouldn't be sitting there in a hotel in
London now.

He shook his head, took another sip of his whiskey.
Really something!

And what about that bastard Mills? He was still alive
when he'd left his house.

What about *now?*

He lit a cigarette and put it all out of his mind. He
needed to start concentrating on what he was going to
do now. He could use this time alone here in the hotel
for that.

He had a lot of thinking to do, plans to make.

The phone rang.

He stared at it, his heart taking a jump and the old
tightness coming back into his stomach. It had to be
Chris, he told himself. She had said she'd call to con-
firm what time she was coming. No one else knew he was
here. It had to be her.

And if it wasn't?

Then he'd hang up, that's all. Hang up and then get
the hell out of here. He picked up the receiver.

"Hello?"

"Mr. Rodman?" Chris said.

Jerry breathed a sigh of relief. He leaned back in the
chair. "Yeah," he said.

There was a slight pause and then, "This is Chris
Altman . . . the nurse?"

He laughed at that. "I *know* who it is," he said to her. "This is Len, the patient, the guy with the hotfoot. Hot feet."

"Well," Chris said, "now that we know who we are, let me ask you—would around eight tomorrow be all right with you?"

"Sure," he said. "That's fine."

"The reason," she said, "is that I have this cat at home and he's alone all day while I'm at the hospital and I feel guilty if I don't go right home after work and feed him and play with him for at least a few minutes. And it'll also give me a chance to freshen up, so I'll feel a bit more human by the time I come to see you."

"Sure," Jerry said, "take your time. Whenever you can make it is okay with me."

"How are you feeling, anyway?" she asked him. "Do you have much pain?"

"Not much," he said. "I took the pills. They helped."

"Good boy," she said. "And remember, try to stay off your feet as much as you can. Read or watch the telly or something."

"The what? The telly? You mean the TV?"

"Yes." Laughing. "The TV. Really, you might enjoy it. It's a lot different over here than it is in the States."

"Yeah?" Jerry asked. "Like how?" Because he was enjoying talking to her, hearing her voice, and he didn't want to give it up yet.

"Watch," Chris said. "You'll see, for one thing, there's no advertisements."

"No commercials! When do you go to the bathroom?"

"You just have to wait," she said, laughing again. "Well, I have to ring off now. I'm up early tomorrow. At five."

"Oh, yeah, sure," Jerry said, trying to keep the disappointment out of his voice. "You better get some sleep."

"All right then, and I'll see you tomorrow night about eight."

"Good night," he said into the phone, because that sounded a lot better to him than good-bye any day of the week.

Since he didn't have a book with him, he decided to take her up on her suggestion and watch the telly. And she was right. It was different. There weren't any commercials, and no time to go to the toilet or not, it was a nice change not to have to watch some goody-two-shoes broad telling her wimpy old man that he had a ring around his collar.

The movie he watched was over at eleven-thirty, and he felt pretty tired, probably because of the pain pills, since he hadn't done a damned thing all day. He went into the bathroom, washed up and brushed his teeth and came back out and poured himself a nightcap from the Daniels. He knew he probably should lay off the booze while he was taking the pills, but he wouldn't have all that much. He wheeled himself over to the window with the drink. The lights of London spread out through the darkness below him, and he sipped the good whiskey and watched them and thought, burned feet and all of it, you're a lucky sonofabitch because you've got a shot at having something now. And all you need is to stay lucky and careful.

He drank the last of the bourbon and climbed into bed and switched off the light. He settled himself in under the blankets and thought about Chris Altman. Knowing that she would be coming to see him tomorrow night made him feel not as alone as he'd felt when he arrived in London. It was pleasant to be able to think about her and wonder what she was like. He knew nothing would come of it, because as soon as he was able, he'd have to get going. There were still way too many complications in his life, dangerous complications, for him to think about taking care of anybody else along with taking care of himself. But he was sure of one thing: He was starting to feel very much that he wanted a special lady, maybe somebody like her, maybe not, but for sure somebody he really cared about. He didn't want to live his life by himself any longer, because no matter how you tried to fill it, there would always be something missing. The pills and the shot of bourbon really began to take their effect then and as he dropped off to sleep, he thought about Vegas and his life there. It all seemed a memory further away than even his childhood somehow.

31

THE FIGURE SLUMPED IN THE large leather armchair slowly opened and closed his lips with a soft smacking sound. The inside of his mouth was gummy, as though he had been chewing on wet clay, and his lips felt crusty and puffed. He did not open his eyes immediately, for as he came back to consciousness, bits and pieces of what had happened to him floated around in his mind, slowly coming together a little at a time, and as the picture became sharper to him so did the pain in his head, a slow, deep ache at first that faster and faster turned into a stabbing fire, and he opened his eyes then and slowly raised his hand up to his head, felt the deeply split flesh, the blood clotted over it and then he let his fingertips move carefully down over his face, searching for more damage, but there didn't seem to be any, on down to the blood that had dried on his lips, and then the picture snapped together suddenly in his mind and with a loud groan, he shoved the exercise weight off his lap, sending it thudding heavily to the floor, the effort firing bright, shooting daggers of light through his head, and he fell back in the chair.

Eyes closed again, he tried to force his mind to focus. He didn't know how long he had been unconscious, but it had to have been several hours because it was almost dark now in the room, the last pale daylight dying outside the window. He wondered how badly he was hurt. Probably bad enough, he thought. The gash in his forehead felt large and deep, and he was aware of a faint but steady buzzing in his ears. He opened his eyes again, let his gaze travel across the ceiling and then on down the far wall. The ceiling and the wall waved in and out of focus and seemed to be trembling slightly. He looked across the room at the telephone by the sofa. He had to get to it, get his number book and call Dowling, get him over here to take a look. Dowling had taken care of him on other occasions like this when he had been hurt, and even though he was a self-righteous bastard considering how corrupt he was, he was still a damned good doctor, and thanks to the money he was paid, he could be relied upon to do what had to be done and keep his mouth shut.

Go! Move! Mills commanded his brain.

He raised his big arms from his side and put one hand on each arm of the chair, gripping the thickly padded ends of it in his fingers. Then, taking a deep breath, he pulled himself into an upright sitting position. A bright glare of pain burst inside his head, and the room in front of his eyes went very white, then very dark, then back to normal. He held on tightly to the arms of the chair and to himself, his breathing ragged and loud in the silent room. He had the feeling that if he tried walking to the phone, he wouldn't make it, he'd pass out, so he scooted his body forward to the edge of the chair and then lowered himself on the rug, groaning aloud suddenly at the pain in his right thigh where the weight must have dropped after Logan had hit him. He sat on the rug for a minute, leaning against the bottom of the chair, his legs spread out in front of him. Then he placed both palms down flat on the rug and slowly rolled over and up on all fours and began crawling toward the direction of the phone, the pattern of the rug swimming under his eyes. Get yourself fixed up, he thought. Eckhart coming soon. And you botched it, lost him his man. He must not let him know that he'd been drinking while he'd had Logan, deny it if Eckhart asked him. Logan would not get far, not with his feet that way. It made him feel better knowing that Logan was in pain, too.

He raised his head then and saw that he was close enough to the sofa to grab the phone cord. He stretched himself out flat on the rug and got hold of it, pulled it toward him until the phone toppled off the edge of the little table and fell to the floor, and he hauled it over to him. He would have to forget about trying to get the book with Dowling's number in it. It wasn't in him to dig the book out and then try to read it. He was in bad shape now. The pain was searing through his head, and as he lifted the receiver he was suddenly sick without any warning and vomiting on the rug. When he had stopped, he lay there sucking in the air, the receiver still in his hand. Several minutes went by. It was almost completely dark in the room now. He put his finger into the slot in the dial, slowly curled it upward and let it go.

"This is the operator," the voice said. "May I help you?"

"I need . . ." Mills said, "the number—Doctor Phillip Dowling—in Grover Street . . . emergency."

More minutes passed while the operator searched out the number, found it, placed the call. Mills felt a cold film of sweat forming over his face in the darkness, and then came the familiar, stiff, dry voice, "Dowling here."

"Mills," he said into the phone, his voice a tight, choking whisper. "My house. *Hurry!*"

And the receiver was still in his hand when he felt his head falling backward, and it seemed to take a long time before the side of his face struck the rug as the buzzing in his ears grew louder and louder.

ECKHART STOOD in front of the door to the house in the chilly night breeze.

Something was very wrong. He had just finished ringing the bell for the third time, and still there was no answer. There was no sound of any movement from inside the house, and there were no lights on in front. He glanced around in the darkness. The sidewalks were empty. The traffic going by in the streets was thin. Most of the people in the neighborhood had gotten home from work by now and were sitting down to dinner. He turned away from the door, crossed the small lawn and headed around to the side of the house. He hoped that nobody next door would happen to hear him, look out the window and ask what he was doing, or not ask what he was doing and just call the police. But if either of those two things should happen, he would tell them that he had come to visit a friend and when there was no answer at the front door, he'd thought his friend might be off in the back of the house and perhaps hadn't heard the bell and so he'd taken a walk around to see.

The entire house was dark.

He made his way quietly through the dead grass back around to the front, the knife already open in his hand. He stepped up close to the door and inserted the thin, narrow blade with the slight nick in the end of it into the keyhole, moved it to the left, then to the right and then to the left again, pressing the blade upward, and felt the soft give of the tumblers. Glancing quickly around, he stepped inside, the knife still in his hand, only with the other blade open now, the special one. He pushed the door shut behind him and stood motionless in the small, dark foyer, listening.

Silence.

The room was warm. Eckhart's eyes began to adjust to the darkness. The knife ready in his hand, he slowly felt his way through the house, looking into every room.

All empty.

Where in the hell was Mills?

He went back into the living room and switched on a floor lamp that stood next to a large armchair. The first thing he saw was the black exercise weight on the rug. The second thing was the dried blood on the upholstery of the big chair. He got down on one knee and looked closely at the dark red smears, scraped at one of them with his thumbnail to make certain it was what it appeared to be. It was blood, all right. The smears spotted several places on one arm of the chair and one side of the seat near the front. Eckhart stood up and walked carefully around the room, his eyes examining the carpet. The stains began and ended on the chair. Whoever had been hurt must have been hurt in the chair and managed to stop the bleeding. Eckhart stared down at the chair, trying to picture what had gone on in the room before he'd gotten there.

Who was hurt, he wondered. Mills or Logan?

He hoped it was Logan. But even if it was Mills, why wasn't he here? He could not imagine Logan getting away from Mills once Mills had him. Wrong, he thought. He *could* imagine it. He remembered how things had gone for the cab driver up to now, and he remembered again Chambers's words back in that crummy bar about Logan still being hot with his luck.

So now what?

If Logan had somehow managed to get away and Mills was out after him, sooner or later, with or without Logan, Mills would come back here, because he knew he'd be waiting for him.

He walked back to the lamp and switched it off again. He felt more comfortable in the darkness now that he knew the house was empty. He would just sit tight and wait for a while. He loosened the big buttons of his top-coat and sat down on the couch. Too many things gone wrong too many times with all of this, he thought. And though he wasn't a gambler, he felt like one, one who was losing over and over again but still staying in the game, praying frantically for his luck to change, for his losing streak to break. He didn't like the feeling at all. He thought of the fear he had seen in Chambers's eyes, the loud-mouthed big shot gone, a scared little fat man afraid for his life in his place. Chambers was a loser now, and he, Eckhart, had mixed himself up in the matters of a loser. He didn't like that, either. He shrugged his broad shoulders under his coat, trying to shake off the feeling.

He'd deal with Logan, get the money, get back to Vegas and end all this. He was impatient to have it all done. A wind had kicked up outside, and he could hear the house creaking in places as it blew hard against the sides of it, and it was a good thing he was sitting quietly, being still and not up and moving around, or he would probably have missed the sound of the key that some-one was inserting in the lock.

Eckhart leaped silently to his feet and moved quickly across the rug to the door, flattening himself against the wall as the bolt turned over and the door opened, cov-ering him, but when it closed again, the figure feeling for the lights was too short for Mills and Eckhart crossed his arms over his chest, pulling them in tight against himself, and threw a solid body block into the man, forcing a sudden, startled yell out of him and slamming him hard into the foyer wall and then down the wall to the floor.

Eckhart hit the light switch and jumped back a step, the knife poised in his hand.

The short, fat man with the salt-and-pepper hair who was now half-sitting, half-lying on the floor gaped up at him, his mouth open wide, gasping for breath, fear and pain on his face.

Eckhart loomed over him. "Who are you?" he snapped.

The man raised one hand, indicating he couldn't speak yet. He put his hand back on his chest.

Eckhart watched him. "Who are you?" he said again.

"Dowling..." the man wheezed tightly. "Dr.... message from Mills..."

"Where is Mills?"

"Hospital," the man who called himself Dowling said, finding more of his voice now. "He knew you would be here. Sent me to tell you. *God!*"

Eckhart said nothing for a minute, only stood looking down at him, his eyes studying the face for even the smallest hint of a lie, of anything wrong.

"Would you mind helping me up?" Dowling said. "I'm a little too old for this sort of thing."

The knife plainly visible in one hand, Eckhart reached down and pulled him up with the other.

"I would've rung the bell," Dowling said, rubbing his side and wincing, "but when there weren't any lights, I didn't think you were here yet." He glanced at Eckhart and then walked past him into the living room and over to Mills's bar, where he splashed some Scotch into a glass and quickly drank it, refilled the glass and walked painfully over to the couch and sat down.

Eckhart did not sit down. He wanted to know what had happened. One thing was for sure, if Mills was in the hospital, then Logan was probably gone. "So what's wrong with Mills?" he said.

The older man drank from the glass, rested it on his knee. His hand was shaking, but his composure was returning as the fear of any danger to himself retreated. He looked directly at Eckhart. "Somebody hit him over the head," he said flatly. "He telephoned me. I came over. He was unconscious. It was a bad gash. I couldn't treat him here so I got him conscious and took him to the hospital. He has a concussion. He told me he was expecting you and that it was important, so I came back here to tell you. He said he'd explain everything when he saw you."

"So when can I see him?"

"Not until the morning," Dowling said crisply. "And when you do, you can tell him this is the last time I'm helping him. I don't enjoy getting knocked about. I'm a doctor, not a thug." His voice had lowered on the last of that so the word *thug* was barely audible, and he glanced quickly at Eckhart to see if the tall man had taken any offense.

Eckhart smiled at him, amused at the man's growing indignation. He could easily guess the type of man this Dr. Dowling had to be. He had seen men like him before. Mills gets hurt. He doesn't call an ambulance. He calls Dowling. And Dowling comes right over. House calls, yet! Eckhart wondered what Mills had on the good doctor or how much he was paying him to get such special treatment.

Dowling reached into his shirt pocket and worked loose one of three ball-point pens and then a small white note pad. He set his drink down between his knees. "This is . . . the address of the hospital," he said, writing. "I'll put the number of the room on here, too— number 1806. You can see him there anytime after eleven tomorrow morning."

"There's no chance I can talk to him tonight?" Eckhart asked.

Dowling shook his head impatiently. "No, no, *no!*" he said quickly. "He had to be sedated, sewn, all of that. Eleven o'clock tomorrow." He jerked the little piece of paper away from the pad and handed it to Eckhart, who put it into the side pocket of his coat. Dowling picked up his glass, drained it and put it down on the arm of the couch. "I have to be going now," he said.

Eckhart nodded. "Sure," he said. Dowling stood up, and they walked back to the front door. "Sorry to have been so rough on you," Eckhart said pleasantly.

Dowling grunted as if to say that he damned well ought to be sorry, and then he buttoned his coat.

"Doctor?" Eckhart said to him.

Dowling turned, his hand on the doorknob.

"Mills say what happened to him, how he got hit on the head? A prowler or something?"

Dowling didn't hesitate, his reply instant. "I've no idea," he said stiffly. "I only treated him. I didn't question him."

And with that he pulled open the door, stepped out into the quiet neighborhood night and closed it in Eckhart's face.

Eckhart looked at the door for a second and smiled. There were so many men like Dowling, he thought. See no evil. Hear no evil. Speak no evil. Especially if the evil happened to be their own. He turned away from the door and walked back into the living room, the smile fading from his lips. He was wondering how it could've happened that Mills let himself be so off his guard that Logan could hit him over the head and get away. He looked over at the bar and wondered if the twisted sonofabitch had been drinking while he was with Logan. He knew that Mills drank only when he was enjoying himself, only when he was doing the one thing in life that really got him off.

Eckhart had never known Mills to be with a girl and long ago had figured him a good candidate for a closet fag. Anyway, Mills did like to drink when he was playing his little pain games, the same way a lot of guys liked to drink before they screwed. It had probably been a mistake, he thought, to tell him he could fix it so Logan couldn't run away anymore, but he had known that the idea would appeal to the man and tend to make him try harder to find Logan. The money wasn't enough. Mills had money. Without the added incentive of a little fun along the way, he might've just driven to the airport, taken a half-assed look around, driven back home, called and said he hadn't been able to find him. A mistake, anyway, Eckhart thought. He should've just leaned on the creep. Told him it was personal or something like that, made it important. Mills was a physical-fitness nut along with everything else, and because he didn't drink very often he couldn't hold it very well. He must have been careless or Logan would never have gotten close enough to hit him over the head. He wondered if Mills had been able to hurt Logan. Dowling had said he had a concussion.

Well, the bastard better get well in a hurry because he was going to need him to find Logan again if it wasn't already too late.

Suddenly a vicious sneer twisted Eckhart's face.

"The stupid sonofa*bitch!*" he spat the words out into the empty room. He *hated* having to work with other people! The minute you involved somebody else in what you were doing, you let things get out of control and took a chance on everything getting screwed up. He looked around the room and for a minute thought about just spending the night here and not going back to his hotel, but no, he didn't want to do that. There was something about the place, about the things Mills had probably done here, that gave him the creeps. He'd go back to the hotel, grab a good night's sleep, then talk to him in the morning, and even if the bastard couldn't get out of bed, he was going to help him. Mills had contacts, eyes on the street, and he was for sure going to need them now. When he left the house, Eckhart turned the lights off and left the front door unlocked. He hoped somebody would come along and rip off everything the fool had!

32

CHRIS ALTMAN ARRIVED a little past eight-thirty. After she had knocked and told him who it was, he yelled,

"Just a minute," wheeled himself over to the door and unlocked it.

"You shouldn't have locked the door," Chris said to him as she came in. "You don't have to keep your hotel door locked." She smiled at him and put the small black bag she was carrying down on the couch. "This isn't America, you know."

"Just a habit, I guess," he said to her. He looked at her as she took off her coat and walked over to the little writing desk and put it over the back of the chair. She was wearing a pale blue turtleneck sweater and matching skirt. The strawberry-blond hair was down to her shoulders now, and it looked brushed and shiny in the room's light. Her face was flushed a faint red from being outside in the wind, and she looked even prettier than at the hospital.

"So tell me," she said. "How have you been? Have they been bothering you much? Were you able to sleep?"

The nurse's uniform was gone, he thought, but the nurse was still around. "Yeah," he said, "I slept okay. I think the pills had a lot to do with it. I don't hurt as much." He grinned at her. "I told you, you make great bandages."

Chris laughed and pointed to the couch. "Sit," she said to him.

He eased himself out of the chair and down on the cushions and said, "Listen, would you like something? Coffee? A drink? I can call room service. Tea? How about tea?"

"This will probably shock you," she said, "but all my life I have hated tea. But if you're going to have some coffee, I'll join you."

"I was thinking about having a drink."

"Not a good idea," she said. "Those pain pills are a rather strong prescription. It's best you don't mix them with alcohol." She looked at him. "You *haven't* been drinking, have you?"

"No," he lied.

"Good boy," she said.

She went over and picked up a wooden footstool covered in red upholstery and brought it back to the couch. She opened her bag, took out a white towel, spread it over the stool and told him to put his foot on it. Then she began taking gauze, dressing and tape from the bag. "Would it be all right if we waited on ordering the coffee?" she asked him. "Until we're finished here. It'll just get cold if we order it now."

"Sure," Jerry said. "I'd rather get this out of the way first, myself." He watched her as she took his ankle gently in one hand, carefully inserted the thin, pointed scissors under the edge of the bandage and slowly snipped it down the center to his toes, separated it in half and removed it. Jerry flinched. God, but it looked awful. The skin didn't look as red as yesterday, but a lot of the big and little blisters had burst under the bandage and the dead, white, blistered skin was flattened out all over his foot and ankle. It looked like he had some kind of damned skin disease. "Beautiful," he said. "Old lizard foot."

"It certainly looks a great deal better than it did yesterday," Chris said. She began applying the burn salve, and though she was being as careful and as gentle as she could, the touch of her fingers on the angry red skin sent sharp, searing pains all through him and brought tears to his eyes. He thought about Mills in the chair with his head bashed in and he felt no remorse at having hit him. The bastard had it coming.

"This is an awful thing to have happen to you on your vacation," Chris said. "Have you ever been to London before or is this the first time?"

"First time," he said. "It's a beautiful city, what I've seen of it, anyway."

"It really is. Too tight?"

"No," he said. She had finished applying the salve and was wrapping the gauze around his foot. "At the hospital, you said you've only been a nurse for seven months?"

Chris glanced up at him, smiled. "Back to that, are we?"

"No," Jerry said, laughing. "I was just wondering—what did you do before?"

"I worked in a law office," she said. "I was a secretary."

"And one day you just decided to be a nurse?"

"No, it wasn't quite like that," she said. "Okay, let's have the other one now." She had finished with his foot. He put the other one up on the stool. "My husband was in medical school," she said, cutting the bandage. "I was working to help with expenses. Then he was killed in an automobile accident and I didn't want to work in the law office anymore. I felt like I wanted to do something more worthwhile." She started applying the salve to his foot. "You wrote on your information card at the hospital that you were a salesman. What is it that you sell?"

Damn! he thought. That was right. He *had* written that down. It had been the first thing that had popped into his mind. "Auto parts," he said now, because that would be something she wouldn't be likely to know much about and so she wouldn't ask him too many questions about it. He didn't like starting off telling lies to her, and he already had a good little file of them going.

"Is it a large company?" she asked him.

"No," he said. "I've got my own little business."

"Where?"

"In Las Vegas."

Chris stopped wrapping the gauze around his foot and looked up at him in surprise. "Las Vegas! Now there is a city *I've* always wanted to visit! I've seen pictures of it in magazines and in the movies. It always looked so colorful and exciting." She went back to wrapping the gauze. "Are you a gambler, Len?"

"Ah, sometimes," he said, glad that she had used his first name even if it wasn't his first name. "Not too much, though. It's different if you go there as a tourist and play and then go home, but if you live there, you have to be careful."

"Yes," she said, thinking about that. "I suppose you would. Too much temptation. I certainly know that it would be for me. I guess I must have some of the gambler inside me. I have to watch myself just playing the slot machines here in London or I'll spend more than I can afford." She finished wrapping the gauze and applied the tape. "There you are. All finished."

Jerry looked down at the two fresh bandages. He felt better now that his feet were wrapped again, the ugly burns covered up. "Can you tell me something?" he asked her. "How long do you think it'll be before I can walk on them?"

"Probably about a month," Chris said. "That is, if you stay off them like you're supposed to and give them a fair chance to heal. When do you have to go back to the States?"

"I've got time," he said, wishing that were true. He wasn't sure he could stand trying to hide out in a hotel room for a month. The longer he stuck around, the better the chance of that tall bastard finding him. But now he smiled at her and said, "See, that's one of the advantages of having your own business. You can hire somebody to watch the store and take longer vacations than other people. How about I order us that coffee?"

She looked at her watch. "Okay," she said. She began putting things back in her bag. "But I can't stay too long. I have to get up so early. That's one of the disadvantages of being a nurse."

Room service delivered the coffee in a large silver pot with two delicate-looking cups, and they drank and talked. Conversation stuff. She told him some things he should try to see in London after his feet were better if he still had the time, and carefully he flirted with her a little, asking her if she would show him around the city, and she laughed and told him that a nurse didn't have any time to be a tour guide. He told her a little about Vegas, about some of the places and people he'd seen while he had lived there, and talking about it made him suddenly miss it, and he thought about being there with her and what a hell of a time they would have especially now that he had money. Chris asked him if he'd ever been married and he told her no, that it had just never quite happened for him. Close once, but not quite. He remembered that she'd told him her husband had been killed. He wondered how long ago it had happened and if she went out much, but he didn't ask her. He'd gotten the feeling at the hospital that it was something she didn't want to go into. They ended up talking for almost an hour and a half and then she had to go, she told him, and after she was gone, he felt sad and frustrated, because he really did like her, but with all the stuff confusing his life now, he didn't see how anything could come of it.

Living in Vegas, driving the cab, he could always be around people when he wanted to and he'd never really been bothered that much by loneliness.

He looked down at the two empty coffee cups on the tray.

Damnit, he really did like her. Sitting and talking to her had somehow made all the trouble he was in not seem so bad, and later, lying in bed, he thought about how women really were what could make a guy's world go around. As corny and old as that was, it was true. The right woman could help make things work in a guy's life. Without her, the rest of it—money, success, whatever— could never be quite as good as if she were around.

BACK HOME, Chris kicked off her shoes and stretched out on the rug and played with Roscoe. The big reddish orange cat rolled over on his back and playfully swiped at her hand as she tickled his stomach and ruffled his heavy fur. Chris really loved the cat. Roscoe had helped her through a lot of lonely hours after the accident, always liking to stay near her while she paced or tried to watch the telly or read, and there had been many a bad night when she had just sat and held him and cried for a while. She got up, went into the kitchen and put the tea kettle full of water over a low flame on the stove. Then she undressed and took a long, hot shower, washing her hair, and when she came out and had dried off, she put on her big heavy yellow terry-cloth robe, wrapped her hair in a towel and went back out into the kitchen, where the water was boiling.

She made a cup of instant coffee and because she felt pretty good, she laced it with a shot of brandy. In the living room she put one of her favorite Miles Davis records on the stereo, turned off all the lights in the room and stretched out on the couch with her coffee. This was a routine that she found relaxing when she was upset, or when she wasn't upset and just wanted to think. And now she wanted to think about this man Leonard Rodman. She snuggled into the heavy robe, loving the softness of it against her freshly showered nakedness. He liked her for sure, was attracted to her. She had seen that plainly in his eyes in spite of how careful and polite he had been back at the hotel. He wasn't particularly handsome, and yet there was something she found very attractive in his rather tough, American-looking face. There was a certain little-boy quality that would come into his face off and on. She thought she sensed real loneliness in him, and something else, too. Nervousness? Fear? She sipped her coffee, enjoying the taste of the brandy. She wondered if she could get involved with a man like him. And if she could, did she really want to? For two years she'd had push-pull feelings inside about wanting or not wanting a man in her life again.

Sometimes she would be fine being alone at night, content even. She would read or play with Roscoe or listen to music and do some of the little things around the house that needed doing, and during those times she would think that yes, maybe she could be one of those women who could learn to live their lives alone, that maybe now, after it all, she was changed somehow, matured in some way, and was, if she chose to be, capable of living without a man.

Then one of the other nights would come along.

And the inside of her neat, tastefully decorated little house would give her the feeling of being inside a comfortably sealed tomb, growing older quickly with the passing of each damned day. She would feel a frightening, urgent need to *do* something, but she would not know what the something was. And then she would become angry at herself because she knew that she was an attractive and intelligent woman who could have a man or men if she wanted to make the effort. She knew she wasn't lazy and she wasn't feeling sorry for herself. Well, she probably was feeling sorry for herself, but not as much as a year ago. Still, making such an effort depressed her. Going out with a couple of friends to some bar where men, their faces smug with unjustified self-confidence, would approach her and say things like, "Hello. I'm Brian. I'm a lawyer. What's *your* name?" Or, "I'm George. How do you like me so far?"

And when you had been living inside the secure warmth of a good relationship with a man you deeply loved and who loved you, and you'd built on that relationship, adding textures to it over the months and years and then suddenly one day it's gone, the idea of going home with a series of these empty suits for a night in the hope that the law of averages would one day give you the real thing was something she simply had not been able to do. Oh, she had gone out a few times, but she'd always ended up leaving early, not having the heart, finally, or the interest or even the just plain horniness to play the whole charade through to its end. She knew that her friends thought she was being too particular, old-fashioned and straitlaced. She'd stand guilty on two of those charges. Particular, yes. And maybe a little old-fashioned, too. But she was not straitlaced. She'd always enjoyed sex. Morality had nothing to do with it. It was just the *degree* of desire that seemed to be missing now. Maybe if she went without it long enough, she'd often thought wryly, then one of these nights, she'd go out and go through with it. But so far, it was an event that she could wait for without any trouble.

But still, on some of those long, restless, bad nights at home, when she couldn't seem to concentrate long enough to read even an entire page in a book, or when the silence in the room would scrape at her nerves as much as the music on the stereo, and playing with Roscoe would bring up images of some lonely old maid and her cat—on nights like that, she would close her eyes and think about how much she would like to be in love again and she would know what was happening to her and she would try to fight it, telling herself all the stuff about how that was what life was all about, having and losing, and losing and having, but those were only words and they wouldn't give her any comfort, and after a while, she would not be able to stop her mind from going back to the still-too-close past, and the tears would come then and the night would close in even more icily around her, and then she would be angry with herself, ashamed at letting herself slip back like that.

But tonight, she drank her coffee and brandy, feeling content, and listened to Miles Davis's soft trumpet in the darkened living room, and thought yes, she definitely did like this Len fellow. She liked being around him. She liked the shy way he was attracted to her, and even if nothing ever came of it—and she knew probably nothing would—she wasn't going to care about that now. She had not felt this way in a long time and she was going to enjoy it while it was happening. She smiled to herself because already she was wishing that she were going to see him again tomorrow night instead of the night after.

33

JERRY LOGAN SAT IN HIS WHEELCHAIR next to the little round wooden table in front of the picture window in his hotel suite, drinking his morning cup of coffee and having a cigarette. He felt calm and rested after a good night's sleep. He sipped his coffee and looked out the window at the city. It was one of London's beautiful days. The sky was a cloudless light blue, and the sun streaming in through the glass was warm on his face. He was really looking forward to the day.

A whole day with Chris.

In the month that she'd been coming to take care of him, they'd gotten a little closer to each other, a little more familiar and at ease. He'd discovered that she had a good sense of humor, and they joked a lot and he was able to flirt with her that way without feeling too self-conscious about doing it. They had talked a little about each other, about their lives, never coming out with anything that was too heavy but still each of them giving away a little. Chris had brought a game of Scrabble one night and a deck of cards on another, and they would play and share a bottle of wine since he didn't need the pain pills anymore.

Now he took a drag on his cigarette and looked down at the thick white bandages on his feet. Carefully he wiggled his toes and felt the familiar stab of pain, only it wasn't as sharp as it had been in days and weeks past, the feeling of pulsing heat not so intense. Under her expert care, he was getting better, and he was happy about that but he was *really* happy about something else.

Now she was coming to see him on nights when the bandages didn't need changing. She was coming because she wanted to see him!

He found that he was sleeping better, and while he was still concerned about the tall man, Eckhart, Mills had called him, and what he might be doing to try to find him, he had even learned not to worry about it all the time like he had been doing. He did not intend to get careless the way he had back in Chicago, but he'd be damned if he was going to let it eat him up. There were a lot of hotels in London. He wasn't registered under his own name, and after the first week, he'd had the hotel manager come up to his suite and given him a story about how he wanted to recuperate from his accident in peace. He had a lot of friends in London, he'd explained, and while he knew they meant well, they were simply bothering him too much, dropping in to see how he was doing, and he wasn't getting any rest. That was why he had moved out of the friend's house where he'd been staying and come here to the hotel. He really didn't want to see anyone for a while, and he would appreciate it if the manager could perhaps say that there was no Mr. Rodman registered at the hotel, should anyone come inquiring for him.

The manager had understood perfectly. He would inform the night manager, too, so he could be on the alert. There was a time to see old friends and there was a time when a man simply had to have his peace and be alone.

Yes, Jerry had told him. That was it, exactly. He was very relieved that the manager understood his position. Would the manager please accept this money as a token of his appreciation and his special efforts? Not necessary, really. No, I insist. Well, then, of course, and thank you. The manager had left, assuring him that he need not have a worry about being disturbed.

So, all things considered, Eckhart was going to have a real hunt on his hands. Especially considering the fact that he hadn't set foot outside his suite since he had checked into the hotel.

He drank the last of his coffee and pushed his cup away from him on the table and lit up another cigarette.

But today, that was going to change.

Today, they were going out into the city.

The whole thing had been Chris's idea, and because of everything she didn't know—because he hadn't told her—it had seemed like a very logical and healthy idea to her. His feet were much better now, she'd told him. It would be excellent for him to get out of the hotel and into the sun and the air. At first, he had tried to kill the idea with the only reasonable argument that had occurred to him. He wasn't up to trooping all over the city on his crutches, and he would feel funny having her push him around in the chair.

But Chris wasn't buying any of it. They'd make it a joint effort, she'd told him. He could wheel himself for a while, and then when he was tired, she would push him. She was a nurse, after all. It would all work out fine. There would not be any problems.

May that be true, he'd thought, smiling at her.

After she had gone, he'd sat down and started thinking about what he could do to give himself a little insurance in the situation.

There hadn't been a hell of a lot of choices.

He'd wear the dark glasses, the only item he'd kept from the blind-man disguise, and he'd only happened to keep them because he found that he didn't have any others. He'd wished that he'd kept the hairpiece, but then maybe it was just as well that he hadn't, because Eckhart had seen him wearing it back in Chicago at the airport and then, too, how in the hell would he explain it to Chris? The major thing that had bothered him were the attention-drawing white bandages on his feet, and then he'd remembered that time he'd gone to visit his grandmother.

He'd just been a kid—seven, eight years old—and his grandmother had been living in a big white wooden house that had been turned into a nursing home, and he remembered seeing all these old guys and old ladies sitting in chairs on the long, wide porch in front of the place, and even though they had shoes and socks on and it was the middle of the summer, they'd all had blankets over their feet, and he'd asked his mother about it and she'd told him that old people got cold easier than younger people, summer or not. Now he realized that he could probably get away with covering his feet with a blanket, too, because Chris had explained to him that his feet, his whole body, in fact, would probably be a lot more sensitive to cold than ever before and that this was a common reaction among burn patients, whose nervous systems were reacting to the shock of the experience. So that would work, he'd decided. He'd complain about that, about his feet being cold and how maybe he should take a blanket to cover them while they were outside. He knew he was going to feel stupid as hell out with this good-looking young woman and her pushing him around the streets of the city with a blanket over him, but then he could live with feeling stupid, he thought wryly.

And so that was it, the dark glasses and cover the feet.

He pushed the negatives out of his mind. Maybe that would turn out to be enough, he thought. He started thinking about spending the whole day in London with Chris, and aside from all the worry, he really felt happy and excited. She'd gotten excited about it, too, talking to him, telling him all the different places she wanted him to see in the city, and he'd told her that for giving up her day off to be his nurse-tour guide, he would take her to dinner at the end of the day at some restaurant that she'd always wanted to go. Chris had protested, saying that he was spending too much money, but he'd held fast, telling her that if she did not accept his invitation to dinner, he wouldn't go out at all, wouldn't leave the room, and she'd laughed and given in. There *was* a place, she'd told him, but he'd better not be mad at her because it really was terribly expensive with the inflation. And he had said to hell with inflation and had loved the reckless, extravagant feeling saying that had given him, the honest-to-God pleasure of not having to worry about money for once in his life, not having to care how much something cost. He had money—plenty of money—and he was sure as hell going to enjoy it!

He looked at his watch. Chris would be here soon. He wheeled himself over to the huge double-door walk-in closet and got the briefcase. He carried it back over to the table and opened it. He lifted the lid and looked at the neatly arranged stacks of bills, feeling again the incredible sense of shock and pleasure that it was all his. He wasn't going to be careless with it, he thought. He'd use his head about it, handle it with some sense. Not that he didn't intend to blow *some* of it for fun. He would do that, too, but he would be careful with most of it. He knew that he didn't ever want to be broke again in his life and if he watched what he was doing, maybe he wouldn't have to be.

He closed the case and made sure it was securely locked. Then he called the hotel manager and asked him to come up and get it. Within five minutes, the manager arrived at his door and Jerry gave him the case, telling him that it contained some important papers and that he was going out today and would like it locked up in the hotel safe. He gave the man a five-pound note, and the manager went away after assuring him not to give the case another thought. The hotel had one of the most secure safes available, the manager had said, and he would personally lock the case inside it himself.

After he had gone, Jerry felt a little uncomfortable. It was the first time the money had been out of his possession, and he wasn't crazy about the feeling. But he sure as hell couldn't leave it in the room while he was gone. It'll be okay, he thought. Don't worry about it. No matter what, he and Chris were going to have one terrific, wonderful day together.

And they did, too.

As he had expected, his wanting to take a blanket to cover his feet had caused no question from Chris. She thought it a good idea, in fact, because even though the sun was out and it was a nice day, it was still December and cold. She had kidded him a little about the extrabig, extradark glasses, and he'd told her just to pretend she was playing nurse to some big movie star who'd been dramatically injured and who didn't want to be recognized and mobbed by his adoring fans. Chris laughed and asked him which film star. "Errol Flynn," he said.

"But he's dead."

Jerry grinned at her slyly. "That's what they all think," he said.

They had a wonderful day.

She took him to all the famous tourist spots in London. He saw Big Ben. Albert Hall, the House of Commons, Piccadilly Circus. She looked incredibly beautiful to him. Yes, *beautiful!* To hell with just pretty. She was wearing a dark green skirt slit up the front to just above the knee and a white turtleneck sweater with a simple gold chain. The strawberry-blond hair looked washed and brushed. He knew he had to be careful, that he was already falling for her, getting too wrapped up in her and that could easily make him careless about everything else and that would be a bad mistake.

Once outside on the crowded walks, he found he was not as uncomfortable or as edgy as he had thought he would be. People would discreetly glance at them now and then, but the simple truth was that a man in a wheelchair just wasn't all that much of an oddity. And Chris seemed to be having a good time, too. She was in the best spirits he'd ever seen her, and her excitement and laughter rubbed off on him, and one time when she was pushing the chair, she had bent down to him and kissed him lightly on the cheek without saying anything and he had reached back behind his head to where her hand was holding the chair and squeezed it lightly and then they had gone on.

Chris had chosen a place called The Marquis, a small and, he noted with pleasure, intimate and romantic little French restaurant. He had felt awkward at first entering the place in the wheelchair, but he appeared to be the only one it bothered. The maître'd took over the chair from Chris, wheeled him over to a table and helped him get comfortable.

The little restaurant was lit almost entirely by the tall, thin candles of various colors that burned in dark, brass holders in the center of each table, giving the effect that each table was alone and separate from the others in a little circle of warm amber light and flickering shadows. They had not talked much during dinner, paying attention to their food, relaxing, letting the crowded day settle, and it was only now after the table had been cleared and they were having the rest of their champagne that Chris surprised him and said, "You said that time at the hotel that you almost got married once. Would you mind if I asked you what happened?"

Jerry smiled at her and shrugged. "No," he said. "I don't mind. It wasn't any big unusual thing, I guess. It's happened to a lot of people. We went together for a couple of years. She wanted to get married, have a family and all of that."

"And you didn't."

"It wasn't that," he said, thinking. "It wasn't that I didn't want it for sure. It was just that I didn't know exactly what I *did* want. I've always had a hard time in my life knowing what I wanted. Anyway, she got tired of waiting for me to make up my mind and she left, that's all."

"Did you see her after you were quits?"

"Nope. She left Vegas. Went to Hawaii, the last I heard."

Chris was silent for a moment. She took a sip of her champagne. "How long ago was all of this?"

"About three years," he said. "Getting close to four now."

"Are you still in love with her at all?"

Jerry laughed and shook his head. "No," he said. "I was for a while, I guess, but you know, when there's nothing to do about it, it fades out after a while."

He pulled the champagne bottle up out of the ice and refilled their glasses while she watched him and then put it back in the silver bucket in the metal stand next to the table.

"You could've gone after her," Chris said.

He shrugged. "Yeah," he said. "I suppose I could've done that, but things still wouldn't have been any different. I still wouldn't have been sure of what I wanted and it would have just happened all over again after a while." He reached for his cigarettes, took one out and lit it. Chris frowned. "I know, I have to quit, right?"

"Right," she said.

"What made you ask me about all of that?"

She smiled at him. "You're a nice guy," she said. "I like you, but I really don't know very much about you except that you have a shop in Las Vegas that sells automobile parts, and you have two badly burned feet. You don't talk very much about yourself, you know."

"I haven't had what anybody would call an exciting life," he said to her, thinking how that had sure as hell been true until recently. The last month or so had been pretty interesting, though, if *interesting* was the right word. He wondered how she would feel, how she would be around him if she knew all the things that were really going on in his life right now. He felt a strong need to come clean with her, to tell her the truth about all of it so he could feel better at just having it out, and because he was feeling more and more guilty lying to her about himself. She didn't even know his right name, for crissake. And it wasn't fair to involve her in his life without at least letting her know what she was getting herself into, especially when it could be dangerous for her.

And wasn't this terrific! he thought. Now you're thinking about involving her in it all, and before, you were going to leave before you would let that happen. He would tell her, he assured himself, but not now. He just wasn't up to it now. He didn't want to risk spoiling the day. He'd tell her one night this week when they were back at the hotel. He knew that what he'd thought when he had first met her was still right. He was in no position to get seriously involved with anyone now, but he'd met her anyway, and if he could just stay lucky for a little while longer, and if she didn't run for cover when she heard the truth, then maybe he could have a shot at something with her. He knew he really wanted that chance. He wanted it even more than the money, but he wasn't kidding himself. He wanted the money, too. He was old enough and practical enough to want both now.

"You don't look very happy," she said softly. "Are you all right?"

He leaned forward on the table and took her hand. "I'm great," he said, smiling at her. "I just didn't expect to meet somebody like you." She laughed and lightly squeezed his hand, and even in the shadowy candlelight, he could see the color rising in her face. "By the way," he said. "I'm not the only one who doesn't talk much about himself. What do I really know about you, anyway?"

"I'll tell you all my dark secrets some night," Chris said. "You'll probably be shocked."

Then that'll make two of us, he thought.

They finished their champagne and left the restaurant. When they had gotten back to the hotel and he was sitting on the sofa in the suite, she came over to him and bent down and kissed him softly on the lips and said, "It really was a nice day. Thank you," and he looked up at her and was surprised to see that her eyes were shiny and he thought for a moment that she was going to cry and he didn't understand that and started to ask her about it, but something told him not to, so he just smiled at her and all he said was, "Best day I've had in years," which was certainly one statement out of his mouth that was the truth. "See you tomorrow night?" he said.

Chris nodded and brushed her hand lightly over his face. Then she turned away and walked across the room to the door and let herself out without turning around again. Jerry stared at the closed door. He was pretty certain that she'd been crying. They both sure had a lot to talk about, he thought.

He reached for his crutches. He had to start getting used to them. Slowly, he got up and made his way over to the door and locked it.

He got ready for bed and fixed himself a short bourbon on the rocks for a nightcap, climbed under the blankets and turned off the lamp. He propped his pillow up against the headboard and, steadying the drink next to his thigh, he set an ashtray on his lap and lit a cigarette. The room was pleasantly warm, and he could faintly hear the sounds of the passing night traffic down on the street. It was a little after midnight. He thought about Chris getting up so early in the morning. They shouldn't have stayed out so late. He looked around the big room in the dark and smiled, thinking how far this suite was from the grimy, depressing room back in Springfield.

God, but you've been lucky! he thought.

He drank the bourbon slowly and smoked in the quiet darkness, letting his mind go back over it all.

Incredible!

And what made it so incredible, he thought, was that you knew that things like this never really happened.

Not *really*. Not to you, some guy off the street. They happened in the movies and that was where you accepted them and they were exciting and then you went back out into the world where they didn't happen.

Except that was wrong.

Things—wild, fantastic fucking things—*did* happen to Joe Blow once in a while.

There really were people who killed other people for money. Sure, you always thought you knew that, but you didn't really know it. And people did buy a ticket and win the Irish Sweeps and were suddenly rich. And you could run for your life clear across the ocean and meet some girl in England who was a nurse and who knocked you out . . .

Jerry laughed aloud in the darkness.

Incredible!

Scary, too.

He put out his cigarette, finished the drink and put the glass on the little table by the bed. He looked at the crutches leaning against the headboard. No chair tomorrow, he told himself. Just the sticks.

He flattened out his pillow and lay down, stretching his legs under the blankets. He felt tired from the day, but it wasn't a bad kind of tired. Chris had been right. It really had been good for him to get outside in the air and sunshine. And he'd liked being on the sidewalks with all the people. There had been some risk in doing it, sure, but thinking about it now, maybe not as much as he had originally worried about. If he remembered correctly, London was the second largest city in the world after Tokyo and anybody looking for him would have to be looking in just the right place at just the right

time and that had to add up to a long shot with the odds
in his favor, but then later in the night when he banged
his foot against the bedpost at the bottom of the bed, the
pain waking him, and he heard the little tick-clicking
sound behind the door and saw it slowly open and the
tall man step silently and quickly inside the room, he
remembered that long shots did come in every once in a
while and he should've known that because after all,
everything that had happened to him so far had been
one.

He lay still as a corpse, staring at the tall man who now
stood motionless in front of the closed door. Jerry
opened his mouth, tried to breathe evenly through it to
imitate the breathing of someone who was still asleep.
His whole body felt rigid under the blankets, and suddenly he was hot and could feel the sweat under his arms
and his pajamas sticking to his back. His right hand
resting against his chest was knotted into a tight fist, and
he felt it trembling through his thin pajama top. His
mind raced, trying to think what to do. The figure in
front of the door still had not moved.

What was he going to do?

Shoot him from over there as soon as his eyes got used
to the dark? No. Probably not. He wouldn't do that because of the money. He didn't know whether the money
was here in the room or not. Thank God he'd had the
manager put it in the safe. Eckhart would have to have
it brought back up to the room, and that would mean the
manager would be in the room and maybe he could do
something then.

Or maybe he could do something now.

If Eckhart got close enough to him, he thought, close enough to the bed, maybe he could hit him, catch him off guard and then maybe make it over to the door, get out in the hall and yell his head off.

Only then he remembered his feet.

Could he run?

He didn't know, but he could probably make it. It was not that far to the door. He had to try it. Let him get close to you, he thought, but not *too* close. Okay, okay. You're scared, but at least you're still thinking.

Then Eckhart started toward the bed.

And keeping his eyes almost closed, Jerry watched him as he brought his other hand slowly up along his side and over his chest out from under the blanket, resting it just below his throat.

Eckhart stopped at the foot of the bed.

He could feel the tall man's eyes studying him. He did his best to keep his breathing steady, even, the breathing of the sound sleeper.

And then, his shoes barely making a sound on the soft carpet, Eckhart moved around to the side of the bed.

The *wrong* side.

Because now Eckhart was *behind* him.

You have to turn over, he thought. Easy—nice and slow. He stirred under the covers, shifting his position, and then rolled over, his eyes shut, expecting suddenly to feel something cave in his skull or worse, but nothing happened and he was on the right side now, and the minute he had done it he couldn't believe how stupid, how unthinking it had been to do that because, Jesus! facing the other way he'd had a clear field to the door! All he'd had to do was roll over to the edge of the bed and run, but no, his mind, his concentration had been so taken up with how he was going to surprise him that he hadn't even realized what he was doing. *Yeah, you're thinking, all right!* Now he *had* to try to get him. He squinted open his eyes.

And saw Eckhart's legs inches away from his face.

The tall man was standing right next to the side of the bed, looking down at him, and now he could hear his soft breathing clearly in the quiet darkness, and he knew that it had to be now, that this was probably going to be the best chance, the *only* chance that he would get, and he tightened his fist, ready to try to hit him one good shot right between the legs only just as he was ready to throw it, the legs turned away out of position, facing the little table by the bed, and he knew then that Eckhart was going for surprise, too, the way he had done with the newspaper back in the airport, that he was reaching to switch on the little lamp by the bed and then he would have him in the light and he couldn't let him do that so he started to go for his ribs, hit him hard, but then he remembered the crutches leaning against the wall and the headboard of the bed, and he threw himself into it, grabbing back suddenly, reaching up, and he felt his hand get one of them in the middle and he grabbed it with the other hand too and swung it as hard as he could in the direction of Eckhart's face, felt it hit, heard him yell in surprised pain, and that was it, all he could do, and he let loose of the crutch and went into his roll over to the other side of the bed and then off it, running like a bastard for the door.

Except he wasn't running.

He was *falling*.

The thick, rounded bandages on his feet took away all of his balance and he went down not more than four or five feet from the bed and he knew it was all stops out now, so he started yelling at the top of his lungs, "Help! Somebody, help!"

But he could've saved his breath.

Because he saw that Eckhart was already running from around the bed and then past him to the door, jerking it open, and he heard his footsteps running away down the hall and he stopped yelling then and just laid there for a few minutes getting his breath and then he looked up at the opened door and saw the old man and old woman, both dressed in nightclothes, peering in at him, their faces white and frightened in the lighted hallway that was now starting to come alive with the sounds of other doors opening, voices questioning.

It was at least an hour before the confusion settled.

The night manager came up, a neatly dressed little man in his late thirties who, with nervous authority, had politely but firmly pushed his way through the people clustered around Jerry's door. Jerry explained the situation to him as simply as possible. A prowler had broken into his room. Yes, the door had been locked. The man must have picked it. No, nothing had been taken. He had woken up, yelled, and the man had run out and down the hall. It had been too dark and with the shock of being awakened out of a sound sleep, he hadn't been able to get a good look at the man.

The night manager listened to all of this tight-lipped, visibly upset that something like this had to happen while *he* was on duty, and then, after making sure that Mr. Rodman was all right, he shooed the people away, apologizing to everyone in the hall for the disturbance and assuring them that there was nothing to be concerned about, telling them all to retire to their rooms. Then he had promptly gone back downstairs to his office, closed the door from the prying eyes of the young desk clerk and downed a quick shot of rye from the small bottle he secretly kept in the far back of a filing cabinet. Then he picked up the phone, called the police and dutifully reported the incident.

Jerry repeated his story for the police, and it was after three-thirty in the morning by the time they departed and he was finally alone again in his suite. Sleeping anymore was out of the question. He had to think. He wondered how Eckhart had managed to find him so quickly. Had he really been so goddamned lucky that he or somebody who worked for him had seen him out with Chris?

Then he remembered that it really wasn't all that quickly. He had, after all, been in the hotel for a month. Obviously long enough for Eckhart, he thought. And too long for you. He looked down at the glass of bourbon in his hand. Burned feet, bandages or not, he had to get going. He had to get out of the hotel and out of London as fast as possible.

And now he would have to be very, very careful. The bastard would be watching the hotel for sure. He'd have to figure a way to sneak out at night. He had to think about that and he had to decide where to go from here. He had to think about those things, only he was having trouble doing it.

Because he was thinking about Chris.

Trouble, *his* trouble, was way too close now, and he couldn't have her involved in it. The best thing to do would be to leave her a letter telling her that he was sorry but there had been some big problem that had developed back home and he'd had to leave on the first plane he could get or he would've called her. He'd write her in care of the hospital. He'd really had a great time being with her and . . .

And *shit!*

He knew there was no way in hell he was going to do that. He had to see her again and at least tell her face to face why he had to go. He'd promised himself that he would tell her all of it; he owed her that. He'd tell her tonight when she came to see him, and after she was gone, he would get out.

He poured a little more bourbon into the glass and wheeled himself over to the window. He was still sitting there when the first gray light of dawn began to show over London.

34

THE COUNTER OF THE little white sidewalk coffee stand in Carnaby Street was only long enough to accommodate the five wooden stools that ran the length of the front of it. A stool at one end became empty, and Eckhart moved quickly over to it and sat down. A tall, skinny kid in his teens, heavily freckled, with protruding front teeth and a shock of brilliant red hair, moved quickly behind the counter, refilling cups, snatching empty ones and wiping off the countertop.

The people who could not get a stool at the counter and who didn't mind standing were served their coffee between the seated customers, the kid handing it over to them with one hand and taking their money with the other. If you were fortunate enough to get a stool, you had the privilege of not paying until you were ready to leave. Eckhart watched as the kid came over to him, and he looked at him and ordered a mug of coffee.

"You want that in the large mug or the small one, sir?" the kid asked him in a piercingly high voice that cut through the noise of the street like a siren. Eckhart wanted a little time, so he ordered the large one. "The large mug, then," the kid shrilled, and he filled a tall, thick-handled white mug with the steaming coffee and brought it back and put it down in front of him.

Eckhart poured cream into the coffee and stirred it slowly, glancing casually around at the other people seated down from him and at the two men standing at the opposite end of the counter who had been following him for at least the past fifteen minutes and probably longer than that.

The two men stood drinking their coffee along with a small handful of other people who had stopped to warm their hands and their insides against the damp, chilling wind that was gusting a course straight down the narrow street, making people pull their coat collars up higher around their necks and hurry faster toward wherever they were going. One of the men was rather stocky and looked to be in his middle forties. The other one was younger, closer to Eckhart's own age. They were both well dressed, and there was nothing about them or their manner to suggest any trouble. They looked like a couple of average businessmen stopping for a coffee break, but they had definitely been following him. He was sure of it. Eckhart was not the least bit worried about handling them, but he was puzzled as to why they were following him.

Who in the hell were they?

He sipped the scalding coffee and tried to come up with some possibilities. The police, of course, came to mind first. They were always a possibility in his life, but not a very likely one here because, even though he might be on some list of theirs sent to them from the States as a shady character (he smiled at the phrase), it was unlikely that they would ever be this alert and waiting for him to land at Heathrow when he had not even been in London in several years. His mind went carefully back to the last time he'd been here, searching the details carefully.

He had flown over on a very special job that time. It had been five, almost six years ago. It was a job that, had it not been for the money and the special circumstances involved, he would never have taken, because matters of someone else's personal revenge were things that he'd always put down as too full of emotion to be safe for him. But this one had been different and had even given him a certain sense of personal satisfaction after it was over.

There had been a skinny, rat-faced man named Dixon, who had been released from prison after serving five years for sexual assault. Dixon had been out less than three weeks when he had abducted a pretty young girl in her twenties off a London street, taken her to a garage, raped her and then nearly beaten her to death. The girl, a college student, happened to be the favorite granddaughter of a very powerful man in Las Vegas named Ulston. Ulston was the major stockholder in a large hotel and casino, a man with a lot of important contacts. The word was sent to Eckhart that Mr. Ulston wanted to talk, and Eckhart had gone to see him.

He knew Ulston by sight and by reputation but had never met him in person. Ulston had a cabin on Lake Mead, and Eckhart had gone there to meet with him. Ulston was up in years then, in his middle seventies, but the moment Eckhart had walked into the cabin and seen him, he knew that here was a man of great force and formidable power in spite of his age. And so he had been surprised, when the two of them were alone and Ulston had told him the story of what had happened to his granddaughter, that his bitterness in the telling of the story so seized control of the older man that by the time he had finished, his tanned, leathery face was twisted into a mask of fury and he was sobbing deep in his throat.

Eckhart had understood immediately that part of this reaction came from Ulston's own frustration at not being able to take care of this man Dixon himself. Ulston asked if Eckhart would see to it that this man was killed. The only condition Ulston insisted upon was that the manner of Dixon's death be particularly vicious. At the time Eckhart had thought it was a perfect job for Mills's special talents, especially since he was already in London, and he mentioned this to Ulston, but the old man had shied away from the suggestion. He did not know Mills, he said. He knew Eckhart.

Eckhart told him that he would accept the job but that it might take awhile for him to locate the man who had done this violence to his granddaughter. The old man had regained his control by then and told him that Dixon had already been located through his people in London. He started to give Eckhart the name of a man that he was to see there, but Eckhart had refused. He would not be involved with anyone else on the matter. Ulston must give him all the information before he left Las Vegas. Ulston was not a man used to hearing the word *no*, but he understood the wisdom of this for both Eckhart and himself. The less people involved, the better. He agreed.

Eckhart left him then, and later that night, around eleven-thirty, an eight-and-a-half-by-eleven manilla envelope was delivered to him by special messenger. Inside it was a sheet of white paper and typed on the sheet in one neat little paragraph was all the information he needed to find Dixon. And along with the white sheet of paper were fifty thousand dollars in one-hundred-dollar bills. Eckhart burned the manilla envelope and the typed sheet of paper in the sink and washed the ashes down the drain. At ten the next morning, he flew to Los Angeles and then on to London.

Dixon was hiding out in a small, abandoned farmhouse in a little country town about twenty miles outside of London. Eckhart rented a car and drove to the town a little after nine that night. He parked the car a quarter of a mile down the deserted road that led to the farmhouse and made his way carefully through a large field of weeds, coming up behind a small shed at the back of the house.

Then he sat down to wait.

Four times he saw Dixon come out on the back porch with a kerosene lantern. He stood and searched the area around the back of the house. Hidden, Eckhart had been pleased. The man was nervous. That was good. He wouldn't go to bed until he really felt that he had checked everything out and that he was safe. Several hours later, Eckhart's eyes followed the glowing lantern from one window of the house to another until finally, in a room at the far back, he saw the flame go out.

Still, he waited.

Another hour passed.

Then he moved.

Even though several windows in the old house were broken, Dixon had locked the back door. The chances were good, Eckhart thought, that he had probably propped something against it, something that would fall with a lot of noise if anyone forced it open. He walked around to the corner of the house farthest away from the window where he had seen the lantern go out. The window was broken and there were still several jagged knives of glass sticking up out of the frame and he'd had to remove them before he could enter.

Once inside, he used his pen flashlight to find his way through the dark house to the room where Dixon was sleeping. He had no trouble finding it. For a nervous and hunted man, Dixon slept well. The sound of his snoring grated clearly through the silent house. The man was not as careful as Eckhart had first thought him to be. The door to the room wasn't even closed, much less locked. For several moments, he stood watching the sleeping figure stretched out on the floor. Then he stepped silently into the doorway, spread his feet and raised the thirty-eight-caliber pistol with the silencer a few inches above his shoulder and slowly brought it down to bear on the sleeping man. His voice shattered the silence of the room. *"Dixon!"*

The man on the floor jerked awake, scrambling to his feet, throwing off the coat he had been using as a blanket. Confused and disoriented, he clutched the knife he had been sleeping with in his drawn-back fist and stared at Eckhart.

"Police!" Eckhart barked. *"Drop it on the floor! Now!"* He made a quick motion with the gun as though he were about to fire it. The knife clattered to the floor. Dixon raised his hands high over his head.

The rest was easy.

Eckhart made him turn around. Then, from his hip pocket, he removed the pair of handcuffs that he had procured especially for the job and handcuffed Dixon securely. He walked the man ahead of him through the house until he found just the kind of room he was looking for. It was a room half the size of the average kitchen and had probably been used for storage. It had only one door and no windows, and it was empty.

By this time, Dixon was already getting nervous, asking a barrage of questions about what was going on. Eckhart ignored him and shoved him into the room. He placed the muzzle of the thirty-eight flush against Dixon's temple and stuffed his handkerchief into his mouth, bulging out the cheeks of his bony face. Then he left him in the room, closed and barred the door, walked out of the house and back across the field of weeds to the car.

To get the dog.

The dog was a full-grown Doberman. Eckhart had bought him for a thousand dollars from a breeder-trainer in London. Better protection than a gun or a body-guard, the trainer had assured him. Eckhart opened the car door, and the dog jumped out and sat beside him on the dark road, the long black leash dangling from his lean, muscled neck. Eckhart picked up the looped end of the leash and walked the dog back to the house.

Inside the room, Dixon was kicking hard at the door. Eckhart gave the dog the *sit* and *stay* commands. He un-barred the door, jerked it open and gave Dixon a shove in the chest, sending him stumbling across the room and down to the floor.

Then he picked up the leash and led the dog into the room.

From the floor, Dixon stared at the animal, his eyes suddenly wide with fear in the narrow beam of Eck-hart's penlight. The gob of handkerchief moved in his mouth as he tried to talk.

Eckhart reached down and unsnapped the leash from the collar. He looked across the room at Dixon, who had now gotten slowly to his feet and was backed up against the far wall of the room. The dog watched him with dark-eyed alertness.

Eckhart gave Dixon a cold smile.

He stepped behind the dog into the doorway, raised his hand and then brought it down fast in a gesture like a karate chop, the fingers of his hand pointed at the man against the wall.

He said only one word.

"Kill!"

Snarling, the black dog lunged.

Eckhart jumped backward out of the room, slammed the door and barred it again.

The whole thing took less than ten minutes.

He removed the cuffs from Dixon's hands along with the handkerchief and dragged the body out behind the house. Then he walked the dog into the shed behind the house, shot it once cleanly through the head and carried it back to the car. Later and miles away, he buried it in a thick woods. He drove into London and got on a flight back to Los Angeles. The London *Times* carried the story on page two. The rapist's death was chalked up to a wild animal, and the writer of the story hinted at some kind of crude justice having been served. Eckhart had only been back in his apartment in Vegas one day when a messenger arrived at his door bearing another manilla envelope containing ten thousand dollars. There was no message, but he understood it was a bonus. Mr. Ulston had been satisfied for his granddaughter.

The two men at the counter were still watching Eckhart, glancing at him quickly, nodding their heads, talking.

No, Eckhart thought. There had been nothing left over from that time with Ulston. The people in that little country burg had been warned to be on the lookout for some kind of wild animal that might be in the woods, but there had been no suspicion of a human being involved in Dixon's death. And he had seen or talked to no one else besides that trainer of the Doberman, and it was highly unlikely that any connection had ever been made between a man purchasing a guard dog for his home and the attack on a rapist in a small country town.

No, there had been no loose ends to that one. As always, he had been very careful.

Suddenly he looked directly over at the two men, and for a second he was looking the older one right in the eyes. The man quickly looked away, and Eckhart saw him mutter something to his companion.

An icy anger began to build in him because all of a sudden, he was certain that he knew who it was that had put the two men on him. The only one it could be.

Chambers!

Chambers, afraid for his money, trying to make sure that Eckhart didn't get any ideas about trying to take off with it after he'd gotten Logan out of the way. Chambers worrying that he couldn't be trusted. Eckhart gripped the edge of the countertop in front of him, his fingers and knuckles turning white. That stupid, fat sonofabitch! His pig brain wasn't logical enough to see that something like that would simply not happen. Never. Half a million was a lot of money, and maybe if his own situation were different, if he, say, really needed the bread, then yeah, he might sit down and give the matter some thought. But that wasn't the case. He had plenty of money, and more important, he had taken on a job, and he had *never* not followed through with a commitment. What that fat fool couldn't see was that he could always be trusted, that his word alone was enough. His carefulness was what made him, goddamnit, one of the best professionals in the country. To blow such a solid and profitable reputation and make himself no less than a fucking sneak thief was out of the question. How Al Chambers had ever been figured as sharp enough to run the Silver Tiara had to be one of the great mysteries of the world.

Eckhart looked over again at the two men. They were not watching him now. He wondered if they had figured out that he was onto them. They were handing their coffee mugs over the counter to the skinny kid and getting ready to leave. And weren't they a pair of fucking winners! So obvious you'd have to be deaf and blind not to know they were following you. Just the type Chambers would hire. Duds attract duds, he thought.

Eckhart paid the kid, slipped off his stool then and started walking again down the street. His eyes burned hate. Come on, boys, he thought. Stay with me. *Stay* with me! They could do him a favor. They could take a message back to that slob. He would lead them, find just the right place and then he would show them just how much he didn't like being followed and after that, after they had come to and seen a doctor, they could call fatso back in Vegas and let him know what had happened to them. Eckhart quickened his pace a little, his jaw locked in grim determination. That would make Chambers sweat. He would wonder and wonder about what was going to happen as a result of his latest stupidity. And he'd let him sweat for a couple of days and then he'd call Vegas and tell him the cost of his latest stupidity. Another ten grand. And he'd tell him that if it ever happened again, he could kiss his own fat ass good-bye because he would drop the whole fucking job and Logan could take the money and go to China for all he gave a damn. That would scare the shit out of Chambers. He would know that he was a dead man if that ever happened.

Eckhart came to a corner and looked off the main street. Yes, this was better. Much better. A few scattered shops. Not too many people out because of the cold. He could hear the two men behind him. He slowed his pace a little. Not too fast. The anger boiled in his stomach. His blood rushed. There would have to be an alley somewhere along this street where trucks could unload their goods for these shops, and because these two stiffs had been hired to watch his movements and report anything he did, anyplace he went that was out of the ordinary, they would wonder what he was doing going into the alley, where he was headed, and they would follow him. The wind whipped into Eckhart's face, but he didn't feel the cold. He would hurt them just enough, he told himself. Today they were going to learn how bad they really were. He walked, listening to the two sets of footsteps. There were even fewer people on the cold street now, and behind him, he clearly heard their voices, back just far enough that if he suddenly turned on them, they would duck into a shop or pretend to be looking into a window or some other dumbass, obvious thing they probably saw on television.

Eckhart's eyes searched the narrow street.

And then he saw it.

Not more than fifty feet ahead of him, the narrow entrance to the alley showed between the buildings at the edge of the street. Now Eckhart went more deeply into his act. He shoved both of his hands into his pockets and hunched his shoulders against the wind and the cold. He pretended to look to the left and to the right as though he were searching for an address.

Twenty-five feet to the alley now.

Eckhart's hand in his right side pocket closed around the heavy metal casing of the knife, his fingers flexing around it. In his fist, it would do fine. It would easily help break a jaw or a nose.

Ten feet and closing.

The two sets of footsteps were clearer now. And he could hear the two men talking, though the wind obscured their words.

And then he was there!

He paused for a moment, looking both ways down the alley, and then turned off the street into it. Perfect. The alley lay empty and deserted in the fast-fading winter light. A little farther in now, he thought, as he heard their footsteps behind him approaching the entrance. Casually he pulled his hands out of his pockets, the closed knife hidden in his right fist and . . .

Eckhart stopped dead in his tracks.

Behind him, he heard the footsteps and the voices going on down the walk past the alley.

He whirled around, walking fast, then running back out to the street. No way! he thought. Even if he had been wrong. Even if they had been smart enough after all to read him and wouldn't follow him into an alley, they weren't getting away. Huh, *uh!* He was out of the alley now, back to the walk, and he turned and saw them moving away down the sidewalk.

And again he stopped, stunned.

Not them!

Eckhart stood, his hands down at his sides, watching the two men walking away down the street. Men, hell! They were both young, not much more than kids. He glared down the street at their receding backs. His teeth were clenched tight. The blood roared in his head. Fool! he thought. You call *them* dumb. You go through this whole fucking…they *made* you! Back at the coffee place, they *made* you, and he knew just when it had happened, too. When he had looked right at the older one. It had been too direct. The look on his face had been too obvious. He turned around, the heavy knife still clutched in his fist, walking fast, and by the time he had again reached Carnaby Street, the fury had faded out of his face, but something else was there.

Fear.

He reentered the busy street and walked through the crowd. He felt it coming slowly up on him, building steadily, growing, the way it had come in the darkness of The Lady's apartment—a feeling of desperate anxiety and mixed with it now was confusion and cold fear. He was no longer thinking about the two men who had been following him nor of Chambers, nor of Logan nor of his meeting with Mills later. Only one question filled his mind.

How had he ever let his anger get so much control over him?

And, he thought with amazement, that was what had happened. He had been out of control. Not thinking or operating at all like himself. He had been running totally on anger, on rage! There had been not any thought as to what he was doing or the possible consequences after it was done. Eckhart swallowed; his throat was dry and tight. The feeling was all over him now and he wanted to just run somewhere or…

…or something.

Why had he reacted like that?

So you were followed, he thought. So Chambers doesn't trust you. So what?

Those things were nothing to him. All shit. He'd been followed before. And he couldn't give a damn about whether that fat ass trusted him or not. But he had been in a blind rage, and now he was filled with a deep relief that it hadn't been the right two men behind him because he knew now for sure that—Jesus!

He had been going to kill both of them!

Never mind what he had told himself he was going to do. What he had told himself was bullshit. He had actually been going to kill two men in broad daylight in an alley in London with the chance of people walking by and seeing him! Maybe even a cop! The wind was blowing stronger than ever now, but his body felt numb. Desperately his mind searched back through memories to find a time he had ever acted like that. He thought of different situations, different cities, different people.

When had he ever behaved like that when he was working?

When?

The anxiety was all over him now, making it hard for him to breathe.

Never!

Not once had he ever lost his control like that.

What's wrong with you? The question was a silent scream in his mind.

He stopped walking and put the knife back in his pocket. There was sweat on his forehead. He had to meet Mills, he thought. Think about business now, about what you have to do. You have to meet Mills. Later you can think about all this, go over it, figure it out. Later, alone.

Trembling, his eyes scanned the windy street for a taxi.

AT THE MOMENT Eckhart was searching for a taxi in Carnaby Street, the two men who had been watching him at the coffee stand were busy at work. They were both employed at the same brokerage establishment, and while they rarely socialized outside of working hours, due mainly to the inability of their wives to get along with each other, they did always take their lunches and coffee breaks together five working days of the week, barring sickness or some other emergency. They were both well read, and though there was a difference of over twelve years in their ages, they found that they each shared an abounding curiosity and a strong, inquiring interest in a great many things. They discussed everything—politics, films, women, inflation—whatever happened to come up. Had they known of Eckhart's certainty that they were following him, they both would have been truly shocked, for in reality, walking down the street behind him, talking as they always did, they hadn't noticed him at all. He had only come to their attention as he was sitting on the stool at the coffee stand where, whenever they occasioned to take their coffee break there, they would pursue a long-standing and for them amusing habit of attempting to speculate on the lives of whatever five people happened to be occupying the stools at the counter.

Studying Eckhart that afternoon, they had concluded that he was probably one of those cold, suspicious types of overly efficient young men who perhaps worked for the tax people or for some other government office, and that he had the look of a man who perhaps had just received some kind of unpleasant news such as, say, being fired from his job or that his wife had left him for another man. But the thing that they had ended up centering on about him was how American he looked, and that led to the question of just exactly what it was that made someone look American. Possible answers to such a question required careful scrutiny of the subject under consideration, and Paul, the older of the two men, had realized that they were being too open in their observation when the American had suddenly turned and stared at them with what could only be called an expression of definite hostility, though it was of course possible that this expression was merely a reflection of the mood the man appeared to be in at that moment. In either case, embarrassed at being discovered, they had both turned in their coffee cups and left the stand. They both agreed that if they were going to continue such observations, they would certainly have to become more adept at doing so undetected. People could be so touchy about these things, and these days you could never tell what someone might do if he misinterpreted your intentions.

35

HIS FACE BURNING WITH anger and shame, Hawker walked through the cold, damp night.

At the corner, he waited impatiently, his eyes fixed on the light, hoping that nobody he knew would come along, that he wouldn't suddenly hear a familiar voice calling his name. His foot had already touched the street as the light went green, and he hurried across to the other side and over the sidewalk and finally he was walking into the soft, grassy darkness of the park. He slowed his pace a little, listening to the wind thrashing the branches of the trees over his head. He walked for a while until he came to his favorite bench: his thinking bench. It stood deserted under the massive, spreading branches of an old, wide-trunked tree.

Hawker sat down and unzipped his coat just far enough so that he could reach his hand inside his shirt pocket and get out his smokes. At first feel, he thought that the pack was empty, but when he stuck his thumb inside it and spread it apart, he found one flattened cigarette remained. He took it out, crumpled up the pack and threw it on the ground, the wind hitting it and whipping it away. Carefully he fingered the cigarette back into its original shape and stuck it in one corner of his mouth. Then he dug a paper book of matches out of his pocket, bent his head forward, struck the match, covered it with his long, bony hands and just caught the flame before the wind blew it out. He straightened up and zipped the jacket up around his neck again. He took a long drag on the cigarette, took it out of his mouth and with his tongue, gingerly felt the cut inside the soft flesh of his lower lip. It was still bleeding a little, but the flow was slowing down.

Damn, what a hell of a thing!

Still, he'd gotten away cheap at that, he supposed. Gently he wiped his face with his hand, running his fingers back through his thick black hair. Bad luck, he thought, that's what it was. He was glad he'd been alone. If any of them ever heard about this one, it'd be a long time before they stopped laughing at him.

Hawker, hit in the face with a cripple's crutch!

God, but they'd be laughing at that one. Old Hawk, they'd say. Losing his touch, that's what's happening to him.

Not true, Hawker thought.

Bad luck. That was it.

The whole thing had looked to him to be as sure and easy as anything, too. He'd seen the woman pushing him in the damned chair, and from the look of them, she wouldn't be staying the night, and he'd been right about that, too. And hadn't he slipped in after them quiet as a ghost without that young sketch of a clerk even blinking one eye at him? And hadn't he waited, watched the bloody room and everything else in the hall until the woman came back out and then he still watched, waited some more until he'd seen the light go out under the door and the man had had a decent amount of time to go to sleep?

Damn right he did all of that!

And the lock—Hawker smiled, thinking of the lock on the hotel-room door. He'd opened it as careful and sure as a surgeon opening up a belly.

Hawker stretched his long legs out on the grass in front of him, took a last pull at the butt of the smoke and flipped it away into the darkness.

A hell of a thing to happen to him, he thought again.

He was going to go in without making a sound, get his eyes seeing in the dark and then pick up whatever looked good. A watch, maybe, if the man had taken it off. His wallet. Maybe even a bottle if he saw one. And the plum part of the pie had been that even if the sketch did wake up, he wouldn't be likely to try and pinch him, what with him being a cripple. There'd be no chance of anybody getting hurt. He'd just take the piece of pipe out of his boot and show it to him, threaten to crack his head like a melon if he made a fuss. Then he'd just take what he wanted and be on his way.

Hawker shook his head, sucked at his cut lip. The branches of the huge tree creaked in the wind above his head.

Bad luck!

He'd seen the crutches there by the bed but he'd been sure the sketch was asleep. Didn't he stand right there by him and watch him to make sure? He surely did! And so he starts to reach down and feel on the little table to see if the watch is there and the next thing he's got that damned crutch in his face and the sketch is trying to run out of the room and then he falls down and starts screaming his bloody head off like he's being murdered, waking up the whole hotel.

Hawker sighed.

And all for nothing, he thought. Didn't get away with a thing in his pocket for his trouble. Except for a lip that would be looking like a monkey in the zoo by morning.

Bad luck. No doubt about it.

Well, he got out of the place, at least, he thought. He'd had a little bit of good luck on that score. Running down all those steps, he could've broken his neck. And then slowing down, trying not to look like he was breathing so heavy when he went back by that dupe of a clerk. The fool'd even nodded at him as he'd passed. Well, he thought, you're here and you could be in the jug. That's something. And at least nobody'll know about it. He'd think up some good story about what happened to his face. Make it interesting and funny so they'd all get a laugh out of it.

He had settled down now. The park was always a good place for him to come to when something bad was on his mind or when he just had a problem he wanted to think out. He got up from the bench and started back across the grass to the street. The wind was still blowing strong, and it seemed to him that it was getting colder, too. He shoved both hands deep into the pockets of his pants and hurried along. A touch of bad luck like that could come along and hit any man, he told himself. Maybe the job had just looked too easy. He'd have to remember that in the future. Watch out for the easy ones. He was sure that there wouldn't be any more trouble after tonight, though. It had been too dark in that hotel room. The guy wouldn't know him from the Queen. Well, he'd go home now. He'd had himself enough of this night. He still had that half-bottle of rye in the drawer by the bed. He'd have a little of that and then get a good night's rest. Hawker walked faster, turning up the collar of his coat around his ears. The cut inside his lip ached in the cold night wind.

Just bad luck, that was all.

The best thing a man could do was to forget about it.

36

JERRY LOGAN SPENT WHAT HAD to be the longest day of his life waiting for it to be night so Chris would be with him. The hands on his watch seemed to move five minutes when he was sure that fifteen or twenty had passed. And to make the waiting all the more unpleasant, his feet had been hurting him all day, the sore flesh throbbing inside the bandages, thanks, no doubt, to his trying to run to the door to get away from that bastard last night. Lying on the bed now, it was hard for him to believe that it had all happened, that Eckhart had actually been here in the room. Well, at least his luck was still holding. He could've *really* been asleep when the bastard came in.

Jerry looked down at the glass in his hand and frowned.

Bourbon, no ice.

He hadn't wanted to call room service for ice because the way he felt now, he didn't want anybody he didn't know coming into his room for any reason at all. He looked at the whiskey in the glass and wondered if maybe he was already on that deceptive road toward being an alcoholic. He didn't think so, but then probably a lot of guys sleeping in doorways this morning with burned-out brains hadn't thought so either at one time or another. He had some of the symptoms, too, he thought gloomily. Like he drank alone a lot and sometimes, like this morning, he had one or two before noon. Still, he had to consider the whole picture. This was a time of high stress in his life and if there ever was a time when he might drink too much, it would be now. And, too, he'd only really started putting a lot of it away since he'd taken off with the money. He'd never drunk this much or this often when he was just hacking in Vegas. He had the feeling that once his life stopped being so desperate all the time, he wouldn't be hitting the booze so heavily.

He looked across the room out the window. The sky was a cold, dishwater gray, and the city looked wrapped in dirty gauze. His eyes fell on the bottle of bourbon on the table, and he decided he wouldn't have anymore until after Chris arrived. This particular bottle had been brought up to his room by the day manager of the hotel, who had appeared at his door that morning to apologize profusely for the "terrible accident" that had occurred during the night. A rare occurrence, he'd assured him.

The manager had wanted him to know that he had telephoned the young desk clerk who had been on duty last night and informed him that he'd better be spending less of his time reading magazines and more of it keeping a sharp eye out for any suspicious-looking characters coming through the door of the hotel, or he'd soon be out looking for a new job! Jerry had immediately remembered how he had taken Eckhart for some hotshot junior-executive type back in the bar at O'Hare and how he'd let him sit at his table. There was little chance that the young desk clerk, alert or not, would ever have taken Eckhart for a suspicious-looking character.

Outside the window, the city was slowly growing dark, and now that it was actually getting close to the time that Chris would be getting off work and coming to see him, he felt the tension starting to take hold of him. He was looking forward to seeing her, was, in fact, almost crazy to see her, but he wasn't looking forward to telling her everything he had to tell her. Especially that he had to leave London tonight and that he didn't know when he would be seeing her again. He wasn't even sure how she would feel about hearing that, how much it would or wouldn't matter to her. Maybe she didn't want anything to come of them. They hadn't had time to get into anything like that. Maybe it just wouldn't be all that much of a big deal to her that he had to leave.

It was crazy, he thought. All of it.

He *wanted* it to be a big deal to her, but even if it turned out that it was, that she was really starting to feel something for him, what in the hell could he do about it now?

Ask her to drop her life and run away with him? Ask her to involve herself in all the trouble that he was involved in? Warn her that there was a chance she could get hurt, maybe even killed? Jerry sighed. No, that stuff was strictly Hollywood. So what could he do? He'd take her address and—*Jesus Christ!* He forced himself to go on with the thought. He'd take her address and he had her phone number and when things were more normal with him, he . . .

He shook his head.

No good, he thought. No good at all.

Because by the time things were normal, if they ever were, it would not be the same with them. He'd write her or call her and they wouldn't even know each other and it would all be embarrassing. Things and people would have come into their lives, changing feelings, dimming memories, and they didn't have all that many to dim. They didn't have enough of anything at this point to withstand the strain of a big time gap in their relationship. So you're just going to have to live with it, he thought angrily. And it's all your own fault. All of it. You knew from the beginning that now wasn't the time for anything like this. No, now was the time for one-night stands, for quick fucks and somebody next to you in bed until morning, not anything like this!

It was dark in the room now. The lights of London glowed mistily through the early night.

You know, he thought, it's really time for you to grow up. You're a man in his forties and it's late for growing up, but you must still have one hell of a lot of it left to do because if you didn't, you wouldn't be finding yourself in situations like this one. You have to learn to really take a good look at the consequences of things before you do them. Make sure you understand what's coming to you if you fuck it up. What you've been doing all your god-damn life is just ignoring the consequences because you wanted to do things so much.

He thought about later tonight, after it was all over and Chris had gone out of the hotel and out of his life.

When the manager had brought up the bottle of liquor, he had talked to him, told him that as much as he hated to do it, he had to go back to the States tonight. Business problems. The manager's face had shown that he was truly sorry to see such a generous guest leave his hotel, and he had expressed the hope that when Mr. Rodman next visited London, he would remember to stay with him again.

Jerry told him that it was still rather painful for him to get around with his injury and asked him if there was maybe a way for him to leave the hotel other than down the steps in front, since they were rather difficult for him. Eager to help, the manager had told him that there was a rear entrance at ground level that led out through the kitchen. And he was most certainly welcome to use it. When he was ready to depart, he should call downstairs, and the manager would arrange to have the taxi come around to the kitchen entrance to collect him.

He had thanked the manager for being so helpful and cooperative during his stay at the hotel, and he could be sure, he'd told him, that he would be back on his next trip to London. Before the manager left, he had tried to give him some more money, a little token of his appreciation, he'd said to him, for all his help. The manager had looked at the money, but a mixture of public-relations sense and decorum had won out over the light of greed that had burned in his eyes, and he had refused the offered bills, saying no, no, it was not necessary. Mr. Rodman had already been far too generous. Then he had promptly given Jerry his card, telling him to write or cable before he returned to London on his next trip and then his suite would be properly prepared for him upon his arrival. They had shaken hands then, the manager wishing him a speedy recovery from his injury, and the man had left.

Jerry then called Pan Am and booked a first-class seat on the midnight flight to Zurich. He had chosen Switzerland because he'd remembered posters of the country plastered on the walls of a travel agency back in Vegas and the place had looked clean and beautiful to him. He felt like he wanted to go someplace clean and beautiful.

So, he thought. Everything was set. He had done everything that he could think of to do now. If Eckhart was having all the exits to the hotel watched, then his ass was in a sling for sure, but he wasn't going to worry about that. He'd just have to take his chances and hope that his luck was still good and if it wasn't, then he'd have to deal with whatever went down. At this point, he didn't really give a damn what happened. He was ready for anything.

Except for Chris.

She arrived a little after seven, and as soon as she was inside the room with him and he looked at her, obviously glad to see him, her face flushed a little from the night cold, her eyes bright, and then her arms around him, kissing him a quick hello—well, for a minute, all logic had gone straight out the window and he didn't think he could do any of it. He didn't think there was any way he could ever leave without taking her with him and so he'd barely said anything to her at all, letting her sit him down and change his bandages, watching her, listening to her talking to him about her day, and that gave him some time to force himself back down to earth, to see again what had to be done because if he really did care about her, then he couldn't risk involving her in anything that might get her hurt. And so when she was through with the bandages and after room service had brought up the little silver bucket of ice so that they could both have a whiskey on the rocks, he'd asked her to sit with him on the sofa because he had something really important to tell her and he saw the wariness that came instantly into her eyes.

"I want you to do something for me," he said to her. "I want you to just listen to me until I'm finished and then we can talk about it all. Okay?"

She leaned back against the arm of the sofa, holding her drink in both hands, resting it in her lap. "All right," she said.

And slowly, taking his time so that he would not forget anything, he told her all of it. He started with his real name and what he'd really been doing for a living back in Vegas, and how he had picked up the thin, blond guy that night at the hotel and everything that had happened after that, up to Eckhart breaking into his room last night, and why he had to leave London right away. He was sorry, he told her, that he had lied to her. He had planned to tell her all of it later, when they'd had some more time together, but now there wasn't anymore time. And then, because he wanted her to know, he told her the newest part of it all. She was the nicest thing that had ever happened to him, he said, and he was already falling in love with her, and he knew she probably didn't feel that way about him, but he wanted to tell her how he felt because it was important for him. He'd like to have her address at home so he could write her later if that was okay, but the truth was that he didn't know when he would even be able to write, but he would do it as soon as he could. And then he was finished and he did feel better that it was all out and that she knew about him and how he felt about her.

Chris listened to it all and she kept her promise and did not interrupt him. She sat there watching his face while he talked, frowning sometimes during certain parts of it, especially during the part when he explained how his feet had gotten burned, and then when she saw that he was finished, she didn't say anything for a minute, took a long drink of her whiskey, then looked at him and said, "May I ask you a question?"

Jerry nodded. "Sure," he said. "Anything."

Chris hesitated a moment and then she said, "What I want to know is if all this is really the truth or is it that you robbed a bank or something like that and the police are after you?"

Jerry stared at her. Then he couldn't help it. It just came up out of him.

Laughter!

He laughed loud and long until he was gasping for breath and the tears were running down his cheeks. Dear God!

"The truth," he said, pulling himself together. "All of it. No bank. No police. Nothing like that." He smiled at her. "Wait a minute," he said. He reached down beside the couch and picked up the tan leather briefcase. He'd had the manager bring it back up to the room because he'd thought he might want to show it to her. He put it down between them on the couch, unlocked it and lifted the lid.

Chris looked down at the stacks of bills and gasped. "My God!" she said softly. "How much is that?"

"Half a million dollars," he said. "Minus whatever I've spent, which hasn't been much."

She reached over and closed the lid of the case. "Lock it, please," she said to him. "Why on earth have you kept all this money in your hotel room?"

He snapped the latches and locked the case again. "I never got a chance to take it to the bank," he said. "I had it downstairs in the safe. I had it brought up so . . ."

"You can't go," Chris said.

"I don't have any choice," he said. "Believe me, I don't want—"

"No," she said firmly. "Now you let *me* talk. You don't know how I feel about you, and I'm rather confused about that myself right now, but I do know that I'm very fond of you and seem to be getting more fond of you every time I see you. And I also know that really doesn't tell you a damned thing, but it tells me an awful lot. It tells me enough to know that I don't want you to go. And besides, you can't even walk. You won't be able to get away from him! Not on crutches, for God's sake! Where can you go that he won't be right behind you? An American, on crutches, with two completely bandaged feet, trying to run from someone in Europe!" She shook her head. "So many people would remember you! Even if this man were stupid, he wouldn't have any trouble finding you. He's *already* found you, in fact! And that's another thing—I could hit you with something! Really! I really could! Why couldn't you have told me all this before so we wouldn't have gone out like we did for a whole day like that? Walking around in public! Damnit! Don't you know that's probably how he found you? Why didn't you tell me? Why did you let me make you take such a risk?"

Jerry looked at her and shrugged. "Because I really wanted to spend a whole day with you," he said. "I wanted to take you to dinner."

"You wanted... We could have spent the whole bloody day *here!* We could have had dinner *here!* What was the matter with you? What were you thinking about to do something that foolish?" She stared at him in frustration, but it was winding down in her fast because, Jesus,

he had taken a chance like that just because he wanted
to be with her!

"I didn't want to tell you any of it then," Jerry said to
her. "I didn't know what you'd think of it all—what
you'd think of me."

Chris took a long drink of her whiskey, looked down
at the floor, shook her head, looked back into his face.
"Do you agree with me that you can't leave like you are
now?" she asked him, her voice a little quieter, more
controlled.

Jerry shrugged. "I know it's going to be tough," he
said, "but I'll just have to try to stay ahead of him until
I can get better and think of what to do."

"Will you stay if I ask you to?"

"Chris, you're just making it harder for me. I don't
want to go, for God's sake. So I stay. What does that do
except make it easier for him to find me?"

Then she really stunned him.

"You'll stay at my house," she said.

Jerry stared at her. "Stay at *your* place? Chris, I am
trying to keep you *out* of it. You want him to come to your
house? Look, I'm not really sure you understand what
I'm talking about here. This guy's not coming just to get
the money back. He wants to kill me *and* get the money
back. If you're with me, he'll probably try to kill you,
too, because he'll figure you know the story. And if he
tracked me here because of us being out together like
that, then he already knows you're involved with me
some way."

"But he won't know who I am," Chris said. "I've
never come here in my uniform. He won't know I'm a
nurse. I could just be somebody you hired to push you

around town for a day. And even if he found out that I was a nurse, do you know how many hospitals and clinics and doctors' offices there are in London? It would take a long time to find me. You'll be safer at my house, don't you see that?''

She took some more ice cubes out of the little silver ice bucket and put them in their glasses and poured them each another drink. She didn't say anything else. She had said what she had to say and now she was waiting for him.

Jerry looked down at the ice in his glass, swirled it around. He was trying not to think about how much the thought of living and sleeping in the same house with her appealed to him, and concentrate on the whole picture. The consequences, remember, he told himself. Except the thing was, her reasoning was pretty sound. She had a good point about all the nurses in London. It wouldn't be that easy to find her and where she lived. And aside from the fact that he didn't want to leave her, especially now that he knew she didn't want him to go, he also knew that she was probably right about him not being able to stay ahead of Eckhart with his feet messed up like they were. Still, Eckhart could get lucky, and if he found them, she would most likely get hurt or maybe even killed right along with him and he wasn't sure he could let her put herself in that position.

He looked at her now, and she was watching him and she knew what he was thinking.

''You're still worried that something could happen to me, aren't you?'' she said.

He nodded. ''That's right,'' he said.

"I think it's my decision if I want to do it," Chris said. "Do you remember why I told you that I didn't think I could live in Las Vegas? Because I like to gamble too much. I'm a gambler, too. I'd think you should be able to understand that." She pointed to the briefcase. "You gambled when you took that money." She smiled at him. "So you can be my gamble."

"I just don't think you fully realize what could . . ."

"Listen, damnit!" Chris said. "Don't you see what I'm trying to say to you? I really care about you. And I haven't felt this way about anybody in quite awhile. Too long, if you want the truth, and if there is a chance that something nice could come from it, I don't want to lose that chance."

He looked at her and he knew that he'd been right about really trying to think things out before he did anything, but now, hearing that from her along with the way he already felt about her—well, it was just too much, and he smiled at her and said, "You sure you got room for me at your place?"

Chris smiled right back at him. "I have this big sofa in the living room," she said to him. "It's really very comfortable. I've fallen asleep on it myself a lot of nights."

And he couldn't stand it anymore then. He reached over and put his arms around her shoulders and pulled her to him, just held her tightly against him for a minute and then he pulled back from her just a little, looking at her face, and kissed her once, a soft, long kiss, and then he let her go. He picked up his glass, raised it. "To good luck," he said softly.

"To *our* good luck," Chris said.

She was already afraid, but she hoped it wasn't showing in her face.

They talked it over and decided that it would be best if they both left the hotel together by the kitchen exit the way he had been going to leave. The only bad part about leaving from the back was that if Eckhart did have that exit covered, there wouldn't be any people around like there would be out in front of the hotel and so Eckhart wouldn't have to worry about witnesses if he tried to stop them before they could get into the taxi. More gambles, Jerry thought. You're spending more of your luck all the time.

He picked up the phone, called Pan Am and canceled his reservations on the midnight to Zurich. When he had made the reservation, they had asked him for a number where he could be reached and he had given them the number of the hotel. He didn't want them calling later when he didn't show up. The hotel manager was too fond of money. The less anyone knew of what he was doing, the better.

They got his stuff together, had another quick drink for the sake of their nerves and then went downstairs in the elevator so he could settle his bill with the young clerk on duty. There was nobody else at the desk when they got there, and the elegant lobby was almost empty. After he had paid, Jerry told the kid he wanted to talk to the night manager.

When the nervous little man came out of the office at the back and saw who it was that had asked for him, a look of worry instantly crossed his face. Had something *else* happened to this unlucky American? Or, worse, was he planning some sort of legal action against the hotel for the fright he had received the other night?

When Jerry explained to him how the day manager had offered him the use of the kitchen exit to the hotel because of his condition, the night manager was visibly relieved. Oh, yes! Of course. The day manager *had* left him a note to that effect. He hurried out from behind the desk, thinking thank God, they were going to be rid of this one! He excused himself for a moment, went over to the doorman and told him to have a taxi come to the kitchen entrance to the hotel. As he came back to Chris and Jerry, a bellhop appeared and, seeing the suitcase, picked it up. The night manager shooed him away. He would handle Mr. Rodman's luggage himself, he said. Chris was carrying the crutches and the tan briefcase. She let the little man take the crutches from her, but saw the look in Jerry's eye and declined the briefcase. Then they followed the night manager into the dining room of the hotel, which, much to Jerry's relief, was empty except for a few couples dawdling over their afterdinner drinks.

The night manager led them back to the entrance to the kitchen and held open the door for them. Jerry saw some of the kitchen help glancing curiously at them as they walked through, and then they went through two large doors at the back and they were outside, in what looked to be the employees' parking lot.

Jerry's eyes searched the cars in the lot. They all looked dark and lifeless. So far, so good.

Then he saw the lights of the taxi and the driver was apparently not sure just where the kitchen exit was because he had stopped the cab about twenty feet away.

The night manager stepped in front of them and waved both of his arms impatiently. The taxi started toward them. Jerry felt his stomach muscles tighten, remembering Mills and the taxi at the airport. But this driver was older, bald, watery-eyed, at least sixty. He got out of the cab, took the suitcase and the crutches from the night manager, put the suitcase in the trunk, tried to fit the crutches in, saw they wouldn't go and then fitted them in the front over the back of the seat. The night manager and Chris helped Jerry out of the wheelchair into the cab, and then Chris slipped in next to him and the night manager closed the door. He would look forward to seeing Mr. Rodman again, he lied, and he was again terribly sorry for the unfortunate incident of the other evening. Then he closed the door of the taxi and watched it pull away.

Done! he thought. He turned on his heels and walked back into the kitchen, pushing the chair. Americans in the hotel had always made him nervous. Problems, the type that you could never predict, always seemed to follow them, he thought. For a while he had hoped that the inflationary economy would keep them in the States, but a lot of them must still have money, because they were still coming. Well, he'd just have to get used to them now, but in a few years, with a bit of good fortune, *he* would be the day manager of some really splendid hotel and he wouldn't have to deal with them face to face so often. They could burden some other poor night manager with their calamities, which always seemed to occur at night.

Now as he went around behind the desk, the young clerk looked at him. "Seems like a nice chap, that Mr.

Rodman," the clerk said. "Too bad he hurt himself that way." The night manager grunted and went into his office, leaving the kid to take care of the wheelchair.

In the smoky-smelling darkness of the back of the taxi, Jerry and Chris sat close together. He held onto her hand, and they didn't talk. In the front, the old taxi driver softly whistled a tune to himself. Jerry listened to it, trying to see if he could place it, but he had never heard it before. He stared at the back of the old driver's head. God, but he was tired! He closed his eyes and thought for a minute how nice it would be to have everything simple and clear in his life again, but he knew that wouldn't happen for a while. It felt good having Chris next to him now, knowing that he wasn't going to be leaving her and knowing that she cared enough about him that she didn't want him to go away. Her being with him had a settling effect on him, but it also was going to make him more aware, more watchful of everything and that was sure good, because now more than ever he would have to be thinking, have to be keeping his eyes open if they were ever going to get out of all of this. He had two lives to worry about now. There was more at stake.

When the taxi pulled up in front of Chris's house, it was the only moving car on the street. The driver carried the suitcase up to the door, and Jerry paid him. The old man smiled, white faced under the streetlights, thanked him and lightly touched the bill of his cap to Chris. Then he went back down the walk and got into his cab, and they watched him drive off, the taillights going away down to the end of the street and then turning the corner, the sound of the car fading. Then they were alone.

Chris reached down into her purse and took out her keys. They made a soft, clear, jangling sound in the darkness. Jerry glanced at her, then looked away again, but he did not move, and she understood and waited with him on the little walk in the chilly, damp night air. He shrugged his shoulders and shifted his position on the crutch pads under his arms. He turned his head and looked back up the shiny, black, empty street in the direction their cab had come.

They stood there for maybe five minutes.

Then he looked at her, smiled at her in the darkness. And Chris smiled, too.

They turned away from the street and went inside to the light and warmth of the little house, and Chris locked the door behind them, telling him to sit on the couch, and she went into the kitchen, stopping for a minute to say hello and pet the big reddish cat that ran up to her.

"This is Roscoe," she said. The cat stayed next to her, staring up at the man on the couch as though it at least expected him to introduce himself and explain what the hell he was doing there.

Jerry said hello to the cat. Chris went on into the kitchen, and Roscoe went with her. When she came back, she was holding two glasses of brandy.

"I've put some coffee on," she said. "We can have another one as soon as it's ready." She sat down next to him on the couch. Roscoe sat down in the middle of the living room floor and looked at them with big yellow eyes. They drank their brandy and talked with a kind of nervous, happy, frightened excitement in their voices.

PART FOUR

37

AL CHAMBERS SAT AT HIS huge desk in his office in the Silver Tiara Hotel and Gambling Casino and thought about how fast a man's life could turn sour on him.

It was really incredible, he thought.

Over the years, he'd worked hard, and he'd done all right for himself, too. He'd learned some things, paid some dues. The road had been laid out all nice and clear.

Now everything was shit.

He took a long puff on his cigar and blew the smoke over the papers on his desk. He looked down at his face reflected in the dark, glossy finish of the wood. The desk was an antique. Roz had found it while she was on a shopping trip to L.A. a few years ago and had bought it for his office. Roz loved antiques. You're a fucking antique, he thought sourly. Well, older, anyway. No kid, that was for sure. And that was why it seemed so unfair that all this bullshit should be happening to him now at this late time in his life. He tapped the ash from his cigar into the ashtray and leaned back in the comfortable, leather-covered chair. Outside the big picture window near his desk, it was getting dark, the lights of the Strip flashing bright colors against the black-edged mountain peaks that rimmed the deep red horizon.

Chambers smiled ruefully. Fucking money, he thought.

He'd been hooked on it, ever since he'd been a kid. And it wasn't just for the things it could buy, either. Not the things themselves. Years ago, it had been that way, but not anymore. He had everything he needed. No, what it was now with the money was—and he realized that he had never told this to anyone, not even Roz—was the feeling the money gave him of having a kind of special insurance against all the bad crap that could come down on a guy's head in his life. If you had the money, you could do things to make it all a little less bad. Without it, you were screwed.

And so when the chance had come along to have that five hundred thousand dollars, he'd grabbed it almost without thinking.

THE WHOLE THING had been so beautifully simple. A setup made in heaven.

There had been a high roller, an Italian millionaire from Rome who came to Vegas once a year for a blast. Through some careful planning, Chambers had managed to get the Italian to spend his week as a guest of the Silver Tiara, flying him to the States with all expenses covered. The man was an incredibly reckless gambler and womanizer. For the week he was in Vegas, money meant absolutely nothing to him. Chambers had been careful to spend a good deal of time with the gambler, from the day he arrived, in order to ensure that when the Italian gambled, he did it at the Tiara. He'd accompanied him to the sumptuous suite that had been reserved for him to make sure that all was to the man's liking. He personally took him through the casino and introduced him to all the pit bosses, and he took him to dinner several times, always arranging for a beautiful girl to be the Italian's dinner date. On one of these occasions, in the tradition of Nate Shapiro, he had gifted the gambler with an antique gold pocketwatch, a token, Chambers had told him, of how special a guest he was.

The Italian's two great passions were gambling and women, and for the five days he stayed under the Tiara's roof, he enjoyed both of them with bright-eyed vigor. His game was the crap table. He loved the wild excitement of his high bets and being the center of breathtaking attention as he made them.

He was one of the unluckiest gamblers Chambers had ever seen. By the time he was ready to leave for Rome, the man had markers due in the Tiara cage totaling five hundred thousand dollars. And because he was only used to dealing with the top people in his life, an unusual thing occurred.

The Italian appeared at Chambers's office to settle his debt with the Tiara, instead of going to the cage as was customary. Chambers welcomed him, shook his hand and poured him a cognac from his special reserve, and had no idea at all of the trouble he was about to bring down upon himself.

Beaming, the gambler had thanked him for one of the most pleasurable times in his entire life, and to Chambers's delight, had assured him that all his future visits to Las Vegas would be spent at the Silver Tiara. Then he presented him with a case containing a half-million dollars in cash. The Italian had sat back in his chair smiling broadly and had sipped his cognac and insisted that Chambers count all the money out on his desk to be certain that the amount was correct.

And while he was counting the money—without giving it the slightest thought beforehand—Al Chambers suddenly saw a way that he could maybe keep all that money for himself and Roz.

When he had finished the count and determined that all the money due the hotel was there on the desk in front of him, he had thanked the Italian, poured him another cognac and then, in his most careful and tactful manner, Chambers had inquired if *he* might now ask a favor of the gambler.

The Italian's face lit up. He made an expansive gesture with both hands, spilling a bit of his cognac on the rug and then fussing over it. Of course! he told Chambers. Of course! What was it!

Chambers gave the gambler a cigar, lit it, and then lit one for himself. Then he asked the Italian if perhaps back in Rome, he had friends, men of wealth and position such as himself, who would also enjoy a trip to Las Vegas with all expenses paid, to be the guests of the Silver Tiara. Men who also, and Chambers had leaned back in his chair and winked at the gambler, might enjoy the company of some of the most beautiful ladies of the Tiara, as he had done.

Most certainly, the Italian had told him, laughing. He had many such friends. Why did he ask?

And by that point, all the pieces of what he was going to do suddenly came together in Chambers's mind, slipping down as smoothly from his unconscious as a silk scarf being pulled from a magician's pocket. For he had closely observed the millionaire during his stay at the hotel and had seen the pride and strong ego in the man. Chambers then proposed that a gambling junket be organized, composed of, say, twenty of the Italian's friends. They would all be flown to Vegas as guests of the Silver Tiara. All their expenses except, of course, their gambling would be on the house. Chambers leaned forward slightly over his desk and lowered his voice as though he feared someone might be listening. He would be doing him a personal favor, he told the Italian, in helping organize this junket of his friends. He started to explain, but the gambler was already ahead of him.

Grinning, he had said that of course the gambling would not be complimentary. His friends could win, but, and he cocked his head at Chambers, they could lose, too. And if they were unlucky, the hotel would make much money, was he correct? Chambers puffed at his cigar and grinned back at him, nodding. And the Italian went on. "Since this trip was your idea," he said to Chambers, "your employer, the owner of the hotel, would be very pleased with you, am I right? Was that not the personal favor?"

Chambers had made himself look a little embarrassed. "Yes," he said, laughing. "Yes, it was."

And as he had expected, the Italian was thrilled with the idea. Thrilled that the president of a large hotel in Las Vegas in the United States had asked him a personal favor. And thrilled too at the prospect of bringing a bunch of his rich buddies to the Silver Tiara and showing how much juice he had that they didn't have. It was a king-size opportunity to impress, and the man had no intention of passing it up. His eyes were brightly alive as he talked excitedly of how it would all be. He began thinking of friends, rattling off names—yes, he would be a good one, no, he would not be good—as though he were alone and planning it all himself. He shook Chambers's hand, slapped him hard on the shoulder. He had to leave tomorrow afternoon, he said. He wanted to try his luck some more. Chambers assured him that all the details of the junket would be taken care of. If he had any questions, he had only to come to his office. It would be a magnificent time! the Italian said. He shook Chambers's hand again and left the office, his mind instantly going back to which of his friends he would bestow the honor of an invitation to Las Vegas!

Chambers stared at the door of his office after the Italian had left. To be that rich, he thought, that you could leave five hundred thousand dollars in cash and not even ask for a receipt!

Then, alone, he had poured himself another cognac, a big one, and holding the glass, he had walked to his big picture window and toasted Vegas, himself and Nate Shapiro. He turned around and looked back at the pile of money on his desk. He raised his glass again and drank.

To the first day in his life that he had made half a million dollars.

Because of certain business commitments on the part of the Italian gambler, Al Chambers had to wait another six months before the junket from Rome arrived at the Silver Tiara.

But it proved to be well worth the wait.

By the time the Italian and his friends had ended their frenzied week of gambling at the Tiara's tables and screwing their brains out in its bedrooms, they had left nearly two million dollars behind them in the casino cage.

And Al Chambers was a hero.

A bottle of expensive imported champagne arrived at his office. Tied around the neck of the bottle with a bright red ribbon was an envelope containing a message from August Gurino, the owner of the hotel. Scrawled in a large hand, the message read, "Well done, Albert," and below it the initials A.G.

Inserted in the fold of the stationery was a bonus check for ten thousand dollars.

Alone in his office that morning looking at the check, Chambers had smiled and relaxed. Then he began making the first of a series of carefully spaced deposits from what he privately thought of as his *real* bonus to his bank in Geneva, Switzerland.

And everything would have been fine if only he had killed Meyer Weiss.

MEYER WEISS WAS a blank-faced little man who wore colorless, ill-fitting suits, and no matter what he was doing, he always seemed to be doing it in a great hurry. Weiss was the hawk-eyed controller of the Silver Tiara's money. He had been at the hotel and casino about eight years. Shapiro himself had lured Weiss out to Vegas from Manhattan, where he had known him through the large bank that had dealt with the Regency Manor.

Meyer Weiss was truly a financial genius.

Shapiro made him head of the accounting department, and using his pencil like a scalpel, Weiss had cut costs to the bone, got rid of a lot of deadwood on the hotel and casino payroll, and the Tiara's books began showing money saved all over the place. Shapiro was impressed, and to show his thanks, he gifted Weiss with some points in the hotel. For eight years, they were a good combination: Nate Shapiro, Meyer Weiss and the Silver Tiara Hotel and Gambling Casino.

Then Nate Shapiro decided to retire and bring Al Chambers out from New York to take his place.

Meyer Weiss was stunned.

For although they had never actually discussed the matter, Weiss had been certain that when Shapiro stepped down, he would become the new president of the Tiara. And the truth was that Shapiro *had* considered him for the job but had decided against it finally, feeling that while Weiss was indeed a capable man within his own financial sphere, he lacked the necessary combination of personality and, if needed, ruthlessness to handle all the varied types of people who came through the Tiara's doors bent on fun or fraud. In the end, Shapiro felt the job would prove to be his friend's undoing. Weiss was a specialist. It was best he remain in his specialty. He was aware that Weiss might be upset by his decision, but he knew the man well. Shapiro felt certain that he could sit down with him in private and make him see the wisdom of his decision. He wanted to do that before Al Chambers arrived in Vegas.

But when he called Weiss at his office to invite him to dinner that evening, Weiss's secretary informed him that the accountant had left for New York, to visit his sister.

Shapiro instantly saw that he had underestimated the degree to which his decision would upset Meyer Weiss. This abrupt departure without a word was proof of that. Finally, after placing several calls, he reached Weiss at his sister's home in Queens. Shapiro was casual, friendly. There was not the slightest trace in his voice of the employer talking to the truant employee. Shapiro said that he should have told him he was going back to New York. He would've gone with him, he told Weiss. They could've had some laughs, seen some people.

Cryptically, Weiss said that he had some things on his mind that he needed to think about. He had the time coming to him, he added. Shapiro laughed and told him that of course he had the time, and even if he didn't, who was counting? Then he asked Weiss how long he thought he might want to stay. Weiss replied that he hadn't decided that yet. Maybe a month, he said. That's good, Nate told him. You relax, visit, play cards, get a little drunk. When you get back to Vegas, we'll have dinner. There's some things I want to go over with you. He had kept his voice casual as though there were no big problems between them, as though things could be straightened out without any trouble. Yeah, Weiss said to him. Okay. We'll get together then when I get back. They ended the conversation on a friendly note with Nate telling him again to relax and have a good time and not to shovel any snow for their lazy friends. After he had hung up the phone, he breathed a sigh of relief. He was again confident that he could make Weiss understand his choice of Al Chambers as president of the Tiara. He would only have to sit down alone with Weiss at dinner. They'd have a good meal, some wine, a cigar, just the two of them talking openly, and everything would be fine.

A few days later, when Al Chambers and Rosylyn arrived in Las Vegas, Shapiro filled Al in on the situation with Meyer Weiss and the delicate nature of it. He impressed upon Chambers that Weiss was a very valuable man to the Tiara operation and that things must be handled carefully so they would not lose him. Chambers said he understood. He hoped things would work out. He didn't want to start his new job with any enemies.

Then three bad things happened.

Nate Shapiro died suddenly.

Al Chambers was forced to take over immediately as the new president of the Silver Tiara.

And Meyer Weiss returned to Las Vegas.

Perhaps if Shapiro had lived, he could have set things right with Weiss. Then again, perhaps not. For even with all his talent for understanding people and dealing with them, there was something present in Meyer Weiss that even Nate Shapiro had missed.

And that something was ambition.

Perhaps Nate had missed it because it was not a quality that one usually had to look for. If it is present in a man, it usually will not remain hidden for very long. But in the case of Meyer Weiss, the seed was planted deep and covered over by his retiring and rather colorless personality. There were no outward signs that it was present, yet it had been growing steadily for years.

Secretly, Meyer Weiss had long hated his own image.

The dry, dull, bookish little accountant sequestered in his equally dry and dull little paper-cluttered office performing acts of mathematical brilliance for other people, making them look good while he remained invisible.

Well now, *he* wanted to be visible!

He wanted to be recognized as a man of respect and power. He wanted to see people looking at him in restaurants, whispering his name, nodding somberly to each other because they knew that he was *Meyer Weiss!* He saw many such men in Las Vegas who got that kind of attention and respect and as president of the powerful and booming Silver Tiara, he could be one of them. He was certain that he could've convinced his old friend Nate that he was the right man for the job. But now Nate Shapiro was dead and already this Chambers was busy taking over everything.

And then, sitting at his desk, Meyer Weiss was suddenly very angry with himself. He wasn't going to settle for whatever came his way, he thought. All his life he had done that. He wasn't going to do it this time!

Godamnit! He wanted to be *somebody!*

And if that was vanity, he thought, then that's the way it was with him. He sat back in his chair and propped his feet up on his desk, the heels of his shoes crinkling papers. If he wanted the job that much—and he *did* want it that much—then he was just going to have to get busy, use his brain and come up with a way to get it. He smiled, nodded to himself. After all, he reasoned, how many men had a brain like his?

A FEW WEEKS LATER, Meyer Weiss began to go out of his way to be pleasant and helpful to the new president of the Tiara.

At first, Chambers was wary of him. He remembered how Nate Shapiro had described the situation as a delicate one. But after a while, Chambers came to believe that the accountant had decided to respect his departed friend's wishes and accept the situation. After all, Weiss did have a damned well-paying job. His salary was second only to Chambers's own, and Nate had left him more points in the hotel. The men began having drinks and lunches together, and in time, Chambers invited Weiss home for dinner to meet Roz.

They got along.

For even though their basic personalities were different, they did have certain things in common. They had both grown up in New York and had come from poor backgrounds. And they had both known and loved Nate Shapiro. They spent many evenings after eating one of Roz's wonderful dinners, sipping cognac and swapping stories about Nate, both somberly agreeing that it was a damned shame that they all three hadn't been able to grow old together in the desert sun.

Six months later the death threat to Rosylyn arrived in the morning mail at Chambers's office.

Chambers stood staring down out of his picture window, his face flushed a deep red with fury, his hands knotted into tight fists inside his trouser pockets to control their trembling. The note was composed in the usual manner of such things, the letters making up the words having been clipped from magazines and newspapers. Using all his will power, Chambers had forced himself to settle down so that he could think clearly. He walked over to the oaken bar that took up nearly one wall of his office, poured himself a large cognac, took it back to his desk and sat down. He fired up one of his favorite cigars, took a long sip of the cognac, sat back and started to dig.

The threat itself had been made against Roz, but Chambers knew he was the real target. The note stated that if he was not out of Vegas in thirty days, Roz would be killed. He knew he had not been in town long enough to make any real enemies, but it stood to reason that now that Nate was gone, there were bound to be guys who would like to move in on the lucrative Tiara operation, and anybody with that goal in mind would naturally want to try to scare him off before he had time to really know the ropes and gain a secure foothold. The first logical place to look, he thought, would be inside the structure of the Tiara itself. Only that wouldn't be so easy. He really didn't know all the people who worked under him that well at this point.

But, he realized suddenly, there was someone who did.

He sat up in his chair, put the cognac down next to the phone and picked up the receiver. Meyer had over eight years at the Tiara. Maybe he would know of anybody who might have big ideas. As he punched out Weiss's exchange, Chambers smiled, thinking that if this shit had gone down a few months ago, Meyer would've been his number-one choice as the guy who . . .

Jesus Christ!

"Mr. Weiss's office," the secretary chirped.

Chambers stared down at the receiver in his hand for a long second. Then he hung it up without saying a word. His hand was trembling again as he picked up the cognac and drank.

Huh, uh! he thought. *No way!*

Not Meyer. And not *now!* They were friends now. And besides, Meyer would never threaten Roz. He was crazy about Roz.

But then he remembered that the threat had not really been aimed at Roz.

At you, he thought. *At you!*

Still, he couldn't buy it. Okay, so Meyer resented him in the beginning and had probably wanted him out. Not hard to understand when you took everything into consideration. But not now. Things were great between them now. The Tiara was booming. It would be a stupid time to pull something like this. No, he thought; he was wrong. He'd get Meyer in here now, show him the note and see what he thought was up. He looked down at the phone.

But he didn't pick it up.

Because it wouldn't be a stupid time, he realized. Not at all.

It would be the perfect time, in fact. Because in the beginning, Meyer hadn't known him, hadn't known then that the person he cared most about in the world was Roz. Now Meyer knew that fact. They were friends now.

Slowly he drained the last of the cognac and put the glass back down on the desk.

The dirty sonofabitch!

Easy, he told himself. Just cool it down now. Okay, it could be, yeah. But he could be wrong, too. Completely full of shit. And you have to be sure, he thought. You have to be absolutely sure!

Late that afternoon, Chambers called Meyer Weiss into his office.

Sitting on the other side of the desk, Weiss read the note and then looked at him. "What the hell?" he said.

"I got it this morning," Chambers told him. "What do you think?"

"You say anything to Roz?" Weiss asked him.

Chambers shook his head, relit his cigar, blew out the burning wooden match and tossed it in the ashtray. "I wanted to talk to you first," he said. "See what you thought. I don't want to scare her if there ain't any reason for her to be scared. She's sick and nervous enough these days."

Weiss nodded thoughtfully. "Yeah," he said. He looked down at the note, read it again, then looked back at Chambers. "Off the top of your head," he said to him, "you know anybody who wasn't in love with the idea of you being in town?" he asked. "In the hotel?"

Chambers shrugged, grinned at him. "Just you," he said.

It had been a subject that he had carefully stayed away from mentioning during the times the two men had been together. He had decided that since the problem was Weiss's, Weiss should be the one to bring it up.

Meyer Weiss laughed, wiped the back of his hand across his lips. His face was slightly embarrassed. "Nate told you about that, huh?" he said.

"He mentioned it, yeah," Chambers said casually.

"Ahh," Weiss said, waving his hand, "for a while, it bothered me. I admit it. I thought I was in line. I wanted the job. Who were you to come in, a new kid who knew from nothing?"

"Yeah," Chambers said. "Okay. I'd have been the same way. Worse, probably." He tapped the jagged gray ash from his cigar into the ashtray.

"Nate knew what he was doing, though," Weiss said. "Your job would've gotten on my nerves. I don't have the patience. I'd have fired half of the hotel by now, the casino, too."

Silence for a minute. Only the soft rushing of the air conditioning coming out of the vents in the floor.

"You think I got trouble?" Chambers asked quietly.

Meyer Weiss made a little sucking sound with his teeth, his face thoughtful, serious. "Maybe," he said. "Then again, the whole thing could be just a bluff, you know. Let me think on it. I'd be careful, though. We can't take any chances. We're talking about Roz here."

"I know," Chambers said. "You think you have to tell me that? You think about it. You come up with anybody, you call me. Anytime. At the house or here, whatever."

Weiss got up from his chair, straightened his suit coat, pulling at the bottom of it with his hands. "I'll let you know," he said. He turned and walked back to the door, started to open it.

"Meyer," Chambers said softly.

Weiss turned.

Chambers reached across the desk, picked up the letter, gestured with it. "Nobody even *thinks* about hurting Roz," he said. "*Nobody.* Look good for me, okay?"

Weiss nodded. "Sure," he said. Then he went out and closed the door.

Chambers sat back in his big chair, swiveled it to the right so he could look out the window. There had been nothing in Meyer's face or in his voice that had been out of line. He had seemed genuinely surprised at the letter, and there had been real concern for Roz in his face. Chambers blew a cloud of cigar smoke toward the window. He was quite calm now. He had to think carefully about what to do next.

He was absolutely certain Meyer Weiss had sent the letter.

He was a crafty sonofabitch, there was no doubt about that. He'd played a damned good show sitting there. But under Nate Shapiro's guidance, Chambers's instincts about people had developed well. His radar was acute. "Always watch the eyes," Nate had told him one night a long time ago at the Regency. "Don't let them know you're doing it. No matter how good they are, sooner or later, if there's something wrong, you'll be able to see it in their eyes if you're looking for it."

And he had seen it in Meyer Weiss's eyes. Only for a second, maybe, but it had been there. It had been a look of caution, the nervous look of the liar in a potentially bad spot.

Chambers swiveled his chair back around to his desk and buzzed his secretary. "No calls, Rita," he said. "Nobody. I'm out. You don't know when I'll be back."

He wanted to be alone now. He needed to be as relaxed as possible so he could think clearly. He went over to the bar, poured himself a cognac and lit up a cigar. Then he sat back down at his desk and thought about what to do with Meyer Weiss.

TWO DAYS LATER, in the morning, Chambers buzzed Weiss and invited him to dinner the next evening.

"Lamb chops," he told him. "Roz don't want me to make a pig out of myself."

Meyer Weiss laughed. "Roz's lamb chops? With me at the table? You'll starve to death."

"I'll tell her," Chambers said. Then, "Anything on the other?"

"Nothing yet," Weiss said.

"Okay. Tomorrow night, then."

He put down the receiver.

He hoped to hell he was playing this right.

THE DINNER, as usual, was a feast.

Rosylyn Chambers was not a woman merely to fix a meal. Food and the preparation of it were two of the great joys in her life. Meyer Weiss liked to eat. Rosylyn had liked him from the beginning. And, too, she had sensed something very solitary and lonely in the man, and her woman's intuition told her that it was probably all connected to the death of his wife. Meyer Weiss was the kind of a man, she thought, who really needed a solid base in his life to feel comfortable and confident. He needed to know that he had a home to go to at the end of the day, with a good woman in that home who cared about him. He did not have that now. He was adrift. Never mind that he seemed to be having a good time with some of the young cuties in town. Rosylyn was convinced he was not happy, and though she had never mentioned it to Al, she always kept an eye out for a woman she thought Meyer might like. If and when she found a good candidate, she planned to carefully arrange for them to meet at the house.

In the meantime, she always enjoyed having Meyer over for an evening, watching him eat, listening to him telling his jokes in his dry New York voice that always reminded her of the old men who used to stand around on the street and talk on summer nights in her old neighborhood back in Brooklyn when she had been growing up.

And Al liked him, too, and she was especially pleased about that. Al did not have any men friends that he was really close to now that Nate had passed away. Rosylyn knew that the reasons for this were tied into her husband's job. ("You gotta be careful who you get close to in this business.") And they were also tied into the rough personality that Al showed to the world when he was outside their home. She sensed that in the beginning, Al had liked Meyer because of his link to Nate. Having Meyer around was like having some of Nate around, and Al had felt good about that. Now he'd come to like Meyer for himself, for his droll sense of humor and his relaxed, unaffected nature. If anyone, including Chambers himself, had told her that Meyer Weiss had been the writer of a note that threatened her life, she simply would not have believed it. She would have said that it was a terrible mistake, that's all. Someone was mistaken.

And knowing her feelings, Chambers had never told her anything. If his plan worked, he would never have to tell her. His relationship with Meyer Weiss would of course never be the same, but if he was careful and it all worked out, Roz would never know anything had been wrong. They had always discussed personal matters together, but this type of thing was something he decided she'd be better off not knowing.

So that night, Chambers worked to conceal his true feelings and things went as they normally did when Meyer was over. All three laughed and talked during dinner and over coffee in the living room. Meyer, as usual, raved about the dinner and about Roz and told Al that he was certainly in the right place living in Las Vegas because he was a lucky man to start with, having a woman like Roz, and Chambers forced himself to smile and laugh as he always did, and he winked at Roz and told her he'd better never come home and catch her alone with this old wolf, and then, also as usual, Roz left them alone to talk and have a cognac, while she went in to clear the table. Chambers said that he felt in the mood to whip Meyer's ass in a game of rotation, so they took their drinks and went into the billiard room. The billiard room was far enough away from the dining room and the kitchen that Roz would not be able to hear anything out of the ordinary.

Chambers sipped at his cognac and shot pool and pretended to joke with Weiss while he went over in his mind exactly what he planned to do.

By the time they had racked for the third game and Meyer had broken, Chambers was ready. As it turned out, he didn't even have to open the subject. Meyer did.

"So," he said, squinting down the length of his cue at the four ball, "I don't know what to tell you about that note."

Leaning against the wall on the other side of the table, Chambers puffed on his cigar and looked at him. "Nobody, huh?" he said.

Skillfully Weiss slammed the ball into the side pocket, walked around to get a bead on the five. "I don't think it's anybody in our place," he said. "Not that I can see. Nate kept everybody pretty happy."

Except you, Chambers thought. "So you think it's somebody on the outside?" he said. "Any idea who?"

Weiss kissed the five into the corner pocket, shook his head. "Don't know," he said.

Chambers took a sip of his cognac. "I been thinking about it, Meyer, you know? And one thing about it all really interests me."

"Ahhh!" Weiss said, missing the six. He hit the edge of the cushion with his fist. "What's that?"

"The threat in that letter wasn't made at me. I mean, not directly. It was made at Roz."

"Yeah," Weiss said. "So?"

Chambers didn't move to shoot. He had let his cigar go out and now busied himself relighting it. "Well," he said, "that makes me think that whoever wrote it must be somebody I know or somebody I used to know." He reached down, picked up the cube of blue chalk from the edge of the cushion and began working it around on the tip of his cue.

"How do you figure that?" Weiss asked, watching him.

"Well," Chambers said as he moved around and bent over the table to shoot, "somebody comes at me head on with something like that, somebody who *knows* me—well, they're gonna know that I ain't gonna show my ass and run."

The six ball was in a tough spot. He tried a bank shot that he knew would miss, and it did. He leaned his cue against the wall and went back around to the other side of the table and picked up his cognac. Meyer Weiss moved to sink the six, saying nothing, waiting for Chambers to go on.

"So they go at me through Roz," he said. "Because if they know me, maybe they know how I am about my wife. They know their shit's in the street if I find out who they are, but they know that while I'm gonna be trying to find that out, I'm still gonna be worrying about something happening to Roz, and I'll have to tell her about it so she'll be careful, and then she'll be worrying too. And all the time I'm looking, I'll be taking a chance that they might pay off on the threat. In the long run, they might win that way. Cause we couldn't go on too long living like that, you know?"

Weiss shot the six cleanly into the side pocket. "Yeah," he said. "It makes sense." He looked across the table into Chambers's face. "So then it's gotta be somebody from New York, huh? Somebody who—what? Knew you back there? Both of you?"

"Yeah," Chambers said. "Somebody from New York." He felt in his shirt pocket for another cigar, knowing he wasn't carrying any more with him.

As he walked over to the little table in the corner where he kept a box of them, Meyer Weiss said, "You got anybody in mind? Anybody from back there who might do something like this?"

Chambers pulled open the drawer, raised the lid of the cigar box, took three out and put them in his shirt pocket. "Yeah, I think so," he said. He reached back down into the drawer, closed the lid of the cigar box, his fingers moving over the top of it to close around the pistol.

"Anybody I might know?" Meyer Weiss asked. There was the solid smack of the cue stick into the ball.

"Yeah," Chambers said.

Then he turned around.

Meyer Weiss went pale. Fear lived instantly in his face. He opened his mouth to speak, but the sudden impact of seeing the gun, of seeing the cold hate on the other man's face froze him and he only stared. This reaction did more to convince Chambers that his instincts had been correct. For even though he had felt sure that afternoon in his office, later, thinking about what to do, he had known that there was still an outside chance that maybe he was wrong, and that chance had worried him because of what he planned on doing tonight. Now he wasn't worried anymore. He felt the anger building in him again and he realized that, goddamnit! He had been hoping he *would* turn out to be wrong! He had wanted to be wrong! Now he walked slowly up to Meyer Weiss, moved very close to him, raised the pistol level with Weiss's face and shoved it forward, stopping it only inches away from the man's mouth.

Meyer Weiss could only look at the ugly black hole of the barrel with the silencer wrapped around it, and then his eyes looked straight ahead into Chambers's face and the fear of dying made him find his voice. "I never meant it!" The words came out full of emotion. "I would never have hurt Roz! I swear it. For God's sake!"

Chambers looked into the fear-contorted face and for a very long moment, he actually wanted to kill him. The anger, indignation and rage were all there for him to do it, but he held onto himself and slowly they subsided. But he had to do *something*. He had to hurt this man.

With a sudden motion, he brought the pistol back across his chest, the muzzle pointing off to the side, and then whipped it forward and down, thudding it hard into Weiss's stomach. Weiss gasped in pain, doubled over and slowly sank down to his knees on the rug beside the billiard table. Chambers stood over him, his beefy face flushed, his lips locked tight in anger and frustration. "You come into my house," he said, his voice controlled but heavy with menace, "and you eat dinner with me at my table. With my wife. You pretend to be our friend. You dirty, two-faced, conning sonofabitch! You told me you were Nate's friend, too. What was it you said, huh? That you *loved* the man? That right? Well, you're full of shit! *I* was Nate's friend. Longer than you. So how in the fuck could you do this to *me?* To a friend of Nate's? Huh? You dirty bastard!"

On his knees on the rug, Meyer Weiss began to sob.

Chambers stared down at the top of his head, breathing heavily, forcing himself to settle down. He had done what he wanted to do. He had made Weiss know real fear. The man was absolutely certain that he was going to die right now in this room. He never had any intention of killing him, but because he knew himself, knew his own rage, the pistol that he now held down at his side had never been loaded.

He knew Weiss had crapped out. He had tried a bluff with nothing at all to back him up if it went wrong. Chambers knew that what Weiss had said about never really planning to actually hurt Roz was the truth. It just wasn't in him. He simply wasn't the type. All that had been behind it had been ambition.

Now came the difficult part. He would have to do something now that, in years past, he would never even have thought of doing because his temper and his sense of being wronged would have gotten the best of him. He must do the thing that Nate Shapiro had always worked so hard to teach him back in the days of the Regency. He must see the whole picture, base his actions on that. He must keep his anger and personal feelings out of it, not let them cloud the issue. He must weigh the situation carefully.

Meyer Weiss would never again threaten him. He was sure of that. The man would leave the house tonight thankful that he was able to leave the house tonight. There would never again be anything between the two men on a personal level. That was over.

"Get up on your feet," he said coldly. He reached down, gripped Weiss under the arm, pulled him up. Chambers nodded toward a chair. "Sit down," he said. Meyer Weiss slumped into the chair trying to regain control of himself. Chambers walked back over to the little desk, put the pistol back in the drawer and closed it. Then he picked up Weiss's cognac from the edge of the billiard table and brought it back to him. "Here," he said. "Drink this. You look like shit."

His hands trembling, Weiss took the glass and drank two quick swallows in succession. Then he sat back in the chair, resting the glass on his leg. He reached up and wiped his face with the palm of his other hand. Chambers picked up his own glass from the cushion where he had left it. He leaned back against the billiard table and looked at Meyer Weiss. "Stop worrying," he said. "Nothing's going to happen to you. Fuck, you're no killer! But you made a stupid mistake. As far as you and me go, you gotta know we're quits."

Weiss nodded, took another drink of his cognac. His composure slowly returned as his fear of death receded.

"From now on," Chambers said, "you're going to stay away from my house. You run into Roz or she calls you on the phone and wants to know why you ain't been around, you make excuses. You're busy. You got a broad. I don't give a fuck what you say, but you don't tell her *anything* about any trouble between us, you got that?"

"Yeah," Weiss said. "It won't take me long. I'll be gone . . ."

"Just shut up and listen," Chambers said harshly. "You know if I want to do it, I can fix it so your ass won't be able to get a job anywhere. But I'm not going to do that. Unless you try to leave."

Meyer Weiss stared up at him, shocked. "What are you saying to me?" he said. "That you want me to stay at the Tiara?"

Chambers made his face impassive, his voice cool and even. "What happened here tonight was personal," he said. "It's over. Settled. This is business I'm talkin' about here. I don't have to like you personally for you to work for me. There's probably going to be a hell of a lot of people in the operation I'm gonna end up not liking after I've been here for a while. You're the best at your job. You're good for the hotel. Nate saw that, and I see it, too. I ain't hurting the Tiara because you did something stupid. You owe me. I need you to stay. You try to leave, I ain't gonna stop you, but I'll sure as hell stop you from working. So just look at it from the business end. You got a good thing here. You make good money. You

got points. You like Vegas. Why leave and bring yourself a lot of aggravation at your age?''

Meyer Weiss swallowed the last of his cognac. He
stood up and put the glass down on the billiard table.
''So . . .'' he said, ''everybody makes stupid mistakes in
their life, right?''

Chambers didn't answer.

''Thanks,'' Weiss said. ''Thank you.''

''Don't thank me,'' Chambers said, and his voice was
ice. ''It ain't for you. It's for me, and for the Tiara. You
just keep doing your job and remember what I told you
about talking to Roz. Now she's probably wondering
what the hell we're doing in here so long, so let's go.''

They went out into the living room then, and Rosylyn
wouldn't hear of Meyer leaving without his usual cup of
coffee, and when he had glanced at Chambers, Chambers had smiled, a signal that he had better do it, and so
he stayed another half-hour or so drinking his coffee,
trying to play out the charade, and then, later, he shook
hands with Chambers at the door, kissed Roz good night
and left the house.

Al Chambers went back and sat down in his favorite
chair and lit a cigar. He felt exhausted. It was over. You
handled it okay, he thought. Nate would've been proud
of you. You set things right on the personal end and you
didn't hurt yourself on the business end.

Roz came over and poured him another half-cup of
coffee. She began clearing away Meyer's cup and saucer, putting them back on the tray with her own, hum-
ming softly to herself. The right woman was all he
needed, she thought again, smiling. She really would

have to keep her eyes open. A good man like that, she thought, with so much to offer—he shouldn't be alone.

MEYER WEISS ROLLED down all the windows in his car before he left to drive home from Al Chambers's house. The road was deserted. He drove slowly, the night breeze blowing in around him. In the light of the pale moon reflecting off the highway ahead of him, his face was expressionless, his eyes on the road, his mouth slack, but inside, his heart and mind were filled to the top with a burning shame and humiliation. The saliva in his mouth was bitter, and he turned his head and spat out the window.

Crying on his knees!

My God!

He had been a fool to try to scare Chambers with a letter like that. What did he know of men like Chambers? Nothing. Chambers was tough. He was not tough. He was just a man who had been born with a very good mind for dealing with numbers and who was confident and at times even arrogant when dealing with men like Chambers as long as they were inside his cluttered little world of pencils, papers and problem solving. But to deal with such men outside that world on other things, on their terms—no, he was not able to do that. All his confidence deserted him then as it had done tonight, and fear and confusion moved in on him like sudden bad weather. When he had seen Chambers, with the pistol in his hand and the silencer on the barrel so Roz would not hear the shot, all he'd been able to think of was that he was going to die.

Now, not dead, the experience over, he knew that Chambers had never planned on killing him. What would he have told Roz? What would he have done with his body? All clear thoughts that logical thinking would have told him, but logical thinking, any kind of thinking at all, had been impossible for him in his fear, and Chambers had known he would be that way, had planned on him being that way. And Chambers had been right about him not being a killer, too. Him, Meyer Weiss, a killer. Absurd! He had never given any thought to hurting Roz. The threat had been a tool, that was all, and not a good one at that. The truth of the matter was that he liked Roz. The thought of anyone, much less himself, doing her physical harm was very nasty and unsettling to him.

When he came to the street where he lived, he drove on past it, deciding suddenly that he didn't want to go home yet. The thought of going into his empty apartment and being alone now with the way he was feeling was something he did not want to do at all. He drove on toward the Strip. Maybe he'd stop somewhere and have a nightcap, perhaps find a girl to share his bed.

The really strange, really incredible thing was that he realized tonight (tonight of *all* nights!) that in spite of his plan, in spite of his desire to get Chambers out of Las Vegas so he could have what he felt he deserved, he had actually *liked* the man. The times they had spent together, the hours talking about Nate, had all been very pleasant for him, comforting even. And that had been why the things Chambers had said about his not really having been Nate's friend, about coming into his house and pretending friendship, had all stung so sharply.

Chambers had shown him tonight that not only was he ambitious—and that had been the main thing, he had admitted to himself, ignoring the rest—but also that he was deceitful and a coward as well. And now he hated Chambers for that, hated him because it was the truth and it was an extremely unpleasant truth to learn about yourself when you were fifty-five and alone. And he couldn't seem to care that it had been his own fault that he had learned these unpleasant things about himself.

On the Strip now, the noises, voices of the street coming in through the open windows with the night breeze, Weiss's eyes flicked back and forth from one side of the street to the other looking for a place to stop and go inside.

He would stay, he thought. He would stay at the Tiara, try to learn to live with it all, to ignore the humiliation that would be a daily feeling. The humiliation that Chambers knew he would have if he stayed, and Chambers knew, too, that he *would* stay because it was the sound thing to do from a practical business point of view.

Especially if you were a coward and needed that practical business point of view to lean on to help hide the thing you knew you should do if you were any kind of a man at all, which was to say, I'll take my chances. I'll look for another job and sooner or later I'll find something, and no matter what it is, it'll be better than being here eating crow.

Another time, he thought.

When he had been younger, perhaps then he could have taken such an attitude, but now, with his later years not that far ahead of him, the thought of leaving a secure job to seek something else was frightening to him.

What if, in spite of his talent and expertise in his field, what if he could not find another place to work because they might not want to hire a new man at his age? Cases like that happened every day. And then there was the threat Chambers had made about seeing to it that he couldn't work anywhere. He didn't know how effectively he could do that, but he was sure that he had the power to make things more difficult for him. So, no. He would not leave, he thought. He would stay. He would hate himself for doing it, but he would stay. He would get used to the taste of crow. He would do his job as he had always done it.

And he would *wait*.

Someday his chance would come along, and when it did, he would be more careful than he had been this time. He would not make any mistakes. Tonight he had found out that he was a coward. That was a problem. But he was very good with problems. You were careful and you used your logic, that was all. And his logic told him that because he was a coward now did not mean that he had to be a coward the next time.

He drove the length of the Strip and back twice before he finally stopped at the Sands and went into the bar for a drink. The bartender was a man about his own age named George, who had once owned his own restaurant and bar back in Jersey. Like Weiss, George was a widower. When his wife had died, he'd sold his own place and moved to Vegas to enjoy the desert sun. George worked at the bar in the Sands because it kept him busy and he enjoyed being around people. George liked Meyer Weiss. He was always glad to see Meyer come in the door. That night the bar wasn't busy. George and Meyer yakked for hours. When Weiss left, he felt better. He drove straight home and went to bed. He didn't remember that he had thought about maybe finding a girl.

MEYER WEISS HAD to wait almost five years before his chance arrived. He spent another two months patiently making certain that he had everything he needed. Then, after fortifying himself with a stiff drink, he sat down and called Al Chambers at his home.

And told Chambers that he knew he was a thief.

He had proof, Weiss told him, that he had kept the five hundred thousand dollars paid to him by the Italian gambler to cover his losses at the Tiara, and that unless Chambers paid him that five hundred thousand dollars, in cash, he was going to arrange a private meeting with August Gurino, and Chambers knew very well how Gurino would react to the news that the trusted president of his hotel and casino had tried to beat him out of half a million dollars. He wasn't bluffing, Weiss assured him. And while he knew how mad Chambers was at hearing all of this, he had just better get hold of that temper of his and forget any stupid ideas about trying to hurt him because if anything like that was attempted now or in the future, all the proof that was needed would go to Gurino anyway.

Tightly gripping the phone, Chambers exerted a terrible effort on himself to stay calm, to keep his voice low so that Roz would not hear him. His voice was ice when he asked Weiss just what proof he was talking about.

And calmly Weiss told him how, before he had left Vegas, the Italian gambler had come looking for Chambers to ask some additional questions about the junket, but Chambers had not been in his office. Roz had telephoned a few hours before. She was having one of her bad days. A migraine; could he come home. Chambers's secretary had referred the Italian to Meyer Weiss. The accountant had received him and politely answered his questions. Then, as the gambler had been leaving, he had stopped and made Weiss a very happy man by asking him for something.

A receipt for the money he had paid Mr. Chambers. For the gambling, the Italian explained.

For a moment, Weiss had only stared at the man. Then he pulled himself together, all his senses suddenly alert, his head starting to pound. He played it well. He did not tell the gambler what Chambers had told him—that the Tiara was wiping out his markers in return for the favor of the junket. Instead, Weiss pretended to be slightly confused. He was not aware, he told the man, that he had paid his debt. He had received no word from the cage. He began shuffling the papers on his desk as though he were searching for some confirmation of what the Italian was saying to him, and carefully covering his movements with the papers, he silently and quickly turned on the portable tape recorder that always stood at the ready on his desk to record any important things that he might want to remember during the course of his working day.

And Weiss was sure that what the Italian was about to say was something he would definitely want to remember.

Patiently the gambler had explained that he had not gone down to the cage to pay his losses. No, he had given the money personally to Mr. Chambers in his office. All of it? Weiss had asked him. The Italian had nodded. Yes, he said. The entire five hundred thousand dollars in cash. Mr. Chambers had counted the money on his desk, and it was all there. Weiss had only to ask Mr. Chambers, the gambler said, smiling. Then he laughed. He and Mr. Chambers, he said, had been so involved in discussing the matter of the junket that he had neglected to obtain his receipt for the gambling losses. It was not important to him, he added, but he had been told that it was best to have it.

Meyer Weiss had given the gambler his most pleasant smile. Of course, he told him. He understood now. And certainly he would give him a receipt. He would inform Mr. Chambers when he returned to the hotel. There was no problem with such things with a customer as wealthy and respected as he was, Weiss told the Italian. He felt like telling the gambler that not only would he give him the receipt, but that he would also buy him dinner, stake him to two weeks in Miami Beach, shine his shoes and press his suit for what he had just done for him.

For there was not a doubt in his mind that Al Chambers had stolen half a million dollars from the Silver Tiara.

And so it was with a delicious sense of revenge at the memory of being on his knees five years ago in Chambers's billiard room that Weiss now told him to just be quiet and listen. Then he placed the receiver of the phone down near the speaker of the portable tape recorder and depressed the Play button.

And when the tape had finished playing, Al Chambers only said, "I pay you the money—then when do you come back and shove it up my ass again?"

Meyer Weiss put shock into his voice. He was talking to him as though he were some cheap blackmailer, he told Chambers. A criminal! He was a businessman, that was all. A man who had seen a good opportunity and had taken advantage of it. 'Like you, Albert,' Weiss said innocently.

Chambers then asked if that was it. He paid the money, Weiss gave him the tape and they were square.

On the other end of the line, Meyer Weiss chuckled softly.

"No," he told Chambers. That wasn't quite it. "You will be writing a letter to August Gurino," Weiss said. In that letter Chambers was to resign as president of the Tiara because of Roz's bad health. "She is nervous. The fast pace of Las Vegas upsets her. You plan to take her to Florida or possibly to the Caribbean," Weiss went on, "but you are a responsible man. You want to leave the Silver Tiara in good, capable hands, so you will recommend someone to replace you. Do I have to tell you," he asked Chambers, "who that someone will be?"

For a long moment, Chambers was silent, and Weiss could feel his hate seething at him through the phone. Then Chambers said, "I can recommend it, but that doesn't mean Gurino will go along."

"And Albert," Weiss said, "whose problem is that, huh? Not yours, am I right?"

Al Chambers knew when his ass was up against the wall. And he knew that August Gurino must never find out that he had stolen money from the Tiara. For even though the Italian junket was a success and the hotel had made a huge profit from it, Chambers knew enough about Gurino by now to know that you did not steal from the man. Nate Shapiro had warned him the night he had taken him to meet the owner of the hotel.

Chambers had gotten along well with Gurino that night at dinner, and Roz had liked him, too. "One classy guy," Chambers had told Nate later.

And Nate had agreed, but he had told him, "You stay straight with Gurino and he'll take good care of you. The best. But if you go against him, you will be in *very* serious trouble."

Now Chambers wondered how after years of listening and heeding Nate Shapiro's advice, he could've forgotten that warning.

But what was done was done, and so he wrote his letter of resignation to Gurino, citing Roz's ill health as his reason for leaving and recommending that Meyer Weiss be the man to replace him as president of the Tiara. Then he withdrew the five hundred thousand dollars from his account in Geneva, telephoned Meyer Weiss and said that he was ready.

Weiss told him that he was to put the money in a locked briefcase and give it to Eric Nichols to deliver to a bartender named George at the Sands. Chambers had no reason to suspect Nichols of anything. He barely knew the skinny, blond man, but as a choice to deliver the money, Nichols seemed a good one. He had worked in the counting room of the Tiara for several years. It was a job of high trust and responsibility, the tallying of the casino's cash winnings, and though all the people employed in the counting room had been carefully screened, the entire operation was still observed on closed-circuit television twenty-four hours a day. So there was no reason to have Nichols followed.

Chambers had him followed anyway.

He would have had Abraham Lincoln followed. Half a million dollars was a lot of money. He told the driver of the car to stay with Nichols to make sure he dropped off the money at the Sands. If anything looked funny, he was to call. Then Chambers lit up a cigar and waited for the time to pass so that Meyer Weiss could call and tell him that he had the money.

Only when the phone did ring it was the driver of the car following Nichols.

Nichols's taxi had just gone by the Sands, the driver told Chambers, and it looked like he was heading for the airport.

And the frustration and anger that had been building up in Chambers exploded. He had been wrong about Nichols. He was obviously in on something with Weiss. Well, he didn't know what the hell was going on, but he was going to find out. There was no way that he planned on letting Nichols just fly away somewhere with half a million dollars of his money. He told the driver to stop the fucking cab if he had to run it off the road and to bring Nichols back to the hotel. Then he would see what was what. Except the driver of Nichols's cab turned out to be another A.J. Foyt and the morons in the car got carried away and ran Nichols down right at the god-damned airport and still didn't get the money back. He had had to call in some heavy favors to get that dumbshit driver out of Vegas and down to Nassau for a while.

NOW CHAMBERS LEANED back in his chair and sighed. It was completely dark in his office now, but he didn't bother turning on the light. He took another small sip from his cognac, knowing that he had been drinking way too much. He felt very tired from too many nights of not sleeping, and his eyes burned.

What a fucking mess, he thought for the thousandth time.

Now his money was way the hell over in London with some goddamned cab driver, and Weiss was crowding him really hard. Chambers glared down out of his window at the glittering Strip, remembering how Weiss had called him that night asking why the money hadn't been delivered to the Sands. He had told the old bastard what had happened with Nichols and the cab driver, and Weiss's only response had been to say, "Well, what can I tell you, Albert? Except that you had better be getting me another five hundred thousand dollars."

Chambers had exploded, yelling at him that that was all the cash he had. The rest of his money was tied up in investments, a fact that Weiss already knew. Weiss had told him that he had best get started talking to the banks, then. He'd give him two weeks. And Chambers had screamed at him that there was no way in hell he would ever be able to raise that much money in two weeks, which Weiss also knew. The man was only needling him and enjoying it. There had been a long silence on the line, and then Weiss had said to him, "Okay, Albert. You have a month. Better?"

"Yeah," Chambers had snapped, and then because he couldn't resist it, he said, "That was a great guy you picked to deliver the money, that Nichols."

Meyer Weiss's voice had been very matter-of-fact and casual. "What can I say, Albert? I picked him because I knew him and I thought I could trust him. How can you know what some people are going to do, huh?" Then Weiss had laughed. "Hey," he said, "maybe it's like those guys that work in a bank ten, fifteen years and then one day they take off with a bundle, you know?"

"Yeah," Chambers had told him dryly, "I know."

"You'll be calling me, right Albert?" Weiss had said. "To let me know how you're coming with the money?"

"You'll hear from me!" Chambers had told him and hung up. He had purposely avoided asking the one big, important question. How had Eric Nichols known there was *money* in that locked briefcase he was carrying unless Weiss had told him?

But Chambers had known there was no point in asking. The whole picture was clear now. Weiss had taken a big chance pulling all this shit. And still he had no guarantee that he'd end up in the top slot at the Tiara even with Chambers's recommendation. So he wanted something for his trouble and effort. He made a deal with Nichols to rip off the money and then he'd deny having any part in it and ask for more.

The balls on that old sonofabitch, Chambers thought.

If Nichols had made it, then Weiss would've had that cash minus whatever he'd agreed to pay Nichols *plus* the new half-million he'd given him a month to come up with. Almost a million bucks!

The balls! Chambers thought again.

So fucking obvious! All of it.

And that's what really got to him, ate away at him like worms. Weiss *knew* his plan was obvious. He *knew* that Chambers would see it.

And he just didn't care.

Because he had all the aces now.

He had the proof that Chambers had stolen from the Tiara. And all he had to do was take that proof to Gurino.

Chambers took another sip of his cognac. He smiled grimly.

At least this cab driver, this Logan, had done him one good thing. By taking off with the money, he'd screwed Weiss out of his extra five hundred grand. It had been two months now since Meyer Weiss had given him one month to come up with another five hundred thousand. Chambers had stalled him, telling him that he was doing everything he could. He was working with the banks, but he needed more time.

And Weiss had given it to him.

But he had had to practically beg the old sonofabitch for it, and each time after he had hung up the phone, Chambers had found himself wishing with all his heart that he had killed the man that night five years ago in his billiard room.

WHAT AL CHAMBERS didn't know was that Meyer Weiss did not care how long it took him to get together the money or even if he got it at all. Not that Weiss didn't want the money. It would help his chances when he went to his meeting with August Gurino.

A meeting he'd always planned on having, whether Chambers paid the blackmail or not.

For he knew that Chambers was right. Gurino might not go along with his recommendation. But if after showing the owner of the Tiara how Chambers had stolen from him, he could then present him with the recovered five hundred thousand dollars—well, his chances of success simply had to increase. And whether Gurino went with him or not, Al Chambers would be out of his life. He would not have to worry about him popping up someday and causing him trouble. He did feel a little guilty about Roz, though. She would suddenly be without a husband.

But then, Weiss thought, smiling, he had always been fond of Roz....

PART FIVE

38

ANOTHER WEEK?'' Eckhart said.

"That's what the doctor tells me," Mills answered. The top half of the hospital bed had been cranked up, and he was sitting with a swing tray pulled over his lap, drinking a cup of coffee. His head was wrapped in a crisscrossed white bandage all the way down to just above his eyebrows.

"You sound okay," Eckhart said to him.

"Oh, I feel all right," Mills said, avoiding the other man's eyes, "as long as I'm lying down, but when I stand up for a while, it seems my balance goes on me and I fall down. But as I said, he told me another week and that'll be under control. Either way, I'm getting the hell out of here before I go crazy." He reached down and took a small serving of cream out of the saucer, peeled the top of it back, poured it into the coffee and stirred it carefully.

Eckhart watched him, saying nothing, and Mills felt the anger and coldness in the silence that Eckhart intended him to feel. Mills looked up from his coffee at the tall man sitting in the straight-backed wooden chair next to the bed, and for a moment a strong mix of his own anger and impatience swept over him, and in that moment, he wanted to suddenly lean forward and drive his big fist right into the middle of Eckhart's face, but he resisted, let the feeling pass. He knew it was his fault Logan was on the loose again and he had apologized for letting it happen. ("Underestimated him, I'm afraid. Didn't think he could go anywhere.")

Mills was not a man who apologized easily to anyone for anything, but once he had put himself through the effort of doing it, he expected the apology to be accepted, the matter dropped. He knew Eckhart had not accepted it and that rankled him. And again, a question he had pondered in the past crossed his mind. One on one, with no weapons except their hands and feet—could he take Eckhart? He thought there was a good chance that he could, for even though they were close to the same height and weight, he was pretty sure he was stronger, in better condition and in such a fight, more capable. With a knife or a gun, no. If the stories he had heard were true—and he had no reason to believe they weren't—Eckhart would win. But man-to-man? He wondered. He was aware that he would probably never know the answer, that such a fight would probably never have a chance to occur. Eckhart was a valuable man to a lot of important people, including the ones he worked for, but still, things change, he thought, and maybe someday Eckhart would botch up and then he wouldn't be so valuable and who knew what could happen then? Now he must stick to the business at hand, so all he said was, "He hasn't shown on the streets. Or if he has, nobody's seen him yet."

"He's got a passport," Eckhart said. "He could already be out of the country."

Mills shrugged. "Possibly," he said. He took a sip of his coffee, set the cup back down in the saucer. "But I don't think so. I don't think he could've traveled right away with his feet the way they were then. My guess is that he's hiding somewhere until they're better and then he'll try to leave."

"It's been almost a month," Eckhart said. "He could be well enough to move by now."

"I've got people watching the transportation," Mills said. "If he shows up, they'll see him."

Eckhart stood up. "I hope so," he said quietly. And Mills looked at him, hearing something in his voice. A threat? Again, he felt the anger rush through him, but he smiled pleasantly at the tall man. "Hope I haven't gotten you in any kind of a flap back in Vegas," he said, hoping just the opposite.

And then something strange happened.

He had expected Eckhart to say something like, "You know damned well you've gotten me in trouble," but Eckhart only smiled down at him. And it was a funny little smile that seemed somehow to change the entire appearance of his face, giving it a frozen look, the eyes going flat and lifeless. It was like, Mills thought, the face of one of those mannequins in department-store windows. The effect was chilling, and he was glad to suddenly hear voices outside his room and then see the nurse and orderly coming in the door. Still Eckhart kept the smile on him for a few more seconds, staring down at him, and then he turned around and looked at the nurse and the orderly, nodded to them, and when he turned back to Mills, the frozen smile was gone, the eyes were alive again, seeing. "I'll be talking to you later," Eckhart said, and then he turned and walked out of the room.

Mills stared at the door, listening to Eckhart's footsteps going away. Damn, he was a strange one! There had to be something amiss deep down at the bottom of a man like that, he thought. A man who killed to earn his living. He wondered what kind of private life Eckhart had back in Las Vegas, what kind of things he did to enjoy himself. Liquor? Mills thought not. He had never seen the man take more than one drink. Women? A good possibility. He smiled thinly. It wouldn't surprise him much to learn that Mr. Eckhart liked to be walked on by some tough-talking bird in spiked heels. It was amusing, really. He had long ago sensed Eckhart's distaste at his own particular fascination with pain. He knew that Eckhart considered him some kind of twisted deviant, and yet the man never saw anything the least bit twisted or warped in what he did—the cold, impersonal killing year after year for money.

"How are you feeling today?" the nurse asked him.

Mills looked up at her, smiled pleasantly. "Oh, I'm fine, love," he said. "Just fine." To hell with Eckhart, he thought. He'd lost Logan, so he'd do his job and help the cold bastard find him. If they didn't find Logan, Eckhart would have no obligation to pay him, but it wasn't really the money. He just didn't want it to get around that he had gotten careless, that was it.

No, it wasn't, he thought.

It was that he didn't want to *owe* Eckhart. One-on-one in that bare room—sure, he'd give that a try—but he did not like the idea of Eckhart going about thinking how he had messed things up for him. Eckhart was a dangerous man. Who could tell what went on in that mind of his? He didn't want to turn around someday and find himself looking into Eckhart's gun or wake up some night as the bastard was about to slit his throat. No, he'd help him find Logan. It wouldn't be all that difficult, providing the man hadn't left London, and he was pretty sure he was still in the city. Nobody on the run would want to risk traveling with burns like he'd given Logan.

And then there was something else, too.

Mills reached up, lightly fingered the edge of the bandage above his eyes. He smiled.

If Eckhart would go along with him, he'd like to spend a little time alone with Jerry Logan. Ten minutes should be enough.

"He looks better every time we come in here!" the orderly said to the nurse. He smiled at Mills. "Come on now. Up we go." He started to help Mills out of the bed, but Mills shrugged off his hand and sat down in the chair while the orderly began changing the sheets. The nurse shook down a thermometer, and Mills winked at her as she put it in his mouth. He wished the nurse had come alone, he thought. The orderly was a prancing little queer if he'd ever seen one. He had been flirting with the nurses ever since he'd begun to feel better. His head might be injured, but there was nothing wrong with the rest of him. He watched her now as she bent over, helping the orderly with the bed. Her ass and her legs looked good to him. He'd heard stories about nurses and male patients and had always wondered if there was any truth to them. Not all that difficult, he thought. Lock the door. Draw the curtains. Have an excuse ready if anybody came knocking. It wouldn't be the best of sex, he

thought. The best was to mix a little pain with the pleasure. Mills blinked, shook the fantasy out of his head.
The nurses were all cold fish anyway. He hadn't been
able to get a ripple out of any of them. Well, he'd be out
of this place in a week, he thought, and Eckhart and
Logan be damned. He was going to have some fun!

39

CHRIS BROUGHT SHEETS FOR HIM and a huge red quilt
that she said her grandmother had made and that had
been passed on to her when her own mother had died.
She set him up with everything he needed in the bathroom, and after their brandy and coffee, they had both
gone off to bed.

She had been right about the couch. It *was* comfortable. He laid there under the heavy quilt in the warm,
new-smelling darkness and he felt more relaxed and
better than he had felt in a long time, and he realized that
part of that feeling came just from knowing that he
wasn't by himself anymore. It was nice to know that just
out of the living room, through the kitchen and down the
short hallway, Chris was sleeping in her bed. And while
he thought about how much he'd like to be in that bed
with her, he was okay for now with things the way they
were and with just being able to think about it. He didn't
want to push her in any way at all. He sensed that to do
so would be a mistake. There were a lot of things they
didn't know about each other, and they needed time to
learn them. He hoped they would have that time.

He fell asleep and slept soundly, not waking until she was leaving for the hospital in the morning. She apologized for waking him and he told her no, that it was okay. There was a fresh pot of coffee on the stove in the kitchen, she said. She hoped it wouldn't be too strong for him. And then he sat up and asked her to come over to the couch for a minute and she came over to him and he took her hand, pulling her down to him and she was all fresh and cologned and he kissed her lightly on the cheek so he wouldn't kill her with his breath and she squeezed his shoulder and told him to take it easy during the day, to rest, and she would be back around five or a little after. Then she went out and closed the door and he sat there listening to her footsteps going away down the little walk to the street and the scent of her cologne stayed in the room.

He laid there for a few minutes thinking about her, about everything, and then he fell back asleep, and when he woke again the sun was bright behind the blue drapes that covered the window in back of the couch.

He got up and made his way into the bathroom on the crutches and washed up and shaved. Then he went out into the kitchen in his robe, poured himself a cup of coffee, carried the pot over to the table and sat down.

He had a lot of things to think about.

He had money. He might, if things went okay, even have a lady. He could already feel his feet getting better, and with Chris's help, they'd keep on getting better. Yeah, he thought. He definitely had some good things going for him.

And a lot of problems going for him, too.

There had to be a way out of it all. He was sick of the goddamned nervousness of being hunted. If things worked out with them, if they managed to get away, he wondered how long Eckhart would look for them.

A year? Two? *Five?*

He had no idea.

Roscoe came into the kitchen from the hallway then. Eyeing him, the big red cat moved out into the middle of the kitchen floor and plopped down. Jerry took another sip of his coffee and wondered how good their chances were if things worked out with Chris. Could they find someplace to go, some country where they could maybe live for a few years until Eckhart and whoever was backing him in Vegas finally got bored with looking for him and hung it up? There should be somewhere they could go, he thought. Back in Vegas, he'd heard several stories of guys who had really been involved with the Mob, had been a part of it, then ended up testifying against them for one reason or another. The government had a special program set up to handle cases like that. They relocated these guys in different places, fixed them up with new names, the works. He'd seen an interview on TV one time with one of the guys who'd done that kind of thing. They'd kept the guy's face in shadow, and they'd done something with the sound to change his voice. The guy had been living in some city in the States, even. He'd been there for almost ten years and the Mob had never found him, so it could be done.

How did they go about pulling off something like that? The trick to it probably had to be that you left no trail at all. Nothing. One day you were just gone. Your old life, friends, relatives, everything was just suddenly finished and you started all over again from square one. It sounded good. What relatives did he have any connection with anyway? None. Except maybe the old man, and even if he wasn't dead, which he most likely was, they wouldn't know one another if they sat across from each other in a barbershop. It was funny, but he had never thought about that before. Not just about the old man, but about how he really didn't have any family ties anymore. He never really knew his mother's family because they'd been way the hell up in Indiana and he'd never lived around them when he was growing up. They'd lived in upstate New York, where the old man was from, and the old man had hated his own family and they'd hated him, so there never were any great relationships formed on that end, either. And as for friends—well, a few in Vegas, but nothing so big that you'd keep up with them if you moved away. No, he was pretty much in the clear on that score. He didn't know about Chris, though, how she was about all that stuff. But if she was okay about it and they decided that they wanted to give it a shot being together, then trying to make it so that their old lives completely disappeared would probably be the way to go.

Or would it be?

Maybe not, he thought. Because even if it turned out to be okay with Chris and they could figure how to do it, to get away someplace and change their names and all the rest of it, he just wasn't sure he could be happy living like that. Not the way he felt now. Because no matter how safe it might look, there would always be that little outside chance that somebody might walk up to you one day on the street or there'd be a knock on the door some night and you'd just open it, not thinking anything, and it would all be over. Maybe you could learn to live with the threat of something like that after a while, adjust to it, but he knew he'd never really be comfortable with it.

No. The best way to be sure that it was all over, that you didn't have to worry about anybody waiting around the corner. But was that possible?

He passed most of the day thinking about it without coming up with any good answers.

When Chris came home from the hospital that evening, she was carrying two big bags of groceries. He headed for the living room when he heard her coming up the walk, and he felt like such a helpless fool because he couldn't even help her with the bags. He followed her into the kitchen and watched her put the groceries down on the table. "There!" she said. She looked at him, smiled. "So how was your day?"

"Pretty good," he said.

"Were you able to get back to sleep after I left?"

"Yeah," Jerry said. "Until after ten. Just like a bum."

"Wonderful! The rest will probably be really good for you." She hung her coat on the back of the chair at the table, took off her nurse's cap and put it over the back of her coat. He watched her as she unpinned her hair and shook it down. "What?" Chris said.

Jerry laughed, embarrassed. "You're just so *pretty*," he said.

She laughed, too, shook her head and started to unpack the groceries.

"Would you come over here please?" he said to her.

She stopped, her hands still inside the grocery bag, and for a minute he was afraid she wasn't going to do it, but she came over to him and he put his hands in her hair, pulled her down to him and kissed her. Her face was still cool from being outside in the cold.

"I missed you," he said, his hands on her shoulders.

"*Did* you? What did you do with yourself all day?"

"I just told you," he said. "I missed you."

"That's all?"

"That's it."

Chris took his hands from her shoulders. "I've got an idea," she said. "Why don't you sit down here at the table and I'll get the Scotch and soda and the glasses and everything and you can fix us both a drink while I put all of this away. You do like Scotch?"

"Sure," he said. He sat down in the chair and laid the crutches on the floor next to it. Roscoe walked over and sniffed at the crutches, looked up at him. "I don't think Roscoe likes me," Jerry said.

"Oh, he'll get used to you," Chris said, looking down at the big red cat. "He's just not used to anybody living here except me, that's all."

"That's good to hear."

She got down the Scotch and soda and two glasses. "You think that I invite every man I meet to live at my house, is that it?" she said to him.

"No. I didn't think you'd invite *me* to your house." He smiled at her. "But I'm sure glad you did."

"Me, too," she said. She put a small silver bowl full of ice cubes down on the table next to the glasses. "Now fix the drinks, please, while I start fixing dinner." She started taking things out of the bags and putting them away in the cabinets. "I didn't know what you like to eat," she said. "So I bought two steaks. Is that all right? You *do* eat steak?"

"Love it," he said, putting the ice into the tall glasses and then the Scotch, measuring with his eye. "You're really going to fix dinner?"

"I certainly am," Chris said. "I don't get to do it very often." She pulled a bottle of red wine out of the bag, held it up and looked at him. "I bought us this, too," she said. "It's burgundy. I don't know how good it is, though. I don't know anything about wine."

"Me neither," he said. Then, "Hey, look, you must've spent a lot of money on all this stuff. You should've told me. I would've given you some before you left."

"I'm not poor," she said.

"Beside the point," he said, stirring the drinks and handing her one. "I know you're not poor, but I also know I can't stay at your house with almost five hundred thousand dollars in a briefcase and still let you buy me groceries and fix me dinner. I'll pay rent, too, if you'll let me." He took out his billfold. "Now come on, Chris. How much did you spend?"

"This time," she said taking a sip of her drink, "let me buy the dinner."

"Chris . . ."

"This one time."

"Why?"

"Because I want to do it," she said.

He smiled at her, shook his head. "You're not one of those libber chicks, are you?" he said, teasing her.

"I just want to treat you to a nice dinner on the first night that you are a guest at my house," she said politely.

"*Last* night was my first night here."

"That doesn't count," she said. "And I am not any kind of a *chick*. How old do you think I am, anyway?"

"Six, maybe seven, tops."

That got her. She burst out laughing. "No, really," she said. "How old? Guess."

He looked at her for a minute. "Twenty-eight...thirty-two. Around there somewhere."

She put her drink down on the cabinet, began unwrapping the steaks. "How do you like your steak?" she asked him.

"Medium rare," he said. *"Well?"*

"Well, what?"

"Am I right or not? Twenty-eight? Thirty-two?"

"I'm certainly not going to tell you *that*," she said.

"Then why did you ask me to guess?"

"I just wanted to see what you thought," she said, smiling. "Now are we agreed on this dinner business? We'd better be or I won't fix it and then we'll both be drunk from these strong drinks and probably starve to death."

"Okay, *okay*," he said. He put his billfold back in his pocket. "But just this one time. And before we get off the subject, will you let me pay you some rent?"

"We'll talk about it later," she said. "Besides, your feet should be a great deal better in about a month."

"And then what? You're kicking me out?"

"Maybe," she said, grinning at him. "Or I'll nail the doors and windows shut so you can't leave."

THEY HAD a great dinner.

Steaks, baked potatoes, a big salad, the works, and it was all delicious and he ate like a lumberjack. After they had finished, they took the rest of the bottle of wine into the living room and he sat on the couch while Chris stretched out on the rug and played with Roscoe. He watched her for a while, feeling content and incredibly glad that he was here with her and not sitting in a hotel room in Zurich wondering what to do next. Chris rolled Roscoe over on his back, patted his stomach and then got up and went over to the small stereo against the wall and put on a record. "Miles Davis," she said to him, coming back and sitting down on the rug again. "Bluesy jazz. Do you like jazz?"

Jerry shrugged. "I guess," he said. "I haven't really heard all that much of it." He listened for a minute. "I like this for sure."

Chris leaned on one elbow, sipped at her wine and looked up at him. "That was quite an incredible story you told me back at the hotel," she said. "Really all true?"

"All true," he said.

"You're lucky you weren't killed."

Jerry nodded but didn't say anything.

"What do you think you'd like to do? After you're well and everything?"

"Keep seeing you," he said, and that sure was the truth.

"That's nice, but really. You won't be able to stay in London. Where will you go?"

"I don't know," he said softly. He didn't really feel like talking about it. He felt so good. He didn't want to start thinking about it all again and spoil the way he felt, but it was already too late.

"I'm not saying that you should do this or anything," Chris said, "but if you gave them back their money, would they still try to hurt you, do you think?"

Jerry laughed softly. He hadn't thought about giving the money back since that night in his trailer in Vegas. "That wouldn't change anything," he said. "It's that I took it and they probably think I might recognize the men who ran that guy down with the car. I wouldn't know them if they were sitting right here in this room, but they don't know that."

But that wasn't all of it.

He didn't want to go into it now, didn't want to try to explain it, but the truth was that at this point, after everything that had happened and as tired as he was of worrying about it all, and even wanting to be safe with her, he still would not give the money back even if that meant they would leave him alone. It wasn't just the money now. It was all that it could help change. He saw Chris watching him, and she moved over then against the back of the sofa and poured some more wine into his glass. He had forgotten he was even holding the wine.

"I don't want anything to happen to you," she said quietly.

Jerry looked down at her, smiled. "Me neither," he said. He thought for a minute. "Would you mind if I asked you something?"

"No. What?"

"You probably won't be able to answer it, but I want to ask you anyway. Right now," he said. "Right this minute, if you had to take a guess, do you think we might have a chance at something together?''

Chris didn't say anything for a minute. Then she said, ''You're right. I really can't answer that now. And even if I could, I might be wrong. But I like you a lot. *Damn!*'' She shook her head. ''I know that sounds like nothing to say, but believe me, it means more to me than it probably sounds to you.''

''Hey, it's okay,'' he said to her. ''I know it's too soon to go into any of that stuff. It was a stupid question.''

''I have a lot of really nice feelings about you,'' she said. ''But I'm not sure of them yet. I'm not sure *why* I'm having them.'' She frowned impatiently. ''I know that probably doesn't make any sense to you. If you knew me better, it would, though.''

''I know what you mean about not being sure how you feel,'' he said to her. ''I've been that way about a whole lot of things in my life.''

''There is something I want you to know,'' she said. ''Maybe it will help.'' She took a little sip of her wine and reached down and scratched Roscoe behind his ears. The huge cat opened his eyes at her touch, then closed them again and stretched contentedly. ''My husband was killed three years ago,'' she said softly. ''I loved him. Really loved him. But I made the mistake of putting my whole life into him instead of keeping some of me separate for myself, and so then when he got killed, I didn't have any of myself to lean on and I thought I was going to go crazy.''

She took another drink of her wine then, and he felt he ought to say something, but he didn't know what, so he just waited.

"I felt sorry for myself for such a long time," Chris said. "I really didn't care if I lived or died, and that's really something, because when I used to hear how people felt like that, I never could understand it. Maybe you've wondered about the men in my life. Well, there haven't been any. There should have been, but I was too wrapped up in being 'Poor Chris' to meet anybody." She shook her head. "I don't know, though. Maybe it was good that I didn't meet anybody then. It would've probably ended in a mess anyway. But finally I started getting myself together, and I decided that I wanted to have a good hold on myself before I got involved with another man. And now I've met you and I'm just not sure that I've got that hold yet." She laughed then. "I'm really botching this, aren't I?" she said. "That's why I became a nurse and not a radio broadcaster." She looked down at Roscoe, asleep beside her knees. "What I am trying to convey to you," she said, "is that I don't know how much of what I feel for you is because of *you* and how much of it might be because I've just been very lonely. But I can tell you this: you're the first man in a long time that I've been glad to meet."

Then she cracked up.

Laughing, she hit the cushion of the couch with her fist. Then she looked at him. "Oh, hell! I go through all of this, make you listen to it all, and what do I end up saying? That *I'm glad to meet you!*"

Jerry was laughing, too, then because he knew about that stuff. You try so damned hard to say just what's on your mind. You're determined to get it out right and it comes out sounding so simple that you feel stupid. He reached out and put his hand around the back of her neck, squeezing lightly. "I'm glad to meet *you*, too," he said. He caressed the back of her neck, moving his fingers up into her hair, looking into her face. Her eyes were shining from laughing. "You make me feel really good," he said to her, surprised because he had only been thinking that and then suddenly he was saying it.

Chris looked at him carefully. "I do?" she said. "Really?"

"Really."

And he pulled her face up to him then and kissed her and the feel and scent of her went straight to his head and for a minute she was with him, her arms tightening around his shoulders, and then he felt her tensing a little and he let go, still holding her, kissing her forehead, her eyes, and there were so many things he wanted to say to her and while he'd sure been getting better at saying the tough things, he couldn't find the words now. They all seemed to run together and so he just looked at her and didn't say any of them.

"I have to go to sleep soon," she said softly. "Would you like a brandy for a nightcap?"

"Sure," he said.

And she went away from being close to him then, and he watched her get up from the rug and walk out into the kitchen and he heard her getting the bottle of brandy and the glasses down out of the cabinet. He lit a cigarette and looked down at Roscoe, who now was sleeping with his big paws over his eyes like he had a headache. Jerry sat back on the couch and listened to Miles Davis and promised himself right then that he was going to do everything in the world that he could to have something with her, and then she was back with the brandy, and they didn't talk anymore, just sat there close, listening to the music, and after a while, it was time for her to go to bed and he thanked her for making the dinner and everything and told her how much he had enjoyed the night. He felt like he should leave the house now, the date over, and go home. He kissed her once more and she went out into the kitchen and down the little hall to her bedroom.

In her bed in the darkness, feeling warm and good from the dinner and the wine and the brandy, Chris turned over on her side, drew one knee up to her stomach and stretched her other leg. She snuggled her head deeper into the soft, fresh-smelling pillow and thought about the man on the couch in her living room. How she liked the feeling knowing there was a man in her house.

A *man?* she thought.

Or him?

Yes. *Him!*

She was pretty sure that she was really starting to care for him, that it wasn't just a matter of the first nice man being nice to her and all of that. And although she certainly didn't know him yet, didn't know what bad aspects of him might surface later after he was more sure of her, she still had the pleasant feeling inside that he would be the kind of man who would really love her and be good to her. Tonight she had felt how much he had wanted to make love to her and he couldn't know how much she had wanted it, too, and yet she still had not allowed it to happen. She thought about that and knew that her own fear was much of the reason. She had not told him how nervous she had been coming home from the hospital. How she had thought she'd seen at least a dozen suspicious-looking faces on the street and in the tube who seemed to be watching her with more than a passing interest, and how, later, when she'd stopped at the grocer's, she had actually jumped and cried out when old Mr. Crocker, who lived down the street, had come up behind her while she was trying to pick out the wine and, grabbing her elbow suddenly, had said, *"Ah! Drinking tonight, eh?"* And even though she believed the incredible story he had told her about the things that had happened to him, it had all seemed so bizarre that she found it difficult to think of it as something that had really happened, and it was not until she had watched him standing there on the walk with the streetlight on him after the taxi had driven away that she had seen the stark tension in his face, the very real wariness in his eyes, and suddenly then she had truly felt his fear, had realized that he really was in danger, that something terrible actually could happen to him and the possibility of that was making her very afraid of giving too much of herself to him. She was afraid for him.

For herself, too.

40

Lots of sleep behind him, showered, shaved and feeling wonderful, Hawker walked through the teeming night street toward the Red Duck.

It was cold as the devil, but he didn't mind the weather. The sharp night air in his face felt good to him. The cigarette he was smoking tasted fresh. Damn, but it was good to be out and around again! That first night had shaken him, to be sure. And was there a man anywhere who wouldn't have been shaken? he thought. Eighteen months in the jug, just out long enough to draw a good breath and your luck comes out sour like it had in that hotel room with the cripple. But that didn't bother him now. No sir! He'd had it right. Bad luck, that's all that had been. The fifty pounds he had in his pocket right this moment was proof enough of that. He'd caused the man to bump right into him there outside the bank and that had been that. The sketch had never noticed a thing. He'd even apologized for not watching where he was going. Hawker smiled, chuckled. Somebody passing waved, called out his name. He raised his hand, waved back, went on. There was a lesson to be learned from that night at the hotel. You took the bad luck for what it was and then went right on, that was the way to deal with it. Yes sir!

Hawker's long, bony face broke into a big grin as he walked through the door and into the warm, smoky noise of the Duck and saw old Dink, fat as ever, a glass of stout in one red beefy hand, a dart poised in the other, taking his aim, his eyes narrowed, concentrating, that little flush he always got in his face when he was hot on his game. Hawker stopped, his mouth open, his eyes going from Dink to the board and back. Somebody slapped him on the shoulder, said hello. He nodded, smiled. Dink's pudgy hand flashed forward. The dart flew. Hawker let out a yell. It mixed with the other yells. Elation from the winners, dismay from the losers who'd been foolish enough to bet against old Dink, thinking he couldn't hit the mark drinking like he did. What they didn't know was that his Sunday afternoon visits to his mum's grave were probably the only things Dink took more seriously than his darts.

Hawker slipped deftly through the crowd, squeezed in between tables and came up to Dink as he finished pulling money out of the outstretched hands of the losers. Dink stuffed the notes into the pockets of his pants and turned around. When he saw Hawker, his red, fleshy face split into an ear-to-ear grin and he roared, "Hawk! Did you see that one? Huh? By God! Did you see that throw?"

"Artistic!" Hawker shouted over the noise. "It was artistic, that's what it was! You're a bloody artist!"

"By God, it's the truth!" Dink bellowed, pumping his hand and pounding him on the shoulder. "Old Hawk!" he said. "Old Hawk! Back from the jug and just in time for me to buy him a drink, too!"

With Dink clearing a path, they pushed their way to a table and sat down. Dink ordered them each a pint and then looked across the table at his old friend, his eyes going carefully over Hawker's face. "Normal, I'd say," he said. "A little pale around the puss, but other than that, normal. Nothing that a few drinks and a little honest sin can't fix." Then Dink leaned forward a little, his face a touch more serious. "You *are* all right, aren't you, Hawk?"

Hawker grinned at him. "Feel twenty-one!" he said. The waitress put their drinks down on the table. "Well, *thirty*-one, anyway!"

Dink laughed, threw some money on the table and made a quick grab at the waitress's ass as she snapped it up and jumped back away from his hand.

There was no sense in telling him about it, Hawker thought. He was fine now, anyway. Eighteen months in the jug and only six along and what do they tell him one day? That he had the bug. The old consumption. And away they sent him to another jug where there's more sun and the air was a bit better and thanks to the good Lord, he shook it off.

Dink took a big drink of his stout, lifted one beefy finger and tapped his lower lip, looking at Hawker's. "Somebody's husband got long arms, Hawk?" he said, grinning.

Hawker grinned right back at him. "Yeah," he said, "but I've got longer legs." That would do fine, he thought. He hadn't decided on a good story to explain his cut lip yet, and an irate husband catching him in the act would be a good one. Dink would mention it around. Then one of these nights when they asked him about it, he'd build it into a beaut of a story. "So…" Hawker said, "tell me some news, Dink. Anything I should know that will interest me?"

Dink always knew the best of what was going on. Before he had settled down to taking fools' money with his darts, he'd been one of the best, *very* best pickpockets in the entire city of London. Now, older, spending his nights in the Duck, his old friends drifting in and out, Dink heard all the news. He leaned forward, his big elbows on the table, the pint between his hands. "It's been quiet as a church," he said. "Until a few weeks ago."

Hawker looked at him, waiting.

And Dink started talking.

When he had finished, Hawker picked up his glass, drained it and said he had to be off.

Dink looked at him shrewdly. "You ain't onto this already, are you Hawk?" he said, amazement plain in his voice.

Hawker looked across the table at his old friend. "Hey!" he said. "Who're you talking to here?"

Dink grinned. "The Hawk himself," he said.

"We'll be having a conversation soon," Hawker said.

"My cut as usual?" Dink asked. "If it's good?"

"As usual," Hawker said. He stood up. "See you, Dink."

"See you," Dink said to him.

Dink sat back and picked up his glass, nodding to himself. Old Hawk. Wasn't he something? Just back on the street and his eyes are working already. He watched the tall figure move away through the crowd toward the door. If Hawk was on it, if he had his teeth into it, this could be the best night in quite a while. Ten percent of a hundred pounds. Dink grinned, finished his glass, looked around the room. With his luck going this way, he thought, it was time to work himself up another game.

41

SWEAT RUNNING COLDLY DOWN his face, Eckhart turned on every light in his hotel room.

He went into the bathroom, twisted the cold-water spigot, cupped his palms under the stream and smacked the water up into his face once, twice, three times. He ran his wet fingers back through his hair, dried his face, quickly used his comb and went back out into his room. He looked out the window. It was just starting to get dark. He glanced at his watch. He'd been asleep almost two hours. He'd go downstairs, he thought. Have a cup of coffee. No. He'd have a drink. Yeah, good. He'd go down and have a short drink at the bar.

But he only stood looking out the window.

Christ, what a nightmare!

They had all come to his house.

He'd never seen the house before. It was little and had a tiny living room and, he remembered now, there had not been any furniture. The house had been empty. He had been standing in the living room and there was a knock on the door and somehow he had known that it was a bill collector. He thought that if he stayed very quiet, the bill collector would think there was nobody home and he would go away. So he just stood there, waiting, listening.

Another knock.

Another. *Harder.*

And then it wasn't knocking anymore. It was pounding. *Boom! Boom! Boom!* And he looked at the door and the wood in the center of it seemed to expand out toward him with every blow like it was made of rubber and he knew that it was not just one bill collector now but many, and outside the door, he could hear a lot of different voices. They weren't going to go away.

They *knew* he was in the house.

He didn't have the money to pay them. That was all there was to it. He'd just have to tell them. If they got mad, that was just too bad. He walked over to the little door, unlocked it and opened it.

Big mistake.

Because they were all there on the step.

All the ones that he had killed!

Some recent, some long forgotten. All of them moaning, screaming at him, screaming his name, waving bills in their pale, dead hands, fighting to get in the door at him.

And the old man made it first. The old man from years ago in Miami, the shock still on his white, made-up, casket face. The two burnt-edged bullet holes in his forehead pouring blood, his arm stretched out, his hand thrusting the bill at Eckhart as he backed away from them into the room.

And they kept coming.

Dixon now, the handcuff prints red circles around his wrists, his face ripped raw by the Doberman, his eyes mad with fear and hate, reaching.

Backing away from them, his arms up in front of his face, his heart pounding . . .

A fat man. His face ballooning out of shape as though it were being pumped full of air, tongue protruding out of his mouth and Eckhart remembered, yes, slipping the wire around his neck, a long time ago, pulling, pulling it.

He knew he had to get away from them and he turned around and ran into the house to the back door, but it was so little, as though it had been built for a child, and he knew he was going to have to duck way down to get through it and he could hear them in the living room screaming his name. He bent way down, almost to one knee, jerked open the door and looked straight into the fear-frozen face of the old waitress from the train depot back in Vegas, and he tried to back away from her but he wasn't fast enough and she reached for him, her white dead fingers clutching his shirt, pulling him in toward her, her mouth open, screaming the way she had screamed when he'd let her fall over the side of the dam, only louder now, and as she pulled him into her, closer, he looked down at her body and suddenly he was screaming too.

Because it wasn't her body.

It was The Lady's body!

Below the old, terror-stricken face was the beautiful, desirable body of The Lady and all his mind kept yelling at him was No, No! That was wrong! Wrong! She shouldn't be here! He hadn't killed her!

Only then it seemed like *that* was wrong.

It seemed that he remembered, *saw* himself doing it . . . yes . . . *yes!* He *had* killed her! That last time. In the morning after he had made love to her again, his hands holding her face, looking at her, kissing her.

His hands twisting once.

And now the face of the old waitress was a breath away from his own, her wide, terrified eyes boring into him, screaming in his face, and she pulled him backward then out through the little door and suddenly they were not in the house anymore. They were falling down the high dam, the wind cutting off their screams, choking him. . . .

Jesus!

Eckhart shook his head, trying to drive away the pictures of the nightmare, the feeling of it. He had to get out of the room. He snatched his coat off the back of a chair, put it on and was all the way to the door when the phone rang. He turned around, went back and picked it up.

"Hello?"

"Mills," the cheerful voice said.

"So what's up?"

"What's up is we've got him, sport!" Mills said, laughing. "We've got him!"

DOWNSTAIRS IN THE softly lit dimness of the hotel bar, Eckhart sat alone at a table and sipped a Scotch on the rocks. He was not thinking about what Mills had just told him on the phone. He was thinking about something else, something he felt he should do.

Ridiculous, he thought.

He took a long sip of the Scotch, looked down at the candle flickering on the table in front of him, the yellow flame slowly melting the wax in a little deepening circle around the dark hair of the wick.

He had her number in his book. It would only take a few minutes to make the call....

A *dream*, damnit, he told himself, hitting the word hard in his mind. A nightmare! You did not do anything like that!

Then why don't you make the call?

And the answer to that made him take another long drink of the Scotch and shrug his shoulders against the chill that was shooting up his back.

Because he wasn't sure.

And because he was afraid.

42

EVER SINCE HE'D BEEN a small boy, Hawker had always loved parks. They had been great places for him to wander around in and play in by himself. He'd always been able to forget he was in the city when he stepped into the park. At around the age of ten or eleven, there had been entire afternoons that he had spent high up in the branches of some tree in the park, watching the people and the goings-on below without anyone knowing he was there. And now, as an adult, he had always gone to the park when something was bothering him, or when he wanted to think without being disturbed. Give him anything serious and he'd pick the park to deal with it in.

Now he sat on his bench, smoking, not minding the damp cold for the cold had never been anything to bother him, and he watched the tall figure of a man walking across the grass toward him. He wasn't all that eager to do business with a man he didn't know. You had to be careful of things such as that, but then he had spoken to Mills on the phone and Mills had told him that *he* was working for this man, an American, and that the man had to hear the story himself before he would do business. Thinking about it, Hawker realized that the truth was, he'd rather do business with this American or almost anyone than deal with Mills in person.

Hawker was afraid of Mills.

And that was saying something, too. He'd met his share of bad ones in his time, no doubt about that, and he was no trembling leaf, but Mills was a bad one. A real bad one. He had worked for Mills several times over the past few years, keeping his eyes and ears open, helping him find this or that poor sketch who'd gambled and then had to run because he didn't have the money to pay up. Riding in Mills's car one time, Mills had told him a bit about his job. When somebody was on the hook and taking too long to pay the casino, Mills would go to see the man at his office or, if he had to, at his home. He was always polite and friendly that first visit, he'd told Hawker. He'd go in, sit down, maybe have a cup of coffee or a drink with the man, and then he'd talk to him in ever so gentlemanly a fashion about his situation. The casino valued him as a customer, Mills would say. And then he would try to work out some kind of plan, Mills would, so the sketch could pay off his debt a bit at a time. That done, they would shake hands and Mills would be on his way. If the man stuck tight with whatever arrangement they'd come up with, then Mills would not call or see him again.

But Mills hoped he wouldn't do that.

Mills hoped that something would happen so the man would not be able to keep his part of the bargain—or better yet, that he'd try to run and not pay at all.

Then Mills would see him again. Sooner or later, he would always see him again. And then, grinning and winking at Hawker, Mills said he could do the one thing that he enjoyed doing the most in life.

Causing pain.

At the time, Hawker had thought that Mills was just trying to frighten him pretty good, scare him about what a bad one he was. And then one time he saw close up, too damned close at that, just what Mr. Derik Mills was really capable of doing.

Hawker winced at the memory, took a long pull at his cigarette as he watched the tall figure coming closer.

A fat man, Hawker remembered. A banker, or at least he'd had something to do with banks. And he'd been really on the hook, too. Fifty, sixty thousand pounds, Mills had said. It had taken months to find the man, but finally, putting together a piece here, a bit there, they had tracked him to a run down hotel in London's East End. Hawker had taken Mills to the place, only that time, instead of just paying him off and letting him go, Mills had told him that he wanted him to be there when he confronted the man. Hawker had not wanted to go, but he was too afraid of Mills to refuse.

And he had never forgotten what had happened in that hotel room.

He had stayed by the door of the room, his back against it, while Mills, holding a gun, had forced the poor sketch to strip down to his shorts, and tied his hands behind him while the sketch went on about how sorry he was about all of it and how if Mills would only give him a chance, he'd set things right. Then Mills tied a handkerchief in the man's mouth and Hawker had felt the sweat breaking out under his arms because he knew the gag wasn't meant to stop the sketch from talking.

It was to keep him from screaming.

Pressed against the door, Hawker had watched as Mills removed his coat and then his belt. A white belt, Hawker remembered, with a shiny silver buckle. A big buckle.

Then it had started.

Mills let the buckle end of the belt hit the floor and started snaking it back and forth around in a circle, watching the man, smiling at him. Then, like lightning, he whipped the belt back in a wide circle and snapped it up from the floor, swinging it hard over his shoulder. The buckle smacked into the man's bare shoulder, the instantly swelling red welt oozing blood, the sketch's eyes crazy, backing away with Mills after him whirling the white belt until the poor bastard backed into a table and fell down on the floor. Mills towered over him, grinning, the belt making a whooshing sound in the air above his head before he whipped it down again and again.

Hawker had seen enough. He turned around, yanked open the door and ran down the steps, his heart pounding in his ears.

Now he pushed the unpleasant memory out of his mind as the tall man came up to the bench and stopped, looking down at him.

"Mr. Hawker?" Eckhart said to him.

"That's me," Hawker said, looking up at him. Younger than he'd expected, he thought. Nicely dressed. Looked like he could afford the hundred pounds Mills had said he would pay if he had the man he was looking for.

Eckhart glanced quickly around the bench, especially at the clump of shrubbery that grew on both sides of the big tree. There was maybe ten feet separating the shrubs from the back of the bench. That was good. Anybody who might be hiding there would have to cross the ten feet and he'd be ready by the time they got to him. He had not liked the idea of meeting anybody in the darkened park. It was too open a place, too full of shadows that could hide things. But Mills had told him that he knew this snitch and that it was some quirk of his always to meet in the park. The man was a street informer, Mills said. There was nothing to worry about from him. Probably true, Eckhart thought, but he'd still keep his eyes open. He said, "I've been told you can help me find a man I'm looking for."

The long, bony face smiled, nodded. "Sit down," Hawker said, gesturing at the bench. Eckhart sat, his body positioned so that he could watch Hawker and the shrubbery behind them. Hawker lit up a cigarette, offered him the pack. Eckhart shook his head. "A hundred pounds. That's what you're offering?" Hawker asked, getting right to business.

"If it's the right man."

"Payable to me in cash as soon as you know that?"

Eckhart nodded again, his eyes glancing quickly at the shrubs. If there was anybody there, he had just let it be known that he had the money in his pocket, but he saw no hint of any movement in the darkness. He put some impatience in his voice. "Let's hear it," he said. It was cold in the damned park and he'd skipped dinner to come here. He wanted to hear what this low-life had to say, pay him off and get rid of him.

Hawker took his cigarette out of his mouth, cleared his throat and spit on the grass. Then he told Eckhart the story he had told Mills over the phone about the American in the wheelchair. How he had thought he was a cripple when he'd seen the woman pushing him, and Eckhart interrupted him, asked him about the woman, what she had looked like, and then let him continue, and

Hawker told him of breaking into the hotel room and everything that had happened after he'd done it and how, as he was running out of the room, he'd seen that the man wasn't crippled at all. That he was injured, had bandages on both of his feet, and Eckhart listened to him, watching his face, and when Hawker had finished, he was sure that the man he was describing was Logan. Eckhart wondered about the woman. A man in Logan's situation might well hire a private nurse to look after him until he was able to get around again. He'd have to do something like that, in fact, or else put himself into a hospital. Still, it was not like Logan to let the woman take him outside into the city, where he might risk being seen. Logan was more careful than that. Unless maybe he was just going nuts cooped up in the hotel room and decided to chance it, or unless he thought that he was safe, that the city was too big. The woman bothered him. What if she wasn't a private nurse? What if she was some friend Logan had in London? How much would he have told her? How would he have explained his burned feet? Damnit! If the woman was a friend, then he'd have to deal with her, too. Logan had obviously not gone to the police or they would've been all over Mills by now, but of course Logan *wouldn't* go to the police. He wouldn't want to risk the involvement because of the money.

"So," Hawker said to him, "do you think this might be your man?"

"It could be," Eckhart said.

"I suppose you'll be wanting me to go along with you back to the hotel then?" Hawker stopped, confused. "But how're you going to get a look at him? Wait for him to come out of his room?'' It was obvious that Hawker looked on having to do something like that as a delay to him getting his money.

Eckhart looked at him, thinking. He didn't want this creep going anywhere with him. He was pretty sure that the guy in the hotel room was Logan. The best thing to do was to pay this snitch off now and get away from him. He didn't care about the money. If by some chance it turned out not to be Logan, so what? Since this Hawker knew Mills, he also probably knew enough to keep his mouth shut. ''You don't have to go with me to the hotel,'' Eckhart said to him. ''My friend tells me that you're reliable, and I think there's a chance that this is the man I'm looking for, so I'll just pay you now. If it turns out that I'm wrong, then that's not your problem.''

''You're saying that if it ain't him, I can keep the money?'' Hawker asked him, wanting to get that point very clear.

''That's it,'' Eckhart said.

''You're a fair man,'' Hawker said, impressed. He wished he had this one to deal with more often. ''And you needn't worry, sir, about a thing,'' he added. ''What happens from here on is none of my concern.''

Eckhart nodded, reached inside his pocket, took out the sheaf of notes, waited while Hawker counted them. Satisfied, Hawker folded the bills, put them in his pocket. Both men stood up. ''A pleasure, sir,'' Hawker said. He turned on his heels and walked off across the grass.

Eckhart stood and watched him. Now he would go somewhere, get something to eat and plan on how to handle Logan at the hotel.

HAWKER HURRIED across the park.

He walked through the wet grass with one hand in his pocket around the hundred pounds Eckhart had given him. *One hundred pounds!* A hell of a lot more than Mills had ever paid him, he thought. And for a lot less work, at that. And there he'd been thinking the whole business in that hotel room had been bad luck! If that sketch had broken open his damned head with that crutch, it still would've been worth it. A hundred pounds! He'd go to the Duck now, pull old Dink away from his darts for the night, give him his share like a gentleman of his word. He was glad to get away from that friend of Mills. He'd sniffed something about that man that he hadn't liked at all. Something bad. Bad like Mills himself, only different. Worse, maybe. He was quiet, the one back there, serious in the face, and Hawker had the feeling that he always looked that way. He'd bet both his shoes and his socks too that the man hardly ever had a laugh, and you for sure had to watch out for that kind. But then you had to watch out for the kind that were always *too* happy. Like Mills. Mills always looked like he was so happy, like he was one of the nicest chaps alive, and just look at the man he was! God, but that sketch with the bandages on his feet had his troubles. That one back there *and* Mills on his tail! But it was none of his affair anymore and he was glad of that. He'd get old Dink and they'd celebrate. Get drunk, maybe. No, not maybe. By God, they'd do it! They hadn't got drunk together in a long time. They'd go looking, too. Find themselves a couple of willing birds, have a time and feel like the devil tomorrow morning. A hundred pounds! The way bad luck could turn out to be good luck, Hawker thought. Really something!

BREATHING HEAVILY, Eckhart leaned back against the tree. The wind was blowing cold over him, but he could feel it hitting the thin layer of sweat on his neck and his chest. He reached up with one hand and wiped his eyes, blinked once, twice, looking around in the darkness.

What's the matter with you! his mind screamed at him.

Well, whatever it was, he had damned well better snap out of it. He hadn't been thinking straight lately. Sometimes it even seemed to him that he hadn't been thinking at all. It was as if he'd been asleep for a few minutes, only he hadn't been asleep. He had been walking, functioning, doing things.

Footsteps, now.

Eckhart straightened up, stepped back and around to one side of the tree. He forced himself to stand completely motionless. Like this tree, he thought, unaware of the little smile that came over his face at that joke. Stand *stilllll*...as this tree. His eyes stared coldly through the windy darkness at the approaching figure.

Maybe fifteen feet away and still coming.

Still as the tree! Eckhart thought.

Ten feet now, and he could hear the sound of the man's swinging arms slapping his coat as he walked.

Five feet...

A little more. A little closer...

Now!

Eckhart's fist flashed up past the side of his face as he took one quick step forward away from the tree, his arm thrusting forward, hard.

Hawker didn't even scream.

He only grunted heavily and stopped in mid-step as the point of the knife went straight into his throat. Eckhart stepped back, his hand jerking. Hawker began to fall, already dying, to the wet grass. Eckhart bent quickly over him, his hands going into his pockets, finding the money, and then he was walking away, blending into the deep darkness, disappearing.

On his back, Hawker's eyes stared up at the dark blowing branches of the tree and the last thing he ever did was give a little laugh at how good luck and bad luck could change places so fast.

But at least he was in the park.

BACK ON THE STREET, walking, Eckhart shivered now in the cold night wind. *Not careful, he thought. Not careful enough! You're not watching, not thinking. Not thinking, damnit! You don't leave strings like that so they lead back to you later. Think! Think! THINK! He saw your face! He knew you were going for the man he saw in the hotel. And who was he? A street snitch! A low-life who'd sell his mother's casket if there was enough money in it for him. And you're ready to let him go! To let him wander around because Mills said he was okay. Mills! Mills, who hates you anyway. Think!* So . . . all right. Taken care of. Mills is minus a street contact. No sweat. It would all make sense. He'd seen the guy, decided the information was good, paid him the money and left. They find him in the park. The money isn't on him. Dumb thing to do, walk around in a park late at night with so much money in your pocket. Even in safe old London. Mills would wonder about it all, of course, but he would never ask. He'd just find himself another pair of eyes on the street.

A short time later, Eckhart was sitting in the shadowy darkness of the bar in the Hilton where Jerry Logan had been staying. On the table in front of him was a whiskey with a lot of ice. He didn't like whiskey and that was exactly the reason he had ordered it. He knew he would only get through part of it. And it would help calm him down.

Logan's luck was still holding.

He stared down at the glass.

Fucking incredible!

Logan should never have run away with the money. He should've just stayed in Vegas that night and taken a fling at the tables. Hell, he'd probably have been rich enough by morning to pay Chambers back and still left town in his own plane. It was clear what had happened. After his thing with Mills, Logan knew there would be eyes looking for him, so he'd hidden himself away in the hotel until he was well enough to travel. Mills had guessed right about that. And then that crummy, low-life snitch breaks into his room. Logan thinks he's probably connected to you and he splits again.

So now what?

So now there were some questions unanswered. Did Logan go somewhere else to hide in the city? Or were his feet well enough by now that he could make a run for it? And who was the woman with him? For a ten-pound note, he'd picked up from the manager that yes, the woman had been with Logan when he'd checked out and that, yes, she had seemed like a private nurse the way she had been looking after him, but then she could've been a friend, too, and taking care of him.

The woman bothered Eckhart a lot.

Because if she was a friend, somebody Logan knew in the city, she would have a house or an apartment somewhere, and that was going to make it a lot more difficult to find him than if he was in another hotel.

And then came the heavy part.

If she was involved with him, how much had he told her? When he finally caught up with Logan again, would he find her there, too? And if he did . . .

A lot of questions, he thought.

He'd gotten from the manager that Logan was using the name Rodman, which could be something or nothing. It was a name to check for plane and hotel reservations, but it was nothing you could count on. Logan could change names without too much trouble.

Eckhart took another sip of his whiskey, realized that it was helping him. He was settling down a little. Easy to see how people could get hooked on booze, he thought. The secret to it was probably moderation. You took it when it helped you to have it, but even then you watched yourself, maybe set up a two-drink maximum for yourself or something like that.

Another sip. A longer one.

Eckhart smiled, leaned back in the straw chair.

And let his mind go away from Jerry Logan to something else. Something that he kept thinking about. If his own circumstances were not so ready to change at this time in his life, he would never have thought about it. It would have been impossible for him to do it and still operate his life on the strict rules that he'd always stuck to.

He lifted his glass, put it back down, his hand still around it.

He would find Logan, he thought. Finish that. Then he would disappear the way he had planned to do for years.

And he would take Al Chambers's money with him.

A half-million dollars to add to what he already had, which was plenty. He would be a wealthy man at the still-young age of thirty-eight. No Howard Hughes or anything that big, but still fat enough that he'd be able to live well in some nice, warm place with a lot of beaches.

Eckhart took another sip of the whiskey, chuckled softly.

It was funny, because if he did do that, it would make old fat ass right about him. It would justify his having him followed the way he had. But the really funny part of it was that he hadn't actually started thinking about taking the money until he found out that Chambers didn't trust him.

And then it had seemed like the perfect thing to do. Because, from his own standpoint, there was never a better time than now. The timing was everything. It was like he had thought back at O'Hare in Chicago, after Logan had gotten away from him. Why should he wait another two years to retire if he didn't have to? A lot of things could happen in two years. Bad things, maybe. Get sick or hurt—his work, after all, was dangerous. There was always the chance that something could go wrong no matter how careful you were.

And lately there had been that other stuff, too.

Scary shit.

Like that night after The Lady had gone to sleep. He took another drink, rolled the whiskey around in his mouth, swallowed it.

Did you do it? Did you *kill* her?

Nerves, he thought. Tension. Too much of it. Dangerous jobs of any kind eventually get to the men doing them, right? Cops. Air-traffic controllers, soldiers, whatever. You live like that for too long and you had to get crazy after a while, that was all.

He waved for the cocktail waitress, and when she came over, he ordered another drink, a Scotch this time. That would take care of his two-drink maximum. You have to stop thinking about that crazy stuff with The Lady, he thought. So maybe you're going through some kind of bad time in your head now. But you're not so fucked up that you could close out somebody and not even remember doing it. And besides, why would you kill The Lady? No reason.

He laughed out loud then just as the cocktail waitress came up to the table with his drink. She put it down, looked at him for a minute like she thought he was going to say something to her, tell her why he was laughing, and then when he didn't, she picked up the check, added the drink to it and went away again.

What had made him laugh was that he had only "hurt" The Lady once. And that had been during that one long day when he had screwed her so many times that she'd told him she was going to be too sore to even walk around her apartment. She had said that to him after he had gotten dressed and was ready to leave and it had turned him on so much that he had gotten undressed again and had her yet another time. So, no, he had to forget that crazy stuff. He hadn't done anything to her. If he did decide to take Chambers's money—and he was pretty sure now that he was going to do that—then when he slipped back to Vegas for the last time, he'd call her. Hell, maybe he'd even see her. She was some hunk of female, no question about it.

He took a sip of his new drink and turned his thoughts back to Logan. When he had first thought about keeping Chambers's money, he had also thought that maybe he would just let Logan go. He had no personal interest in killing him. If anything, he had begun to feel a certain admiration for the guy. He had a lot of moxie. You had to give him that. But then he'd thought more about it and decided that Logan could be of some use to him dead. It would help create a puzzle for Chambers, throw the fat slob off the track when he decided to track him down, which he was sure to do. Not that he worried about Chambers ever finding him. There was no chance of that. He had planned his getaway from Vegas for years. But it wouldn't hurt to throw a little confusion at him anyway. He would be gone. Logan would be gone. He would make sure Logan's body was never found. Chambers would not know what had happened. Which one of them had the money? Did Logan get away with it to some other part of the world? Or did Eckhart take it and run like he'd worried about him doing? Chambers wouldn't know. Maybe something had happened to him while he was chasing Logan. Maybe an old enemy had caught up with him along the way. That kind of thing happened now and then, and Chambers knew it.

Yes, Logan had to go.

And the woman, too, if she was with him.

He wondered how much Logan's feet had healed. Would he still have to wear bandages? Well, there was nothing to do now but sit and wait. In his years of sniffing out guys who'd run from their gambling debts, Mills had acquired a small army of eyes and ears on the streets. He could only hope that if Logan showed, they'd spot him.

He finished the Scotch, paid his check and left the hotel. Outside, it was cold and misting rain. He had the doorman get him a taxi. The driver had the heat on full blast and the inside of his cab was warm. Eckhart gave him the name of his hotel and settled back in the seat. The two drinks had done a lot to relax him, and now inside the heated cab moving through the late-night streets, he felt drowsy. He'd log some real sack time, he thought. Not leave a wake-up call, sleep until he woke up in the morning. He closed his eyes and thought about how his life was going to be changing soon. He felt good about his decision to get out. There were some things you were stupid to try to do for too long. He felt himself dozing, and as he did, he wondered if anybody had followed him when he had gone into the hotel or when he'd come out of it. He didn't think so. He woke up when the driver stopped the cab and turned on the inside lights. He paid him, got out and went into the hotel.

It didn't start to get him again until he was on his way up in the elevator.

He felt the muscles in his back and shoulders tighten and suddenly his heart was beating a little faster, then a lot faster, and it seemed like it was getting harder for him to breathe. He felt a deep feeling of nervousness rising up in him that made him want to scream or throw something.

Nervousness about *what!* he stormed at himself.

But he didn't know.

Only the feeling itself was there with nothing behind it to make any sense. Nothing to help him understand it so he could fight it, do something about it. The elevator doors opened and he stepped out, hurried away down the hall to his room and then had trouble with his key in the lock. Rage boiled in him because of that and he wanted to step back and put his foot through the door, but then he got it, the key turning all the way, and the door was open. He went inside, slammed it shut and flipped on the lights.

So *quiet!*

The room was so quiet. He glanced at his watch. Of course it was quiet. What the hell did you expect? He took off his coat, threw it at a chair. He looked around the room. No magazines, books, nothing. Not even a fucking newspaper! He went over to the TV and turned it on. He didn't care about watching it. He just wanted the sound of it in the room. He walked slowly over to the window, breathing deeply through his clenched teeth. He parted the curtain and looked down into the lights of the city. Rain was starting to fall now, streaking against the glass in front of his face. The city looked cold and ugly to him. He let go of the curtain, turned around and looked at the room. There was a movie of some kind on the TV, and the sounds of the actors' voices, the words in the room, were irritating to him, but he didn't want to turn it off. He thought about going out again, but he didn't know where he wanted to go. Eckhart swallowed, unclenched his fists at his sides, concentrated, forced himself to take several deep breaths. This-is-enough-of-this-shit! he told himself, hitting each word. You have got to pull it together and you've got to do it now. A hot bath might help, he thought. Make it as hot as you can stand it and just soak for a long time. You have done that before when things really got to you. It always helped a lot.

But this time it only helped a little.

Wearing only his shorts, he stretched out on the bed, his back and head resting against the two pillows he'd propped up against the headboard. The bath had helped ease the tightness a little in his back and shoulders, but the deep feeling of nameless dread stayed with him. He could feel that his body was tired, but his mind was so awake. He wondered if he just got up now, turned off the TV and lights and got back in bed, he might be able to go to sleep. He lay there and thought about that.

He stared at the moving figures on the TV screen and the memory of the nightmare he'd had came back to him again.

And so did the long, bony face of that street snitch in the park, his eyes popping in surprise, his mouth open, the knife in his throat.

Two, almost three hours later, he finally slipped off into sleep, the TV screen long blank and buzzing static, the lights in the room glaring.

43

CHRIS ALTMAN WAS THROUGH for the day.

Now she was anxious to check out and get home, take a shower, put on some cologne, brush her hair, slip into something comfortable.

And be with Jerry.

Jerry was changing the way she felt these days about a lot of things. Jerry was making her feel good. She was happier. Things, little irritations at the hospital that before would have bothered her, didn't faze her now. She found that she wasn't having to remind herself off and on throughout the day to perk up and be happy.

God, but she loved having him in the house!

And the house itself—that was another thing. It wasn't frightening to her anymore. Sometimes, especially on cold, ugly, gray winter nights, the empty house had looked sinister and frightening to her in the darkness and she hadn't wanted to go inside. But not anymore. Jerry was there now, waiting for her, and she could always tell by the look on his face how glad he was to see her. Now as she came out of the last room on her rounds, she frowned and stopped because she ran right into Nancy McLain.

Nancy liked to gossip.

No. Wrong. Nancy *loved* to gossip. It was a passion with her, like food or sex might be to someone else. As a nurse, she already had over ten years' experience, and at thirty-one, she was only three years older than Chris. Chris thought of Nancy as an excellent nurse, but as a woman, she could often be one real pain in the ass. She took a daily pleasure in learning little tidbits of infor-

mation about the personal lives of the other nurses who
worked around her. Short, a little heavy, with very
brightly alive dark eyes, Nancy would have been the
ideal gossip columnist if the hospital had had a newspaper. The odd thing was that almost everybody liked
her. Women who gossip are normally not popular, but
because Nancy was so pleasant and because she never
gossiped about anybody with malice in her face or in her
voice, she tended to be thought of only as a nice girl who
happened to be very nosy, a colorful character in the
otherwise formal atmosphere of the daily hospital routine. Nurse Madden had called Nancy into her office on
several occasions and talked to her about it, and then
Nancy had promptly gone out and gossiped about what
Nurse Madden had said to her. And when the other
nurses would openly tease her, Nancy would always
cheerfully defend herself by saying that she just happened to have a very "inquiring mind" and was very
interested in people, that was all, and what was so bad
about that? Nancy had at one time or another gotten
every one of the nurses on the floor to tell her something
about their personal life.

Everyone except Chris Altman.

Chris was Nancy's Mount Everest. She was determined to learn something about her private hours after
work. Oh, not that she didn't know her past. But *everyone* knew that Chris's husband had been a doctor and
that he had been killed in an auto accident, and that
Chris didn't seem to be interested in meeting any new
men, even after so long a time. The latter Nancy had
learned from various other girls on the floor, who had

attempted to get Chris to go pub crawling with them for hunting purposes.

But Nancy was after something *new!*

And now, looking at her, Chris saw that she had that certain sly look in her eyes. Chris had come to know that look. It broadcast to all that Nancy had acquired some piece of tasty information, and she braced herself because she could guess what had happened. There was only one other nurse on the entire floor that Chris shared details of her life with over an occasional cup of coffee at break or at lunch in the hospital cafeteria, and that girl was Millie.

"So . . . Chris," Nancy said, her smooth-cheeked, round face just barely holding back a big grin, "I hear you are taking in lodgers these days."

Damnit! Millie had fallen.

Nancy kept her for fifteen minutes.

At first, Chris had tried to save herself. She would like to talk, she'd said, but she *really* did have to leave. She was in a rush. But Nancy had looked her directly in the eyes, and she hadn't been able to hold back the grin any longer, and putting a look of mock amusement and astonishment on her face, she'd said, "Can't wait to get home these days, huh? Well . . . isn't *that* interesting!" The grin widened, the dark eyes sparkled.

And in spite of herself, Chris'd had to laugh. So yes, she'd told her. She *did* have a new boyfriend, as a matter of fact, and yes, he was an American, and yes, she had met him one night in Emergency, and yes, his feet had been badly burned, and yes, he was staying at her house, at least until he was better. And then Nancy had made her laugh again, saying that she was really lucky that he hadn't had an awful toothache or he'd most likely be living in some sexy dental technician's house instead of hers.

After Nancy had been satisfied and Chris was finally on her way home, she thought about how she really did feel lucky meeting Jerry, even if there was trouble connected with him. They would be careful. They would find a way to get away from it all. She had been careful of what she had said to Nancy, not telling her any of the important things. She'd given her the story of the auto-parts shop owner from Las Vegas on vacation in London. She was certain that there wasn't anyone Nancy could talk to who would find that information of any special interest, and she was right about that, because a short while later on Floor Six, the nurse that Nancy was telling about Chris and Jerry was also anxious to get home and she didn't know Chris Altman all that well anyway, so she wasn't very interested, not nearly as interested as the male patient with the head injury in the room just off the hall near where they were talking, and who probably would never have paid any attention at all to their conversation except now that he was better, he was also bored silly with being in the hospital and so he had just laid there, listening to them, thinking that maybe he might get an idea of the private life of the nurse Nancy was talking to, and who had been taking care of him for the last month, but had shown no interest at all in his advances.

AND LATER, as Chris Altman was hurrying up the street to her house, Derik Mills was talking on the phone, his pale blue eyes shining, his voice low but very cheerful.

44

IT WAS RAINING HARD. The window was misted up, and the wind blew the rain against the glass. Jerry Logan watched the drops run down behind the mist to the bottom of the window. Wearing his white terry-cloth bathrobe, he sat at the little table in the kitchen of Chris's house, lingering over his second cup of morning coffee and having another cigarette. It was only a little past eight, but already Chris had been gone for nearly two hours. The day stretched out before him. He took a drink of his coffee and turned his gaze again out the window at the old tree that grew behind the building. The kitchen window was too high up in the wall and he couldn't see the trunk of the tree, so he watched the black branches blowing against the dull gray sky and thought about what Eckhart had said to him back in the airport bar in Chicago. Eckhart had called him a thief.

True or false, he wondered.

True. If you looked at things for just what they were. Money was left in his cab. The money didn't belong to him. He had taken it anyway. And that was stealing no matter how you looked at it and so, yeah, that made him a thief.

So why didn't that bother him?

It probably doesn't bother you, he thought, because of the kind of people you stole the money from. There was probably a good chance that they had stolen it in one way or another from somebody else. There were a lot of ways you could steal. He would never have gone in to rob a bank, for instance, or say, some guy had just been riding in his cab, some regular fare, and when he'd dropped the guy off, he'd discovered that he'd left his briefcase behind, he would've turned it into the cab company and forgotten about it.

Yeah, he thought, but would you have turned it in if you knew there was a half-million bucks in cash in it?

He tapped the long ash off his cigarette end and thought about that one for a minute.

Yeah. He would've, he thought. He would've turned it in anyway. Not that he wouldn't have been tempted by it all. That was one hell of a lot of money and he was sure as hell no saint, but he was pretty certain that even though he might have thought about keeping it, those would've been only fantasy thoughts and he would've turned it in. So, he thought, what you're saying is that it's okay to steal, depending on whom you were stealing from?

He took another sip of his coffee.

Yeah, he thought, grinning. That was it. You're a thief, but you've got standards!

He listened to the soft, steady hum of the electric clock in the oven behind him and took his thoughts away from the question of his own morality or the lack of it and turned them to everything that was right now because those were the important things he had to deal with. He had been here a little over three weeks. His feet, thanks to Chris, were almost well. He wasn't wearing bandages anymore. He wore only white cotton socks. His feet and his legs halfway up his calves were a hairless, dark brownish color and looked like they'd been dipped in furniture stain. Using tweezers and a lot of careful patience, Chris had peeled away strip after strip of dead skin. He could walk now without the crutches and with only a little discomfort, a word he had picked up from Chris the Nurse and had teased her about. (''You mean *pain*. Why don't you say *pain?*'') So you can move now, he thought. It's time to quit messing around and get your act on the road.

He was in love with her.

There was no doubt about that in his mind. He wasn't falling anymore. He was there. The sight of her when she walked in the door in the evenings always sent the blood straight to his head, and though he was surprised at himself, surprised that, at his age, he could still feel that way, he liked the feeling.

And he hadn't kept his feelings from her, either, and he was proud of himself for that. He thought about the night she had told him that she was falling for him too. He had lain awake for hours hearing her words over and over again in his mind. It had been a long time since he'd felt as warm and as good as he had felt that night. Incredibly, he still had not made love to her. They both wanted to and they had talked about it. And too many nights he had thought he would go crazy, explode or something if he couldn't feel her all over him, feeling himself going into her. But he had stayed on the couch and in a strange way, it had been okay because—and he really wasn't too clear about this—he felt that it had to do with everything being so uncertain with him, and thus with them. Making love to her with all of that was scary for both of them because it represented to each a kind of final giving up to the other, a commitment and that was frightening and difficult for both of them for their own reasons.

Chris had told him all about her life before she met him, and listening to her, he had known that she was telling him all of it, really being honest with him, telling him the good parts and the bad parts too. She had told him of her own weaknesses. The way, after her husband had died, she had shut herself off from the world and spent too much time licking her wounds, feeling sorry for "poor Chris." He had a lot of respect for her. It had to have been a bitch pulling yourself out of something like that.

He had told her about himself, too. What there was to tell, which didn't come to a hell of a lot when you considered the years involved. The few affairs. The one very-close-to-marriage thing. Then a lot of time just moving around from one place and thing to another, all the time thinking that the day would come when his life would finally straighten out and have some direction and some meaning and then finally ending up in Vegas, just living, not thinking very much about things, dulled without really realizing it.

It was raining harder now, and he watched it slanting down through the black, bare branches of the old tree and he thought about what he had to tell her tonight, and he wondered again how she was going to react to all of it.

Today was Monday. He had lain awake most of Saturday night and Sunday night in the warm, now familiar smelling and sounding darkness, and smoked and thought about it and had come to the conclusion that it was the only way anything could ever be settled. It had all been suddenly clear to him and it had scared him then, thinking about it in the stillness of the night and it scared him now even more in the daylight.

He had decided not to run anymore.

Thinking about it, he could see that there was no real future in running. So they stayed lucky and managed to get out of London, out of England. So they went from country to country, city to city. There would always be something that they wouldn't know and that was whether or not there was *still* somebody after them, and the only way to really know that was to show your ass and then wait to see if somebody popped up and tried to blow it off.

Lovely. A great way to live, to start a life.

No, he thought again. He had to know they were okay, and there was only one way to know that.

He had to let this Eckhart find him. And see if he might go for a deal.

You're crazy, he thought, and that was how he had felt late in the night, lying on the couch when he had thought of it. Nuts! You are nuts! Why should the guy even listen to any kind of a deal with you?

And after a while, he thought he had an answer.

Because he wants the money.

And when he finds you, *you won't have it.*

He was pretty sure that Eckhart wouldn't do anything to him until he had the money. So he had to make sure that when he found him, there would be no way that he could get at it unless he was alive and well. And once Eckhart saw that was the way it was, he would go along with the deal.

Or rather, Eckhart would *pretend* to go along with the deal.

And *you'll* pretend, too, Jerry thought.

Then, somehow, you have to try to kill him.

He picked up his pack of cigarettes, shook one out and lit it. He stared down at the now-cold half-cup of coffee in front of him.

Aren't you something, he thought. Aren't you just something? And even as he thought about what he was— a forty-six-year-old man, a little overweight, a whole lot tired and a whole lot scared, who not too long ago had been pushing a hack around Vegas hustling for a living—even as he thought of all that, he knew, too, that in ways he didn't even understand now, he was not that man at all. He was somebody different.

He had formed a plan that he thought might work. A week ago, he had taken the money into the city and put it in a safe-deposit box at the bank, so it would be out of the house. He had arranged it so that nobody but Chris and himself could get into that box. He was going to start spending some time in the city. He would show himself around, be obvious, and sooner or later, Eckhart would find him. He had a feeling it wouldn't take him very long. Then he'd tell him first thing that he didn't have the money. He'd offer him half of it. And after that, he'd just have to play it all as it went down.

He put out his cigarette and went into the bathroom and showered and shaved. When he had finished and dressed, it was twenty-five minutes to eleven.

Chris wouldn't be home until around three-thirty.

He tried to read. No good. The TV. No good either.

The day crawled by.

He waited until they were through with dinner and were in the little living room having their usual brandy and coffee, with Chris stretched out on the rug, Roscoe beside her, dozing near her legs as she scratched behind his ears. Then, carefully, taking his time, he told her everything he planned to do, and after he had talked for a few minutes, he saw that she had stopped scratching Roscoe and that her lips were pressed tightly together and he thought she was going to cry.

He was wrong.

"You're going to let him find you?" she said when he had finished.

He nodded. "Yeah," he said quietly.

"You spend all this time hiding from him," Chris said, her voice slowly rising, "so you can get well. So we can figure out what the hell we are going to do and now that you're better and we can do that, you tell me that you're going to let him find you!"

"It's the best way," he said. "We can't—"

"It's *not* the best way!" she snapped at him. "What's the matter with you? Are you insane!"

Roscoe opened his eyes at her voice.

Chris stood up, looking down at him on the couch. "These people," she began, shaking her head, "how do you know that they don't have ways of getting into a safe-deposit box like that? You *don't* know! He could kill you in some stupid, bloody, goddamn hotel room and then just get the money and…" She stopped, glaring at him, but her eyes were bright with tears now and her hands at her sides were shaking. "Do you know what the hell I'm talking about?" she yelled at him. "I'm in love with you! Goddamn you, you bastard! I'm in love with you! I'd go anywhere with you. I'm ready to do something that crazy. And so now you tell me that you're going to

do something that might get you killed and—! Shut *up!*
I don't want to hear all the logical reasons why you're
doing it! It might get you *killed!*'' She was crying now,
tears running down her cheeks. "Then," she said,
"then what? Then where would it all be?"

He looked up at her, at her face, the way it was full of
fear for him, and he didn't say anything at first. He
picked up his brandy and took a long drink of it. He
wanted to make sure she had gotten it all out. Chris
reached down and picked up her glass from the rug and
drank, too, holding it, her eyes looking at Roscoe,
around the room, back at him. He motioned to the couch
next to him.

"Sit with me?" he asked her.

She only looked at him for a minute. Then, angrily,
wiping her eyes with her hand, she came over and sat
down next to him.

He reached over and took her hands. They were cold.
"I want you to know something," he said calmly. "I love
you. And I'm not sure I've ever been able to say that in
my life when at least part of it wasn't bullshit, but now
it's the way I really feel. I love you and I want to have a
life with you."

She started to pull her hands away, but he held her,
looking into her face. And then slowly he went over it
all again. The thing she was worried about, he told her,
him getting killed—well, if they just took off, that could
happen anyway. Maybe a year, maybe even five years
from now, but it could still happen. You can't stay lucky,
he told her. And he knew what she was thinking and he
said, "And no, I don't know for sure that we'd be followed for that long, but we *might* be. There'd always be

the chance of that and I don't want to live that way. This way, if I face up to it now and try to make some kind of deal with him, then maybe it'll work out okay."

Only he had trouble with that last part.

His voice wasn't convincing enough because this was the lying part of it and he tried to hide that, to keep it out of his eyes that he really wasn't telling her all of it, but she asked the question anyway. "How do you know," she asked him, "that if he makes a deal like that with you, he will keep his portion of it? That he won't just take his half of the money and still be hunting you?"

And for a brief second, he almost told her.

He almost yelled, I know he's not going to be following us because I'm going to kill him! But of course he couldn't say that to her so he held on to himself. He would never want her to know that he would think about doing something like that. In spite of how much you wanted to be honest with people, he thought, you still always ended up having some little secrets. She was really afraid for him, that something would happen to him, and she was scared for both of them about that. Seeing the way she felt about him, the fear and caring in her eyes, he felt rotten and guilty that he couldn't tell her the truth, which was that his chances of getting hurt or killed were even greater than she thought because of what he now planned to do. He had come into her life and she was loving him and now he was going to lay her open to maybe having a lot of pain and grief in her life again.

He forced these thoughts out of his mind, but they would come back at him later. He knew that.

From now on, he had to concentrate only on what he had to do. So now, he told her, there wasn't any guarantee that Eckhart wouldn't come after them once he had been given the money, but if he didn't try to make a deal, if he didn't give that a shot, then he would for sure be following their footsteps. It was a crapshoot, he said, but he felt like it was better than not trying anything at all.

As he talked to her, he worked hard at looking and sounding convincing. "Who knows?" he said. "The guy's over here in London. A chance at all that money. He could make up a story to give to the people back in Vegas who hired him. He could say—what? He could say. . . that he had just lost me over here. Yeah, he could call back to Vegas and tell them that he had lost me and that I could be anywhere in Europe, for all he knew.

"He might go for it," he said earnestly. "A quarter of a million bucks—not small change . . ."

Chris listened to all of it, and while there was a part of her that almost hated him for even thinking about taking such a risk, there was a bigger part of her, she realized for sure now, that loved him, and from his face and his voice, she knew that he had made up his mind about it. And she knew, too, that she would go along with him and not run away like the scared part of her wanted to. That was one of the things about falling in love that people always fooled themselves about, she thought. They always tried to be careful about it, especially if there had been a bad time before. But that was only a game because you could only be careful *before* you were in love. Once it had happened, it overpowered the being careful without any trouble and made you not care about it even if you wanted to. Now she took another drink of her brandy and began to get control of herself. She stopped crying and her hands were not trembling quite so much anymore.

She sat back on the rug and ruffled Roscoe's thick, reddish fur with her fingers. The big cat yawned and stretched himself out full-length. Jerry was waiting, sipping at his brandy, smoking, watching her, his face shadowy in the dimmed light of the room. "When are you going to do this?" she asked quietly.

"Tomorrow," he said. "I don't want to wait around about it. There's no need to drag it out and make it any harder for us. I got a bag packed. I'll go into the city in the morning and find a hotel."

"Then I'm not going to see you for a while?"

"Not for a while."

"How long do you think it will take?" she asked him.

"I don't know," he said. "Probably not too long, though, if I'm out and show myself around."

"I'm going to miss you."

"I miss you already."

"I guess I don't have to tell you to be careful," she said to him. "Please, *please* be careful!"

"Don't worry. I can't let anything happen to me now."

"I keep thinking that we should *do* something—I don't know—something ordinary, like call the police and have the man arrested or something."

He smiled at her and shook his head. "We can't do that."

"I know. Will you call me from the hotel?"

"No," he said gently. "I can't. It's not a good idea. And besides, there's something I want you to do for me."

"You can't call me to let me know what is happening! I'll be crazy!"

"I can't call you. Now, listen to me. Can you get a few days away from the hospital?"

"Why?"

"Can you? Tell them you're sick. Or do you have some vacation you could take or something, however they work it?"

"Yes. Why?"

"Because I want you to go away for a while until I call you. Do you know somewhere you could go?"

"I think so, yes. But you've got to tell me why you want me to do that. And what about Roscoe?"

"He'll be okay. Can't you just do it without making me explain it?"

"I could do that," she said. "But I won't. Why do you want me to go away?"

Jerry sighed. "Chris, I don't know how much ground they've gained on me by now. I don't know if they've found out about you or not, but I don't want to take any chances if they have." He looked down at his cigarettes on the couch cushion and picked them up. "This creep will probably make a deal with me," he said, still trying to sound convincing. "They're all hungry for money anyway. But I don't want him to have a choice. I don't want him to think that he can have it all by getting to me through you."

"You're afraid they might still come here after you're gone?" She was trying to keep the fear out of her voice, but it was there.

"Look," he said to her, "try not to worry that much about it, okay? They probably don't even know about you. I don't see how they could, as a matter of fact, but

NIGHT OF THE RUNNING MAN   365

I want to be careful, that's all. I'm going to have a lot of things on my mind. It'll help me if I know you're out of here and away somewhere.''

"I've got a friend," Chris said, "in Sussex. I could go there.''

"A friend that's a girl, I hope?"

"You're jealous?"

"Picked right up on that, huh?''

She laughed softly, looking at him. "I'm really in love with you,'' she said.

And the way she said it—the way she was looking at him—well, it really did something to him all of a sudden and he just sat there and looked at her like an idiot.

"You know something that's really too bad?'' she said.

"What?''

Chris took his hand in both of hers and brought it up to her face. "Love's out of style now," she said. "Do you know what I mean? I don't mean that people don't still fall in love. They do. But nobody talks very much about *romance* anymore. It's like you're supposed to be embarrassed if you talk about it, if you feel romantic or think something is romantic, then you're being silly or not acting your age or not being realistic or sophisticated or all of that.''

He nodded. "Yeah," he said. "I think I know what you mean.'' He knew what she meant all right. He knew because that was just the way he had been for how long now? A long time, anyway. Love. What was that? That's the way he had been about it. Love was sweet sixteen and meeting some chick at the football game in October and giving her your ring on a chain to wear around her neck. You grew out of that stuff.

Right, he thought. And look at you now, baby! Just look at you now!

"Well?" Chris said to him.

"Well, what?"

"Are you sure you're in love with me?"

Jerry nodded. "Very," he said.

"Say it. I want to hear it again."

"I love you," he said, and he was a little surprised at how easy it was for him to just say it like that, and then he let her have it all. "It's like this," he told her. "I just look at you and no matter what's bothering me, what's on my mind, it goes away. I'm not kidding. It's everything. The way you look. The way you talk to me, listen to me. I kiss you and you leave the house and I go nuts all day wanting you to come home . . ." He stopped himself then, shaking his head, laughing, not believing he had said all that to her, and then his arms were around the back of her neck, pulling her to him.

He kissed her and she held onto him hard for a minute, then pulled away, her face close, and she whispered, "I have this special bottle of wine. I've been saving it."

She slipped out of his arms and away off the couch and he leaned back and looked up at the ceiling. He felt good. Even with everything that was coming up, he felt good! Man, you have been so lucky! So lucky! he thought. And then along with the warm, beautiful feeling of all of it came the reality, too. The way things were. The way they had to be taken care of, and he thought, *Lady, stay with me for just a little longer, okay? Just so nothing can hurt all of this for us. I won't ask for anymore luck after that. No more. Zip. We'll be square.*

He was suddenly aware that he hadn't heard her in the kitchen, and then he heard the soft pop of the cork as she pulled it out of the bottle of wine and the clinking of the glasses and then she was standing in the doorway to the kitchen, the wine bottle in one hand, the glasses in the other, her two fingers holding them together at the stems. But he only saw the bottle and the glasses for a fraction of an instant and then his mouth was suddenly dry and he felt a rush of electricity pass all through him.

She had changed clothes.

The strawberry-blond hair had been given a quick brush and now swirled down around her face and shoulders. The nightgown was a filmy baby blue and went all the way to the floor. She looked stunning, sexy, beautiful, exciting—the adjectives clicked through his head.

"Do you like it?" she asked, coming over to him.

"Wow!" he said softly.

Chris laughed. "I don't really know if it's a *wow* or not," she said, but the pleasure was there in her voice that he thought it was. She put the bottle and the glasses down on the little drink table in front of the sofa. "I just didn't feel like lounging around in my blue jeans and blouse," she said as though she felt she had to try to offer him some kind of explanation even though they both knew it was a lie. Carefully she tilted the bottle, and the wine splashed softly into the tall, clear glasses, turning them red.

"Thank you," he said.

"Don't thank me so quickly," she said. "You may not like it. I don't know that much about wine, really, but the man at the shop told me it was good."

"I meant for putting that on for me. You look really beautiful."

"Thank *you*," she said. "That's enough of that, please. Here."

He took the glass from her, and she picked up hers from the table and sat down next to him on the couch. The closeness of her in the thin blue gown and the scent of her perfume was really more than he could handle and he was glad that they were both holding glasses of wine or he would probably have made a fool of himself.

Chris raised her glass. "To good things," she said softly, looking at him. "And that," and there was no keeping the worry from coming into her voice, "you'll be safe and all right and everything."

"To us," he added. "To everything down the road."

They brought the two glasses together, and on the rug, Roscoe looked up sleepily at the sound and, seeing nothing that interested him, closed his eyes again and rested his chin back down on his big paws. The wine tasted as good as it smelled, and as he drank it, Jerry was aware that the rain had started up again. He could hear the wind blowing and the drops hitting the window behind the couch.

"Do you like it?" Chris said.

"It's nice," he said. He set his glass on the drink table. "Would you put that down please?" he said to her. She smiled at him and the glass had barely touched the table before he was pulling her to him. He kissed her gently a couple of times and looked at her, smiling, running his fingertips slowly over her face and she watched his eyes and knew that he had not been lying to her. He really did love her and that made her happy, but it made her feel desperate and scared, too, and she felt again that she needed to do something so he wouldn't go away from her and maybe change things, but she didn't know what she could do and then he was kissing her again, his arms around her bare shoulders and she felt a lot of things finally breaking loose inside her and she held onto him and forgot about everything but being with him now and holding onto him, and then he was picking her up and carrying her into the bedroom and they made love fiercely at first and then he held her under the sheet, her head resting on his chest, his hand lightly caressing her hair, talking softly in the warm darkness and he told her that if a guy could be sure of having a few times like this in his life, it would all be worth it, and they made love again, slower this time, more gently, and then he pulled the blankets up close around them and they fell asleep.

HE WOKE SUDDENLY sometime deep in the night, and the wind was blowing very hard, and he could hear it whipping the rain against the bedroom window. He snuggled down a little more under the blankets and Chris stirred slightly, moved closer to him in her sleep. He looked down at the end of the bed and saw the round form of Roscoe sleeping on the top of the blankets near her feet. He wondered how late it was, how long before daylight. And that started things running through his head that he didn't want to think about now, and to keep them out of his mind, he turned his head on the pillow and looked at Chris, listened to her steady breathing and thought about the way it had been tonight and how much he wanted everything to work out. He looked at her face and thought, *Jesus, don't let this go to hell on me!* and after a while, he was able to fall asleep again and the next time he woke up it was daylight and Roscoe was gone from the bed.

He glanced at Chris's clock and knew the alarm would be going off soon and he slipped quietly out of bed and, shivering a little in the chilly room, put on his pants and shirt to go in and make coffee for them and as he walked into the kitchen he saw Roscoe running to him because he was hungry and then he looked over and saw Eckhart sitting at the kitchen table with the gun in front of him.

45

JERRY FROZE. Roscoe rubbed against his legs, meowing softly for his breakfast.

"Don't do anything stupid," Eckhart said, looking at him. He motioned to the chair at the opposite end of the little table. "Just sit down. We've got some things to talk about."

Jerry hesitated, and Eckhart read his mind. "I'm telling you," he said. "Don't do anything stupid." He pointed to the gun. "This is ready to fire, and I can hit you long before you could do anything anyway, so sit down. If I wanted you dead, I'd have shot both of you back there in the bed."

Jerry pulled the chair back from the table and sat down. Roscoe looked at him, disappointed, and walked over near his dish and spread himself out on the floor. "How did you get here?" Jerry asked him.

Eckhart rested his hand on the table near the gun and shook his head. "Not important," he said quietly. "I'm here. You know why I'm here. I want the money you stole." He smiled, and across the table, Jerry felt a chill pass up his spine. There was something wrong with the smile. It was like a smile on the face of a dead man. "I'd like to kill you," Eckhart said. "You've caused me a lot of trouble." He nodded slowly and the smile went away from his face. "A lot of trouble," he repeated, "but then," he sighed, "it's like I told you back in Chicago. I've been hired to get back the money you took, that's all. Now why don't we just go get it and I'll leave before your girl friend wakes up." He glanced at his watch. "She'll have to be getting up soon to go to the hospital."

So he knew about Chris. That was how he got here. "I don't have the money," Jerry said. He was afraid, he realized, but it was different now. He wasn't terrified anymore. He was just starting what he had planned on starting anyway, only he was starting it earlier.

"You don't have the money," Eckhart said, and his voice sounded tired. "*Why* don't you have the money? With your feet the way they've been, you haven't been in too great shape to run around spending it all."

"I don't mean I don't have it anymore," Jerry said. "I mean I don't have it *here*. After you broke into my room at the hotel, I knew I'd probably be seeing you again, so I put the money in a bank. In a safe-deposit box."

"I don't think so," Eckhart said quietly. "And I never broke into your hotel room. It was somebody else." He saw the look of disbelief come into Jerry's face. "I'm not lying to you," he said. "It wasn't me. But I think you've got the money. I think it's probably in your briefcase, put away somewhere here in the house."

And again, the dead man's smile was back.

Eckhart picked up the gun. "I told you that I wasn't hired to hurt you or kill you," he said softly, "but if that's what I have to do to get the money back from you, that's what I'll do. You've been a very lucky man up to now, so don't start being stupid." The smile faded again. "I want to tell you something," Eckhart said, "and I want you to know I mean it. If you don't get up with me right now and go and get me that briefcase, I am going to shoot you in the legs and then I'm going to drag you in there and you are going to watch me shoot your girl friend. Now don't be stupid. I'm telling you."

For a moment, Jerry couldn't find his voice. The terrible cold-blooded bluntness of the threat had silenced him. He took a deep breath and looked across the table. "The money's in the safe-deposit box," he said. "I can show you the receipt."

Eckhart looked at him for a minute, his eyes boring into him, and in that minute of cold silence, Jerry heard something he had been dreading to hear.

From the bedroom came the muted ringing of Chris's alarm clock.

"I think your girl friend is getting up," Eckhart said.

"You want to see the receipt or not?" Jerry snapped at him, because now he did not feel fear for this sonofabitch. This sick sonofabitch! He was not going to shoot Chris, he thought. He was not going to do anything to Chris and those thoughts had only just gone through his mind when something inside him slapped him hard and told him that he had to stay as calm now as he could, not let his temper, his anger get the best of him or everything would probably be over for him and for Chris, because he told himself, this guy is a killer— one of those guys who kills for money and this ain't the movies. You try to be a tough guy or a hero or something dumb like that and you're going to be dead. So okay, okay. . .

"I've got it in my billfold," he said.

Eckhart nodded.

He raised up on the chair and pulled his billfold out of his back pocket. He opened it and quickly flipped through the little plastic holders—where did he put the damned thing? And then he found it, spreading the plastic, sticking his index finger inside and pulling it out. He dropped the billfold on the table, tossed the receipt over to Eckhart.

Eckhart picked it up, read it.

"Let me stop her," Jerry said. "I don't want her to see you. She's not really part of this."

Eckhart dropped the receipt on the table. Television, he thought. Everybody watches too much television. His girl friend doesn't see me, then nothing will happen to her. "So stop her," he said. "From the *door!*"

Jerry pushed his chair back, got up and walked down the short hall to the bedroom. Behind him, he heard Eckhart turning his chair at the table so he could watch him. He looked into the bedroom.

Chris was sitting up in the bed, leaning back against the headboard, trying to wake up. She saw him and smiled. "What're you doing?" she said. "I wondered where you'd gone to. I thought you made love to me and then ran away."

"Listen to me, okay?" he said to her, and she really looked at him then and she knew something was wrong.

"What?" she said. "What is it?"

"There's somebody here," he said quietly. "That man I told you about."

Chris jerked forward, away from the headboard, her face instantly afraid. "What do you mean?" she said, looking at him then in the doorway where he was standing. "He's *here?* What do you mean?"

"I have to talk to him now," Jerry said. "Don't worry. I have to talk to him about some things. I don't want you to come out. I want you to stay in here. I'm going to close the door and I want you to stay in here."

She started to get up from the bed.

"Chris!" he snapped at her, his eyes glaring. "I don't want you in it!"

She stopped moving then, staring at him, her eyes frightened, confused.

"I don't want you to see him," he said to her, his voice quieter again. "If you don't see him, it'll be okay." He looked at her, hoping his voice sounded convincing.

Because he knew that whether she saw Eckhart or not wouldn't make any difference. He only wanted her in the bedroom so if things did go wrong, she wouldn't be right there, close, where she was sure to get hurt. *"Please!"* he said to her, and he was raising his hand to point to the window, to motion for her to try and get out of the house through it, but he pointed at her instead.

Because he'd felt Eckhart move up behind him.

As he started to turn around, Eckhart shoved him in the back, sending him stumbling off balance into the bedroom. Chris let out a short scream. Jerry kept his balance. Eckhart stood in the doorway, looking at them.

"I am *very* tired of messing around with you, you dud!" Eckhart said. "Now you are going to find something, a piece of rope, some neckties of yours, something, and you're going to tie her up, and then we are going to that bank and you are going to give me that money. Now get your ass in gear!"

Jerry looked at Chris sitting up on the bed, holding the blankets close around her, her eyes staring at him, wide with fear, her face pale in the gray light of the day coming in through the bedroom window, and he knew in an instant that there was no way he could let any of this happen. If they left her tied up here in the flat, there was a good chance that Eckhart had somebody waiting to come in as soon as they were out of sight, somebody to kill her. And he had not yet spoken a word about the deal he'd planned. He knew and Eckhart knew, too, that if he went to the bank with him now he'd have to give him the money because of Chris being here. That he'd probably tell him she'd be killed if he didn't, when the truth of it would be that she'd be killed no matter what he did. And then once the bastard had the money in his hands, once he had what he'd come for, Jerry was sure he would kill him, too. So now he looked away from Chris and over at the tall man standing impatiently in the doorway. And his voice was dead calm when he said it:

"No."

Eckhart raised the gun. "You really want to make me kill both of you, don't you?"

And watching him, Jerry could see that Eckhart was searching his face, looking for the fear he was trying to build. "Don't do anything stupid," he said evenly. "You'll never get into that safe-deposit box without me. I've got a proposition for you. Why don't you listen to it?"

Eckhart looked at him, surprised and even impressed, though he kept his face impassive. He had really been right about this guy. He had read the situation and decided to take his chances. Well, let's see, he thought. He turned the gun straight at the woman on the bed. "I told you what would happen," he said quietly.

And just as quietly, Jerry Logan said, "If you do anything to her, you sonofabitch, I can promise you that you'll never see that money. None of it. Because I won't give a shit what you do to me."

Well! The guy had come a long way from when he'd had him in that bar at the airport, Eckhart thought. But then there hadn't been a woman involved back at that point. Really something, he thought, the things a man will do sometimes for a woman. But he'd played his hand. Now he'd listen. He really wanted that money. This thing could wait. Slowly, he lowered the gun to his side. "So talk," he said. "I'm listening."

"Not in here," Jerry said, because he really didn't want Chris to hear any of it.

Eckhart shrugged and backed out into the hall.

Jerry looked quickly at Chris. "I'll be back in a few minutes," he said. Then he went out of the bedroom in front of Eckhart and closed the door behind him.

They sat back down at the kitchen table, and Jerry told Eckhart just what he had planned to tell him. He forced himself to be calm, to speak quietly, to make it all sound very matter-of-fact. "You want the money," he told Eckhart. "And I think that as soon as you've got it, you'll kill me and probably her, too, since she's involved with me and you don't know how much I've told her. So the money is all I've got to cover my ass now. That's why I have to make you this proposition. I don't have any choice," he said to him. "So I'll give you half the money—two hundred and fifty grand. I'll go to the bank and get it today, but I'll go *by myself* or I won't go at all. You come back here tonight at eight and I'll give it to you. Then that's it. You leave and you stay off my ass."

Eckhart listened, and he thought how funny it was the way things could work out sometimes, the way things could change. If everything was the way it had been originally, if he was just out to do this job for Chambers and get his money back instead of keeping it himself like he now planned to do, and if he hadn't been thinking about getting out of it all and disappearing—well, things would be very different now. He would just take the woman and keep her until Logan got the money. He was sure that would work in spite of what Logan had said about him never seeing any money if he hurt her. The guy was obviously crazy about her. He wouldn't be able to stand the thought of anything happening to her because of him.

But things *were* different now. And doing that whole number with the woman would take time and trouble, and then, too, he knew there was no telling what kind of crazy thing Logan might try. He might even bring the cops into it then. So he said, "Just for conversation's sake, what makes you think I could go back to the people who hired me with only half of their money? What do I tell them happened to the rest of it?"

Jerry Logan smiled at him. "Stop fucking around with me," he said. "I don't give a damn about who hired you. I'm offering *you* the money. What you do with it and what your problems are ain't shit to me. You'd be here in Europe with two hundred and fifty grand. Who's to know that you ever found me or the money?"

Eckhart looked at him thoughtfully. "How do you know I won't come after you anyway? Once you've paid me."

Jerry shrugged. "I don't," he said, "but I can tell you that you're going to have a hard time getting the rest of that money if you do, because I won't be carrying it with me anymore. I'll just have it transferred from one bank to another, wherever I go."

Eckhart almost laughed. Not stupid, he thought again. It was a good plan. He looked at Logan, tossed the receipt for the safe-deposit box back over in front of him. "This stuff is just business with me," Eckhart said simply. "You know what I mean? You've been lucky, but you've used your head, too. And the way it is— you're right about the situation. It's got some good points. A quarter of a million dollars is better than nothing, right?"

"Right," Jerry said, not believing a word of it.

The dead man's smile was back on Eckhart's face again. "You know," he said softly, "back there in Chicago, in the airport at the gate—" The smile widened. "I was going to kill you," Eckhart said. "I had a knife."

Jerry only looked at him.

The glaze passed out of Eckhart's eyes. The smile faded again. He pushed back the chair. "Eight tonight?" he said.

"I'll be there," Jerry said.

"I want to tell you something," Eckhart said. "You fuck me over—you don't show and you run—money or whatever, I'm going to kill you." He turned his head quickly and looked toward the bedroom. "And I'll kill her, too. Now, you think about that."

Then he got up and walked out of the kitchen into the living room, and Jerry heard him open the door and then there was the sound of it closing, and for the first time, he realized that he didn't even know how the bastard had gotten in the house. A window, maybe, or he'd worked the lock on the door. It didn't matter now. He looked down at the receipt for the safe-deposit box. Then he got up and went into the bedroom to see Chris.

She was still sitting on the bed, only she had put on a pair of jeans and a light blue turtleneck sweater. She jumped when he came in the door and looked behind him to see if Eckhart was coming in after him.

"He's gone," Jerry said to her.

She came off the bed then and he was holding her. "Oh, God, I was so afraid!" she said. "I was wondering where you were after that damned alarm went off and then you came in looking that way and said we had company! I was still half-asleep and when he pushed you like that and he had that gun! I thought he was going to kill us both! When he pointed it at me . . ."

"I know," Jerry said, holding her. He could feel her back trembling under his hands. "Don't talk about it."

Guilt was running through him because she was so frightened. She had thought she was going to be killed, shot right here in her own house. It was his fault, he thought angrily. This was *his* trouble, not hers. He had no right to subject her to any of this, but he had known that before and he had done it anyway and it was way too late to be worrying about that now.

"How did he get in?" Chris asked him. "Did you hear him?"

"No," Jerry said to her. "I didn't even know he was here. When I got up and went into the kitchen, he was sitting at the table. I don't even know how long he was here before I saw him."

She pulled back from him a little so she could see him, keeping her arms around his neck. "When you told him no—about the money—did you really know he wouldn't shoot us?"

Jerry nodded. "He has to have the money," he said. "And I showed him the slip for the box at the bank. He knew he wouldn't be able to get near it without me." He didn't want to tell her the rest of it about what might have, what probably *would* have happened if he'd done what the bastard said and tied her up and gone with him. There was no need to tell her that.

"When you talked to him out there—after you went back out—did you do what you were going to do?"

"Yes."

"And he agreed to that?"

"Yeah," Jerry said quietly, "I'm giving him half the money."

"Jerry, for God's sake!" And she let go of him then and stepped back, looking at him. "Why don't you just

give him *all* of it! That's what he wants! Give it to him!
We don't need it. It's not worth getting killed for!''

"Look," he said patiently. "I explained all that to you.
Once he's got the money. . .''

"But you don't *know* that!" she said. "You don't *really*
know that! How do you know for certain that it's not like
he told you—that he was just hired to get the money
back, not to kill you?"

Jerry sighed. "I just know," he told her. He thought
about what she had said about the money not being
worth getting killed for and he knew she was right about
that, but in another way, she was wrong, too, because it
wasn't greed for the money. It had to do with the money
and his whole life from now on. His *time*. "I never did
get any coffee," he said to her.

She looked at him for a long minute without saying
anything, and he could see that she was fighting with
herself not to go on with what she'd been saying about
him just giving up the money, to not push that harder
and try to convince him, but then she said, "Come on,
I'll fix us some. And I don't care how early it is, I'm
putting some brandy in mine!"

While they were having their coffee, he told her that
she had to go away like they'd talked about before and
that she had to go today, this morning. She said that she
would just call in and tell them that she was sick. Nurse
Madden wouldn't like it, but it would be all right. They
would probably be calling before too long anyway, she
told him, to find out where she was. "Do I have to go
away though?" Chris asked him. "Couldn't I just stay
here? I'll be going crazy wondering what's happening
to you."

Jerry shook his head. "I want you to go," he said to her. "I don't want you around for any of the rest of it. I want you to be far away because there's always the chance that he still might try to use you to get to me, and I don't want to have that on my mind."

But that was only part of it.

The rest of it was that there was no way she could be in the house with what he planned to do tonight, and no matter how it came out, he wanted her miles away so that if she ever had to, she could prove that she didn't have anything to do with whatever happened. And he felt the guilt come at him again then because he knew that the whole thing should not be happening here in her house. He had told Eckhart to meet him here tonight because he had not known any other place, and with the bastard showing up like he did this morning, there was no time to search one out. He had never intended on getting a hotel room like he'd told her. A hotel was no good. He had hoped that he could find a house somewhere out in the country and then it would've at least been away from her if things ended up going bad for him. Now she would be away at her girl friend's house, worrying about him, waiting to hear from him, and if he did blow it tonight, the next thing that she would hear about him was that his body had been found in the house. And wasn't that a great thing to do to her! He fought back the anger at the way this had happened. More than at any time before, he knew he had to stay calm now. He had to make sure things didn't go wrong.

"When do you want me to go?" she asked him quietly.

"Right away," he said. "Go to work, and then when you go to lunch, don't come back."

"I'll write down the address and the telephone for you," she said.

"No, not the address," he said. "Just the number." Chris got up and went over to the little phone table, wrote the number down on a pad, tore off the sheet and brought it back to him. Jerry put it in his billfold. He would memorize it after she had gone and then throw the paper away.

"What time are you meeting him?"

"Eight o'clock tonight. I'm going to the bank this morning."

"Wouldn't it be better," Chris asked him, "if I just went to visit somebody here in the city or got a hotel room?"

"No," Jerry said. "I don't trust him. I want you gone until we decide what to do."

"You'll call me as soon as you've given him the money?"

"You know it."

She had been standing looking at him after she had given him the phone number of her friend, and now she sat down on his lap and put her arms around his neck. "What *are* we going to do?" she asked him.

"You mean afterward?"

"Yes."

He put his hand on her thigh and squeezed, smiling at her. "Make love a lot, I hope."

She tried to smile. "What else?"

"Well, I know we have to talk about it and everything, but I was hoping that maybe you'd go away with me and we could travel and . . ." he shrugged. "I don't know—*do* things together."

She looked at him, not saying anything.

Say it! he yelled at himself. *Damn!*

"I really want you to marry me," he said. "Or think about it, at least."

"Think about it?" Chris said, laughing, but there were already tears in the corners of her eyes. "I don't have to think about it."

He looked at her face for a minute. "Wow!" he said softly.

Chris laughed again, shook her head. "Yes," she said. "Wow!" Softly, too.

IT WAS STILL RAINING when they took a taxi into the city. They sat close together in one corner of the backseat and looked out through the rain-spattered windows and didn't talk. Now and then during the ride he would turn and look out the rear window to see if he could spot any car that might be following them, but with the traffic and the rain, he couldn't tell. So far, things had gone the way he'd expected them to. He was sure Eckhart had only pretended to buy the deal. He only wished he knew just what the sonofabitch had planned for tonight.

When the taxi pulled up and stopped in front of the hospital, Chris kissed him quickly and then got out, hurrying away down the walk and then up the steps in the rain without looking back. He was thankful she had left that way. He wasn't up to any dragged-out good-bye.

He gave the driver the address of the bank and sat back in the seat and lit a cigarette. He was glad to be alone. He had a lot of things to think about.

At the bank, a guard led him to his safe-deposit box and then showed him into one of the little private enclosures. He put his empty briefcase down on the floor, and though there was no need, he used his key and opened the box. In the heavy stillness, he looked down at the stacks of bills and wondered how much of the half-million he had spent. He hadn't bothered to count it since that night in his trailer back in Vegas. He closed the box and locked it again.

He stayed in the booth for another ten minutes and then he opened the door and gave the box and the money back to the guard, thanking him. He walked back up to the entrance to the safe-deposit area, and another guard buzzed open the gates, and then he was back in the main part of the bank. As he walked past the tellers' cages to the door, he felt the tension starting to grow inside him. His eyes automatically checked out the faces of the other customers in the bank. And then he was through the door and back out on the rainy street. He tightened his grip on the empty briefcase and brought it in closer to his leg. He really didn't think that Eckhart would try anything here in the middle of the city with these people, but then he reminded himself he had thought the same thing back in the airport in Chicago, too.

He walked several blocks, keeping his eyes open, looking carefully at the people around him when he waited for lights to change at different street corners. He was sure he was being watched. He saw a pub called The Country Squire and went into it. He wanted to get out of the rain and cold, have a drink and go over what he had to do.

Thanks to the early hour, The Country Squire was not crowded. He started to take a table, but then he changed his mind and walked down to one end of the long wooden bar and sat down. The bartender, a thin-faced man wearing a white shirt with red stripes, came over to him. "Good morning, sir," he said. "What would you like?"

"How about a big mug of coffee with some brandy in it?" Jerry said to him, thinking of Chris.

The bartender nodded. "A good choice on a day like this one," he said and went away to get it.

He lit a cigarette and dropped the pack on the counter next to the ashtray. The bartender brought the coffee over in a black mug and put it down on a coaster in front of him. He could smell the brandy in the steam rising from the cup. He picked it up, sipped some of it from the edge and set it back down. He was cold from being outside in the damp rain, and all of a sudden he felt very lonely and afraid. He touched the empty briefcase on the floor in front of the barstool with his foot and turned his mind away from Chris, whom he wanted to think about, to what he had to do tonight, which he didn't want to think about. He took another little sip of the coffee and kept his hand around the side of the warm mug. Only one question stood out in his mind.

Would he be able to do it?

What had he ever killed in his life? he thought. Rabbits, hunting with his old man in the winter snow back in upstate New York and he hadn't been crazy about doing that. He'd gone because the old man made a big thing out of it. He'd only been twelve years old. The old

man was already putting away the booze pretty heavily
by then, and the rabbits didn't have a lot to worry about
since they were usually gone by the time the old man had
shoved his half-pint back in his pocket and raised his
shotgun. But he had gotten a couple himself and found
that he wasn't all that hot about shooting anything.

Rabbits . . .

And then there had been the war and that had been a
lot of scared guys shooting because they had to shoot and
you were never even sure most of the time if it was your
shot that had made the guy fall down, and you always
hoped that it wasn't.

Not much killing, he thought.

And how about Eckhart?

Probably a lot of killing. A lot of people. He knew the
guy hadn't been hired just to track him down. He was a
contract killer. He took lives for money, Jerry thought.
And he knew that he was trying to use that as a reason
now to justify what he was going to do tonight. Eckhart
killed a lot of people so it's okay if you kill him.

No good, he thought.

It was probably reason enough for Eckhart to die, but
it wasn't reason enough for him to kill him. No, he
thought, your reason is that if you don't stop him now,
he'll more than likely kill you sooner or later. And Chris,
too. He had to free them of that threat.

He brought the dark mug up to his mouth and drank
several swallows of the coffee. Then suddenly he set it
down, took out his billfold and laid some money on the
bar. The bartender saw him and came over. He looked
in the mug and then down at the money. "Have to rush
off, eh?" he said. "I know how it is." He looked at the

briefcase Jerry was holding. "I used to work in the business world myself when I was a younger man. I'll get your change for you."

"Keep it," Jerry said to him. "And thanks."

"Thank *you*, sir!" the bartender said.

Outside, he hurried down the walk looking for a taxi. You think too much, he told himself. You think too much about things that you have to do after you've decided to do them. No more of that. No more thinking like that. You know what you have to do, and you know what will happen if you don't try to do it. You want Chris and you want a life. Eckhart will stop you from having both of those things if you let him, but you are not going to let him!

A taxi was parked at the curb. He opened the door and got in. The driver, a short, chunky-looking man with a deeply wrinkled red face, turned and looked at him. He gave him Chris's address. The man had been asleep. Slowly he smacked his lips and rubbed his forehead with the palm of one beefy hand, trying to think if he knew how to get to the address he'd just been given. Then slowly he nodded to himself and turned back around to the wheel and without a word started the engine and pulled the taxi away from the curb into the slow-moving rainy-day traffic.

Jerry lit a cigarette. His feet were hurting him a little from walking. The rain began to come down harder, and the glass in the window of the cab looked like it was melting. He tried not to think about the night ahead of him. He thought about Chris and saw her face in his mind. He had the feeling that he wanted to say some kind of prayer for everything to come out all right for them, but he couldn't do it. How could he say a prayer for what he planned to do? He put out the cigarette and closed his eyes. He tried to make himself concentrate on the sound of the rain pounding down on the roof of the cab. It seemed like it didn't take any time at all to get back to Chris's house.

AND CHRIS ALTMAN, standing in the little line of people waiting to board the bus to Sussex, thought about this man who had come into her life and whom she had fallen in love with and she wondered again if she should be leaving him in spite of his reasons and his insistence that she go. He could be in trouble, meeting this man, and if he were in trouble, shouldn't she be with him? Shouldn't she be there to help him if he needed her?

Inside the bus, the driver opened the doors and the line began to move.

PART SIX

46

ROSYLYN CHAMBERS LAY AWAKE in the deep darkness of the bedroom. She thought that it must now be about three-thirty in the morning. She had been up once earlier in the night to go to the bathroom. Al had left his watch on the counter next to the basin, and for some reason she had picked it up and looked at the time. It had been just a few minutes past two. She didn't think she had slept longer than an hour and a half so, yes, she thought, it was probably around three-thirty. She hated waking up off and on in the night like this. She needed her rest these days.

She sighed, remembering the way she used to sleep when she had been a young girl. Back when she'd met Al. They'd go out on a Friday night, eating, dancing—he'd liked to dance then—and most of the time, she would not walk back in the door of her apartment until almost daylight and she would go to bed and not wake up sometimes until twelve, one-thirty in the afternoon. No trouble sleeping then. Of course, that was only on the weekends. She smiled to herself in the darkness. Those times when she'd been working in the gift shop of the Regency Manor, when Al was the manager of the hotel, had been really good times. Nothing had ever seemed to bother him then.

Not like now.

Something very serious was bothering him now. She had been aware of that for a couple of months. He didn't talk very much at dinner, always a sure sign that he had something serious on his mind. He was hardly with her at all when he was home. He spent most of his time upstairs in the little office, and on a lot of nights after she had looked in and said good night to him and gone to bed herself, she would wake up later in the night and he would not be next to her, and she would hear him walking around in the office and smell the smoke from his cigars that drifted out under the door. She had waited for him to talk to her about whatever it was. If something was really bothering him, something serious, sooner or later he would always talk to her about it, usually at night after they had turned out the lights and were in bed. He would lie awake and talk in the dark, and she would listen more than discuss anything with him. Especially if it was something that had to do with the Tiara. Talking like that always helped him put things together, he'd told her.

But not this time. And that worried her.

He had started acting strange around the time he had gotten the call from Meyer that night, so maybe there was some kind of serious trouble at the Tiara. She wondered what Meyer had said to him on the phone, and a few times she had actually thought about calling him and meeting him somewhere for coffee or lunch and confidentially asking him, but she had never done it. She didn't feel close to Meyer anymore, the way she had when they first came to Las Vegas and he would come to the house. She had never understood the way he had just drifted away after being their close friend. He was still friendly when he saw her, but he seemed to always have things to do, and when she'd mention something about getting together, he would say yes, that was a good idea, they would have to do that, but then he would hurry away before they could set a night and it just never happened. She had mentioned it to Al, and he'd told her that Meyer was, after all, a bachelor and he had his own life, so she'd let it go and stopped asking him after that.

Rosylyn pushed the blankets down around her waist. She felt like the bedroom was too warm. She was always either too hot or wanting a sweater to put on. She heard a low, whistling noise outside the house and knew that another desert windstorm was starting up. She liked everything about Las Vegas except the wind. It would just kick up sometimes out of nowhere and blow the sand at you so hard and so thick that it stung your face, and a lot of times, if you were driving, you'd have to pull over until it stopped because you couldn't see. And when it came in the night like now it always woke her and kept her up and made her more nervous.

She listened to Al's deep breathing next to her and was glad that he was asleep. She didn't know what time he had finally come to bed, but she was sure it had been after midnight. Well, she was just going to have to do it, she thought. Enough was enough. She couldn't have him being the way he was, so upset all the time. Tomorrow night she'd just wait up for him and tell him that she had to know what it was that was bothering him so much. She had hardly ever pressed him that way in the years they had been married, so she felt justified in doing it this time.

The whistling of the wind around the house was deeper now, and behind the shutters of the window she could hear the sand hitting the glass. She had to get back to sleep, she thought, but she was very awake now and with the wind blowing, she knew it would never happen unless she took one of Dr. Jacobson's pills. She didn't like taking the pills. They did make her sleep, but they were so strong and the next day it always seemed to take her half the morning to wake up. She reached over to her little night table and picked up the bottle, worked off the plastic cap, kept it in her hand so she wouldn't lose it in the dark and tipped the bottle until one of the capsules fell into her palm. She replaced the cap, put the bottle back on the table and picked up the glass of water that she always put there each night before she went to bed. She took the pill and then sat holding the glass in her lap for a minute, took a couple more swallows of the water and then replaced it next to the bottle of pills. She eased herself back down under the covers and tried to get comfortable.

The pill worked fast.

She felt the wavy drowsiness spreading like a heavy pressure all over her body and she closed her eyes and the pressure seemed to hold them shut and she felt like she couldn't open them again and as she began to slip away, she thought how it was a good thing that when Al did finally go to sleep, he always slept soundly because with all of her rustling around every night, he would never get any rest.

The very last thing she was aware of was the wind whistling louder and blowing something with a thump against the side of the wall. She never saw the big man standing in the dark over her husband, who now brought the short, heavy piece of pipe down on his head a second time. And she never knew or felt anything after he had moved around to her side of the bed.

47

THAT SAME NIGHT August Gurino, owner of the Silver Tiara Hotel and Gambling Casino, had his own troubles going to sleep.

In his early seventies now, tall and slender, with a full head of thick gray hair and a neatly trimmed salt-and-pepper mustache, Gurino gave the sedate appearance of perhaps a retired banker or politician. Both his appearance and his refined manner were two things he had carefully cult.vated over the years as he had begun to grow in wealth and power, and now he was a long way from the old days in Detroit, when he had been known as Augie Gurino and had been a key figure in the gambling and loansharking in that city. Then his tastes had leaned more to flash, his manner had been more explosive than refined. Augie had had a reputation for being a fair man in his business and personal dealings. In fact, fairness was one of his obsessions. "I treat square, I want to be treated square," he was often heard to say. But of course there were times when it didn't work out that way.

And because of those times, Augie Gurino had been a man widely feared by other men.

For on those times, he had shown himself to be savagely ruthless to anyone who he felt had not treated him fairly. A story had gone around for years about how Gurino had dealt with a man known as The Gypsy, who had been the head of one of Gurino's many lucrative bookmaking operations. There had been an attempt on Gurino's life by a rival gangster named Salvatore Valenti. Gurino later found out that The Gypsy had been in collusion with Valenti, that he had made a deal with his rival and had supplied him with certain information that had almost made Gurino vulnerable to the attempt on his life.

Gurino did nothing for three months so that The Gypsy might feel more secure that he had gotten away with his treachery. Then one night all the other heads of Gurino's bookmaking operations were summoned to meet in an abandoned warehouse. Stonily Gurino had greeted the men and then he had led them to the far back of the building.

To where The Gypsy had sat tied and gagged in a chair.

Gurino had produced a baseball bat and told each of the men to step in front of the chair and swing it once. The deadly coldness of the order had convinced each man that he himself might end up in the chair if he refused.

The Gypsy had given up the ghost and still three men remained.

Grimly Gurino had forced each of them to take his swing with the bat. Gurino had walked over to the chair, looked down at the dead man in it for a moment and then viciously spit in his face. Turning, he had looked into the faces of the other men.

And his message had needed no words.

BUT ALL THAT WAS decades behind August Gurino now.

Today, thanks to very careful planning and equally careful spending of money in the right places over the years, he was a respectable businessman, the wealthy owner of the booming Silver Tiara. He contributed heavily to his chosen community. He made lavish contributions to charities, helped build schools and churches. Mention the name of August Gurino in Las Vegas and all you would be likely to hear were comments like, "A good man! A real gentleman!"

And, putting certain limits on definition, those statements held some truth.

But also true was that deep within August Gurino, pillar of the community and soft-spoken gentleman, there still lived some of Augie Gurino.

And tonight the two parts mixed.

Unable to sleep, Gurino paced the floor of his huge living room, wandering out to the kitchen several times, Scotch in hand, to open the refrigerator door and then close it again without taking anything. Conflicting thoughts and emotions churned restlessly through his mind.

He had *liked* Al Chambers, goddamnit to hell!

And he'd liked Roz, too.

Ever since Nate had first introduced the two of them, he'd liked them. His instincts had told him that Chambers was a much more complex man than he appeared. He was a little rough around the edges, not as smoothly polished as Nate, but when Chambers was being friendly, his rough exterior added to his charm. He had done a damned good job running the Regency back in Manhattan, and Gurino had agreed with Nate that, groomed correctly, he'd make a damned good president of the Tiara, too. And they'd been right. Al had done well in the spot, especially considering that he'd had to take over suddenly after Nate had died, losing the benefit of Nate's experience and guidance.

Al Chambers had been a close friend of Nate Shapiro's. They'd been in the war together. And Gurino had loved Nate Shapiro like a brother.

He reached down to his side and with a jerk, knotted the sash of his robe more tightly, paced.

But call it like it was, he thought.

Al was a thief.

Maybe it had all gotten to him, Gurino thought. Some men could handle it—the power and having access to so much money. He had thought Al Chambers could handle it. Nate Shapiro had thought so, too.

But they had both been wrong.

Five hundred thousand dollars. Al had cheated the Tiara out of five hundred thousand dollars. Gurino's lips tightened in a frustrated frown. Stealing from the Tiara was the same as stealing from him personally, goddamnit! He wondered if Al had ever thought of it that way. What the hell had gotten into him to make him do a stupid ass thing like that? And it didn't matter about the fucking junket either, Gurino thought angrily. Sure Al made the Tiara a lot of money on that one. But that's what he was supposed to do. He was supposed to make money for the operation. That's why he'd been hired in the first place. And it wasn't that what he'd done hadn't been appreciated, Gurino reminded himself. He'd given the man a ten-grand bonus. He shook his head at that thought. Al steals half a million from him and then he *keeps* a ten-grand bonus along with it.

You couldn't let something like that go, Gurino told himself.

Because if you did let it go, you could bet your ass that someday the guy would do it again. Maybe not right away. Maybe three, five years down the road, but he would do it again. He had seen it happen too many times to believe differently. It wasn't the money that mattered. The money was shit to him. It was the act itself and all that it finally said about the man.

Al Chambers . . .

Sonofabitch!

Gurino walked from the kitchen back into his silent living room, turning his mind to this Meyer Weiss.

From the very day he'd met him, he had not liked the man.

He had gone along with Nate about bringing him in because Nate had said the Tiara needed a guy like Weiss behind the books. He was the best with the money, Nate had told him. And he'd been right about that part of it. So he'd kept his personal feelings about the man to himself. Weiss looked harmless enough, like any clerk, but he was one of those sneaky-eyed, peasant Jews who, if it weren't for his head for numbers, would probably be working in the garment district hustling notions or down in the fish market stringing up those filthy carp. And it wasn't that the bastard was Jewish, either. Nate Shapiro had been Jewish. There were Italians like that, too, the kind of guy who always acts as harmless as he looks. Just a quiet little Mr. Nobody who does his job, takes his check and goes home. No trouble. No waves.

NIGHT OF THE RUNNING MAN

But all the time, all the fucking time, the bastard's got those sneaky hawk eyes open, just looking out for that big opportunity to get his ass up there in the money with the big boys.

Gurino stared angrily down at the thick, rust-colored shag rug on his living room floor.

And Al Chambers had been Weiss's big opportunity.

He'd been surprised when Weiss had called him at home. Surprised and angry because he wondered how in the hell he had gotten his number. His private line at home was confidential. Only a select few had it. Al Chambers was one of those few, but he couldn't imagine Al giving Weiss the number. When Weiss had told him that he wanted to talk to him about something very important, about someone who had stolen from the Tiara, someone in a high position, he had agreed to see him. Weiss was the money man, and he was sharp. If there was a thief and he'd spotted him, Gurino wanted to know who it was.

But not once had he thought it would turn out to be Al Chambers.

Weiss had come to his home one night a week ago, and Gurino had welcomed him politely and shown him into the library. He offered Weiss a drink, but the accountant had prudently refused it. There were only a few minutes of small talk. The two men had only met before when there were others present so they had never had any real direct contact. Alone in a room together, they were strangers. To show how he wished things, Gurino sat down behind his desk and waited.

And carefully Meyer Weiss told him the story of the Italian gambler and how Al Chambers had pocketed the five hundred thousand dollars the man owed the Tiara for his gambling losses.

When Weiss had finished, Gurino had looked at him and, barely keeping the contempt out of his voice, said, "You have proof of all of this?"

And Weiss understood it was not a question.

He had better have the proof. And he had better be right.

Gurino sat silent as Weiss opened his briefcase, removed the portable tape recorder and carefully placed it on the desk in front of him. Weiss was very afraid of Gurino. He had heard the stories about the man's past, but he was confident his proof was rock solid. Wordlessly he pressed the Play button.

And the cheerful voice of the Italian gambler broke into the silence of Gurino's library, damning Al Chambers.

When the tape had finished, Weiss followed through with the rest of his plan. He picked up a large brown leather satchel from the floor next to his chair and brought it over to Gurino. The satchel contained the five hundred thousand dollars that Al Chambers had finally managed to raise. Gurino dumped the money out on his desk, looked down at it, then back up at Meyer Weiss. "How did you get this?" he asked quietly.

Weiss was sweating. He worked to make his voice sound coldly matter-of-fact, businesslike. He told Gurino how he had pretended to blackmail Al Chambers in order to recover the money for the Tiara. Weiss looked at the older man, half smiled, shrugged. An unusual method, he explained, but he had thought that it might work and it had. Chambers had delivered the money last night.

Gurino's eyes studied him. "Chambers brought this money to you?" he asked.

Meyer Weiss raised his hands, dropped them to his side, shook his head. No, he said. Frankly, he was afraid of Chambers. He had set it up so that Chambers had delivered the money to a friend, a bartender at the Sands. Then the friend had brought it to him.

He did not tell Gurino the story of Eric Nichols and the first five hundred thousand dollars or anything about the cab driver who now had that money. Then, his plan finished, Weiss returned to his chair, sat down and looked at Gurino, waiting.

August Gurino looked at him across his desk for a long minute, not saying a word, and for an instant, Meyer Weiss experienced a cold chill of fear at the look in the older man's eyes. Then Gurino had pushed the money away from him and said, "You have nothing more to do with this. You forget about it. You say nothing. It's all out of your hands now. Do you understand that?"

Weiss knew he had just been dismissed. He stood up, nodding vigorously. He understood perfectly, he told Gurino.

And after he had left the house, Gurino knew that Weiss had not understood at all.

Now GURINO PULLED back the sleeve of his long blue silk robe and looked at his watch.

Four-thirty in the morning.

It would be done by now, he thought.

He walked over to the bar and picked up a large glass, poured from the bottle of cognac, his face expressionless. He stood there for a moment, tall and dignified in the quiet living room. Then he looked down at the glass in his hand, lifted it and drank.

In his mind, he hoped that Al would understand about Roz. That he would know it had not been an easy decision for him to make, but that he had thought it over very carefully and decided that she would not have lived too long without him anyway.

LATER, UPSTAIRS in bed, his wife snoring loudly into the pillow next to him, Gurino experienced a feeling of satisfaction thinking about Meyer Weiss. The whole picture had been very clear to him when he had received Al Chambers's letter of resignation in the mail. He knew just what it was that this snake snitch wanted.

And so he would see to it that he got it. The announcement would be made. Mr. Meyer Weiss would become the new president of the Silver Tiara.

But one thing was certain. The new president's term of office would be short.

Gurino closed his eyes, and the smile that came over his face in the darkened bedroom was the chilling smile of another man, a younger man, from another time.

48

THE RAIN WAS REALLY GETTING on his nerves.

Jerry Logan stood in front of the window in the kitchen of Chris's house and watched it. It would slow down and then after a few minutes, start up again with a heavy rushing sound and then slow down, and start up again. The sound of it beating down on the roof made him grind his teeth. He turned away from the window and went back over to the table and picked up the cup of coffee that was strongly laced with brandy. He looked around the kitchen. The house seemed so goddamned empty! Different than when Chris was away at work. He had tried putting some music on the stereo, but that had bothered him, too. He walked into the living room and looked over at Roscoe on the couch. The big red cat was curled up, his head buried in his front paws, sleeping. He would have to do something with him later, he thought. Put him down in the basement or something, get him out of the way.

He took a big sip of the coffee and looked at his watch for what had to be the fucking ten thousandth time.

Four o'clock.

Four more long fucking hours before the bastard was due to show up. Why hadn't he made it earlier? For later this afternoon?

Because there were some things that just seemed better suited for happening at night.

Why was that, he wondered.

Why was that? Why was this? Who knew? Who the fuck knew the why of anything? You think too much, he told himself again. Always thinking. He was tired of thinking. But then he wondered if Chris had gotten to her girl friend's yet. He didn't know how far away Sussex was from London. Mentally he repeated the telephone number she had given him.

God, he missed her!

Thinking about Chris didn't comfort him much now. It just made him wish she were here with him. He took another big swallow of the coffee, turned around and went back through the kitchen to the bedroom. He thought he could still faintly smell her perfume. He walked over to the bed and sat down, looking at the pillow on his side. He drank more of the coffee, thinking again that he really had to watch the booze, not have too much of it today. He set the cup down between his thighs and reached under the pillow with one hand.

And brought out the long thin ice pick.

He had thought about buying one after he had left the bank this morning and then remembered that he had seen this one in the drawer in the kitchen. He looked down at it in his hand, tested the flexibility of the point with his two fingers, seeing how much it would bend. It would do okay, he thought. He would've felt better with a gun, but buying a gun left records. Only guys like Eckhart knew how to get guns without leaving records. He smiled grimly. Maybe he should have asked Eckhart for the name of a good gun dealer. He would have to be *very* close to him to use this. One quick thrust in the right place. Surprise. He would need surprise. He had heard a story a long time ago back in Vegas, about how ice picks like this one had been one of the favorite weapons of the old Murder Incorporated, back in the thirties, when guys kept showing up dead all the time. He looked around the little bedroom at Chris's things on the dressing table, feeling the delicate, feminine atmosphere of the room. He put the ice pick back under the pillow and went out into the kitchen with his coffee.

He should've bought some magazines, he thought. Because now, with the time and nothing to do, it was starting to come at him again.

Could he do it?

Yes, he told himself again. Yes. Yes!

He didn't know.

He waited another hour before he fixed himself a drink.

Above his head, the rain never stopped pounding.

49

ECKHART HOOKED THE TOE of his shoe under the man's ribs and turned him over. He glanced quickly around the little parking lot, but there was nobody to be seen in the driving rain. He looked down at the man on the ground, his face turned toward the hubcap of his car, the front of his suit jacket and his pants stained dark from the water and smeared with gravel and mud.

Hit him too hard, Eckhart thought. He couldn't wait around for him to wake up. He studied the man's face, trying to see if it rang any bell in his mind. No, he'd never seen him before. He was probably from over here. He hoped the creep wasn't dead. He wanted the word to get back to Chambers that he had been the one who'd hit the guy. That would scare the shit out of the fat slob.

He would worry about all kinds of things when he heard that. Eckhart only wished he could see the look on his fat pig face when he found out. If he was going to hire somebody to follow him, he sure should've chosen sharper men than this one or those other two duds who had been at that little coffee joint. At least the other two had had the sense to cut out after they knew he'd spotted them. But not this one. He comes after him anyway and then when he'd just stopped and turned around and started walking toward the guy, *he* turns around and starts hotfooting it away like a bat out of hell to his car.

He looked down at the man on the ground again. He was really out. He would've liked to have said a few things to this jerk. Things that would've gotten back to Chambers. He wondered if the man on the gravel in front of him was free-lance or if he was connected to anybody in London. He stepped forward and kicked the wallet in closer to the body. He had gone through it. The guy's driver's license said his name was Harold Dawkins, and there had been a business card that said he was promotional director for some restaurant chain, but that didn't mean anything. Well, the hell with it, he thought. He couldn't stand around here all day. He was already soaking wet.

He turned and began walking out of the parking lot. He'd go back to the hotel, grab a shower and change into some dry clothes. Then he'd get something to eat before he went to his meeting with Logan. That whole deal Logan had laid out had been a real ditch-out desperate move. But when a guy had his ass really flat up against the wall the way Logan had his now, you had to play it all very carefully. Especially now that there was a woman involved.

Eckhart picked up his pace, hurrying to get in out of the rain.

If everything went the way it should tonight, he would have Chambers's money, or rather, *his* money, and he would have *all* of it, not just half, by tomorrow morning, and he would be on a plane out of London by tomorrow night.

Smiling, Eckhart walked faster.

Smiling because he realized something.

He felt happy!

Even with the rain beating down on him, and shivering inside his wet clothes, the water dripping out of his hair and running down his face, he felt *happy!* He walked still faster and by the time he got to the corner, he was laughing out loud. The smile on his wet face seemed frozen, the smile of a wax figure, his eyes wide and shining. He began to wave both of his arms in wide, fast circles above his head and a taxi pulled up and stopped. He jumped in and gave the driver the address of his hotel and sat back in the seat. The night traffic was heavy, and the taxi moved slowly through the wet, glistening streets.

The driver looked straight ahead out through his windshield. He wished it weren't raining so he could hurry along. The way this one was chuckling to himself back there was giving him gooseflesh on the back of his neck . . .

50

HE WAS OKAY AT SIX-THIRTY. He had not had too much to drink during the day. Only two, waiting until later when he might really need one strong one.

At seven-thirty, he went into the kitchen and fixed it.

In spite of the drink, his hands were shaking and he kept listening for the sound of footsteps coming up the walk outside and he kept checking to make sure that his shirttail was pulled down far enough over the top of his pants pocket so that the point of the ice pick didn't show when he stood up. He remembered a time when he had felt this way before. It had been during the war, the first time he'd had to jump out of a plane at night, and when it had been his turn and he'd come up to the door and set himself, staring out into the blackness, he had been so scared that he'd held onto the sides of the door of the plane too long and the leader had booted him in the ass to get him moving.

Nobody to boot him tonight.

Don't think, he told himself, sitting on the couch. Just wait. You know what you have to do. Work on that. Keep your mind just on that. Had he done everything? Yes, yes. He had changed into the long shirt. He had put Roscoe, protesting, down in the basement. He nursed the drink. The glass was nearly empty. Should he go ahead and finish this one and make another one? He might need it. Jesus! His hands were shaking badly enough to make the ice bang around in the glass. He didn't want Eckhart to see. No. He'd better wait on the drink.

Just wait . . .

Twenty minutes past eight.

Nobody.

No sweat, he thought. No big deal. Traffic. Hard time getting a taxi. Something like that.

At five minutes past nine, he started getting this very bad feeling in his stomach that something was going to happen that he didn't know anything about.

At nine-thirty, he went into the kitchen and fixed that other drink. Not thinking now, not even shaking that much anymore. He was just waiting, his whole body highly tensed, aware. He watched everything. The front door. The back. The windows. His ears alert for any sound, he walked back and forth through the house, the drink in his hand and as he came back into the kitchen, the phone rang loudly and his hand gave an involuntary jerk, spilling some of the drink on the floor. He stopped and looked at it, not sure if he should pick it up or not.

Chris? he wondered.

The ringing continued.

Some friend of hers, maybe, just calling to say hello?

Four more rings.

Eckhart?

In three quick steps, he was up to it, jerking it off the hook.

"Hello?"

Silence.

But the line was *alive*.

"Hello!" Louder.

Nothing for a minute.

Then, click, and the dial tone.

He put the receiver back, heart pounding.

Okay…okay…he thought. So something was up. The bastard had something on his mind.

But what?

Never mind, he told himself. Never mind what *he's* going to do. Think what *you're* going to do!

And standing there in the kitchen, he knew what that had to be.

He couldn't watch everything at once. Trying to, walking all over the place from one room to another, only made him more nervous. The doors were all locked. The windows, too. He had to fix it, he thought, so that if the sonofabitch came at him, he wouldn't have too many ways to do it.

He set the glass down on the kitchen table and walked back into the living room.

To turn off the lights.

Then, moving carefully in the darkness, he went over to each of the three lamps that were connected to the wall switch and removed the bulbs, dropping them behind the couch.

Okay. Good.

Now into the kitchen, unscrewing the bulbs, putting them in the sink.

He moved into the bedroom in the darkness. Chris had only the one lamp on the table by the bed. He knelt down on the floor and following the cord with his fingers, he pulled the plug out of the wall.

There! He stood at the foot of the bed, listening. There was only the sound of the rain still coming down. He pulled up the tail of his shirt, pulled the ice pick out of his pocket. He moved around to the head of the bed and took the two pillows out from under the spread, propped them up against the headboard.

Then he stretched out on the bed to wait.

Maybe an hour passed.

Nothing.

His eyes adjusted to the bedroom darkness. He could see the outline of the curtains around the only window, heard the rain hitting softly on the glass.

Maybe another half-hour.

Still nothing.

And then through the closed door, he heard the phone ringing again.

Fuck you, he thought. He held the ice pick in his lap. Three, four, five . . . he counted the rings.

At twelve, they stopped.

Then there was only the darkness and the sound of the wind and the rain. He stayed there on the bed, tense, ready, his eyes going back and forth from the door to the window, listening, concentrating hard, trying to hear the sounds of someone forcing a door or a window in the silent house, but he never heard anything.

Until the footsteps were right outside the bedroom door.

He sat quickly up on the bed. *Jesus Christ!* How could he have . . . but then the door was opening and he gripped the ice pick tightly and heard, ''Jerry . . . ?''

He couldn't believe it.

But it was her and he almost yelled with relief, and he didn't even care that she was supposed to be gone, not be here at all and he said, ''Chris! Wait a minute!'' Down on the floor by the bed then, finding the cord, trying to plug it in and he couldn't find the damned holes in the socket and then he had it. He jumped up and switched on the lamp.

Chris stood in the doorway looking at him and he saw that she was crying, her face scared from the dark house, and of course he hadn't heard anyone forcing the door because she had her key, and as he went around the foot of the bed, she came to him and he saw her open her mouth and he knew that she was going to say that she was sorry, that she knew she hadn't done what he'd told her, but he didn't even care, he was just so glad to see her, and so he was caught flat when he reached out to hold her and suddenly she screamed, *"Run!"* into his face. He stopped, confused, his hands around her arms, staring at her and then he looked past her and he knew that when it got right down to it, you really couldn't count on anything all the way and he wished he hadn't just dropped the ice pick on the bed, not that it would've helped him any.

The gun was aimed straight at the back of Chris's head.

Jerry looked into the face that he had been sure he would never see again in his life.

Derik Mills flashed a big smile. "Surprise!" he said.

THE BULBS WERE REPLACED. The lights were turned on. Mills brought them into the living room. Sitting in the chair across from the couch, Eckhart looked at them as they came in.

Mills pointed to the couch with the gun. "Sit down," he said pleasantly, and as they did, Jerry realized that one of the main things that made this man so frightening was his always-happy manner. It was so out of place for the kind of guy that he was, like an undertaker who walked around cracking jokes while he was doing his job. He moved his feet inside his shoes and felt his skin crawl.

Mills looked at Chris, then at Jerry. "She was going to *leave!*" he said, mock surprise in his voice. "She was about to get on a bus and leave when I found her!" He shook his head, clucking softly. "Couldn't let her do that!"

"They had me called over the speaker at the bus terminal," Chris said, the frustration and fear plain in her voice. She sat close against him on the couch, one hand tightly holding his arm. "I thought it was you."

"Why were you back in the bedroom?" Eckhart asked quietly. "And why did you have all the lights out like that?"

Before he could answer, he heard Mills say, "He had *this* back there with him," and they all looked at him. He was holding the ice pick up in the air by the point, moving it back and forth like the pendulum of a clock. He had picked it up off of the bed as they had all left the room.

Jerry felt Chris's grip loosen a little on his arm and he could feel her staring at him, but there was no time to say anything to her now. He looked into Eckhart's face, tried to keep his voice calm and even. "You didn't show up," he said. "Then the phone rings and there's nobody there." He shrugged. "I got nervous."

Eckhart looked at him and saw past the controlled voice, saw the fear in the man's eyes. This time it would all be settled, he thought. He might have settled it this morning. He could probably have done it himself, but he had never enjoyed that type of thing. He'd needed

Mills. Mills was very good at that kind of stuff. He enjoyed it. And he had wanted Mills there for another reason, too. In Mills's car, he had followed them this morning, and his first thought had been that they were headed for the bank and then out of the city and he had even felt disappointed in Logan for thinking he could get away with something like that, something that obvious. But then, when the taxi had stopped in front of the hospital and he'd seen the woman go up the steps, pinning on her nurse's cap, he knew he'd been wrong. Logan was doing the smart thing, the careful thing. He didn't want her in the house when they met tonight. That would be too risky. He didn't know for sure what would happen, and if anything went wrong, he wouldn't want the woman there because that could work against him. Eckhart had been sure the woman would not be back at the house until Logan called her. She would probably go somewhere, a friend's, and wait for him to call when the meeting was over. And so he'd sent Mills to watch the hospital, grab her when she left work that evening and bring her to the house. A good thing, too, since she had left the hospital early, and since she'd been trying to leave town. Logan's idea, too; he was sure of that. They had kept her at Mills's house.

And then they had all waited.

He'd wanted Logan to sweat, to be unsettled. That would put him off his guard. He knew that he would start to worry when he didn't show up for their meeting. All kinds of things would go through his mind. The two phone calls to the house had been Mills's idea, and they had been a nice touch. That kind of thing, picking up a phone and knowing that somebody was on it but not having anybody speak, that unnerved a lot of people.

And all of it had worked.

The lights out and Logan in the back bedroom with an ice pick was proof of that.

Now, he thought, looking at the man, this fucking Vegas cabbie who had caused him so much inconvenience—now everything was ready. And quietly, Eckhart said, "I'm going to tell you something. You've caused me a lot of trouble, a lot of hassle and time." Eckhart spoke slowly, hitting each word heavily. "There's not going to be any goddamned deal with you. See, you made a big mistake. You thought you were smart, when all you were was lucky." He leaned forward in the chair, looked dead into Jerry Logan's eyes. "Now this is what's going to happen here, you sonofabitch! You're going to give me the money that you brought back from the bank this morning. Then we are all going to stay here tonight in this house, and first thing tomorrow morning, we're going back to that bank and you're going to give me the rest of it." He pointed at Chris. "She's going to stay here with my friend. When I call him and tell him I've got the money, he'll let her go."

"How do I know that?" Jerry said, looking at him, not even caring about the answer to the question, but only buying time to think.

"Hey, chump!" Eckhart said. "You don't know shit! You just have to take your chances that that's the way it's going to be! And I'll tell you something else," Eckhart hissed. "You better really think about your answer or things are going to get very unpleasant here for you. See,

I don't give a fuck what happens to you. Or to her. I'll get into that safe-deposit box with or without you. There are ways to do that that you're too fucking stupid to know about. And," he pointed at Mills, "my friend here has really been pushing me for some time with you."

Jerry flicked a glance at Mills.

Mills grinned at him. Then he began to whistle softly.

Jerry turned and looked at Chris then. Her face was pale, tired and very frightened. "Do it!" she said to him. "Give him the damned money!"

Jerry looked away from her, put all thoughts of her out of his mind. He was surprised at how clearly he could think. He was deeply afraid, but there was so much more at stake now. There wasn't just himself to look for. There was Chris.

He played the whole picture through again in his mind very fast, and things really weren't any different from the way they had been early this morning in the kitchen, when he had offered Eckhart the deal. The money was still in the safe-deposit box, and all that about him being able to get into it anyway was most likely pure bullshit, but even if it were the truth, it wouldn't be easy. It would take time and trouble. The only thing that was any different from this morning was that Eckhart now thought half the money was here in the house and he'd decided to bring along his sicko buddy as a threat to help him get the rest of it.

But the money wasn't in the house. And there was no way in hell that he was ever going to leave Chris here with Mills. Not a chance. He would do anything to prevent that. He knew that as soon as he had turned over the money at the bank and Eckhart made the call back to the house, Mills would kill Chris and then Eckhart would kill him. No, he thought, Eckhart was bluffing. He still needed him unhurt and alive to walk into that bank and open that safe-deposit box, and if they did anything now to Chris, he promised himself that they'd never see a cent of the money, no matter what else happened.

"Well?" Eckhart snapped.

Mills stopped whistling. There was only the sound of the strong wind and the rain hitting the window behind the couch.

Jerry looked at Eckhart, concentrated on keeping his face blank. "I thought you might pull some shit like this," he said evenly. "I didn't get any money at the bank this morning."

"What you're telling me," Eckhart said, "is that you were waiting here for me to come and make a deal with you, and yet you didn't have the money for that deal? You went all the way into the city to the bank, went back where the safety-deposit boxes were—and I know that's what you did because I saw you—you did all of that and then you came back here without any money in that briefcase?"

Jerry only looked at him. He was going to have to lay it all down, he thought. Chris or no Chris.

"Bullshit," Eckhart said. "You made the deal. It was your idea. How were you going to do it without the money? Huh?"

"I wasn't going to make any deal," Jerry said quietly.

"What?" Eckhart said. "What do you mean you weren't going to make any deal?"

"I was going to kill you," Jerry said quietly.

Eckhart stared at him.

Mills started whistling again.

Jerry didn't look at Chris.

"Where's the briefcase?" Eckhart said, his eyes studying Logan's face.

"In the bedroom. Under the bed."

Eckhart looked over at Mills, reached out his hand. Mills went over to him and handed him the gun. "Get it," Eckhart said to him. Mills walked out of the living room.

They waited.

Mills returned with the tan briefcase. He put it on the rug, knelt down, opened it. He turned it around so Eckhart could see that it was empty. Eckhart glanced at it, then he looked back at Jerry. "Where's the money?" he said.

"I told you . . ."

"Where did you put the money? We'll find it anyway."

"I didn't get any. . ."

"*Bullshit!*" Eckhart yelled at him. "Now you listen to me, you sonofabitch! You did *not* go all the way to that bank to not come back here with the money! Okay, so it's not in the case. Where is it? Where *is* it?"

"It's in the bank," Jerry said.

He saw Eckhart look at Mills, saw him nod, and then Mills kind of ran the few steps to him and there was no getting out of the way. The punch got him solidly in the nose with a bright burst of light and pain and he heard Chris's scream as his head snapped back against the couch, the warm blood instantly running down over his lips, and Eckhart's, "Where did you put it?" The *Where did you* soft and far-away sounding, and then the *put it?* suddenly very loud.

He sat up, wiped under his nose with the back of his hand and then wiped his hand on the thigh of his pants. *"It isn't here!"* he shouted. "Look! Go look!" He leaned his head back against the couch, his hand covering his nose, feeling the blood running into his fingers.

"Here," Chris said, and though her voice was strained, she wasn't crying. He took the handkerchief from her, held it up to his nose, kept his head back, hoping the bleeding would stop.

Then he heard Eckhart's voice again, a little quieter now, a little more controlled. "Look in the bedroom first," he said to Mills. "It's probably there, in the back of a closet or somewhere."

No reply from Mills. Only the sound of his steps leaving the room, entering the kitchen, going away down the hall.

Then silence.

Jerry sat up, took the handkerchief away from his nose, put the fingers of his other hand up to it. It was sore and already swelling, but the bleeding was slowing down. He put the handkerchief up to it again and looked at Eckhart. "He's not going to find anything," he said to him. "I told you the truth. I didn't get the money this morning."

Eckhart crossed his legs, rested the gun on his knee, and as he did, something happened that made Jerry's skin crawl and a chill shoot up his back.

Eckhart smiled.

A smile without any amusement in it. A smile that came from some secret the man was thinking about. The eyes above the smile were slightly glazed and far away, and looking at him, Jerry felt a colder, deeper terror than he had ever felt before about this man because, up to now, he had been counting on logic—on the fact that Eckhart had been sent to get the money and to kill him and that he would not do the latter until he had accomplished the former—until the money was in his hands, but now, looking at him, at the smile, at the eyes, he realized for the first time that this might not be true.

Eckhart looked at them, the two of them, sitting close together like that, both of them scared shitless, scared of what was going to happen to them.

They were, he thought, in love.

You could see it if you paid attention. The way the woman had given him the handkerchief. The way she was sitting so close to him. And you could see it with Logan, too. It was right there in his eyes. He was ready to do anything to stop her from being hurt. Eckhart stared at them, thinking back. Had he ever felt like that? No. What was that like? He'd always had to be careful, he thought. *Sooo* careful. Because the only one that you could really, *really* trust all the way, the only one that you could know would never, never screw you up, was only yourself.

It would've been wonderful, he thought, to have been with a woman and have her feel and look at you like that.

But a woman was the most dangerous.

Oh, yes! He knew that for sure. Because you got your emotions wrapped up in a woman when it was like that, and once your emotions were going, really moving— well, then you were off your guard, your head just couldn't be as sharp as you needed it to be and you were on your way.

To dying. You were on your way to the box with the velvet lining and being cold and dead.

In love, he thought again.

And people can get desperate when they're really in love. That's what Logan was now. He was desperate. So he says that he never got the money from the bank. That he went all the way to the bank and walked out with just an empty briefcase so if you were watching him, you would only *think* he had the money.

And then, he said, he was going to try to kill you.

Eckhart felt the smile getting bigger on his lips.

And see, he thought, that's the way it was when your emotions got wrapped up in what you were doing. Logan thought he had really made a deal with you. He'd thought maybe he'd worked a way out for him and the woman. He hadn't been able to get to the bank fast enough this morning to get that two hundred and fifty thousand.

And then things don't work out tonight the way he thought they would. The way they were supposed to work out. And as he looked at Logan's face, he knew the two things that were scaring him the most now:

That maybe he hadn't hidden the money in a good enough place and Mills would find it.

And that you might not be greedy, he thought.

That you might settle for just the two hundred fifty thousand and finish this business right here. That you might kill them both tonight.

And he wouldn't tell him, Eckhart thought. He wouldn't tell him right away.

That he was right!

Jerry and Chris sat very still. They were both listening to the sounds in the back bedroom of the little house as Mills searched, pulled out drawers, dropped them, threw things out of closets, looked and looked.

Then Mills was standing in the doorway to the living room, his face slightly flushed under the heavy white bandage that was wrapped like a turban around his head. There were sweat circles under the arms of his shirt, and Jerry could see the powerful muscles of his shoulders and biceps. He saw Eckhart look at him, and in an instant, the strange, terrible smile was gone, the eyes alert. "I can't find anything," Mills said.

Eckhart looked back at Jerry.

"I don't have any more patience for you," he said quietly. "I won't ask you again. Where did you put the money?"

This was getting bad. He had to do something to make him believe he was telling the truth. "The money isn't in the house," he said. "That's the truth. It's still in the bank. But, okay," he hurried on, "you can have it, all of it, but we *both* go with you to the bank in the morning. I'll get it out of the box and give it to you."

Once they were there, Jerry thought, once they were out of the house and inside the bank, he would think of something.

But right away he saw it wasn't going to be like that.

Eckhart leaned forward, uncrossed his long legs, put his feet flat on the floor. He stretched out his arm, pointing the gun. Jerry looked straight into the little dark hole of the muzzle. "Do it!" Eckhart said sharply.

And Derik Mills started toward them and Jerry's brain tried to tell him what to do, how to handle it, but all the messages were coming too fast and all at once. He won't kill you he thought—beat you, but not kill you . . .

All wrong.

Because Mills's big hand snaked down, his fingers going around the back of *Chris's* neck and she screamed as he jerked her forward to her feet and into the middle of the room. Jerry started to jump up.

"Go on!" Eckhart's voice was like a whip in his face.

Jerry stared at the gun, his whole body burning, his mind racing. *Think! Think! Think!* He shoots you, it's over. Just Chris, then. With them. *"It's not here!"* he screamed at Eckhart. *"You dirty sonofabitch! Don't you think I'd tell you!"*

Eckhart didn't say a word. He got up and came over to the side of the couch next to Jerry, went down on one knee and then the muzzle of the gun wasn't more than three, four inches from Logan's face.

"Do it!" Eckhart said again.

And then Mills began to go to work on Chris.

And for a terrible moment, the stark horror of just seeing it happen froze him and he stared as Mills suddenly hit her hard in the stomach and Chris cried out, doubled over, gasping, the wind knocked out of her, and both of Mills's big hands were in her hair, tangling it around them and then his arms were going up over his head and he was lifting Chris off the floor by her hair, and she was trying to scream, but she couldn't catch her breath, and then her head dropped to one side and she went limp, fainted. Without even thinking, Jerry heard himself yelling, "*In the basement! It's downstairs in the basement!*"

Mills dropped Chris in a heap on the rug, pulled his hands out of her hair. His face under the big bandage around his head was a bright red and his eyes were shining.

Jerry looked away from her to Eckhart, feeling the icy cold hate starting to take him. Eckhart looked at him and knew that everything he had thought had been right. Logan by himself would have toughed it out or at least tried to, but you add the woman and the emotion, and everything changed. Now he would take the two hundred and fifty thousand and to hell with the rest of it. That amount, added to what he already had, would be enough. You had to be careful and not get greedy.

Like Mills, he thought.

Oh, he knew about Mills. Mills didn't think he knew, but he did. He knew that Mills had some plan in his twisted mind to take the money once they'd gotten Logan to show them where he'd hidden it.

But Mills wasn't careful enough.

He got too confident, too sure of himself. He didn't watch everything all the time and that was what you had to do, and so when he looked at Mills now, Mills started toward Logan, thinking he wanted him to go down to the basement with him and get the money and there was nothing but total surprise on the handsome face as Eckhart swung his body away from Logan, took one step toward Mills and fired the gun straight into his face, the bullet hitting him under his left eye close to his nostril and Mills stared at him for a second, terrible shock in his eyes, his hand going up to his face, and then he was falling, already dead before his knees, his face, smacked down into the rug.

And it was then that Eckhart realized he had made a mistake.

Because one of the really bad and dangerous things about people who reach the breaking point and suddenly go berserk is that you can never depend on them to do anything logical, like run, which Logan should've done then only he didn't, and because he was out of position, Eckhart wasn't ready at all when Logan screamed and landed on him.

They both went down hard on the floor, the gun flying out of Eckhart's grasp, and Jerry smashed his fist hard into Eckhart's face, not thinking or caring about anything then, his hands going for the man's throat to kill him—*to kill him!*—the rage surging through his body, taking him.

Only his rage wasn't enough.

The gun was gone from Eckhart's hand, but he was bigger, younger, stronger, and he jerked Logan to his feet and hit him hard on the side of the head, but Jerry held onto the front of Eckhart's shirt, ripping it, pulling him as they crashed into a lamp and he felt the shade crush against his back, then the sound of the lamp breaking, and they were back down on the floor again only this time Eckhart was the one on top, and Jerry thought, *you have to get away from him!* only then Eckhart's fingers snapped around his throat, squeezing, his thumbs pressing down into the flesh just below the Adam's apple and God, was he strong! Jerry grabbed a handful of hair and yanked hard, but that didn't do anything, and Eckhart's fingers just kept squeezing and pressing and it was harder for him to breathe now and then he felt a tingling rush of heat pass up through his body and suddenly he was very lightheaded and he knew he was going out.

Except then he thought of Chris.

Chris, hurt on the floor, unconscious, and if he went out now, it would be all over for him and Chris might wake up to see him dead on the floor and this bastard coming over to kill her and there was no way, goddamnit! that he could let that happen, and the lightheadedness was getting worse now and he could feel his tongue being forced out of his mouth and he had to do something now and fast, and he saw only one thing that was worth a shot and he made a fist and drove it hard down over his stomach between the legs that straddled him and heard the sharp cry of pain, felt the death grip around his throat loosen, the air rushing into his lungs, and he spread the fingers of one hand wide then and brought it up hard, the heel of his palm catching Eckhart under his chin, knocking him sideways and off him, and then he was scrambling up on his feet, running, not looking at Chris on the floor, just running straight out of the living room, hearing Eckhart panting in pain behind him, to the basement door. He had to get down into the basement.

So he could knock out the lights!

He jerked open the door and, holding onto the railing, he half-ran, half-fell down the steep steps in the darkness, ducking around under them at the bottom, moving to the wall and feeling flat-handed along the gritty, cold concrete for the power box, finding it, clawing at the lever, pulling it down, leaning against the box, his forehead touching the wall, trying to listen upstairs over the sound of his own gasping.

Eckhart stood in the middle of the dark living room, his head bent over almost even with his waist, his hand between his legs, massaging gently and slowly as the sharp pain began to subside. He straightened up, listening. He had heard Logan running down the steps to the basement. Eckhart smiled in the darkness. He could've run out the front door, he thought, but he didn't because of the woman. Now he had to make a fight of it. He would stay down there in the dark waiting for him to come after him and it would be in Logan's mind to take him by surprise only Logan didn't really know who he was dealing with, didn't know that he didn't have a chance in the dark.

For Eckhart was very good in the dark.

It didn't bother him that the gun was gone. He wouldn't need it. Guns were no good in the dark anyway.

But his knife was.

He walked over to the woman, bound her hands with his belt, her feet with his tie. She was still unconscious. She would be no problem later, but he didn't want her coming around and complicating things. Logan was the important one now.

Eckhart sat down on the living room rug and removed his shoes. Then he stood up and moved silently into the kitchen to the open door of the basement, stopped still and listened. All he could hear was the deep rush of the wind outside and the steady beating of the rain on the kitchen window. He reached down and unbuttoned the cuff of his shirt, rolled the sleeve up to his elbow.

Then he took the knife out of his pocket, picked open the special blade.

In the darkness below, Jerry Logan stood against the wall next to the power box. His body was drenched in sweat and his nose throbbed from where Mills had hit him, the clotted blood thick in his nostrils when he tried to breathe.

Ten seconds, maybe twenty...

Nothing. Not a sound.

And then he heard it.

Faint, and if you weren't really listening, really trying to hear, you would miss it.

The soft, giving sound of wood under weight.

Eckhart was coming for him.

Jerry swallowed and the pain seared his throat from where Eckhart had choked him. You can't fight him, he thought. You have to find something to use on him. You've been down here before. Think! What's where? Slowly, up on his toes, he stepped away from the wall, his hands feeling ahead of him in the darkness and then something moved near him and there was no keeping back the little yell as Roscoe rushed by him, running up the steps. He had forgotten the cat even existed. Frozen, he listened.

And what he heard made his skin crawl.

From somewhere up on the dark steps came soft, breathy laughter. Then Eckhart's voice, very quiet, almost whispering, the laughter still in it.

"Did the kitty scare you?"

Jesus!

Jerry stared through the blackness. The sonofabitch was crazy. Out of his fucking mind. He had seen it, too. That smile on his face upstairs and his eyes, the way they looked at you only you could tell they were seeing something else.

Move! he yelled silently at himself.

He took steps again, bent way over, arms out in front of him, fingers feeling.

And then his knee bumped into something.

He stopped, reached down, and his hands touched the cool, rough wooden surface of the barrel. He lifted it. It was heavy. Cider, he remembered. Chris had said it was full of apple cider. She loved apple cider.

Maybe, he thought.

Silently, carefully, he bent down, picked up the barrel.

Eckhart stopped on the third step, one hand on the railing, the smooth, heavy casing of the knife in the other.

He was having trouble with something.

It was crazy, but he just couldn't help himself.

He wanted to *laugh*.

He kept his lips pressed tightly together, but damnit, it was funny! It really was!

He was going after Logan one *step* at a time!

That was so funny! But, no, he thought. Don't do it. Don't laugh. He turned his head slightly, closed his eyes, listened.

Not a sound from below.

Logan was being *soooo* quiet, he thought.

But Eckhart could feel his fear. Things always went better when he had fear working for him. Nice and easy, he told himself. Nice and slow. Make him sweat. By the time he got there, Logan would be ready to go. He wouldn't have the nerves for this. He knew he was going to die.

Eckhart smiled, opened his eyes, breathed in the basement dampness. All his senses felt so charged, so alert. He would wait at the bottom of the steps for what he needed to hear. It didn't have to be much.

A little rustle of clothing, maybe.

Or an intake of breath.

Almost everything was done now, he thought. Mills was dead. He was sure of that. God, the look on his face! Was he ever surprised! The woman was unconscious, hurt. She would be no problem. And now he had Logan. You've been so careful, he told himself, and soon all this hassle will be over, finished, and you can relax. You won't have to be so careful with your life anymore. He stared down into the darkness and wondered if Logan had found himself any kind of a weapon. It didn't matter. He wouldn't know that, but it didn't matter at all. He ran his thumb lightly over the blade of the knife. He was so good with this. There had been three of them that one night in Paris, he remembered, in a narrow alley. And they'd all had weapons, too.

Jerry Logan waited in the darkness, his eyes, his ears, all his concentration fixed on the steps, listening.

And again, the soft squeak of the wood.

Eckhart wet his lips. "Going *downnnn*," he whispered softly and he took another step.

Jerry held his breath, waiting.

Silence.

Eckhart didn't feel like laughing anymore. Now he felt like business. Carefully he stepped down, felt the cool of the wood through his sock.

And Jerry Logan reached up through the space between the steps and grabbed him.

Eckhart gasped aloud as he felt the hands grabbing at him, one at his ankle, one on the calf of his other leg.

Standing on top of the upended barrel under the steps, Jerry's fingers locked tight and he threw himself off it, felt the legs in his hands wobble for a fraction of a second and then they were both torn out of his grip by his own falling weight as he fell headfirst onto the basement floor.

Eckhart's hand flew away from the railing and he might have grabbed hold of it again with the other one, but there was the knife in that hand and he let go of it, reached out.

Way too late.

He felt his fingers close on themselves and then his head was going over and down.

Eckhart screamed.

But only for a second.

And lying in a heap under the steps, one side of his face flat against the cold concrete floor, Jerry Logan heard it and it was like the sound of a very heavy, big bag of laundry being thrown bouncing and thudding every which way down the steep steps only it was like there was something breakable in the bag because when it finally hit the floor, he heard a soft but very clear *cracking* sound in the darkness.

Then only silence.

Except for his own quick breathing and the heavy pounding of his heart.

EPILOGUE

CONSIDERING EVERYTHING that had happened, what followed was nothing at all.

Not that there weren't some bad, nervous moments.

Like the unpleasant business of cleaning up the house. He wouldn't let Chris come back until he was done. He got Mills and Eckhart into the car in the middle of the night and hoped that there was no old lady peeking through her drapes watching him, and then, after he had them in the car, Mills stretched out on the backseat and Eckhart leaning against the door in front, he had driven off with them, sure that he would be stopped and that it would be all over.

But fortunately there was still the rain.

It was coming down harder than ever and it helped keep people off the streets, and those that were out were more concerned with their driving and getting home than paying any attention to some man who happened to be sleeping against the window of another car that was stopped next to them at a light.

He left them and the car at the back of a parking lot of a movie theater.

And still he was worried. He didn't want to swap Eckhart being after him for the police being after him. They talked it over and decided to stay another scared month in the house, waiting to see if anything would happen, but nobody ever came around.

THEY HAD NO WAY of knowing it, but they really didn't have anything to worry about.

Because the truth was that the police simply weren't all that excited about finding the two bodies, once they had been identified. Derik Mills was already known to them as a shady sort connected to gambling and the underworld in London, and as for the other one, an American from Las Vegas, information had it that he was strongly suspected of being a contract killer for organized crime. Both of them had been found in an abandoned car in a parking lot. Certainly not an unusual occurrence. An investigation was made, of course, but it was not all that vigorous. Violence leading to violence and all that. In time, the case was stamped Unsolved, filed and forgotten along with many others.

Chris left her job at the hospital and sold the house.

She felt some sadness cutting those ties, but she knew it had to be done. The job, the house—well, they were all part of before and it was time to leave all that behind her now. They were going to just travel around for a while, see some of the world, and after they had done that, then they could choose where they finally wanted to settle and what they wanted to do. They decided not to get married in London but to pick a place along the way somewhere, some country that appealed to them.

Chris wanted to go to Greece first.

But they went to Switzerland.

Because Jerry had something to do there. In the time since that windy October night when, scared to death, he had left Vegas on the train, he had come to believe that you could never be too careful, and so he only really began to relax and feel a little comfortable when he was finally sitting in the luxuriously appointed office in Zurich, looking across the highly polished desk into the ruddy, smiling face of the silver-haired man who was purported to be absolutely the very best, most discreet plastic surgeon in the world.